Alexandra Carew worked
years launching entertainm
Europe and the Middle
approached she quit her job
in the south of France to wr

Also by Alexandra Carew

What Goes Around

Getting Away From It All

Alexandra Carew

PIATKUS

Copyright Alexandra Carew © 2004

First published in Great Britain in 2004 by
Judy Piatkus (Publishers) Ltd of
5 Windmill Street, London W1T 2JA
email: info@piatkus.co.uk

This edition published 2004

The moral right of the author has been asserted

A catalogue record for this book is available from the British Library

ISBN 0 7499 3431 X

Set in Times by
Action Publishing Technology, Gloucester

Printed and bound in Great Britain by
Bookmarque Ltd, Croydon, Surrey

I'd like to thank my agent, Brie Burkeman, and editors Alice Wood and Emma Callagher at Piatkus for their faith, support and encouragement. I'd also like to thank friends too numerous to mention for making my life in France such a joy, and my mother, for never trying to dissuade me from doing the ridiculous.

Alexandra Carew

For Claudia

Chapter One

Lia Scott would never forget the moment she realised that everything in her life was wrong – from her stuffy boyfriend to her stifling job, her orderly beige flat to the drudgery of her daily commute – she realised she'd outgrown the lot, and that it was time to do something about it.

It was as she was arriving with her boyfriend Jonathan at an Indian restaurant in an exclusive street off the Fulham Road. They had had to park two blocks away and had run through the rain, their umbrellas bending backwards in the wind. She'd entered first, climbing down the basement steps, the welcoming smell of fresh coriander and spices wafting up to greet her. As the waiter took her dripping umbrella and helped her out of her raincoat, she spotted the large party seated at the centre table. They included faces she recognised from *Hello!* – a thirty-something heir and his supermodel fiancée, a gallery owner, a bit-part TV actress and an It girl more famed for her disastrous love life than for any particular achievement.

Lia felt herself brighten, as if mere proximity to this group would bring her closer to the London that still eluded her after almost fourteen years: the London of the

1

wealthy and chic – the beautiful people who shopped and snogged for England, whose every moves were detailed in the gossip columns; the people for whom London made itself available, for whom life was always the best table in the most fashionable restaurant; the people who could find taxis in the rain and wore skimpy dresses in winter. In short, the people who conspired to make her own life seem rather dull.

She pulled in her stomach and, hoping her suit didn't look too last season, ran a hand through her tousled blonde hair. It was at that moment that Jonathan, struggling with his umbrella, made his entrance. Striding enthusiastically downstairs, he slipped on the finely worn tread and tumbled down the remaining steps, to land in a tangle of green barbour and brogues on the restaurant floor.

Amidst the stifled giggles of the main table, Lia, to her shock, realised that she was more embarrassed for him than concerned and, as no less than three waiters rushed over to help, could feel her cheeks reddening. It was at that point that she realised that just about everything he said and did irritated her, and had done for months. In those few seconds she could see her career tumbling down towards redundancy, and knew she didn't care. And as he brushed himself down, angrily pointing out the worn-out tread on the stairway, she suddenly felt the full force of her dissatisfaction, and knew that if she were ever to feel truly happy, she'd have to reinvent herself, and her life, completely.

But she didn't – not immediately. First, she had to be sure of exactly what she did, and did not, want.

The *did nots* were easy: she *did not* want to stay in London – she'd lived there too long, rarely went to the theatre or any exhibitions and hadn't seen the inside of a night club since Madonna was in conical bras. She hated the weather, loathed her District Line commute and was sick of her regular morning view of terraced houses under an overcast sky. She'd lost her appetite for shopping, could no longer face the West End and found most restaurants self-conscious and overpriced.

She *did not* want to continue at the *Staying Alive* lifestyle channel where she produced *Miracle Mick's Gardening Tips*, a half-hour daily show. In the early days she'd loved the buzz of working in broadcasting and the thrill of a shoot. But now, as a reluctant member of middle management, her routine seemed to consist mainly of checking invoices, typing numbers into a spreadsheet and overseeing others who did all the fun stuff. The show had a structured format, which she herself had created, but by now it was a question of slotting in the components factory-style – something her junior producer was more than capable of. Lia missed being creative, missed the process of writing and missed the hands-on cooking and gardening she used to do.

But not only that, in recent months the channel had suffered numerous budget cuts and redundancies, with original programming being replaced by cheap American imports. How long, she often wondered, before her own show was canned and she, too, became the proud owner of a P45?

And finally, the hardest *did not* of all, Lia *did not* want to stay with Jonathan, her boyfriend of the last six years. Yes, he was still good looking; yes, he was successful and highly regarded at his management consultancy; and yes, he came with a Fulham flat she could never have afforded by herself. But no, she did not love him – a sentiment she had known for some time but chosen to ignore, at least until that cruel, slippery piece of carpet that sent him crashing down into the restaurant entrance.

He was a handsome man – tall and slender, thanks to hours in the gym, with broad shoulders that made his jackets hang nicely. They'd met at a cousin's wedding in Hampshire, and he'd immediately been taken by Lia's clear, tanned skin and the large blue-green eyes that seemed to find in him something the others all missed. There was something vulnerable about the way she ran her fingers through her hair as she talked, and something about her body which implied she was comfortable within it, and

3

would be fun to have dinner with, and not fret about forbidden foods and hidden calories. Lia, on the other hand, had been strangely drawn to his intellect and seriousness, finding it refreshing after years of creative types who thought Conrad was the bloke behind Habitat and Heal's. She had enjoyed teasing him and making him laugh, and for the first few years they'd been genuinely happy. Yes, there'd been problems, but then weren't there in every relationship?

He was cheap – earning almost twice as much as she did yet expecting her to pay half of practically everything. At first she'd thought it fair enough – they weren't married, after all, and she was in a full-time job. But it was the minor things that got to her – his rage if she used a first-class stamp when a second would have done, his disapproval of any expensive clothes, shoes or make-up she bought herself and his occasional offering to treat her to a meal, only to balk at the price and ask for a contribution instead.

She'd lived with it all for a while, but then there was a subtle shift in their relationship – she couldn't place exactly when it happened – and she found that far from being in thrall to his intellect and careful financial management, she'd begun to rebel against them, flaunting unnecessary purchases, revelling in gossip columns and chick-lit novels, and listening to George Michael rather than Mahler.

But the one thing they'd never done, the one thing they'd studiously avoided doing, was discuss their differences. It had been a *did not* that they were both reluctant to face. They'd put up with each other for the sake of stability, going through the motions of a relationship that neither was particularly comfortable with; neither wanting to be the first to disturb the balance.

And as for the *did wants*? Lia *did want* to be in the warmth – she wanted to wake up each morning rejoicing in a beautiful, sunny view, rather than in the relief that it wasn't *actually* raining again. She wanted a garden of her

4

own full of fruit and vegetables, but not the carrots and sprouts of the studio garden – she wanted aubergines, peppers and citrus fruits, she wanted herbs and tomatoes and peaches – and she wanted to cook, preferably with all the colourful ingredients of the south.

And she *did want* to write again, finding numerous different projects floating through her mind each day as she checked edit schedules and holiday leave requests. The one which kept coming back, though, more persistently than the others, urging her to pay attention, followed a year in the life of a busy Mediterranean garden, examining how the produce was nurtured and covering everything from sun-drying tomatoes to making fig jam with the results. As the idea kept interrupting her staff meetings, distracting her reading on the tube and popping into her mind whenever Jonathan tried to be amorous, so it developed a title, *The Sensuous South*.

It could become a book, she thought initially, based on her own experiences in the little garden in southern France she'd fantasise about in her lunch breaks.

Her friend Jules, whom she'd met several years ago at the channel, was now in publishing, an assistant editor at a company specialising in lifestyle titles, and although Lia had a natural aversion to seeking favours, it would surely do no harm to ask her opinion?

But the very thought of getting a deal, leaving Jonathan, finding somewhere to live, throwing it all in – it all seemed too arduous and unrealistic. That was the kind of thing other people did, surely, but not her? It was better, perhaps, to take the easy option, and devise it as a TV series instead, with the pleasant distraction of a nice overseas shoot for a few weeks.

So one particularly mind-numbing Tuesday afternoon she began to create a treatment, which she then worked on sporadically over the next few weeks. Finally, when she thought she had the makings of a pretty decent twelve-part series on her hands, she made an appointment to pitch the idea to her boss, the head of programming.

Rebecca Johnson was somewhere in her forties and had dedicated her life to keeping a selection of low-budget cable channels on air despite nominal audience figures and a distinct lack of advertising. She had never married and had no apparent boyfriend, but was known to get drunk after work from time to time and end up bedding a lowly technician who'd quietly lose his job weeks later.

She had started off in production herself, many years before, but had ended up being promoted to a level just beyond her competence, and acted as though terrified of being caught out. The decisions she took were cautious, the proposals she accepted safe and the channel she ran lacked flair and character as a result. Lia lived in fear of becoming another Rebecca – it was yet another *did not* to add to her list.

Inside the grey office full of files, videos and a selection of dying pot plants, Lia handed Rebecca the proposal, neatly collated and ring-bound, complete with the overall concept, a programme format and ideas for each episode. She then sat down, waiting for her boss to pause the preview cassette of an American talk show she'd been watching. To her mild indignation, however, Rebecca kept it on, actually turning back occasionally to watch, leaving Lia to fight a myriad of American housewives and a face-lifted hostess for her attention.

Share It With Sara screamed the logo in the top right of screen, with the episode title *I'll Never Forgive You* in bold orange along the bottom.

'I had a daughter, she was three years old,' a member of the audience, a woman with badly dyed blonde hair and heavy bags under her eyes, started saying after some fervent clapping. 'And my mother was with her one afternoon, supposedly looking after her.' Tears started welling in the woman's eyes, and Lia stopped, her ideas for a summer fruits and jam-making episode seeming suddenly trivial.

'They were in the garden. She got distracted and turned her back, she said it was only for a minute or two, but my

6

little girl drowned in the pool. I don't care what anyone says, and I don't care what anyone thinks, but I will *never* forgive her for that.' There was a collective intake of breath followed by a sigh from the audience.

Sara, the hostess, looked pained. 'Do you still have any kind of relationship with your mother?' she asked.

'Absolutely not,' the woman replied. 'I changed jobs, moved state, found a new life, and I will *never* see that woman again.'

'Bloody great stuff,' Rebecca turned back to Lia. 'And I can get it pretty cheap, too, five shows a week. As opposed to a lovely shoot in St Tropez. Dream on, Lia. What little budget I have is tied up with our existing programmes, and I'm going to have to cut them back by next quarter as it is. You're still with Miracle Mick, aren't you?' She frowned, rubbing her forehead. 'Just keep on as you are.'

Biting back her anger and disappointment, Lia retrieved her proposal and turned to leave.

Rebecca, possibly regretting her tone, suddenly called out, 'I'm sorry, Lia, it's a great idea and all that, it really is. But I've got no choice, I'm sorry.'

Lia just nodded and walked away. But *The Sensuous South* – the book – kept going.

Chapter Two

'It's got potential,' Jules Neville lit her cigarette and inhaled deeply. She claimed rarely to smoke yet this was her third that night, and Lia found herself likening her to someone who fervently insisted she was vegetarian, yet still ate fish, chicken and the occasional pepperoni pizza. 'I'd have to see an outline and three sample chapters first, of course, and I couldn't give you any preferential treatment.'

Lia frowned. They were sitting in a Soho wine bar having the quick drink that would inevitably turn into a late-night dinner followed by a long wait for a taxi home. 'I wouldn't expect you to,' she told her friend curtly.

Jules paused. She had shoulder-length auburn hair, full lips and the longest eyelashes Lia had seen outside a transvestite club. She played a lot of sport – tennis and hockey mostly – and had well-defined arms, a full bust and the kind of pert bottom men adored. 'But are you seriously thinking about doing all this? I mean, France? Leaving your job?'

'It's all I *have* been thinking about for months now. Believe me, I've given myself plenty of time to change my mind. But instead of going off the idea, I just get more and more into it.' She lowered her voice as if imparting a state secret. 'Miracle Mick's meeting the BBC next week – he told me a few days ago. If he leaves, the show will be cancelled, and with it my job. It's only a matter of time.'

'You could follow him, couldn't you?' Jules suggested. 'Or take your redundancy money and set up a production company, make it as a series with him fronting it?'

Lia shook her head. 'It's not just my job that needs changing, it's my whole lifestyle. I mean, why do I need to be in London? I never *do* anything. I used to, but I just don't have the energy any more. I want simple things now, like a garden. I'd honestly rather be growing my own veg than traipsing around the V&A or watching some obscure Russian art-house movie in Camden Town. London's a fabulous city, you can do anything here, but I *don't* any more. I want out.'

Jules nodded. 'And what about that man of yours? Where does he fit in with all this?' She had never liked Jonathan, and made no secret of it, barely even bringing herself to say his name.

Lia's face fell. 'I've talked it over with him,' she started. 'It's very hard, and it's very painful, but – ' she paused, the words still sounding strange in her mind '– we're splitting up.'

Jules went to say something but was distracted by her mobile beeping. She grabbed it off the table, studied the screen, a wry smile forming on her face, and began tapping out a reply. 'About time, too. I never thought he was right for you, you know.'

Lia sighed. They'd met as researchers on the morning show, *Coffee'n'Biscuits*, and despite Jules being several years her junior, Lia had quickly taken to her warmth and to the sense of humour that had rescued many a potential disaster in the studio. But as much as she admired the focused brain that had got her through Oxford, she could live without the straightforward honesty that accompanied it.

'There's something superior about him,' Jules continued. 'Like we're all lesser mortals around him.'

9

'I know what you mean,' Lia agreed reluctantly. 'High on intellect but low on charm. My mum and stepdad came over for lunch the other day and Mum was going on about all her usual stuff, you know, the catering business, the weddings she's done lately and who was wearing what frock, and J was like, "Do you mind if I go to the other room and read Joyce?"'

'And what, your mum thought it was a new women's magazine?' Jules quipped.

'Nearly,' Lia laughed. 'Oh God,' she rubbed her eyes. 'I think I was suffering from mid-life crisis when I met him. I was thirty and everyone around me was getting married and having babies and I thought he seemed the ideal prospect, you know? That he had all the qualities you look for.'

'Except a personality,' Jules interjected, stabbing at her mobile.

Lia smiled miserably, wishing she had her friend's full attention. 'I wanted to be part of this dynamic corporate couple – to have a career, a couple of kids, a nanny. I was on such a birth wish in those days.'

Jules looked up from her text messaging. 'Well, that quickly died a death, didn't it?'

Lia frowned. Every now and then she wished Jules could just switch off that quick wit of hers and allow others to speak without having to fight the steady barrage of quips and one-liners, not to mention the mobile. 'So maybe we should have got married,' she pressed on. 'And I'd be broody for babies by now, maybe that's what should have happened. But it didn't. And it's not babies I want any more, it's freedom.' She stopped, frustrated. 'Who exactly are you messaging now?' Here she was, trying to explain a major life-change and all Jules could do was text flirt with someone whose name she'd probably have forgotten by the end of next week.

'No one special,' Jules told her huffily, putting the phone down. 'So why didn't you ever marry?' she asked suddenly.

'I don't know, he never asked me,' Lia shrugged. 'I wanted to, a few years ago, that was exactly what I wanted. But something always held him back.' She paused, toying with her glass. 'Too mean to buy a ring, probably.'

'And weddings cost a fortune, let's face it,' Jules agreed.

'And a honeymoon? We're looking at a man who'd rather buy an ISA than a trip to Ibiza,' Lia laughed sadly.

'But he's OK about all this?' Jules persisted. 'He understands?'

Lia nodded cautiously. 'I think he's coming round to it. He'll miss me paying half the bills, of course, and he'll miss having his meals cooked, and the sex, I suppose; but I don't actually think he'll miss me. I don't think he's realised that yet, though. Right now he's angry and hurt, but only because he'd rather have been the one to make the decision, that's all.'

There was a pause while Jules ordered another bottle, and Lia asked, 'So you'd be prepared to help me? With the book, I mean, look at a few chapters? You seriously think it could have a future?'

Jules straightened up, and Lia got a taste of how she might come across in a meeting. It was a far cry from the girl she remembered years ago, all ripped jeans and hair falling out of a bun, climbing up a stepladder in search of missing tapes. 'Like I said, I'd be willing to check out a synopsis and some sample chapters, but don't expect me to push something through that I don't believe in.'

Lia recoiled, wondering whether she'd honestly be able to take her friend's criticism. But if she wanted the project to work, Jules was her best chance.

'So how would you fund all this?' Jules asked. 'I mean, I know you've been at the channel for a while, but you're hardly going to get a massive pay-off, are you?'

Lia leant forward and lowered her voice again. 'I've got some money put away, enough to last a few years, if I'm careful. When my grandmother died she left me a chunk. And my mother, quite astutely for her, made me promise

11

not to tell Jonathan. She's always had this thing, ever since my dad left, about a woman keeping her independence. She'd had to learn the hard way, after all. She was left with no money and two kids to feed. Got the job in catering and years later started up on her own, but it was tough going. So she was adamant that I kept this to myself. Kind of *fuck you* money, though those weren't the words she used, of course. So we opened a separate bank account and sent the statements to her house. And it's there, waiting for me to do something stupid like run off to France and write a book that no one's going to publish.'

'I didn't say that,' Jules tutted. 'Look, you really think you're up to all this?'

'Yes, I do,' Lia said emphatically. 'It all falls into place. Don't forget, I know France quite well – I au paired there once and taught English as a student. And I've been cooking for years, helping my mum out and then at the channel. Gardening might not be my strong point, but I'll learn. And as for the writing – I miss it, and I know it's something I'm good at. I'm ready to get my teeth into something bigger. It all falls into place, it really does. I've just got to make the move.'

Jules sat back, impressed. 'You know something? I've spent the last two hours trying to talk you out of this and picking holes in your plan. But you've thwarted me. It's obviously something you've just got to do. So got for it, girl, and I'll be as supportive as I can, I promise.' They chinked glasses in celebration. 'So what kind of a place are you looking for?'

'Something in Provence,' Lia started excitedly. 'Say, within an hour from Nice airport. I've started looking at things on the Internet, but they're mostly flash flats on the coast. What I want is something simpler, something more rural, nothing fancy. I don't want to spend all my money on rent.'

'Hang on a sec,' Jules started thoughtfully. 'I'm sure I remember one of my authors – funny woman, writes obsessively on stencilling, can't stand blank walls – I'm sure she

12

mentioned some place she rented near Nice once, did some sort of course there, can't remember what in. But I remember it sounded pretty ideal, with lovely gardens and views. I could contact her if you like, try to find out a bit more?'

'And what, I'd have to do courses in home decorating or something?' Lia asked doubtfully.

'No, they have places to rent, I'm sure that's what she told me. Over the winter. It had a gorgeous garden, that's what I remember her saying, really stunning.'

'Hell, call her, then, if you don't mind,' Lia said, her eyes lighting up with excitement. 'I'm willing to explore everything. You know, I just feel that this is the start of a major adventure – a huge turning point in my life. I just want to try everything – I'll make mistakes, I'm sure, but they'll be *mine*, you know, something I'll learn from. I feel like this is going to be the most positive thing I've ever done in my life. I've been so bored I can't tell you. But now I feel like I'm about to throw myself off the edge of the cliff, you know, and just see where I fall.'

Jules looked at her quizzically. 'Let's hope you don't have a bumpy landing,' she joked.

Chapter Three

Through the plane window, Lia could see her new life spreading out in front of her like the hills above Nice and its romantic Bay of Angels. She could picture a beautiful cottage set in a garden bursting with fruit and Provençal vegetables, a kitchen full of warm and inviting smells and a haphazard work space centred around her laptop, books and countless notes. And somewhere in the middle of this picture was Lia herself, snipping fresh herbs and stirring vast pots of ratatouille, a modern-day Felicity Kendall enjoying her good life.

Sure enough, Miracle Mick had switched to the BBC and her redundancy followed shortly thereafter. She'd lost count of all the evenings she and Jonathan had spent discussing their relationship, and what each of them really wanted. He'd finally admitted that their differences had been getting to him, too, and that whilst he'd certainly miss her, the last thing he wanted was to hold her back. And on their final morning, as Lia's stepfather loaded her belongings into the back of the catering van, Lia had been gripped by a sudden panic that she was making the biggest mistake of her life. Jonathan had held her then, whispering that he'd always be there for her, and somehow another thought had superseded the first, and she knew that she wouldn't need him.

Now, more than ever, she sensed that again – she felt liberated, as if she'd finally cut herself free from a series of Houdini-style chains and escaped from the coffin that lay twenty metres underwater. As the plane finally touched down at Nice Côte d'Azure airport, she almost expected the other passengers to burst into applause at her achievement.

But then, this was a good day – there had been plenty of bad. For every now and then her euphoria would descend into terror, and the magnitude of what she was doing would hit her with all the force of the high-speed London to Paris rail link. Then, she'd imagine a bleak future, penniless and unpublished, remembering when she'd seemingly had it all and inexplicably let it go.

She passed through immigration, collected her luggage off the carousel and joined the queue for taxis in the warming January sunshine. When it was her turn, she gave the driver the name of the village and sat back to watch as the modern coastal towns disappeared through the rear window, and they climbed up, towards the mountains and round the twisting roads and hilltop villages that were soon to become her home.

'I spoke to that author,' Jules had told her one evening in between phone calls and text messages. 'You know, about the flat? Turns out it's in some funny spiritual centre just up from Nice. They run courses in the summer—'

'In what, astrology and caftan-making?' Lia had interrupted. 'Not exactly my kind of thing.'

'Will you let me finish? In the winter they rent places out, very cheaply, too, I gather. And it sounds like it's closing down anyway – the guy had a stroke, or something, and they might be looking for full-time tenants.'

'I don't know, Jules, it doesn't sound like me.'

'You'd be renting a flat, Li, not learning how to knit your own yoghurt. And anyway, what was all that about exploring everything and jumping off the cliff? Apparently it's in a beautiful spot, the woman who runs it's some dotty

American and there'll be a few English speakers around – even if you don't stay long it'll be a good start.'

'True,' Lia mused, knowing that the reality of her move might well mean long nights alone drinking too much *vin de pays*.

'Look, I've got this woman's number right here.' Jules rummaged for it in her bag. 'Her name's, wait for it, Peaches,' she smirked, handing Lia a piece of paper. 'At least give her a call. She might not even have anything left, but it's worth a try.'

So Lia did call, and Peaches did have something: a tiny pink cottage set away from the rest of the complex. It had one bedroom, one bathroom, a living and dining area and a small kitchen, but best of all it had a large terrace and a view down the valley towards the sea, and all for a rent that was well within her budget.

Despite her initial misgivings, Lia thought Peaches sounded warm and reassuring, the sort she could chat to over a coffee; the sort who'd cheer her up on the inevitable bad days when she found her confidence had got up without her and disappeared for a day on the beach.

'I'm expecting a number of people to join us over the next few months,' she'd told Lia. 'We have quite a little community going on here. A couple of Brits, for example: Chloe, who lives here permanently now and teaches yoga and does massage, and Ben, who's a photographer, and stays here between assignments. I'll be hearing from others, no doubt, but there are plenty of English speakers in the village. I'm sure you'll settle in and have a wonderful time.'

Lia took it immediately. It would only be for the winter, she told herself, and then she'd find something more permanent, with its own garden. Peaches had faxed her a hand-drawn map of the village, including references to restaurants, a garden centre and some local shops. It all looked charming: the stuff of dreams, a place where nothing bad could ever happen, and Lia couldn't wait to get there.

16

She'd moved her belongings to her mother's house in Sussex and endured a Christmas of people telling her she was insane. What was she doing, throwing away a perfectly good career like that? Didn't she know that every relationship had its problems? And wasn't it terribly hard to get a book published these days, especially as she'd never been on TV? She felt as if she was killing time, waiting for the festivities to end so that she could get on with the rest of her life and prove them all wrong.

Her mother had been supportive, though, as always. 'You've got so many more opportunities these days than I ever had,' she told Lia over a glass of champagne on New Year's Day. She'd catered for two parties the previous evening and had just finished a lunch for twelve. Now she'd kicked off her shoes, put her feet up on the sofa and was beginning to unwind. 'Take them, I say, or you'll only regret it. In some ways I don't know why you didn't do this earlier. Jonathan was never the one for you. I didn't think it would last. I always thought he held you back, or maybe it was you holding yourself back because of him? Whatever, enjoy yourself, Lia, work yourself hard, but *make* something of your life while you're still young. It's one thing to take a chance and then get it all wrong, but quite another to do nothing at all.'

Her mother had taken her chances, after all, she thought admiringly, and they were all beginning to come good for her. She'd set up her own business and then married Brian, a decent, steady sort who adored her and took care of the administration. She'd built a loyal team around her and was fast becoming an established name in the county. Lia had sometimes wondered if, when the time was right, her mother didn't secretly want her to become a partner, but appreciated how she'd never once tried to influence her.

They were almost there now and the driver asked for directions, interrupting her thoughts. Lia guided him using Peaches' map, and they turned left just before the village – a pretty, haphazard cluster of buildings perched on a hill – and then entered a lane dotted with pink and caramel-coloured houses hiding behind olive trees and old stone walls. Finally they came to a sign marked Les Eglantines, or wild roses, and pulled up outside.

'Amelia? Is that you?' A voice cooed at her, and there, waiting under the archway, stood a vision in red and gold Indian print, dirty green gardening gloves, some green wellies and a pair of baggy black tracksuit bottoms. Her orange hair was covered in a floppy hat, and as she leant forward to kiss her on both cheeks, the smell of patchouli oil filled Lia's nostrils. This, of course, had to be Peaches.

'How was your flight?' she continued. 'I can't bear flying myself, the thought of being trapped in a steel tube thirty thousand feet above ground fills me with horror. Can you manage those cases? My, you have travelled light. I can't even go to Paris for the weekend without at least six bags. Now let me show you to your cottage, it's just along here.'

As Peaches paused for breath, Lia tried to take in her new surroundings. The path they were on took them past a small, kidney-shaped swimming pool, an orchard of citrus trees and a huge weeping willow tree which hung dreamily overhead. In the distance Lia could see her cottage – not quite visible from the main house – a former barn to which a modern bathroom and kitchen had been added.

'Get out of here!' Peaches suddenly shrieked at a bad-tempered-looking tabby which was about to leap on to an extremely fat ginger tom. 'You just get out of here, I tell you!' Peaches flung herself in the direction of the cats, scattering both. 'He's a dreadful bully, you know, belongs to the neighbours, who refuse to have him fixed. He just terrorises my boys, so if you see him, just chase him away, and for goodness sake don't feed him. There, there.' Peaches went up to stroke the other cat, which was now hiding under a garden table. 'Don't let that old bully bother you.'

She petted him for a minute before opening a small iron gate, and leading Lia on to what was to be her terrace. Producing a key from somewhere within the folds of her top, she unlocked the cottage door and Lia found herself in

18

a dining room with a solid wooden table under which six elderly chairs stood. Beyond that was a cosy sitting room, complete with a sofa, two velvet armchairs, a wooden coffee table and a couple of standing lamps with warm orange lampshades. Scattered throughout were pieces of leopard-skin print – a throw over one of the chairs, an ashtray on the coffee table, a vase in one of the many nooks and a rug on the floor.

'I so like to theme a room, don't you?' Peaches trilled approvingly. 'I go to all the *brocantes* around here and find pieces. There's one in one of the neighbouring villages in a week or so, you could come with me if you like. Will you be getting a car?'

Without waiting for an answer, Peaches had moved to a green velvet drape to the left, which acted as a barrier between the main room and the kitchen. Inside was a gas oven, a sink and some open cupboards filled with kitchen-ware and crockery, none of which appeared to match.

'All my crockery comes from *brocantes* too – it's amazing what people will throw out.'

'A *brocante*'s a kind of antique fair, isn't it?' Lia tried to remember.

'Less sophisticated than that, dear. Garage sale, more like, or I think you might call it a car boot sale. You never know what treasures you might find, though. Now, upstairs you have a bedroom and a charming bathroom.'

She charged up, knocking her hat off the beam above the staircase, and as she turned, Lia saw that Peaches must once have been quite a beauty. She had large, twinkling green eyes, high cheekbones and a heart-shaped mouth. Now, Lia estimated her to be in her late sixties, and the sun and good food had begun to take their toll, but without removing the brightness in her eyes, or the girlish enthusi-asm in her voice.

To the right of the stairs was the bedroom, painted yellow with golden wooden floorboards and a roomy double bed. In one corner stood a chest of drawers, and in the other a fitted wardrobe.

'Have a look at this bathroom,' Peaches called out. 'It was done up just two years ago.'

To Lia's delight she found a warm, terracotta-tiled space with a creamy white bathtub, impressive-looking shower, a loo, bidet and a basin.

'I was thrilled with this room.' Peaches continued. 'But I love the cottage as a whole. I often think that when Felix dies I might just move in here. It's so much cosier than the main house. He's been ill, you know, though he's getting better. Now, I dare say you'll want some time to settle in. The supermarket stays open until seven, so there's plenty of time to do any shopping.' She had started moving downstairs by now. 'But I was hoping to offer you a welcome supper tonight. I've invited Chloe and Etienne along, too. They both work and live here, a charming couple, you must meet them.'

'I'd love to, thank you. How kind.' Lia was touched.

'Splendid! The supermarket's a five-minute walk away. Oh, I should show you things – the phone's over there – I get detailed bills so there'll be nothing to worry about. The switch for hot water's on the wall here somewhere.' She started fussing around the drape looking for it. 'And there's a heater over in that corner. Do let me know if you get too cold, and I can try to arrange something else.'

'But it's so mild here, far warmer than it was in England.'

'You wait until the sun sets, then there's a sudden drop and you'll need all the heating you can get. Be sure to close the shutters, won't you, as they make a huge difference. Now, was there anything else?'

'No, no, I'll find everything, don't worry.' Lia was keen to get on alone, to start unpacking and exploring her new home.

'Very well, I'll leave you now, and see you around seven?' She trotted off, not bothering to wait for an answer, and paused to examine a plant beside the gate. 'Well, aren't you just doing so much better?' Lia heard her say. 'My lantana,' Peaches added as if this would explain

20

everything. 'I'd had it over there, by the summer kitchen.' She nodded towards a building covered in ivy near the pool. 'But it was in too much shade. Now it's looking far happier. You're writing about gardening, aren't you? So you can give me plenty of advice.'

Lia just smiled as she watched Peaches tripping down the path towards her own house, pausing to chat to an African daisy as if they were old friends. Lia returned to the cottage, and to her lovely bathroom. She ran a comb through her hair and washed her hands, which felt dirty after all the travelling. It was odd to think that only this morning her mother had driven her to the airport, tearfully hugging her goodbye, and now here she was, just a few hours later, enjoying the glorious southern France sunshine.

She took another look around the cottage, thrilled with its eccentric décor and warmth, far removed from the neutral beiges Jonathan had insisted on in their Fulham flat. Secretly she had always loved leopard skin, but he had dismissed it as vulgar, something suited only to a tart's boudoir. She checked out the mismatched crockery in the kitchen, remembering the cool white dinner set they had bought in Habitat. Everything about the cottage was fun and forced her to smile – it had a distinct charm of its own.

She started to unpack, arranging her toiletries in the bathroom, pleased with how they looked against the terra-cotta backdrop. She unpacked her clothes, filling the drawers of the antique chest and hanging anything creasable in the fitted wardrobe. There were several paintings on the walls she hadn't noticed earlier – presumably found in the *brocantes* Peaches frequented: oil paintings of flowers and a still life of some fruit, a sentimental depiction of three cats and a delicate watercolour Lia realised was of the entrance to Peaches' house – an archway covered in pink wild roses with the sign marked Les Eglantines beside. In the bottom right was an unassuming signature, not flamboyant, not rushed, just perfectly normal: Bella DeVere.

21

Bella DeVere – what an extraordinary name, Lia thought idly. It sounded theatrical, dramatic, although the signature was anything but. Lia could imagine a woman flouncing down a stairway, hand outstretched, ready to be questioned by an awaiting Hercule Poirot. Had she poisoned her husband, as suspected, or was she a grieving widow to be pitied?

She was wasting time, she told herself, and should do some shopping before it got dark. Stepping out onto the terrace, Lia paused to admire the view again in the fading light, and the hills cascading down towards the valley below. She didn't think she had ever felt so content before, or so positive. She grabbed her bag, threw on a warm jacket and locked up the cottage, before retracing her footsteps along the pool and the side of Peaches' house, then down to the gateway and into the lane.

The air was getting cooler now as the sun dipped behind the mountain to the west, and she pulled her jacket more tightly around herself. Examining her immediate surroundings, Lia delighted in the thought that soon this walk would be commonplace to her. Soon she would have friends, she thought, and might even be visiting people in these houses; soon she'd have a car and be expertly negotiating each bend and exploring the neighbouring towns and villages.

In the gaps between trees she could make out other gentle hills and valleys, studded with houses with no obvious signs of access. How did people ever get to them, she wondered, deciding to explore as soon as she could. To her left, a hedge of rosemary tumbled down from a wall. She paused to touch it and inhale its fresh smell, wondering if anyone would notice if she pinched a bit to take home. It was definitely getting colder now; she shivered, hurrying on, admiring the medieval village up ahead of her, with its narrow streets and tiled roofs.

Before that stood a fairly recent development comprising the supermarket, a beauty salon, a bar tabac, bakery and a bank, which seemed to cover all Lia's needs for now. She took a trolley and made her way inside the supermarket, stopping first at the fruit and vegetable counter to buy mixed salad leaves, some tomatoes and garlic. Then to the dairy counter, where she picked up a round of goat's cheese which looked like it was about to melt, and a Brie. Then some ham, a salami and some pâtés.

As she explored the aisles her trolley became enticingly full with pasta, warming tins of soup and *cassoulet*, orange juice, milk, jams and bread. And wine, of course, she had to get wine. She settled on a Bordeaux and a Côtes du Rhône, and bought a Provençal rosé for the fun of it.

It was only as she made her way to the checkout that she realised how heavy everything was going to be to carry back. She struggled down the lane, surprised at how quickly darkness was falling, and pleased to be having dinner with Peaches and the others later. She could imagine the scene: a homely fireplace, a tureen of warming soup and a large pan of steaming *cassoulet*, perhaps? Or would Peaches be vegetarian, and into wholefood and brown rice? Either way, she thought hungrily, there was bound to be wine: thick, dark, feel-good, red wine, poured slowly out of a carafe, easing the atmosphere and bringing colour to the cheeks.

The life of a struggling writer, she laughed to herself. And they said she was mad.

Chapter Four

'You'll have some wine, now, won't you, Amelia?'
Peaches poured some into her glass.

'Lia, please, do call me Lia.'

Peaches paused. 'Ah, that makes quite a difference, you
know. In terms of numerology. I did a little research
before you arrived,' she added with a faintly defiant cheek-
iness.

'Research? On me?' Lia was puzzled. 'What, to make
sure I was suitable?'

'Oh no, dear, nothing like that. Just a character analysis, just to get an idea of how you might settle here.
Nothing sinister. You see as Amelia your destiny number
is one, which very much relates to looking after number
one. You can't bear restrictions, and have to live life on
your own terms. Number one types are usually creative
and need their own space.'

'That sounds pretty accurate,' Lia admitted, but Peaches
had turned to the thick velvet curtains, and was looking out
impatiently.

'Now, where are the others? I quite clearly said seven,'
she tutted, peering into the darkness beyond.

They were in Peaches' living room, a cluttered space

full of bric-à-brac with a vaguely North African theme. Along the mantelpiece stood a selection of brass jugs and coffee pots under a painting of two veiled women in a souk. The wooden coffee table was inlaid with mother-of-pearl patterns and in one corner sat an elaborate-looking hookah pipe. Lia sat on a deep orange sofa covered in cushions, and at the foot of one of two armchairs was a faded leather pouf, which smelt of old goat.

Two cats jealously guarded the fire: a small tabby and an all black with two white paws, whilst the large ginger tom Lia had seen earlier had sprawled out across one of the armchairs. Peaches introduced them as if they were children.

'Now you've met James, haven't you? He's the most inquisitive of the three. He was born on the roof of your cottage, you know, and adopted us the minute we moved in. And by the fire are Timothy the tabby, who's getting on a bit now, and Keith. He doesn't go out much. They're named after old boyfriends of mine, you know!' She giggled.

There was a knock and the door opened. 'Ah, there they are!' Peaches exclaimed, getting up as an attractive woman in her early thirties appeared, unwrapping a scarf from around her neck and removing a beige-coloured anorak. She was followed by a stocky man wearing a battered leather jacket.

'Sorry we're a bit late, Peaches,' the blonde said in what Jonathan would have dismissed as an estuary accent. 'Hi, I'm Chloe.' She approached Lia with a smile and a handshake. She was petite and pretty, with a straight blonde bob and neat turtleneck sweater and jeans. 'And this is my boyfriend, Etienne.'

Etienne, Lia could see now, was slightly younger than Chloe and had a stud just below his lower lip. His thick dark hair was drawn back by a red bandanna. He wore a faded blue checked shirt, some old jeans and a pair of heavily scuffed boots. He smiled and shook her hand, revealing a large gap between his front teeth.

25

'So you arrived today, did you?' Chloe asked, a warm smile on her face. 'God, the temperature's dropped, you must have brought it over from England.'

As they chatted, Peaches fluttered around, a bottle in one hand and some mismatched glasses in the other. Chloe sat beside Lia, giving off a waft of sweet but reassuring perfume as she did so.

'So you're writing a book, are you? What's it about?'

'The produce of the Mediterranean,' Lia said self-consciously, reminding herself that she would have to get used to discussing it some time. 'You know, gardening and cooking with the seasons.'

'A sort of *A Year in Provence*, then, is it?'

'Well, not exactly, though I imagine there may be some anecdotes. It would be more practical.'

'Well, I wish you luck,' Chloe raised her glass, clearly having heard enough. 'You're a brave woman for doing it. I wouldn't know where to start, I wouldn't.'

They toasted her future success. Etienne had sat down in the armchair and raised his scuffed boots onto the pouf, as if at home, while Chloe sat upright on the sofa, clutching her glass.

'Lia?' Peaches paused, a plate of *charcuterie* poised mid-air. 'That's what you like to be called, is it? L-I-A? Yes, that does change things, though of course you'd still keep the characteristics of your full name.' She offered Lia the platter and waited while she helped herself to two pieces of finely sliced *saucisson*.

'She's onto numerology again, isn't she?' Chloe mocked, her eyes rolling. 'Can't stop herself, can you Peaches? I'm a seven myself, bit dreamy, a good teacher and very musical, apparently, not that you'd know it.' She helped herself to some of the meat.

'Lia Scott becomes a nine, if my calculations are right,' Peaches continued, ignoring her. 'Now nines make quick decisions and are very impatient.'

'Well that sounds a bit like me, too.'

She offered the platter to Etienne, who scooped up five

or six slices and began chewing loudly. 'They like change, challenge and variety, but can find it hard to form relationships.'

'Are you into all this?' Chloe asked. 'Numerology and all that?'

'I'm open to it, I suppose,' Lia said carefully, not wanting to alienate them all just yet. 'I've never really thought about it before.'

'I never believed in it, myself,' Chloe began. 'Thought it was a load of old nonsense. But when my marriage was breaking up a friend persuaded me to come on one of Peaches' courses here, and I just thought, Why not? I didn't get on with the astrology or past-life regression sessions, but then I really got into yoga. Never went back!'

'That was three years ago, wasn't it, dear? We had a wonderful summer that year,' Peaches reminisced. 'There were fourteen on that course, and it was such a lovely group. Oh, do I smell burning?' She sprang up from her chair and rushed to the kitchen, which was just beyond the sitting room.

'You say you never went back?' Lia turned to Chloe, intrigued.

'Nah,' Chloe giggled. 'My marriage was dead. His business was having problems and he was in terrible debt. He had no time for me or my needs, so I thought, Sod it, and stayed on. It was a spiritual thing,' she added, without a trace of irony. 'I wanted to get in touch with myself, you know. I'd got too bogged down in all his problems. Then Etienne started working here in the garden, and everything fell into place, didn't it, Babe?' She smiled at Etienne, who had finished most of the *charcuterie* and was refilling his glass.

'And so you teach yoga and massage?' Lia remembered.

'Nearly – I give yoga classes twice a week in the village, and do massage in people's homes. It's a good way of getting to know everyone around here, you know? It's a bit like being someone's hairdresser, they trust me and open up. You should hear some of the things I've been told,' she

27

laughed, and Lia wondered if she might just start telling her.

'Good for you. So it's really worked out here, then?' Lia was intrigued. Already she was mentally writing her first e-mail to Jules, describing Peaches and the pink cottage, Chloe's spiritual quest and her poor deserted husband in England. 'And Etienne? What is it you do again?'

'He does bits and bobs about the place,' Chloe said for him. 'Some gardening, light building work, decorating, that sort of thing. He doesn't speak much English,' she added, scrunching up her nose. 'He does other jobs in the village, though, quite a busy boy.'

'And, so you both live here, in the complex?'

'Yes, just below the pool, there's a little path that leads to a row of studio flats; we've got one of them. Bit lonely down there, as there's no one else here yet, but no doubt someone will turn up soon.'

'There, supper's ready,' Peaches called. 'Do sit yourselves down. I'm afraid Felix won't be joining us tonight, it's his night for fasting and meditation.'

Lia tried not to laugh out loud. Inside the spacious kitchen a round dining table had been laid with a somewhat stained tablecloth depicting lavender and herbs. Each place setting had been given its own battered silver cutlery and a chintzy plate. Etienne pulled out a chair for himself and reached for a ceramic bowl of sleek black olives, smaller and less wrinkled than the Greek ones Lia knew.

'How are you finding the pink cottage?' Chloe asked as Peaches darted between them, laying out salad and a pissaladière. As Lia chatted, Etienne went to help himself, but as if suddenly remembering his manners, offered it to Lia first, and then Chloe. It was delicious: a crisp light pasty base covered with caramelised onions, more of the tiny Provençal black olives and thin slivers of anchovy.

'Did you make this yourself, Peaches?' Lia asked approvingly. 'It's wonderful. You must give me the recipe.'

'Oh no, dear.' Peaches laughed. 'I got it from the *traiteur* in the village. They do the most marvellous dishes. But everything else is mine, though.'

The pissaladière, Lia thought, was a must for her book. So she would have to grow her own onions and learn to caramelise them to the exact right degree, and perhaps include it in a chapter about olives, along with tapenade paste and olive bread? And oil, of course, or perhaps that would merit a chapter in its own right? Her book was coming to life – though still an untamed mass of ideas, recipes and research, waiting to be put into some kind of order. The main idea was to base it around the seasons, which would then be broken up into different categories for each of the produce.

'The wicked witches, I call 'em at that shop,' Chloe confessed, dabbing her mouth with her napkin. 'You shop anywhere else and they'll put a spell on you.'

'Now, now, Chloe,' Peaches scoffed, presenting the table with an aubergine gratin and a pot-roasted rabbit cooked with herbs which smelt heavenly. 'You have such an overactive imagination. They are no such thing. They're charming ladies who make an honest living and cook divinely.'

'They give me the shivers,' Chloe insisted, as Peaches began serving. 'They do practise witchcraft, you know,' she added quietly. 'I know they do.'

Peaches laughed. 'Don't you listen to her,' she said, checking that everyone had a full plate. 'She's been watching too many movies. Now, Lia, you must give me your date, place and time of birth.' She made it sound like a formality, like handing over a passport or driving licence as ID. 'And then I can do your chart. I used to charge ninety-five dollars for them, you know, but it's more of a hobby these days.'

'I think I'm a little scared to,' Lia joked, enjoying her food. If anyone seemed like a witch right now, Peaches did. 'I'll have no secrets left.'

'There are always secrets, dear – unfortunately we all have them!' She broke into a chuckle and Lia couldn't imagine her ever managing to keep one herself – she was too open, too much of a chatterer. Warily, she gave Peaches her date of birth. 'I'll have to ask my mother for the actual time,' she added. 'But that makes me a Cancer, a home-maker, a shy crab.'

'Yes, that's right, ruled by the moon. But do ask your mother, won't you, or else I can't do your chart properly.' Peaches told her, pausing to think. 'Now in numerology that date makes you a three-two-five,' she continued excitedly. 'Lively, creative and artistic, you hate routine and need constant change. You're lucky and adventurous, love to travel and would do well in any form of communications, like publishing. Well, that much is true, isn't it? But you could become addicted to food, drink, sex or drugs, though, so you must watch those areas, and you'd also do well to meditate, which would be good for your nerves.'

'My goodness,' Lia tried to laugh off her embarrassment. 'I sound a bit of a wreck.'

'Nonsense, dear, they're just areas to watch, that's all. Now, tell us all about this book you're writing.'

Not really feeling like going into it again, Lia gave the outline she'd rehearsed a few times before.

'*The Sensuous South*,' Peaches repeated. 'I rather like that. *The Sensuous South*.' A faraway look came over her face again as Etienne took a second helping of rabbit. 'That works out as a six, so it should be attractive and money-making, bravo!'

The phone started ringing and Peaches tossed down her napkin and stood up, tutting and clearly disapproving of the interruption.

'What did you do before?' Lia turned back to Chloe, grateful for a chance of normality.

'I was in recruitment consultancy,' Chloe told her proudly. 'Temps, mainly, for all the big city firms.' She began explaining in far more detail than Lia needed, but was mercifully distracted by the sound of Peaches' thrilled voice on the phone.

'Ben?' she started excitedly, as if the caller were a great

distance away. 'Is that you, dear? Where are you calling from? ... Oh my, you be careful, now ... Oh how wonderful, we'd love to see you ... Yes, yes, we still have places, Chloe's here of course, with Etienne, and a charming girl called Lia arrived today, she's in the pink cottage ... in February? Of course, dear, how marvellous ... Well, we look forward to seeing you ... Yes, yes, I'll prepare everything ... OK, see you then ... Bye, dear, bye.'

She returned to the table. 'What wonderful news,' she said. 'Ben's coming over at the beginning of February. He's such a handsome boy,' she turned to Lia. 'A war correspondent, or photographer, I forget which, now. He's seen and experienced some dreadful things, of course, but has a wonderful charm and sense of humour. You'll adore him.'

'He was pretty cut up when he first came here, wasn't he?' Chloe started. 'He'd been in Afghanistan or somewhere like that, found it all a bit much. Didn't he get close to getting killed or something?' she asked.

'He came here seeking spiritual comfort,' Peaches speared a bit of aubergine with her fork. 'And he found it here, as does everyone at Les Eglantines.' She laughed proudly. 'But did you know there are many Brits and Americans around here? A delightful couple, Tristram and Elspeth, living in a darling cottage further down the valley, then there's James and Margaret Caversham in the village, oh and Nick Delaney.' Her eyes lit up. 'He's a dotcom millionaire! He has a wonderful house on the road directly above this, you can see it from your cottage, dear. He's an American, terribly dashing—'

'What about Bella, isn't she coming down, soon?' Chloe interrupted her.

'Yes, dear, I think she may be. Bella's renovating a house about a half an hour away,' she told Lia. 'I think she'll be down in the spring, but she hasn't confirmed yet.'

Peaches didn't seem too enthusiastic about this new arrival.

31

'Is that Bella the artist?' Lia asked.

'Oh, that's right, her watercolour's in your bedroom, isn't it? Bella DeVere. She was married to a wealthy businessman, but they're divorced now. She paints and dabbles in interior design, a very bright woman.' Coming from Peaches, this description was almost damning. 'Now, anyone for cheese?'

She stood up to make for the kitchen as the others began clearing away the plates. 'Oh good, Ben's coming,' she continued from the kitchen. 'Such a lovely man, he just makes this place, you know?'

Lia caught Chloe rolling her eyes again, as if she sometimes found Peaches too much. What characters they all were, she thought, clearing away the plates and cutlery; so far removed from anyone she'd ever met in London.

Life might certainly be different here, she told herself, but by the looks of things, it would never be dull.

Chapter Five

Lia woke late the next morning, unaccustomed not only to the hour time difference, but to the shutters which blocked out the morning sun. Once she'd opened them, it streamed into the east-facing bedroom which overlooked the weeping willow and the citrus orchard. She climbed out of bed, pulled a fleece on over her nightie and put on her socks and slippers before tiptoeing down the stone steps, where she found to her delight that the cottage, *her cottage*, was just as enchanting as she'd remembered it. Through the dining area she went, pausing to admire her little sitting room, before pulling open the drape and entering the kitchen. She poured herself some orange juice and put the kettle on the stove to make tea.

Through the window she noticed a scrubby patch of land, just rocks, a few weeds and soil, and Lia wondered idly if she could develop it, grow a few herbs perhaps. A washing line hung between two trees and there was a small path which ran around the back of the cottage. The area, which was a lot smaller than the terrace to the front, was sealed off by a tall fence which ran the length of the garden down the terraces, and high above it she could make out an elegantly terraced garden and a lovely toffee-coloured house with pale green shutters.

As the kettle warmed up, she took another look at her property, throwing open the shutters and peering at her terrace, which was bare except for a handful of terracotta tubs. There was a sage, a daisy and a couple of sorry-looking geraniums, and along the fence climbed a tired clematis, which she wondered whether to cut back. At the far end, on either side of the gate, was a mandarin tree and an oleander bush. She could put more tubs on this terrace, she thought, fill them with pansies and primula, and then develop the scrubby bit at the back.

Beneath her terrace was an overgrown patch of land which looked like it had once been a vegetable garden, but that had been allowed to grow wild, and she wondered whether she might be able to do something with that as well. Beyond that she could see nothing but gently cascading tree-covered hillsides which met in an obscured valley and led towards the sea. The eastern side was still in shade, she noticed, whilst the west was bathed in golden sun, which only a handful of houses were enjoying. Beyond the hills the sea twinkled in the distance. The cottage was everything she ever wanted; and she could barely believe her luck.

She made her tea and took a gloriously hot shower, loving her new bathroom. From the window she could just make out the neighbouring house beyond the tall fence and its prim garden, lined with roses. She decided to have a proper look round the village before unpacking her laptop and starting to work. Ideas would come as she walked, she told herself, so she would in fact be working anyway.

The morning air was cool and fresh as she made her way along the narrow lane towards the village, but the sun warmed her face. If winter stayed like this, she thought – dry, sunny and cold – then life would be blissful. It was the eternal rain that had depressed her so much in London, the eternal grey drizzle. She'd far rather a sudden downpour, a dramatic storm, to that relentless dampness, but now it seemed she'd found the climate of her choice.

34

She paused to admire the other houses, some right there, on the road, in full view of passers-by, and others tucked away more discreetly. As she walked she had to avoid treading on stray olives which had fallen, reminding her of the chapter she had thought about the previous night. She'd heard of olive groves and mills that were open to the public somewhere north of Avignon, and thought how she must get a car soon and go there, learn about the process and immerse herself in the subject. Hadn't the goddess Athena planted the first olive tree in Athens, she tried to remember, and wasn't the olive tree a symbol of wisdom, peace and light? For her book to work, she knew she had to understand every aspect of the fruit.

The lane took her gently uphill until it met the main road, off which more lanes and terraces lay. She climbed up until she reached the modern complex, but this time continued on to the village itself, up the narrow twisting lanes full of terraced houses, their washing lines and hanging baskets fluttering overhead. Stray tabby cats, one of which looked suspiciously like the neighbouring bully, skulked in corners before disappearing off down alleyways as she came closer, and there was the occasional sound of dogs barking or the cry of a child.

She passed many villagers carrying *banettes*, the smaller and more manageable version of a *baguette*. Everyone said *bonjour* with a polite smile, even the children, and despite the darkness in the narrow streets, the village itself felt warm and sunny.

At last she reached the top, where she found a small post office, a pharmacy and the *traiteur*, where two women worked, cutting hunks of cheese or slabs of meat for their customers. One had a thick, plain face with long black hair pulled severely back in a ponytail, and until her face broke into a huge warm smile Lia could see why Chloe thought she might be a witch. Their shop was an Aladdin's cave of vegetables, fruit, cheese, meat, tinned goods, wines and general groceries, and judging by the queue waiting to be served, it was clearly appreciated by the locals. It was the

35

sort of place where buying onions would take half an hour, Lia thought, but it would be a pleasurable half hour, full of gossip and chatter, if she could ever penetrate their thick southern accents.

Having spent two separate years in France she had once considered herself pretty fluent, but by now Lia felt decidedly rusty. As she walked she rehearsed standard phrases or questions she might need, realising to her disappointment how much she'd lost. It was there, she knew, the vocabulary was there somewhere, hidden in the recesses of her mind; waiting, no doubt to pop out about half an hour after she'd needed it. She would study, she told herself, she'd read the papers and watch TV and converse with the locals until she'd got it; until the day came when she realised she understood it all as effortlessly as she did English, and no longer had to concentrate or rehearse each sentence before speaking.

Further along the lane she came to a newsagents, and paused to study the magazines. She could buy an *Elle*, she thought, or the *Nice-Matin* for the news. Or what about *Paris-Match*, or *Le Figaro*? Her eyes fell on two familiar-looking magazines which featured Hollywood stars on their covers: *Ola!* and *Gala*, which bore a striking resemblance to *Hello!* and *OK*, and chose them over the others, reasoning that she stood a better chance of grasping an interview with Julia Roberts than she did with Jacques Chirac. You could take the girl out of London, she laughed at herself, but you couldn't turn her into a Francophile overnight.

She passed two pizzerias and a busy bar, stopped to have a quick look inside the church and came across a panorama, with views across the valley and down to the sea. She could make out her lane, but not Les Eglantines itself, only the attractive toffee-coloured house above her kitchen garden.

Her kitchen garden – she must get to work immediately, ask Peaches if she could plant things there and find the garden centre on her hand-drawn map. It was too late to plant basil, of course, but she could find more sage, perhaps, some parsley, thyme and rosemary. Maybe she should plant garlic, too, and some basics?

She turned around and made her way back, through the village and down past the supermarket. Outside the hair-dressers she watched two satisfied customers leave, each with newly coifed bright orange hair like Peaches', and wondered whether this was a fashion Peaches had started, or just a prerequisite of living there. She could picture herself in thirty years' time, her French fluent and her hair bright orange, a shelf full of books to her name, and smiled.

She continued towards her own lane, thrilled that this was her home, and privileged to be a part of it. *Her home!* She would make coffee, read her magazines and then send a few e-mails to let people know she'd arrived safely.

She'd just sat down with her Julia Roberts interview when Peaches appeared at the door, her hair looking slightly wild, as if she'd just been dancing.

'I just popped in to see that you're all right,' she started. 'It can get a bit lonely up here sometimes.'

'No, I'm not lonely,' Lia assured her. 'I'm very happy, believe me. I just had a nice walk around the village and am looking forward to getting on with some work soon.' She glanced guiltily at the magazines on the dining table, betraying her.

Peaches didn't notice. 'Good, there's the spirit. Well, if there's anything you need, or anything I can do, you know where to find me. Or even if you just want a chat, I'm always here. Oh, James, did you follow me?' She dropped to stroke the large ginger tom, who was brushing up against her leg. 'You are a naughty boy! You don't mind him, do you? Only he's terribly friendly, just loves to meet new people.'

'No, I don't mind at all,' Lia told her. 'Peaches, can I ask you something? The patch of land, outside my kitchen,' she led her outside to show where she meant. 'Could I do something with it? Grow herbs, for example, or vegetables?'

'Why of course, dear. I used to do just that but you know, you can't expect others to look after things all the time and so they all died. But do, I'd be thrilled if you would. And you know you can hang your washing out here? It doesn't get much morning sun, I'm afraid, but it's so much more discreet than the main terrace.' She nudged Lia and pointed up the hill. 'That's Nick Delaney's house,' she said conspiratorially. 'The dotcom millionaire I told you about. Very handsome and charming.'

'Maybe I don't want him seeing all my undies hanging there, then,' Lia suggested with a giggle.

'Oh he's not here very often, he commutes between Paris and London and New York and, oh, all over the world. He comes here once or twice a year, that's all. My dear friend Binkie Hardcastle shares the same cleaner, and apparently his house is exquisite, all Moroccan in style, very exotic. He has a beautiful French girlfriend, of course, Elodie, very glamorous, who travels the world with him.' She paused, as if lost in thought, and then remembered something. 'You must talk to Etienne about the garden, you know, that's what he's here for. He only does a few hours for me a week, unfortunately, as he has other commitments. But you see the land below you?' She indicated the wild-looking terrace beneath Lia's. 'I'd planned on creating a lunar garden there, but what with Felix's stroke and all the ugly business with the neighbours, I've rather let it go. In fact, now you've reminded me, I must get Etienne to work on it straight away.'

She turned as if to go and Lia had to call her back, intrigued. 'Ugly business with the neighbours?' she asked.

'Oh yes,' Peaches sighed. 'I'm sorry to say it, as they're British. But they took umbrage at James using their garden as his bathroom – they even threatened to put poison down, can you believe that? So we had to build that ugly fence to deter him. Well, I must get on, I have an apricot tart in the oven and it's time for Felix to take his pills.'

With that she fluttered, like a bird, across the terrace and into her own garden, pausing only to pick up a stone

38

and hurl it at the neighbour's cat, who'd started prowling around the pool house.

Turning back, Lia glanced up at Nick Delaney's house and wondered if she might ever get to meet this extraordinary man. It struck her as funny that it was here, in this tiny village, and not the sophisticated metropolis of London, that she might meet interesting people, and that it was here that she might finally become the person she'd almost forgotten existed, trapped by the need for security, a steady job and a reliable boyfriend. Here she would mingle with artists, writers and even millionaires, and here she would achieve something in her own right, be her own person. And yes, eventually, here she might find love, although this wasn't a priority just yet, she reminded herself, but yes, here she might find love.

But in the meantime, the sun was getting stronger and her coffee and magazines lay untouched, so she pulled up a chair outside, and in doing so successfully delayed the moment when she'd actually have to start living out the fantasy instead of dreaming it, and get on with some proper work.

Chapter Six

Lia found the garden centre, and bought herbs, lavender and some daisies, which she then carried home, her arms feeling longer by the minute. Etienne agreed to dig over the little garden for her, stopping for frequent cigarette and coffee breaks, and Chloe popped up from time to time to check on their progress and have a chat.

'You know he's going to start growing vegetables with Peaches in that patch just below you?' she asked, sipping the coffee Lia had made her. 'She was on about it the other day, wants to create a lunar garden, or something. You could probably work with them on that, too.'

'Yes, she mentioned it to me.' Lia sipped the mint tea she'd bought as an experiment. She'd always been fascinated by herbal teas, but had never tried any before. This seemed to be the perfect place to start, and now her cupboard boasted several packets, including lemon, blackcurrant and orange and cinnamon, but still the only one she found vaguely appetising was the mint.

'I've got to be honest and say I don't want to have to do all the work myself,' Lia admitted. 'I just need to know how things are grown, you know, the right circumstances, and the timing, so that I can do an overview in the book.'

'Never really saw all the fuss about gardening, myself,' said Chloe slurping her coffee. 'What's the big deal? I mean, you just buy a few packets of seeds and read the instructions on the back. It's hardly brain surgery.'

'I'm not sure Alan Titchmarsh would agree with you on that one,' Lia laughed. 'But there's something magical about when it all works out, you know, when you realise that things you've planted are happy and thriving. I never had more than a window box in London,' she admitted. 'But in my old job, I worked with quite a few gardeners, and was just blown away by their passion and knowledge.'

'In my old job all we had were a few houseplants, and most of them died,' Chloe cut in, before beginning a monologue about whose job it had been to water them, and how their leaves dropping off would start the burglar alarm; and the time when the office manager once cleaned them with Jif. When she paused for breath, Lia found herself starting a revenge monologue, if anything just to see how much she could get away with before the next interruption.

'When I was younger I spent a lot of time with my grandparents, especially in the summer,' she began. 'They retired to Devon and had a fabulous garden. My grandfather used to spend hours talking me through what plant was what, testing me, and then once I knew them all, teaching me all the Latin names. It was a real passion for him, that garden, and a magical place for me. I'd forgotten that feeling until I came here, and seeing this place, it all came back.'

'Don't think my granddad ever left the pub, let alone do anything in the garden. I've got an uncle, though, who's got an allotment, and my Ian always talked about growing things one day.'

'Your husband? He must miss you.' Lia conceded defeat, but consoled herself with a more interesting subject.

'He's all right,' Chloe tutted, not seeming particularly bothered. 'I think the kids took it badly at first, though, but they're coming round.'

41

'Children?' Lia spluttered on her mint tea. 'You have children?'

'That's right, a boy and a girl. Nickie and Samantha.'

'And you, left them?' Lia was incredulous.

'They're with their dad,' Chloe countered before bursting into raucous laughter. 'Your face!' She started heaving, trying not to spill her coffee. 'I'm only joking – we never had kids. Your face, though, it was a picture!'

Lia was hardly disappointed when, minutes later, Chloe realised she was running late for a massage. She began to appreciate Etienne's monosyllabic answers and gruff suggestions on how best to position the herbs. As he planted a backdrop of lavender against the wall, she broke up a garlic bulb and planted each clove, sticking some twigs in the soil to remind herself where they were.

A while later Peaches appeared, followed by James the cat. 'Chloe just told me what you're doing,' she started, a worried look on her face which made Lia wonder if she'd somehow misunderstood their agreement. 'If you'd just wait another week, dear,' she carried on solemnly. 'When the moon's in the descendent, then everything would be so much happier. It stimulates the roots, you see.'

Lia tried not to laugh out loud. 'I'm afraid I can't really wait,' she told her patiently. 'I just need to get on with it.'

Peaches tutted. 'I know you do, but with earthly matters, you're far better off following the moon. That's what we're going to do with the other terrace, isn't it, Etienne, plant and cultivate, everything in accordance with the planets, it's by far the best way. And whatever you do,' she said, wagging her finger like a deranged Sunday schoolmistress, 'be sure not to garden on Saturday, when the moon's node is in the ascendent.'

'Peaches!' Lia laughed out loud. 'I worked in a studio where we put out five half-hour shows a week. We couldn't wait for the moon's nodes to change, or whatever they do, we just had to get on with it. I can't honestly say it made any difference.'

'Oh, but I'm sure it did,' Peaches said in a mock serious

tone. 'We must all follow the moon, to some extent, and be in tune with it. You especially, as a crab. Do you know, for example, the right time to cut your hair?' She was giggling now, backing off towards the terrace and tripping over the cat, who'd started digging a shallow hole. Lia shook her head, baffled.

'If you want it to grow quickly, you cut it during the new moon, and if you want it to grow more slowly, you cut it around the full moon. Oh James, what are you doing?' She cried as he squatted to pee in the hole. 'Come along, you naughty boy!' Defiantly the cat scraped some earth over the damp patch, before turning to follow his mistress towards the terrace.

As Peaches disappeared, Etienne just rolled his eyes. 'She's a crazy woman,' he muttered in a thick, soupy accent, tapping the side of his head. 'Crazy.'

Chapter Seven

Lia created a garden diary on her laptop, so that she could keep track of everything she planted and its progress. She set up a workspace at one end of the dining table and started creating *The Sensuous South*, naming her chapters and grouping food types together. It had to be seasonal, she'd decided, so she needed to focus on warming foods first: soups, *cassoulets*, lentil dishes, flageolets, coq au vins – and then explore the gardening that each might entail. For the spring section she would include lamb with garlic and rosemary, various chicken dishes and whatever vegetables seemed to be appearing in the markets.

But summer – that was the section she most looked forward to – with lots of fresh herbs and vegetables, not to mention all the fruit. She thought she might do a special chapter on jams, and then of course on tarts and puddings. It didn't matter if each season wasn't just the one chapter, she told herself, it was more a question of responding to each season and its produce. Summer in the Med was obviously going to be a highlight.

And then the autumn, with wild mushrooms cooked in crème fraiche or sweet Marsala wine, or turned into risotto or made as stroganoff with mustard and tomato purée –

mushrooms would surely deserve a chapter in their own right? And as she was looking at the Mediterranean as a whole, she had to remember not just to focus on France, but to explore the rest of the region as well: the delicious pastas and fricassées of Italy, the tapas of Spain and all the Middle Eastern and North African specialities.

It was all a bit daunting, really, she'd think from time to time, trying to work out how to pull together all the strands she wanted. But gradually her files built up, full of different chapter headings, ideas, notes to herself and reminders of certain recipes.

Her days fell into an easy routine. She'd spend the mornings either shopping or cooking, then have some lunch on the terrace, noting how the light changed throughout the day, and how at times the sea seemed to merge with the sky. Then she'd sit at her makeshift desk all afternoon. Sometimes James the cat would join her, insisting on kneading her stomach as she typed, otherwise her only companionship was the Internet, which provided a vital link back to the UK.

She'd read the papers, catch up on the gossip and exchange e-mails with friends. Jules was her most regular correspondent, and she'd keep Lia up to date on her chaotic social life, which seemed to involve having quick drinks with acquaintances after work, moving on to supper with friends by nine and then ending up with more drinks well into the early hours, her mobile constantly buzzing with invites and coded text messages. Lia used to rather envy her friend's lifestyle, not to mention energy, feeling rather staid with the simple weeknight pasta suppers she used to cook Jonathan; but now, as she pictured the nightmare of simply getting from one place to another, or going through her credit card statements at the end of the month, she was grateful for her new life.

It occurred to her though, one crisp February morning, that she was not only getting a little tired of her own company, but that she'd been cooking nothing more challenging than a few pasta dishes and the occasional roast chicken. What about all the more complex dishes she needed to try out? She would throw a dinner party for all the others, she decided, stretch herself a bit. She could have them round on Saturday evening, do everything from black olives in garlic and parsley over drinks, to warm *gesier* salad or some soup for starters, chicken and chorizo stew for mains, a cheese platter and perhaps a pear Tarte Tatin for pudding.

Excited by her plans, Lia put on her fleece and headed for Peaches' house to invite her and Felix. Felix was still a bit of a mystery to her – Lia had only seen him once or twice, just to say hello and shake hands. He was clearly still recovering from his stroke and taking life gently. Tall and thin, he had fine grey hair which was just starting to cover his collar, and spoke slowly in a crisp English public school accent. She was intrigued by what might have led him down the mystical path he was travelling, if that was the right term, and looking forward to getting to know him better.

Opening the gate she caught sight of a figure she didn't recognise, a thirty-something man with wavy brown hair wearing jeans, a navy sweater and a roomy leather jacket. He was carrying a travelling bag and what looked like camera equipment on one shoulder. He had been heading towards the studios, but on seeing her, stopped, nodding in acknowledgement.

'You must be Ben?' She approached him and he broke into a warm, welcoming smile. It was the kind of smile that lit up his whole face, every bit of it seeming to join in – it was impossible not to warm to a smile like that. He looked tanned, the deep, rich tan of someone who'd spent most of the year abroad, and his hair was long overdue for a cut. He dropped his bag and held his hand out to shake hers. It was a strong handshake, not so strong as to be overpowering, but strong enough to reveal character, a certain confidence.

'Lia, isn't it? Peaches has just been telling me all about you: how charming and talented you are and how you're writing this wonderful book that's destined for the best-seller list.'

Lia laughed, embarrassed. 'Does Peaches ever say a bad word about anyone? You're the charming, talented and brave war correspondent, aren't you, who dashes around from one war zone to another, bringing the truth into people's homes?'

'Not exactly how I'd put it,' he smiled and Lia knew immediately they'd be friends. More than that, with any luck, she realised with a flush to her cheeks. 'I'm a photo journalist, which doesn't necessarily mean going into war zones, but Peaches gets a bit confused. In the end I let her think what she wants.'

'And where have you just come from now?' she asked.

'Kosovo,' he told her. 'Watching the place rebuild itself. It's a very positive thing, seeing somewhere you've known in a complete state of chaos start to turn itself round. Gives you hope for everywhere.'

Lia nodded, but couldn't think of anything intelligent to say apart from 'I bet' with what she hoped was a sensitive nod. 'So you're down for a few weeks, then?' she asked, trying to subdue the little butterflies that seemed to be flitting around inside her chest, stealing her breath.

'Looks like it. I like the winters here.'

They stood there, Lia slightly awkward, not knowing what to say but not wanting to leave him just yet, either. Ben, on the other hand, looked perfectly composed and at ease.

She hadn't taken Peaches' comments that seriously, Lia realised now, and had expected a gaunt and earnest Ben to arrive; a Ben with a nervous tick or a stammer; a Ben who didn't wash very often or who'd look at a full plate of food only to start lecturing on starvation and third-world debt relief. The last thing she'd expected was this seriously gorgeous Ben who stood before her now.

'Well, I'll let you settle in.' She started to move off, embarrassed by the series of dirty fantasies that had just flashed through her mind. 'But do come up for a drink, or

47

something, won't you? I'm always at the pink cottage.'

It was only after he'd taken the path down to the studios that Lia kicked herself for not having invited him to join them on Saturday. Now it would look like she'd only decided to throw the party because she fancied him, in a sad attempt to get to know him better. All it would have taken, she chided herself, was a casual 'oh, I'm having a dinner party Saturday, in fact I'm just on my way to invite everyone, and I'd love you to come' and everything would have been all right. She was wondering what to do when Peaches appeared, a trowel in one hand.

'Well, hello, dear, did you know today's an excellent day to sow your perennials? The moon's in Libra, you see. Now, did you just meet Ben?' she continued, unperturbed by the look of amusement on Lia's face. 'Such a lovely man, so warm and friendly.'

'Yes I did,' Lia told her. 'In fact, I'm just kicking myself. I was on my way to invite you and Felix to dinner on Saturday, and I should have invited him too.'

'Oh, but you must,' Peaches implored. 'Ben is such good company. Saturday, was that, dear? Well we'd love to, what a treat.'

They established that Felix couldn't eat fish, which wasn't a problem, and that Peaches was trying to avoid cheese that week, but apart from that they could eat anything she offered. Lia took a deep breath and started on the path which led to the studio flats, six in a row, tucked below the pool. She rehearsed over and again what she might say to Ben, and how she might laugh off not having mentioned the dinner before.

Chloe and Etienne's flat was at the far end, so she had to walk past Ben's to reach them. She looked away, not wanting to pry. The front door was open, she noticed, and she could hear sounds of zips being opened and hangers shuffling. At the end flat she rang the bell and had to wait a few seconds until Chloe appeared, wearing a loose green tracksuit.

'I was just doing my yoga,' she explained apologetically.

48

'I'm starting a new course next week, so I've got to prepare it. Why don't you join us? It would do you good.'

'Yes, perhaps I should,' Lia said doubtfully, knowing how pitiful she was at keeping up any exercise, and remembering the three sessions at the gym which had worked out at £72 each before she'd cancelled her membership. 'Anyway, I'm having a dinner party on Saturday,' she said, changing the subject. 'And I'd love you both to come.'

'Oh, that sounds great, we'd love to,' Chloe said enthusiastically. 'Are you inviting Ben?'

'Yes, I thought I would,' Lia said loudly, hoping he might hear. 'I met him just now and completely forgot, though. So I'll ask him next. Now, is there anything you can't eat?'

'Well,' Chloe thought for a moment. 'All dairy produce, wheat, meat, and I can't stand root vegetables,' she told her, before bursting out laughing. 'No, Babe, we can eat anything, though I can't bear all those brains in aspic and pigs' trotters and stuff like that,' she added.

'They weren't on the menu,' Lia assured her, before heading towards Ben's open door. She knocked, and he swung round from his unpacking, the welcoming smile automatically on his face.

'Sorry to disturb you,' she started, before extending the invitation.

'I'd love to come,' Ben smiled and Lia wondered why she'd ever been so worried. They established that he ate everything but had lived on bean soup and bread for the last few months, so Lia promised to do something more interesting.

It was only later that she kicked herself again for not having offered him some teabags, or a cup of milk, or some bread – something nice and neighbourly to see him through until the supermarket opened again after lunch.

And it was hours later, as she poured herself her second glass of wine that evening, idly stirring a broccoli, chilli and anchovy paste sauce, that she realised that all she'd

49

thought of that afternoon was how to arrange dinner, what exactly to serve and where everyone should sit, and that ultimately all her thoughts were leading to Ben, and how to create the right impression.

She couldn't remember the last time she'd felt like this about anyone.

Chapter Eight

Lia was sitting in the sun on her terrace, working through her table plan for the following evening's dinner party over a glass of rosé. She didn't normally drink at lunchtime, but had been overcome by a sudden feeling of well-being and, spotting the opened bottle in the fridge, had found it hard to resist. It was so warm that she'd had to take off her jumper and socks, and she could see bees buzzing around Peaches' lavender as if it were spring. She'd had to remind herself that this was the beginning of February – a month when she was more used to shivering by radiators and trying to keep her hands from going numb. It had to be the sun, she told herself, guiltily having a sip of the wine – it was leading her astray. And all she could think about was Ben, and she felt heady with excitement at the prospect of seeing him again.

Everything around her seemed to be pushing her, urging her towards a big new romance: from the moon at night, which seemed to be lower and brighter than ever, to the dazzling sun by day; the cold crispness of morning to the hazy warmth of the afternoon; everything felt alive; everything she touched, smelt or ate seemed more purpose-ful, somehow, more definite. She had never known such prettiness in her surroundings before, far preferring the tree-covered hills and the turquoise sea to the gentle landscapes of her childhood in Sussex. And as for the terraced streets of Fulham – she'd barely given them a thought. Had she really spent, wasted even, so much of her life there?

Even shopping now, browsing round the village stores and the little supermarket, was a pleasure. Never before had she known such high standard of produce. Gone were the days when she'd a buy cellophane-wrapped vegetables and pre-packed cheeses from vast supermarkets – now everything was hand selected from the counter, along with personal recommendations, friendly advice and a bunch of fresh herbs thrown in.

She had done all the food shopping that morning and even splashed out on candles: four tall orange ones for the mantelpiece and dining table, and two thick vanilla-scented ones for the coffee table. She'd filled her vases with pale orange roses and bought some pretty floral paper napkins. Everything was going to be perfect, she told herself – good company enhanced by warming, nutritious food. And as for the seating arrangements, she'd put herself at the table head nearest the kitchen, with Felix opposite. Ben would be to her right and Etienne left, with Peaches beside Etienne and Chloe by Ben. But that would mean Peaches and Felix would be sitting together, so perhaps that didn't work, after all? She was just reworking it, being careful to keep Ben to her side, when she heard the gate creak, and suddenly there he was, on the terrace.

'Lunchtime drinking?' He smiled, surveying the scene. 'You'll never get any work done that way.'

She leapt up, thrilled to see him but embarrassed at being caught out. 'I don't normally,' she insisted. 'But it's such a lovely day and I thought "to hell with it all" and had a glass. Can I get you one?'

He smiled sheepishly. 'A small one then,' he said, pulling up a chair.

She rushed to the kitchen and fetched a glass and the bottle, hurriedly putting it in a cooler. 'So, are you all

52

settled in, then?' She filled his glass, trying to sound calmer than she felt.

'As much as I'll ever be. How about you, you enjoying it here?'

Lia told him how much she'd fallen in love with her cottage and the village. 'You've been here a few times, I take it?'

'Two or three, since last summer. It's a good place for clearing the mind. If I stayed in London between trips I'd go mad. This place helps me relax.'

'And how did you first hear about it?'

He looked slightly embarrassed. 'I came on one of Peaches' retreats.'

'You did?' She leant forward, intrigued. 'And did it, do much, for you?' she asked hesitantly, wondering what on earth he would have got out of it.

'It did actually,' he told her with an air of surprise. 'It opened me up, made me see the bigger picture. You get a bit bogged down in my job, you know? You see things that make you wonder, you know.' He shrugged, as if he couldn't find the right words. 'What it's all about. Sounds a cliché, I know. But you need to put it in some kind of perspective.' He sipped his wine thoughtfully. 'I've got a lot of time for Peaches,' he continued. 'She can be a bit of a silly old thing sometimes, but there's a goodness there, and she's surprisingly intuitive. There've been days when she's pinpointed exactly what was on my mind and said just the right thing at the right time.' He noticed the scepticism on Lia's face. 'It's hard to believe, I know, when she witters on like she does, but it's true. She's got a good heart.'

'Oh yes, I don't doubt that,' Lia gushed, feeling suddenly rather tipsy. It couldn't have been the wine, she thought, as she'd barely had a glass, so it had to be the excitement of his visit. The thrill of finally talking to him, rather than just imagining it, as she'd done for the last couple of days. To her annoyance, though, she could hardly think of anything articulate to say. 'It was her

53

warmth, that attracted me, when I spoke to her on the phone.' She told him about Jules, and her introduction to Les Eglantines.

'So you just decided to throw it all in and come here?' he asked. 'That's impressive.'

'Not really,' she shrugged. 'I had to do something, you know? Had to challenge myself, try something different before I got bogged down.' She hoped a word like *challenge* might impress him; that he would relate to it. 'But you, though, you put yourself through far more than that.'

He leant down to pick up the bottle from under the table and refilled both their glasses. His action thrilled her, suggesting that they were in for a long chat.

'Yes, there are challenges, certainly, but then the very thing you're witnessing tends to belittle the job itself. You see kids with their legs blown off by landmines, boys who've gone out fighting at the age of twelve, families devastated by war – and you're powerless. Sure, you can send the message back home, but ultimately, you're not going to save any lives. So you sometimes wonder what the point is.'

He took a large swig of wine and Lia wished she could come up with something appropriate and intelligent to say, as Peaches apparently could.

'In many ways I suppose you're privileged,' she tried. 'Because you get to witness history all over the world, and there aren't many people who can say they've done that.'

'That doesn't make me feel any better,' he laughed. 'I get to witness history and record it. I make a living out of witnessing and recording people's misery and deprivation, but without actually doing anything tangible to alleviate it. Nice, eh?'

'I didn't mean it like that,' Lia said quickly, kicking herself. 'And even if you're not making a tangible difference, surely you're contributing to some long-term benefit? I mean, ultimately, your photos could lead to world powers getting together to make a difference?'

'That's a nice thought,' he smiled. 'But I don't flatter

myself. To be honest, there's just nothing else I'd rather be doing. I can't imagine a desk job, or photographing people's pets for a living. But having said that, I really appreciate days like this, when the sun's shining, French life continues at its best, and the only problem I have is the bottle running out.'

'Talking of which,' Lia topped up their glasses, relieved that he'd let her off. 'So how long are you down here for this time?'

'A few weeks. I'm not sure. I was asked to go to the West Bank, but I think Afghanistan's coming up, and I'd rather wait for that.'

She suddenly felt anxious that he might go before they'd become close. It was strange to have a deadline – it made every minute seem significant, and she hated to waste time. But bar dragging him upstairs to her bedroom, there was not a lot she could do.

'So how do you spend your days down here?' she asked, resisting the urge to touch the hairs on his arm, or to send him a discreet but unambiguous signal.

'Sleeping. Catching up on my reading. Hanging out in cafés drinking coffee and beers. Busy doing nothing, but the days go by.' He turned to her, and the look on his face suggested he knew exactly what she was thinking, and that he wasn't averse to being dragged up to her bedroom, either.

He asked about her book, and she explained how far she'd got, carefully omitting how much of the work was still in her mind, and not yet on screen, and then offered him some lunch, pulling together a selection of cheeses, some smoked ham and salami, a fresh *banette* and a salad.

'To be honest, I've been thinking of doing a book myself, perhaps, or setting up an exhibition,' he started. 'I've got so much material, I'm just trying to collate it all. That is, actually, the main thing I do down here – I'm not an entire slouch.' He smiled, slicing into a hunk of cheese. 'But I've been thinking about changing the way I work completely. I reckon I've had enough misery to last me a lifetime, it's been doing my head in. So I'd like to do something more positive, and maybe find people I've photo'd in the past and see how they're doing now, show how aid and relief has either helped, or maybe even hindered them. I just did that in Kosovo: I managed to trace some of the refugees I'd met during the war, and found them back in their farms, rebuilding their lives.'

'That sounds wonderful, Ben,' Lia enthused. 'A really wonderful project.' Her own seemed trivial by comparison.

They finished the bottle, and at around four, as the sun dipped behind the mountain, leaving a sudden coldness in its wake, Ben began to get up. 'I'd better leave you to it,' he said, and she wished he'd stay. They could open another bottle, she thought, a warming red, and then transfer to the sitting room, talk until midnight and end up in each other's arms, and preferably, her bed.

'You know, I'm not going to get any work done now,' she tried.

'I'm sorry for distracting you. But I'd better get going.' He yawned. 'I'm feeling a bit tired, actually, I might have a nap.' He stood up and stretched, and she caught herself wondering what he'd look like naked. What he'd be like under the duvet, napping, his hair all messy on her pillow.

'I don't know, you get a girl tipsy and then you just walk away,' she teased, and he laughed, more out of surprise than because it was funny, and reached across to ruffle her hair, as if she were a mischievous child who'd just said something naughty.

Suddenly noticing the seating arrangement she'd left on a spare chair, he frowned, picking it up. 'So I'm next to you, am I, which is nice, but opposite Etienne? Have you seen his table manners lately?'

Embarrassed, she pulled the paper out of his hands, feeling like a provincial housewife throwing her first dinner party. She should be more bohemian, she told herself, and let people sit wherever they wanted. If only she could rely on Ben to sit next to her.

'I'll change it,' she promised, adding, 'it's not important.'

'Thanks for the wine, and lunch,' he kissed her on either cheek, and she wished she had the nerve to hold him, and kiss him properly. 'It was great.'

'Pop up any time, won't you?' Lia told him, trying to disguise her disappointment. 'I'm always here.'

He smiled, that warm, broad, open smile of his, gave her a last wave and then left through the gate. She watched as he forked right down the path, towards the flats, and then slumped into a mild depression. As the sun had gone in, so had it taken him with it, and the cottage and terrace suddenly felt empty and grey.

She washed up the lunch things and made herself some apple and cinnamon tea and, knowing that she couldn't work now, wandered aimlessly about the place, shivering. It was extraordinary how quickly the atmosphere had changed – just half an hour ago the sun had been at its strongest, giving out a lovely golden light before dipping behind the mountain, and now it was that strange twilight hour when it was too cold to sit outside, but not yet dark enough to close the shutters and light candles.

She pulled on another jumper and settled into one of the armchairs, the table lamp merely accentuating the lack of light inside and lack of darkness out, and decided to have another go at a novel Jonathan had bought her two years ago. When, some half an hour later, she realised she'd re-read the same two pages several times and still hadn't a clue what they said, she decided to call Jules, and tell her all about Ben.

'So which agency does he work for, then?' Jules asked abruptly, after Lia had finished.

'I don't know, it never occurred to me to ask,' she told her, slightly taken aback.

'And why does he keep going to France?' Jules sounded suspicious, which rather threw Lia.

'I don't know, it's nicer than London.'

Jules hummed. 'It just sounds a bit odd to me. I mean, he went on a retreat? Bit girlie, isn't it?'

'He needed to clear his head, Jules, get a different

perspective on life, that's all.' Lia couldn't understand her friend's attitude.

'So how exactly does he make a living, again?'

'I've told you, he's a photographer—'

'Come on, Li, they don't make that much,' Jules said scornfully. 'How will he finance this new project of his, all that travelling? Are you sure he hasn't got some sugar-mummy somewhere? And if he's freelance, how can he just turn down an offer like the West Bank? It doesn't make sense – it's like there's something he's not telling you.'

This was neither the response Lia was expecting nor wanting to hear. 'He's a great guy, Jules,' she tried. 'But like me, he's just trying to change his life.' As she said it, she felt a bond of solidarity with him, and felt herself grow stronger. 'I don't know anything about his finances, it's not my place to. But he's trying to do something different.'

'Yeah, right, and he'd rather be in some dodgy French retreat than out there working? I'm sorry, Li, I don't mean to put him down, but he sounds a bit precious to me, you know, the sort who witnesses something nasty and goes into counselling for days.'

'Jules!' This was frustrating, and Lia began to wish she'd never made the call. She'd assumed Jules would just be happy for her, share in her excitement.

'Oops, better go, got a meeting,' Jules said suddenly. 'How's the book coming along, anyway? Got any chapters for me, yet?' She made it sound so easy. 'Drop me a line and tell me what's happening, won't you?'

Lia hung up, feeling decidedly deflated. It was as if she'd fancied a movie star for years and had just heard he was gay. Had she missed something about Ben? Was he indeed precious, or hiding something? She tried to go over their conversation again, and found herself wishing that he'd just show up and spend the evening with her. Then she could grill him properly, and turn Jules around. But instead, all she had right now were hours, at least sixteen before she might see him again and over twenty-four before he'd be round for supper.

She sipped her tea grumpily. Had he not come over, she thought, she would have had a perfectly nice lunch on the terrace, stopped at just the one glass of wine and then continued working all afternoon. How ironic, then, that the arrival of the man she lusted after should now have put her in such a bad mood.

She finished her tea and made another cup, bullying herself to be productive, and spent the next hour or so until dark toying with her seating plan, fantasising about an evening playing footsy under the table and making quiet eye contact when no one was looking. It killed the hour at least. Just another twenty-four to go.

Chapter Nine

'I have two gifts for you, dear.' Peaches and Felix were the first to arrive in a noisy chaos of chatter and the removal of coats, gloves and scarves. They'd had to walk all of fifty metres but seemed to have dressed for a ten-mile trek across the Arctic. Once they'd stripped off, however, Felix was still in the tracksuit he'd been wearing earlier in the day, while Peaches looked splendid in a deep-orange cowl-neck jumper and long black woollen skirt. She'd applied some make-up, too, black eye-liner which emphasised the almond shape of her eyes and some red lipstick, and she smelt musky and warm.

'Some lavender, snipped from the garden,' she presented Lia first with a bunch of pale purple flowers tied together with twine, their muted scent redolent of warmer times, and then with a look of delight handed over a dossier. 'Your chart,' she whispered. 'I hope it encourages you with your endeavours.'

'Peaches, how kind!' Lia gushed, wanting to read through it immediately.

'Are we the first? Not too early, though, I hope. I hate lateness, you know. But as Felix is always late, and I'm always early, somehow between us we usually manage to be on time! My, the cottage looks darling, look at all your candles and roses.'

'You even match my colour scheme, Peaches,' Lia smiled, handing her a glass of Bordeaux. She ushered them into the sitting room and began to look through her chart, reading certain items of interest out loud. Peaches had started it with some keywords before going into a more in-depth analysis.

'Sensitive, vulnerable, nurturing,' Lia read. 'Loyal clinging, possessive. Not sure if I like that so much.' She paused to have a sip of wine. Perhaps reading it out loud wasn't such a good idea, after all. 'Sentimental, creative. Well, that's not so bad, is it? So my Moon's in Virgo, is it, making me self-critical, hard working and interested in health and diet,' she continued. 'And Venus is in my fourth house, giving me an enjoyment of home entertaining and an interest in gardening. That's certainly true, isn't it?'

There was a tap on the door and with a jump Lia went to open it. The others were all there, waiting in the cold, and Lia had to go through the motions of kissing Chloe and Etienne on both cheeks and welcoming them inside before finally greeting Ben himself. His cheeks felt icy against her lips, and he smelt clean and wholesome. Gratefully she accepted their offerings of wine and then removed their coats, excited even to be touching his battered leather jacket, imagining how it must have travelled the world with him, like an old friend. Peaches greeted them all as if she hadn't seen them in weeks, and they took their seats, filling her little sitting room with their warmth and voices.

In the kitchen she poured three more glasses of Bordeaux, and as she turned, Ben was there to help her. It was such a simple act, she thought, a minor detail, but she couldn't help but hope it implied something more than just good manners.

'So how's your chart, then?' Chloe asked, perching on the arm of Etienne's chair, as Lia handed her a glass. 'Does it say you're going to be a successful cookery writer?'

'Haven't got that far, but there was a reference to creativity,' Lia assured her, picking up the papers again. 'You see?' she said, triumphantly, though not altogether seriously. 'Mercury in Gemini, meaning I communicate ideas articulately and accurately.' She scanned through the pages, looking for anything that might impress Ben. 'Jupiter in Virgo means I'm capable of detailed and careful work,' she read. 'And Saturn in Aries means I use my initiative and am self-reliant in life.'

She skimmed over phrases like 'easily hurt in love', 'not completing projects once started' and 'moody and unpredictable' but, as Chloe began describing key factors in her own chart, she realised she wasn't particularly impressing anyone, and quietly put it down, deciding to go and check on the food instead.

In the kitchen, the chicken and chorizo stew bubbled away happily. It was a wonderful dish, becoming tastier and heartier the longer it cooked, and so ideal for a supper party. She'd changed her mind about the starter, and had made instead some hummus and aubergine dips, which she'd experimentally warmed up, rather than serve cold.

She laid out the bowls, no two of which were the same, in the centre of the table, along with a basket full of bread, satisfied with how warm and welcoming it all looked. Ben offered to open another bottle and she had to squeeze past him as she arranged things, fantasising that they were a couple, and hosting the dinner together.

'Oh my, this all looks divine!' Peaches cooed as she found her seat. Despite her earlier reservations, Lia had left a card on each plate, so as to avoid confusion. Felix still managed to walk in exactly the wrong direction around the table, however, a puzzled look on his face, until he found his seat. She was at one head, with Ben comfortably close to her and Felix on her other side, leaving Etienne at the other head, where his table manners could amuse Chloe and Peaches. He lunged into the bread first, dunking it into the hummus without even thinking of offering it around, and started chewing before Chloe had even sat down.

'You've been slaving, haven't you?' Chloe said approvingly, tucking her blonde bob behind her ears. 'I hate cooking, myself. We live off spaghetti and salads, don't we, Babe? And then every now and then Etienne goes spare and has to have a steak!'

As Chloe described her every cooking disaster, they ate heartily, helping themselves to more spoonfuls and greedily tearing off chunks of bread. Every now and then Ben's knee would meet her own, sending a tremor of excitement through her body, but Lia had to accept that they were accidental, and not necessarily evidence of his own desire. He enjoyed the food, she noticed happily, and was the first to top up glasses and ensure that everyone was catered for.

The perfect host, she thought dreamily – with her cooking and his manners they'd make a wonderful couple. Jonathan had been frustratingly slow to pour more wine, she'd always noticed, failing to spot an empty glass or one with only a polite mouthful left in it. Ben was more aware and less disapproving, Lia thought, willing it only to be a matter of time before he was hers.

When the first course was pretty much demolished, Lia cleared the debris and prepared for her *pièce de résistance* – the chicken and chorizo stew, served with a simple rice pilaff. Peaches clapped enthusiastically as she brought it to the table, having transferred it into a large earthenware pot she'd discovered under the sink, and began to serve it with a soup ladle.

The table fell into a satisfied silence as everyone began eating their tender chicken thighs, and all that could be heard was Etienne's sucking on each mouthful, hoovering the meat off each bone and slurping up the chickpeas in their fresh tomato sauce.

Lia turned to Felix. 'Tell me more about the retreat – what exactly was it all about?'

'Well, it was quite a set-up,' he started gently, and she could see what a steadying influence he must have been on Peaches, how calm and good-natured he was. 'In a good summer we'd have fourteen visitors a week, you know.

63

There was no obligation to do anything, of course, the guests were free to sit by the pool all day if they so wished, but we'd offer them various lectures and practice groups throughout the day, and for the most part, people would join in.'

'Felix would start them off with a guided dawn meditation each morning,' Peaches cut in excitedly. 'And once Chloe had joined us she'd take yoga classes, too.'

'And then, after breakfast,' Felix continued quickly, as if terrified that Chloe might interrupt, 'Peaches would go straight into a dream analysis group.'

'That was always riveting,' Peaches started. 'You can tell so much about a person through their nocturnal adventures. It was quite an eye-opener!'

'Next she'd take her astrology or numerology classes,' Felix went on. Lia noticed how similar his and Peaches' accents had become – hers was more toned down, leaning towards English, with token 'British' phrases thrown in, whilst his had a slight transatlantic drawl she hadn't noticed at first. It was as if they'd met each other halfway.

'Then we'd have a nice long break for lunch,' Peaches took over again. 'So that the guests could go to a restaurant in the village if they wanted, or spend time by the pool.'

'Yes, and then each afternoon we'd run a different course: crystal healing, elementary tarot or runes, they were all Peaches' specialities,' Felix continued. 'While I'd lecture on automatic script and past-life regression.'

Lia nodded, trying to suppress the smirk that was trying to spread across her face. It was as if he'd just spoken about bee-keeping to a women's institute group. Had Ben really gone through all this? 'Past-life regression I understand,' she started. 'I remember reading a magazine article about it somewhere, about discovering past problems that can then help the present, or something.'

'That's right, dear, look to the past to heal the present, and indeed the future. It's very effective. I used to practise it as well, but that was an additional charge.'

64

'But automatic script,' Lia pressed on, willing her face to keep straight. 'Now that I'm not familiar with.'

'That's when you go into a trance and a spirit chooses to channel itself through you as a vehicle, and you write their words, usually which offer guidance and spiritual insights,' Felix told her carefully.

'And so, do you – automatically script-write?' she asked, not knowing how to phrase it.

This brought a smile. 'I have been known to in the past,' he told her. 'But it hasn't happened for a while now.'

'I see,' she nodded. 'And so, what's happening now, the retreat's come to a close?'

'Not entirely, dear, we've just wound it down some-what,' Peaches told her. 'It was awfully hard work, and I'm not sure if Felix is up to it this year. Still, we've had some interest from a group for the middle of August, so who knows? Of course, the hardest part is having to lose our friendly winter tenants, like yourself – it's always such a wrench, and then having to find someone else in the fall. So we've yet to make a decision this year.'

Noticing that everyone had finished, Lia piled up their plates and took them to the kitchen, as Ben picked up the empty serving dishes and followed her in. 'Why am I having such a hard time imagining you at one of these retreats?' she whispered, willing him to tell her it had been a joke.

He just smiled, that big warm smile of his, and she felt herself melting, rather like the cheeses on their wooden platter. As she carried them out, Lia could hear Peaches saying, 'I see they're doing some work on Nick Delaney's land. Building a pool house, Binkie says. Or at least, they were there yesterday, though I didn't see anyone again today.'

'Is he back now?' Lia asked, vaguely interested, offering everyone cheese biscuits.

'I don't think so, dear. I'd be disappointed if he was and hadn't popped round to see me. I think this is just work he commissioned last summer. It must be so hard managing a

65

property from abroad, I'm surprised Elodie doesn't come down here more often. You haven't heard from her, have you, Chloe?'

'Peaches, they broke up, I keep telling you,' Chloe sounded exasperated. 'I know you don't want to believe it, but it's true – she left him.'

'Oh, but why would she do a thing like that?' Peaches cried. 'Why would anyone want to leave someone like Nick?'

'Peaches, people leave one another,' Chloe started irritably. 'It was a very hard decision for me to leave my Ian, but I did. He wasn't there for me any more; he wasn't putting me first. Maybe it came as a shock to some people, but I had to go.'

As the monologue continued, Lia disappeared into the kitchen to retrieve the Tarte Tatin. It was extraordinary how Chloe could hijack any given conversation and turn it round to herself, oblivious to the polite silence around her and the distinct lack of interest. She'd have to test her, she decided, start up conversations on the most abstract of things, and see how quickly she could bring them back to the more important subject of herself.

There was a palpable sense of relief when Lia returned with the pudding.

'Have you thought about getting a car yet, dear?' Peaches asked, neatly slicing into a pear with her spoon.

'I have, yes. I just haven't got round to it yet. I've looked a bit in the classifieds, but, you know, how can I go and see a car when I don't actually have a car to get to it? And to tell you the truth, I've never actually bought one before, so I'm a bit nervous.'

'Etienne's friend, Jean-Marc, he could find you something, couldn't he, Babe?' Chloe suggested, and Lia wondered whether she might perhaps start describing her driving lessons next. 'He's got his own garage down the road, hasn't he – I'll talk to him for you, if you like.'

'That would be great,' Lia said doubtfully.

'I'll take a look at it with you,' Ben suggested. 'I mean,

66

I'm not a mechanic but I can certainly give it the once-over for you.'

Suddenly, getting a car became Lia's highest priority. How could she *possibly* have gone so long without one? She would have to badger Chloe until she'd spoken to this Jean-Marc person and something could be arranged.

'That was absolutely delicious,' Peaches said emphatically as she finished her dessert. 'My, is it that late already? Felix, time for bed, dear.'

Obediently he went to retrieve their coats. Ben jumped up and helped Peaches into hers, passing her scarf and gloves, and then disappointingly reached for his jacket as well.

'You're off, too, Ben?' Lia tried to sound unconcerned.

'It was lovely, thank you.' He reached forward and kissed her on both cheeks. 'But I'm up early tomorrow. The forecast is good so I'm hoping to go skiing.'

'Are you, dear?' Peaches interrupted. 'My, I haven't skied in years. When was the last time, Felix?'

As Felix tried to remember, Lia held back her disappointment. She'd hoped he might stay on a bit later than the others, help her with the washing up, or suggest they had lunch or something tomorrow. Instead he was off, up on the slopes, and with whom?

'Lucky you – have a great time,' she told him.

'Thanks,' he said warmly. 'Come on, Peaches, take my arm.' Carefully he led her out of the cottage, and towards the gate, with Felix trotting behind. Lia turned back, expecting to find Chloe and Etienne pulling on their coats, but instead they were still in their chairs, and looked like they had no intention of going anywhere.

'Is there any more of that wine, Lia?' Chloe asked, waving her empty glass. There was, and Lia poured her some.

'I love staying behind after a dinner party and talking about the other guests, don't you?' Chloe laughed. 'I'm in a bit of bother with Peaches at the moment, to tell you the truth. She wants me to get more involved, you know, take bookings for the flats, do the changeover, that sort of thing. Even if they don't do the retreat from now on, she'd still like to rent them out and get some money in.'

'So, isn't that a good idea?' Lia asked, willing her to finish her glass and get going.

'I just don't know where I'd find the time, that's all. I mean, the whole point of my being here is to develop myself spiritually, and I can't see how I'm going to do that by taking bookings and changing sheets. She doesn't seem to understand. I mean, I've got to meditate first thing, then I do my dream analysis, my crystal healing – I can't just drop all that for her.'

Lia, trying not to yawn, wondered again who Ben might be skiing with.

'And I mean, I don't know what she does all day that's so important,' Chloe continued. 'Sits around gossiping with Binkie Hardcastle if you ask me. Loves to know what's going on everywhere. Someone building a new house, renovating some old cottage, all that stuff. And as for Nick Delaney, you'd think he walked on water.'

'She's terribly impressed by him, isn't she?' Lia said without thinking. Did Ben have a girlfriend? Is that who he was skiing with?

'I told her last year that Elodie was leaving him, but she just won't get it. She's got this image that he's this perfect man, and it couldn't be further from the truth.'

'I think everyone gets a bit exaggerated with her, don't you?' Surreptitiously Lia looked at her watch. If there were a girlfriend, then why wouldn't he have said anything? Why wouldn't Peaches have mentioned her?

'Yeah, but him especially,' Chloe drained her glass, and promptly topped it up again. 'He's a dark character, that one. And it's all hidden behind closed doors.'

'What on earth do you mean?' Lia was tired now and just wanted to go to bed. 'Is he in league with the village witches or something?'

'No,' Chloe shook her head, oblivious to Lia's sarcasm. 'Worse than that. He's a wife-beater, that's what he is.'

'What?' Lia frowned, fearing yet another long and unbelievable story.

'Elodie, his ex, she used to come to me for massages. So I used to see the bruises.' Chloe reached across the table for Etienne's glass. He was too far gone to notice. 'But that's not all,' she carried on dramatically. 'He was married once – she told me all about it. His wife committed suicide, and he drove her to it.'

'This all sounds very melodramatic, Chloe,' Lia said evenly, waiting for her to burst out laughing and admit it was another joke.

'God, you're as bad as Peaches, you are. Elodie was terrified. She was planning on running away when he was on a trip. I haven't heard from her, but I hope to God she made it.'

'So, Peaches doesn't know about any of this?'

'No' Chloe shook her head. 'She wouldn't believe me if I told her. She only likes to see the good in people. But that man is evil – he might pretend to be all charm and charisma on the outside, but he's pure evil, really.' She looked across at Etienne, who'd slumped on the table. 'Come on, Babe, don't fall asleep. We'd better get going.'

At this suggestion, Lia jumped up, hoping to encourage them. Chloe shook him awake, and reluctantly they pulled on their coats, eyeing up one of the unopened bottles on their way to the door.

'That was a lovely dinner, Babe, thank you,' Chloe hugged her. Her eyes were half-closed now and her hair dishevelled. Etienne just nodded in acknowledgement and tripped over the rug on his way out.

Once they'd gone, Lia shook her head, feeling suddenly depressed. There were two reasons why, she told herself, piling the plates into the sink and clearing the debris off the table. First it had been Chloe, boring her until she'd virtually lost the will to live – how could she not feel depressed after that? And secondly, it was the idea that Ben was skiing the next day, and more than likely with a girlfriend. Or perhaps even the sugar-mummy Jules had talked about?

There had to be someone, or why else would he keep coming back to France? She'd been too thick to realise it before, she chided herself, but now it was clear. He'd deliberately kept it from Peaches and Chloe because they were such gossips, and he wanted to remain private. It was obvious, when she thought about it.

So Ben had a girlfriend and now there was a wife-beater living right above her cottage. Nice. But at least her dinner had been a success, she laughed gently, putting out the gas fire.

At least that much had gone right.

Chapter Ten

Lia took the next day slowly, washing up and drinking endless cups of lemon verbena tea. She'd put a load of washing on, and as she hung it on the line, found herself drawn to Nick Delaney's lovely toffee-coloured house in the lane above, with its pale green shutters. Could Chloe have been telling the truth, she wondered, and if so, was that where his wife died, and the scene of many a battering? Or had Chloe just been watching too many movies again?

She was depressed: caught in a post-party, pre-period slump and feeling anti-climatic after all her efforts. She wished Ben would appear from nowhere and tell her his skiing had been cancelled, and then suggest a long and lazy lunch somewhere, or a walk in the hills. All she could think of was where he might be right now, and with whom. What an idiot she'd been to think he was single, she told herself, straightening the cottage out. What an idiot to think he'd be free.

She decided that a walk would do her some good, and was heading towards the village when a tired-looking Chloe appeared, wearing jeans and a jumper, her hair scraped back into a ponytail. She wore no make-up and was looking pale and rather fragile.

'Lia, Babe, how are you?' No one had ever called Lia 'Babe' before, and nor did she want them to start now. 'Are you off to the village? Good, I'll join you.'

Inwardly Lia groaned. A bad day had just got worse.

'Look, I'm sorry,' Chloe started. 'I drank a bit too much last night. Went on a bit. How are you doing?'

'I'm fine, thanks, taking things a bit slowly.'

'I know I get a bit gobby after a few drinks, but last night I said some things I shouldn't have.' The last word was pronounced 'of'. 'All that stuff about Nick Delaney, I shouldn't have said anything, really, you know. It's private, not something to be bandied about.'

'Well, I'm hardly going to tell anyone,' Lia started, resenting the implication that she might.

'Especially not Peaches,' Chloe said quickly. 'Or anyone else, for that matter. I'm just worried that if it got out, Elodie's life might be in danger.'

Suddenly Lia developed a headache, the village road seemed longer than usual and the climb steeper. If only she'd have left a few minutes earlier. 'Well, it won't get out,' she said tersely.

'Good, I just wanted to check on that. He'll probably be down in the summer, and so I'll find out about Elodie then. I'd just like to know she's safe.'

They walked in silence for a couple of minutes, which felt almost more uncomfortable than listening to another monologue. Briefly Chloe greeted a woman coming towards them. She was in her fifties with a saggy, lined face, and had a lit cigarette in one hand and a *baguette* in the other.

'That's Maureen, have you met her?' Chloe asked afterwards, and Lia shook her head. 'Maureen and Eric, they're your neighbours.'

'The ones Peaches had trouble with? So what's their story, then? Bodies under the rose garden? Or are they really aliens from outer space?'

'No, nothing like that,' Chloe told her in all seriousness. 'They're just wasters, sit around boozing all day watching

72

Sky TV. He loves his garden, though, and works on it most mornings, but then they open a bottle at twelve and it's downhill from there. Some nights you hear them rowing. Bit sad, really.'

'So what, they don't work?'

'No, he retired early. Bought this place and now they don't know what to do with themselves. There are quite a few like that around here.'

They arrived at the complex, and Lia turned to her. 'So, we've got cat-poisoning alcoholics, a witches' coven and a wife-beater in the village – anything else I should know about?'

Chloe laughed. 'No, I think that's enough, isn't it?' She looked at Lia awkwardly. 'You couldn't do me a favour, could you?' she asked. 'Only the bakery's run by Etienne's ex-girlfriend, Hélène, and her mum, so I don't really like going in there. You couldn't just nip in and pick up a loaf for me, could you?'

At this, Lia had to smile. She went into the bakery and was served by a pretty girl with dark hair. This was Etienne's ex?

'She hates me, that Hélène,' Chloe confided as Lia handed her the bread. 'They were childhood sweethearts, and she thought they were going to get married and have kids. She and her mum must slag me off, I'm sure, but what can you do? It was love at first sight. You've just got to go with it when it happens, haven't you? I know he doesn't speak much English and my French is pretty awful, but it doesn't matter, we still understand each other. Anyway, this village gives me the shudders.' She started backing away. 'It's a full moon on Tuesday, so that'll mean another coven. Watch out for the signs,' she added. 'You know, arrows, markings. There's a lot of strange stuff going on around here, I mean that.'

Lia told her she'd walk on for a while, and, grateful for her own company, began exploring the lanes and alleyways she'd often passed, hoping to clear her mind and cheer herself up. *They're all mad*, she started mentally writing

73

another e-mail to Jules. *It must be something in the water*.

Where was Ben right now, the only sane one among them, and with whom? If he were at Les Eglantines today she'd feel better. How much nicer if there were a chance she might run into him somewhere, even just catch a glimpse of him in passing. But knowing he was somewhere up in the mountains, either throwing himself down a piste or sipping warming brandies in the snow, just made her feel emptier.

Wandering around the narrow lanes, Lia found herself peering at a spot of graffiti on a wall, and a chalk marking on the pavement. Could these be the signs Chloe had talked about, or was she just being ridiculous?

The village was buzzing, full of church-goers pouring through the church door and heading for the bakery and *traiteur*, where the ladies were serving. Everyone was chatting and laughing, warmly greeting one another and living normal lives. It was nonsensical to think that there were witches, she laughed – of course it was all a joke. Nothing Chloe said could be trusted. Didn't the very fact that she'd even asked Lia not to say anything about Nick hint that it was all lies?

But still, she shivered. What if a man she was with turned violent, what would she do then? She tried to imagine the fear, the nightmare she'd be living. If it happened to her, she'd pack her bags and leave one day while he was at work. Jump in a car, catch a train, go anywhere, but she'd be sure to disappear and never come back. She'd have had to plan it, days or even weeks in advance, packing discreetly bit by bit, making preparations he could never trace. Gradually she'd empty her bank account, change the billing address of her credit cards and fill the car with petrol. And then, Lia could feel her heart quicken as she thought it all through, then she'd wait until he'd left, until she'd seen his car disappear down the lane, or driven him to the airport, and then she'd do it, throw the last of her belongings in a case, throw the case in the back of the car and drive off, head for the autoroute and drive west towards Avignon, or Toulouse. There she'd stay in guest houses and find a job, create a new life for herself.

That's what she'd do, she kept thinking, running the scene over and over again in her mind; if it happened to her. That was exactly what she'd do.

But then, this was all fantasy, as was just about everything Chloe said. The couple next door were probably no more alcoholic than she was, and Nick would no sooner hit a woman than Ben would not be with a girlfriend right now.

Ben, she sighed to herself. Lovely, funny, handsome Ben. There was no getting away from it. All her thoughts were still leading to him.

Chapter Eleven

A couple of days later, Lia was on her way to the post office when there was a shout behind her, and there was Ben, running to catch up. 'How was the skiing?' she asked with excitement tinged with a vague sense of resentment.

He told her about the slopes and conditions, and it emerged that he'd gone with some friends, five of them in all, piled into an old Citroën. From the sound of things it had been very much a boys' trip, and Lia wondered what he'd think if he knew how much she'd tortured herself over it.

At the supermarket complex he announced that he needed a haircut and disappeared into the salon, and Lia caught herself envying the lucky girl who'd get to run her fingers through his hair.

A little further on, a scrawny tabby scowled at her, and right behind it on the pavement, marked in orange, Lia noticed an arrow. It was pointing to an alleyway, and out of curiosity, she went down it. There was nothing odd about the alleyway, with the inevitable washing fluttering overhead, but the sun hadn't yet reached that point and it felt cool and dark. At the end, another arrow pointed towards the right, and Lia found herself descending the village on a route she'd never come across before. She continued following the arrows, until one pointed down a path through some scrubland, so she gave up and went back the way she'd come.

Was Chloe right, then, she shivered, suddenly glad not to be living inside the village itself, but a safe distance away. What if she'd stumbled upon the coven by mistake one night, she started to wonder, climbing back up to the post office. What if they'd seen her, these mysterious figures in black, chanting their devil-worshipping incantations? What if they'd come after her, what if she realised they were the same people she said *bonjour* to in the mornings? She was just on the point of being made into some kind of human sacrifice when she spotted Maureen right below her in the car park, dropping bottle after bottle into the recycling bins, and had to laugh.

She posted her letters and made her way back, amused at the sight of a cyclist carrying a *baguette*, a dog running alongside him, trying to snatch a piece out of his hands. This was not an evil village, she told herself, still somewhat unsettled by all the markings. Chloe was just having her on.

She wandered home, admiring the sudden flashes of yellow which had appeared almost overnight everywhere she looked. The mimosa trees were in full bloom now, contrasting dramatically with the purple African daisies which were cascading down stone walls as if determined to cover their grey stones. She walked past several orange trees, heavy with fruit, and spotted primroses for the first time in the hedgerows. Had she missed all this on Sunday, she wondered, too preoccupied with Chloe and her own gloom, or had they really only just appeared?

There were lemon trees everywhere too, now that she was looking – she'd heard of the lemon festival coming up in Menton, and remembered she had to ask Chloe about the car. So would lemons come in her winter section, she reflected, or were they more appropriate in the summer? She could always preserve some, she thought, Moroccan style, and have a nice tajine in the winter section, but then weren't lemons invaluable in jams, for their pectin, and so better off in the summer?

It seemed that with every fruit she thought about, and every vegetable, the gardening process somehow failed to tally with the types of recipes she'd use to illustrate them. The olive harvest, for example, which she'd spectacularly failed to witness for herself, happened in January, and yet most olive and olive oil recipes were more suited to the summer.

Lia knew her structure was flawed, but was unable to see any way out of it. Back in the cottage she started going over it again, hoping that something would spark an idea which would bring it all together. It *had* to be seasonal, surely, to create a sense of what happened when. It was slotting the recipes in which was the hard part.

As she sat, frowning at one of her numerous lists of contents, she heard the gate open and wondered immediately if it could be Ben. She froze, deciding in that second that it was better he saw her working away instead of applying lipstick, which is what she felt like doing. So she frowned at her screen and wrote some notes in her IDEAS file, waiting for the visitor. There was a knock on the window and she looked up to see Peaches standing there, a large bunch of mimosas in her hand.

'I'm not disturbing you, am I?' she began, walking inside. 'Only I just wanted to pop up to thank you for the other evening, which was lovely, we thoroughly enjoyed ourselves. My, if you cook like that all the time your book will be unmissable! Did you see the mimosa's out at last? Here, I brought you a bunch, snipped off my tree this morning. Oh, and I almost forgot, here's some mail.'

She handed over two envelopes, which, Lia noticed, had been forwarded from Fulham by Jonathan. They were junk mail, she could see, nothing important. She checked the back, but there was nothing, no word of encouragement or greeting. She'd hadn't heard anything from him since she'd left, despite having sent him a card. So it really was over, then. Or perhaps he was just sulking?

'Oh James, are you following me again?' Peaches cried out as the fat ginger tom strolled into the cottage, brushing itself against one of the table legs. 'He used to in real life, you know,' she giggled. 'I mean, James, my boyfriend. I was never that interested but he pursued me, followed me around all over the place.' She laughed, enjoying the memory.

'And did you fall for him in the end?'

'I'm afraid not. We dated a few times – of course it was all quite innocent in those days – the movie theatre, ice-cream parlours, that sort of thing, but it never got serious. Now, what else was I going to tell you?' She looked vaguely in the distance before remembering, her whole face lighting up. 'Oh, that's right, did you hear about the new comet coming into our solar system? Levin-Bayes, it's called, after the astronomers who discovered it. It'll be visible from the end of May, and is going to bring about great change and revelations!'

Lia thought she vaguely remembered it from a newspaper article months ago.

'It'll be a positive force in the world and will root out all evil,' Peaches continued excitedly.

'Just what we all need,' Lia said, feeling like she was on the set of a sitcom. All they needed now was the canned laughter.

'Well, I must let you get back to work. How is the book coming along?' Peaches didn't wait for an answer, just called out 'Good, good' from the path as she left, and then stopped to encourage some bulbs which were starting to show. 'Well, hello again,' she started. 'My, you were so pretty last year. I just hope we don't get a cold spell now.'

Lia chuckled, thinking how delightful Peaches' world was, with plants and cats to talk to, and men pursuing her in the past. Had she ever known what Lia was going through now, she wondered idly, snipping off the ends of the mimosas and filling a vase with water. Had she ever

79

gone through this strange uncertainty over a man, unable to work or think about anything else?

Change and revelations, she thought over Peaches' words. Change would certainly be good, or at least an improvement on the state of limbo she was currently in, but revelations? She took the vase into the sitting room. Now they sounded altogether more scary.

Chapter Twelve

To Lia's surprise, Chloe actually got back to her with news of a car, a Peugeot that would make an ideal runaround. Etienne offered to take her in his truck, Ben agreed to give it the once-over and Chloe decided to join them all for the ride.

'So this is a friend of yours, Etienne?' Lia asked as he pulled out of the drive and veered into the lane with just a cursory glance in either direction.

'That's right,' Chloe answered for him. 'Jean-Marc. His girlfriend's a client of mine. I've been helping her out with her cellulite – all over her thighs, it is.'

Lia caught Ben's eye and he shook his head in despair. Etienne turned into the main road which led east out of the village.

'Don't drive too fast, Babe,' Chloe told him as he over-took a Renault, narrowly missing an oncoming lorry.

'So it's his garage, this bloke?' Lia pressed on, her grip tightening on the seat.

'Yeah, well, he works there, anyway. They get a few cars in, and this one sounds right up your street. I'd buy it myself if I had the money, but as it is, Etienne has to drive me everywhere, don't you, Babe? Still, not that I'd want to drive on these roads, the way they go.' As she said this, Etienne had started tailgating the car in front. 'They never indicate, do they, and what is the point of pedestrian crossings? I mean, no one ever stops. I was waiting outside the supermarket for ages the other day, loaded down with shopping, but did anyone stop for me? It took forever before I could cross; they're all so selfish. All they think about is themselves, and getting from A to B as fast as they can.'

Lia caught Ben rolling his eyes, and as Chloe paused for breath, asked him quickly, 'So you're not tempted to get a car, then?'

He shook his head. 'I'm not here often enough. A friend of mind lends me his bike from time to time,' he added. 'But for this favour I think you could become my full-time driver in future.'

They arrived at the garage and Jean-Marc took them to the car. It was a few years old and had some minor scratches, but these didn't bother Lia, who was convinced that it would only get a few more, anyway. As Etienne and Ben scrutinised the engine and the body, Lia and Chloe examined the interior. It had a radio, some innocuous grey seats and a stale pine air freshener hanging from the mirror. Whatever was the point, she thought, taking it down, when opening the window did the job for free?

She test drove with Ben at her side, helping her to negotiate the twists in the road and the erratic traffic all around. As she pulled into a layby, delighted to have been at the front of a wheel after so many years, Ben took over, testing its reactions.

'It's fine,' he told her. 'It's got a few more years in it. For the price he's asking, I'd go for it.'

Jean-Marc said he'd organise the paperwork, suggested an insurer and promised to deliver it by the end of the week. When they returned to Les Eglantines, Lia thanked Chloe and Etienne, making a mental note to buy them a decent bottle of wine for their trouble.

'Have dinner with me tonight,' she suggested to Ben

when they were alone, and to her delight he readily agreed. She had already planned a possible menu on the drive back – something to take her mind off Etienne's driving. She wouldn't need to go to the shops either, as she already had everything to hand: couscous, some vegetables and a tub of chicken livers that she'd dip in Moroccan spices.

She prepared the basics and spent an hour or so tidying the cottage: hoovering and washing the floors and re-arranging her scented candles, all the time congratulating herself on having taken a major step – she'd bought a car, after all! Now the whole of Provence was at her disposal – finally she'd be able to visit the olive groves of Nyons, the fish markets of Marseilles and the herb gardens of Salagon. She could see the lavender fields in Haute Provence, snuff out the truffles in the market at Carpentras and sample the goat's cheese of Banon.

She'd just finished brushing her hair and touching up her make-up when there was a tap on the front door, and there was Ben, clutching a bottle of Côtes du Rhône Villages.

'Recovered from the ordeal?' He leant forward and kissed her on both cheeks, before making for the kitchen and opening the bottle. She loved the way he seemed to feel at home with her. How could they *possibly* go on like this without getting together, she asked herself? It just *had* to happen.

They talked about the car, and Ben told her certain things to look out for and the garages to avoid. 'Jean-Marc seems to be one of Chloe's more reliable contacts, though,' he was saying as Lia suddenly interrupted him.

'You know something? I saw them! The signs Chloe's been on about!' Ben looked puzzled. 'In the village,' she continued. 'She told me there were secret signs, for the witches, showing where the next meeting is. Well, I hate to say it, as I'm the last person to believe anything she says, but I actually think I saw them.'

'Come on,' he scoffed. 'Whereabouts in the village?'

'On the roads, the pavements. There were markings, loads of them, pointing the way.'

Ben's face changed, as if she was actually onto something. 'They weren't in orange, were they?' he asked.

'Yes!' she said breathlessly. He had to know about them, probably from some group or other he'd photographed in the past. He would have seen similar signs in other countries; no doubt, heard stories.

'And what, they were arrows, were they?'

'My God, yes!' He knew about them, all right, she thought wildly. He must have seen similar things in Kosovo or Chechnya.

Ben shook his head, a worried look on his face and paused, giving her a clear indication that they were in some kind of trouble. He took a deep breath before asking quietly, 'Lia, have you ever heard of the Hash House Harriers?'

Her face fell. 'The running group?'

He smiled patiently. 'I heard it on the radio the other day. They were having a run through this village and the surrounding area. I think you'll find that if you follow the arrows they lead to a trail to the next village, and ultimately, instead of any coven, or cauldron, or witches' den of any kind, you're more likely to come across a bar, where they drink themselves stupid and sing silly songs.'

'Oh no!' Lia shrank back into her chair, covering her face in embarrassment. 'Tell me you're not serious?'

He threw back his head and laughed. 'You're so gullible,' he chided her gently. 'Of course I'm bloody serious. There are no witches in this village, Lia – where do you think this is, Salem? Though I'll give Chloe this, it was a Protestant village, and so always considered highly suspect by the Catholics. But there's nothing like that going on now, for goodness sake, there hasn't been for years.'

'I feel such a prat,' she groaned. 'Bloody Chloe, why do I listen to her?'

'You don't get much choice, usually,' he smiled.

She got on with the cooking, which seemed the most sensible thing to do under the circumstances. She checked

84

on the courgettes and peppers which were bubbling away in a spicy tomato sauce, and stirred some hot stock with butter into the couscous, leaving it to fluff up. All she had to do was fry the chicken livers, which had been marinating in their spices, and be careful not to overcook them.

Ben laid the table and they sat down to eat, the flavours reminding him of meals he'd eaten in the past, and he began describing vegetable curries cooked on an open fire in India, the layered feta cheese pies he'd snack on in Macedonia and the lemony-flavoured chickpeas in yoghurt he once had for breakfast in Damascus. His life sounded mysterious and exotic, and she felt parochial in his presence.

'What I haven't mentioned are the bugs, the dysentery, the often appalling conditions, the rabid dogs and occasionally the soothing sound of gunfire in the background. Believe me, coming here is bliss. I bet I'm enjoying myself far more than you are.'

'What about London, though?' Lia asked nervously, doubting it. If ever there was an opportunity to find out about his girlfriend, if indeed she existed, then this was surely it. 'Don't you enjoy being there, too?'

'It's a bit difficult,' he admitted and she felt her chest tighten. 'I usually stay at my sister's – she's got a nice house in Battersea – that's where all my stuff is. But she wants the room back. She's got a couple of kids and I wouldn't be surprised if they don't have another one soon, so I need to make some decisions pretty quickly.'

'And are there any, friends, you could stay with there?' she asked, wondering what more she could get out of him without shining a torch in his face and threatening to remove his fingernails.

'No, not particularly,' he shrugged and she felt a glimmer of hope.

Inside her mind, the words pounded to get out. *So, Ben, do you have a girlfriend?* Or, *So, isn't there a girlfriend hidden away somewhere?* Or even, *Is it true you've got some sugar mummy picking up your living expenses?*

Instead she found herself veering onto another tricky subject. 'I've got to say,' she started awkwardly, 'I can't imagine you on one of these retreats, I mean, taking part in Peaches' crystal therapy or Felix's scriptwriting stuff. It just doesn't sound your sort of thing.'

He laughed and looked slightly embarrassed. 'I'd had a bit of a rough time last year, and I just needed to get my head together. My sister read an article about it somewhere, and thought it would be a good place to chill out. She probably just wanted to get rid of me for a while. I didn't do much of the group stuff, to be honest, but I found myself spending a lot of time with Peaches and Felix. And I like it here, I mean, what's not to like? So I've been back a couple of times.'

He paused to look at his watch and, for a moment she was worried that he might leave. 'This is a terrible thing to ask, but d'you mind if we have the telly on in the background? Only there's a Champions' League match on I wouldn't mind having a look at.'

'Oh, of course,' she jumped up, disappointed that he would rather be watching twenty-two men kick a ball around than flirting with her.

But instead of watching, Ben carried on talking, pausing to keep an eye on matters from time to time. His father, a doctor, had been a keen amateur photographer, he told her, and had always encouraged Ben to take up the hobby for himself. On his gap year he'd travelled around India, where he found himself obsessively photographing everything he saw – from the grand monuments and palaces to exotic festivals and rituals – yet it was often just the simple aspects of everyday human life that interested him the most. At college, where he studied civil engineering, he'd started entering shots in various competitions, and from the assorted trips and equipment he kept winning, knew he was on to something.

'While I was at college there was the Bhopal disaster followed by Chernobyl two years later. Each time I just wanted to pack my bags and head off to the airport.

86

Suddenly I was passionate about something; suddenly I had something to be passionate about. And you know, all these years later, that passion's still there. I'm lucky, I don't think there are many people around who can say that about their work.'

She wanted to ask why he wasn't working now, and why that passion seemed somehow to have left him, but they were distracted by a roar from the crowd and the excited frenzy of the commentator as a goal was scored.

They turned, just in time to watch all four action replays and enjoy the satisfying thwack of the ball hitting the back of the net each time.

Lia topped up their glasses. She remembered Jules once complaining about an ex of hers who only wanted sex when Crystal Palace won, and wondered if this goal might just clinch it for her.

The match ended in a draw, and Ben got up, straightening his jeans, and stretched. 'I'd better get a move on,' he told her. 'But thank you so much for dinner.'

'Oh God, don't thank me, we should do this more often,' she said with a hint of desperation. It wasn't too late, she told herself. Their goodbye pecks on the cheek could still lead to something more.

He reached for his leather jacket. 'Well I'll be off, then.' He made for the door. 'Beware of any strange witches in the village,' he kissed her on either cheek. 'And thank you again.'

'My pleasure,' she smiled, trying to hide her disappointment, until he held her, awkwardly, for a second, before letting her go. It had only been brief, but Lia was sure it meant something. In that second he'd told her: *I want you, but not yet, let's give ourselves a bit more time and not rush into anything*, or so she told herself. Or perhaps, she started to think minutes later as she got on with the washing up, what he'd really been saying was: *I want you, but I have a girlfriend, and so we'll just have to stay friends*.

She imagined herself walking through Peaches' garden

87

one day and spotting him and some girl laughing together and making their way to his flat. Holding hands, just to rub it in, and carrying a supermarket bag full of smoked salmon and champagne and ice cream and all the *fuck me* foods that lovers fill their fridges with. And there she was, silly, foolish Lia, cooking her couscous and her courgettes and trying to win him over with naïve stories of witches' signs and secret covens.

If there wasn't a girlfriend then there had to be something wrong with him, her mind continued. Hadn't he had some kind of breakdown last year, after all? He'd as much as admitted it. Perhaps Jules was right, and this really wasn't the sort of man she should get involved with; someone who'd be moody and unpredictable, who couldn't make a decision?

Getting ready for bed, Lia took a deep breath. It was time to admit defeat. She would carry on exactly as she was, she told herself. She would get her car, get out and about, and get over him. Now was not the time for a boyfriend, anyway – she had to prove herself first. Get the book out, make it a success, and *then* think about a love life.

But it would just be so nice, she sighed, climbing into her spacious bed and lamenting the untouched other half. *It would just be so nice.*

Chapter Thirteen

Jean-Marc delivered the car a couple of days later, and Lia had her first trial drive that lunchtime, when there was hardly any traffic on the roads. The exhilaration she felt after years of taxis and public transport in London was muted only by the thought that Ben was now firmly out of bounds, and should henceforth be demoted to 'interesting friend' rather than 'potential lover'. She was not to make a fool of herself by chasing after him, she told herself firmly, negotiating the car onto the main road, and should act friendly but distanced.

Every now and then, though, she'd feel a terrible pang, missing all the fantasies she now refused to indulge in: exploring Provence together, taking the car up to the mountains and finding cosy little hotels, picnics on the coast and even just snuggling up on the sofa together – she missed the fantasies almost as much as she missed the man himself.

She explored three of the neighbouring villages, trying to work out which roads led to which towns and how she might one day get on to the motorway. She would have a little drive every lunchtime and explore, but was not to get carried away – her real work was in the garden or kitchen or at her laptop. Happy that she was finally getting her bearings, Lia turned back towards the village and into her lane. There, walking ahead of her, was Ben. Her first test. She slowed down, tooted the horn and wound down the window.

'Want a lift?' she asked cheerfully, just as a friend would.

His face opened into a broad grin, and he climbed into the passenger seat. 'How are you getting on?' he asked. 'Been anywhere interesting?'

She told him about her drive, crunching the gear awkwardly into second as she did so, and headed slowly towards Les Eglantines. Once they'd arrived, she parked opposite and jumped out, but instead of inviting him in for tea or a coffee, as she normally would, she simply smiled and said goodbye. He looked a bit confused, but she was determined. She was only doing this to protect them both, she reminded herself, not to mention his girlfriend.

She got on with some e-mailing, letting Jules know the latest, and busied herself with recipes, gardening tips and a bit of weeding outside. Etienne was clearing the terrace below, an industrial-sized weedkiller pump strapped to his back, and as a row broke out between Maureen and Eric next door, he laughingly threatened to spray their roses if they didn't stop.

By mid-afternoon, as Lia was trying some insipid pear and vanilla tea, Ben appeared on the terrace.

'Do you want a cup?' she offered with a smile. 'I've got some others, if you like: blackberry and apple, peach and something—'

'Don't you have any builders?' he asked, frowning.

She laughed, made him a cup and they sat down on the terrace. 'Look at all the blossom on the trees.' She gazed out across the view. 'They're almonds, aren't they? I just hope it doesn't rain soon and wash everything away.'

He nodded without saying anything, which rather spoilt matters. She was supposed to be the one being aloof, after all.

90

'So, anything happening?' she started fishing. 'Any new assignments, anything in London?'

'Not yet. I've been offered things – I told you, didn't I, in the West Bank, but I just feel a bit burned out at the moment. I do want to go back there some time, but not now, not with all the current upheaval. I'd rather go when things have calmed down a bit.'

He looked troubled, and she didn't know how to deal with it. What had happened to him, she wondered, not liking to ask.

'Lebanon is more interesting to me right now,' he went on. 'Now it's settled down. I'd like to go back and see some people from before – that would be interesting.'

'So what's holding you back?' she asked.

'I have to plan these things,' he told her. 'If I'm going to get a book together then I can't do all this randomly. Right now I suppose you could say I'm selecting the "before" shots, but if I don't find enough there that I like, then I can hardly justify a trip back for the "after" stuff. I've got to look at the whole before I can plan where to go and when.'

'But financially,' she began, wondering how to put it politely, knowing that someone like Jules would just storm in and ask anyway. She was just putting her sentence together when Chloe appeared at the gate.

'Just wondering how the car's going,' she called out, clearly delighted to be seeing them together.

'It's great, thank you, I love it,' Lia told her, willing her away.

'Chloe,' Ben jumped up, welcoming her. 'We were just talking about the Lebanon, and the war there,' he started, and Lia knew instantly what he was up to.

'Bit gloomy, that.' Chloe frowned, before brightening. 'You know, there used to be a Lebanese takeaway near me, run by a bloke called Sam. He had quite a thing for me at one point, he did – used to give me one of those little pastry things with every order. Come to think of it, he bought a car off my Ian, a little Beetle it was.'

'She's masterful,' Lia whispered once Chloe had gone, having spent five minutes describing Sam's beetle, Ian's business collapse and her quest for spiritual peace. 'How does she do it?'

'There's got to be something,' Ben started earnestly, sipping his tea. 'Something even she can't turn around.'

'How are you on nuclear physics, or the state of the world economy?' Lia suggested.

'Physics might be a good one,' he nodded. 'But the economy she'd only turn round to how much she charges for her yoga classes. There's got to be something else, I don't know, like, the end of apartheid?'

Lia shook her head. 'She'll only have black friends.'

'Then, the handover of Hong Kong?'

'She'll tell us how much she likes Chinese food.'

'God, ditto India, and the creation of Pakistan. There's got to be something.'

'Cloning?' Lia suggested off the top of her head. 'Dolly the sheep?'

'No, she'll just tell us about how her mum does a mean leg of lamb,' Ben said wearily and suddenly they began laughing: raw, uncontrollable laughter – the kind of laughter that becomes funny in its own right, the kind that Lia wanted any man who'd ever hurt her to witness. She couldn't remember when she'd laughed so much, or so loudly. They'd reach a point where both were calming down and then one would get another fit, infect the other, and so it would go on. There were tears streaming out of Lia's eyes and her chest was beginning to ache, she'd laughed so much. They didn't notice Peaches arriving until the gate made its distinctive click.

'Christ, it's like Piccadilly Circus round here,' Ben muttered, and through her laughter, Lia thought how sweet it was that he didn't consider himself another piece of traffic.

'It's probably rude, so I won't ask,' Peaches said with mock primness. 'There's a phone bill for you, dear, I'm afraid, nothing interesting. If you'll just pay me, preferably in cash, and then I'll send the company a cheque.' She turned to go, almost awkwardly, before tripping on the ginger cat. 'Oh James, do you have to follow me everywhere?' she tutted.

'Peaches,' Lia felt slightly guilty. 'Why don't you stay and have some tea?'

'Oh, no, dear, I'd better not,' Peaches smiled. 'Oh, but I must tell you that this Saturday there's a marvellous pagan festival in the village – did you know?' They shook their heads. 'It's about chasing the moon away and heralding the start of spring. You must both come.'

'What exactly happens?' Lia asked curiously.

'Flour throwing, so be sure to wear old clothes. Then there's free wine and food and lots of dancing – it's terrific fun. It'll start late, around nine or ten o'clock, I think, but do remember protective clothing. I know, why don't we have a drink at my place first, and then we can all go together, say around eight o'clock?'

They said they'd be there and Peaches left, firmly taking the cat with her.

'Why would I need protective clothing for flowers?' Lia asked. 'I don't know, this place is mad, isn't it? I think I'm the only sane one around – well, possibly along with you.'

'And sometimes I think that's questionable,' Ben agreed. He picked himself up, as if to leave. 'So what do you think, should we have dinner tonight? Us two sane ones? Something in the village?'

She paused, fighting the urge to cry out 'yes' happily and throw herself back into her lusty fantasies. Or could they just be friends who saw a lot of each other? But the minute she'd asked herself that, Lia knew it would be too hard.

Taking a deep breath, and, hating herself, and every word she was about to say, she told him, 'I can't, I'm afraid. I've got so much work on, I really must just get on with it.'

A few minutes later Ben left, looking vaguely hurt.

93

Chapter Fourteen

On Saturday evening Lia turned up at Peaches' house at the appointed time, to find Chloe and Etienne already there but, worryingly, no sign of Ben. Had he decided against going, she asked herself as Peaches fetched her a glass, or was he just late? Without him the room seemed empty, somehow, and she chided herself for not simply being able to enjoy the others' company in the meantime. Chloe had her hair tied back in a ponytail, with the excess bits clipped back with grips. She was wearing an old tracksuit and some trainers, whilst Etienne had put on some paint-splattered jeans and a grey fleece. Felix was wearing a pair of battered beige cords and a green jumper with holes in each elbow, while Peaches was resplendent in a turtleneck sweater under an old man's shirt and some cords that were a size too big for her. Holding her hair back was a green bandanna Lia had seen her wearing in the garden before.

'You don't know what you've got in store, tonight, do you?' Chloe asked with a knowing smile. Lia admitted she didn't. 'I think you're looking a bit too smart if you ask me.'

Lia gulped her wine and ate a couple of olives. What was the big deal about a few flowers? She'd put on some jeans, a cream turtleneck and a black fleece. She might not exactly be ready for the garden, yet she was hardly dressed for the Cannes film festival, either. But more importantly, where was Ben? Was he doing something else, or worse still, was he even going with someone else? Perhaps his girlfriend had come over for the weekend, her mind raced, and he was taking her?

If she didn't fancy him, she thought crossly, she would simply have asked the others where he was and it would have been perfectly natural. But she *did* fancy him, and so she couldn't possibly ask because everyone would then realise she did. *Where's Ben?* She tried it out in her mind, a mildly puzzled look on her face. Or, *isn't Ben coming?* Was that any better? The thing was, she sighed quietly, that as Peaches had invited them together, might it now reflect badly on her that he had chosen not to go? Did it look like a snub and was everyone feeling sorry for her? She was just beginning to sink into a confused and lonely depression when there was a bang on the door, and there he was.

'Sorry I'm late, Peaches,' he said with an affectionate kiss on the cheek. He looked around, his face lighting up as he found Lia, who was now holding on to the back of a chair to steady herself. It felt as if the room had brightened. The waiting was over, and everyone seemed more animated and happy. Peaches poured more wine, topping up everyone's glasses, and Etienne nibbled four olives in a row, spitting the stones into the fire.

'Did you find what you was looking for today, then, Ben?' Chloe asked him, before adding, 'I bumped into him in the chemist this morning.'

'Maybe Ben doesn't want the rest of us to know about that,' Lia said quickly, wondering what exactly he *had* been looking for.

Ben just looked amused. 'Yes, I did, thank you, and Lia's quite right, it's not for public consumption.'

What was he buying, she asked herself. Did he have a medical condition, or had he just run out of deodorant? It

95

was odd, getting to know a man. They were mysterious creatures to her, needing strange things from all the boring counters at Boots she'd normally walk right past. Jonathan, for example, got through tube after tube of Savlon and was addicted to various anti-fungal powders, whilst Lia didn't even like to think what he might be doing with them.

Ben was by her side, and she could smell his shampoo, or perhaps it was shower gel. It wasn't the smell of after-shave, that she was sure of – he wasn't the type to wear it. He was in some fading blue jeans, a worn-out but soft-looking shirt and a jumper she hadn't seen before. She noticed it was fraying at the bottom.

Despite herself she chatted with him warmly, relieved to be with him again after the emptiness of the last few days. She told him about the driving she'd done, and how she'd explored a village that specialised in crystallised petals and fruits, and how she was wondering whether to include them in her book or not.

'Now, are we all ready?' Peaches chirped excitedly. 'Amelia, are you sure you'll be all right like that?'

'I'm sorry, I don't get it,' Lia said, exasperated. 'It's a flower festival, so what's the worst that can happen? I get a few petals thrown at me, that's all.'

There was a startled pause, and then Chloe began to laugh. 'Not flowers, flour!'

'No, *flour*, dear,' Peaches began, as if explaining something to a small child who was partially deaf. 'As in bread making. You're going to end up looking like a ghost.'

Only Ben didn't make her feel stupid. He was grinning at her affectionately, whilst Etienne clearly thought this was the funniest thing he'd ever heard, and as he laughed, tiny fragments of black olive shot out of his mouth.

'Oh I see,' Lia tried, seeing the funny side. 'Well, all of this is washable, so it's no big deal.'

'I should have thought,' Chloe said in a vaguely patronising tone, 'that you might have misunderstood. So you thought everyone was going to be chucking flowers around.' She laughed again, and Lia wanted to kick her.

'No, it's a pagan festival to shoo away the moon and the ghosts and to herald in the spring,' Peaches explained. 'But there certainly aren't many flowers around, yet.'

How long would it go on, Lia thought to herself. How long before they grew tired of the joke?

'Chloe, I was reading this really interesting article about Robert Mugabe the other day,' Ben started, and Lia had to smile. How sweet he was to take her attention away, and how clever to continue their game.

'Never heard of him,' Chloe interrupted, shaking her head. 'I've got a cousin called Robert, though, he's a hairdresser in Chigwell. You know I once thought about taking up hairdressing, myself, only I'm a bit allergic to the chemicals they use.'

Trying hard not to laugh, Lia turned to Felix. Peaches had disappeared upstairs and he'd been left on his own. 'So you enjoy this festival, Felix?' she asked.

'It's quite fun,' he said simply. 'Gets a little boisterous, though, so I shan't stay long. How's your book coming along?'

That seemed to be everyone's stock question. 'A bit of a mess at the moment,' Lia told him truthfully, 'but I'm getting there.'

'Well, are we all ready?' Peaches had emerged from the stairs and the room filled with stunned gasps at the sight of her. She was wearing an all-encompassing white shellsuit with the hood up and an underwater mask shielding her eyes. Around her shoulders was a pump contraption similar to Etienne's weedkiller, which led to a plastic bag full of flour, which she was holding protectively. 'Come along, then, time to go.'

Chloe applauded excitedly, while Felix looked on proudly, as if she was wearing a ball gown in his eyes. Ben was smiling that warm, affectionate smile that Lia was dying to see close up, preferably a few inches above her own face, in a horizontal position, and Etienne was using the distraction to top up his glass and quickly knock it back.

Together, they made their strange parade towards the village centre, where the action was to begin. Ben and Lia walked slightly behind the others, wondering what could possibly be in store. In the village centre, by the newsagents, a large crowd had gathered: children with bags of flour and some adults who were already dusting themselves down. Peaches sprang into action, spraying first Felix and then Etienne, before turning to Lia and Ben and covering them.

There was the sound of bells and singing, and a group of what looked like Morris dancers appeared, in a procession, bashing tambourines and doing various jigs. One victim was dunked upside down in some flour, and then the newsagent produced vats of wine and slices of pizza and tart. Ben and Lia kept slightly away from the action, and were grateful when Etienne arrived with two plastic cups of wine for them. Around them, children were running in and out of the crowds, tossing flour in people's hair before disappearing behind an obliging adult and then re-emerging to have another go.

The procession moved on towards the *traiteur*, where the same thing happened all over again; the song, the jig, the dunking followed by wine and snacks. Every now and again Lia caught sight of Peaches, madly squirting flour at anyone who looked vaguely untouched, laughing demonically as she did so. Somewhere between the fourth jig and wine-break at the post office, and the fifth, outside the church, Ben held Lia's arm protectively, allowing a determined group to push past. His hand then dropped down to hers, holding it comfortably, and they walked, wordlessly, behind the throng.

Was this simple act confirmation that he was single, or was he one of those men who'd bed her first and *then* admit to having someone else?

The novelty of the event was wearing off. Lia felt she knew the song by heart, even if she couldn't exactly understand all the words, and was getting tired of dusting flour out of her hair and off her clothes.

'I think we go to the chapel next,' Ben told her. 'For the full-on dancing and food.'

'There's more?' she wailed, not wanting to seem unenthusiastic, but tiring all the same. It was getting late, and her legs were beginning to ache.

A group of flour-covered teenagers knocked into them, pushing their hands apart, and Lia wondered whether to take his back or not. Why was she so useless at times like this, she chastised herself? Jules wouldn't have thought twice about it, but would probably be snuggling up against his neck by now and suggesting they got an early evening. Lia just felt unsure of herself, and the last thing she wanted was to start something they couldn't finish.

They followed the procession to the little chapel, and watched as each participant was shaken upside down before being allowed in. Coins were scattered, one man lost his glasses and a woman with orange hair showed more of her knickers than she probably would have liked.

'I don't think I can bear to go through all that,' Lia whispered.

'Me neither. What do you say? Home for a nightcap?'

She nodded in relief, wondering whether he considered the pink cottage home. They walked back through the village, and as they left the noise and the crowds, he took her hand again, pressing it gently in his. It was now around one o'clock, and the night sky was twinkling with stars. Outside the village it suddenly felt colder, and Lia could see her own breath.

'I'd forgotten what stars looked like in London,' she said quietly. 'But here they're beautiful, so clear. Has Peaches told you about her comet? It's coming around the end of May or something, supposed to bring change and revelations, or so she says.'

Ben laughed, and Lia wondered what revelations he might be about to make himself. They arrived in Peaches' garden, and were at the point where he would normally turn left, when they stopped.

'Goodnight, then,' he said, rather disappointingly,

before kissing her gently on the lips. She leant in towards him, and they kissed again, and then again, until finally his tongue was inside her mouth and their hands had found each other's shoulders, and backs, and sides, and they were kissing, revelling in the warmth of each other's touch. Worrying that the others might arrive at any time, Lia pulled back.

Do you have a girlfriend? she wanted to ask, but the words refused to come out, possibly because she feared the answer. She took a deep breath. 'So whose bed gets messed up with all this flour, then, yours or mine?'

'Yours,' he smiled, leading her towards the pink cottage.

Inside her bedroom, Lia thought it might be awkward, undressing for the first time, but the flour made each of them look so ridiculous that they did it with giggles and laughter, and then fell on the bed in their underwear. He kissed her neck and her lips and his hand gently teased down the strap of her bra, until, when she didn't resist, he'd dragged the cup down and was kissing her nipple. Then he pulled away.

'You remember Chloe announcing to everyone that I'd been to the pharmacy earlier?'

'Yes,' Lia said, panicking for a second. 'So what unpleasant medical condition do you have, then? Herpes? Genital warts?'

'No,' he laughed, pulling himself off her, his penis peeking quickly at her through the gap in his boxer shorts. He reached for his jeans, and fumbled in the pockets, until triumphantly he produced a condom. 'I was buying these,' he told her, and she laughed in relief.

'What foresight,' she congratulated him. 'I'm glad you did.'

'Me too,' he said, with a smile and a kiss. 'Me too.'

Chapter Fifteen

They spent the rest of March in bed. Two days after the flour festival heralded the start of spring, the heavens opened and torrential rain lashed the entire region for weeks. If this was spring, Lia thought, give her winter any day. Not that it really mattered, because as Peaches' kitchen flooded and a river ran through her ground floor, Lia and Ben were making love. As Etienne almost caught pneumonia digging over the lunar garden, because Peaches had determined that that was exactly the right time to do so, she and Ben were making love, and as Chloe's yoga class disintegrated into a soggy mass of raincoats and umbrellas, she and Ben were making love.

Some mornings Peaches would tap on the front door and push letters and bills through the gap in the shutters, and guiltily they'd feign sleep, holding each other tight and not wanting ever to crawl out from under the duvet again. The phone would occasionally ring and they'd begin to whisper, as if the caller could hear them in the cottage. When all was calm Lia would tiptoe downstairs and make cups of tea, or boil some eggs for breakfast, and carry a tray upstairs. Usually they'd get up for lunch, and twice a week she'd battle the weather and head to the supermarket for supplies. Some afternoons Ben would check his post and make sure his flat wasn't under water, and quickly she'd e-mail Jules and read her replies, waiting excitedly for his return.

In the evenings, safely behind the shutters, they'd cook and eat supper, opening bottles of wine and snuggling on the sofa in the sitting room as the rain beat down outside. Lia started off counting the times they'd done it, keeping track: a silly mental diary that for some reason was important to her, but once she'd got to eleven or twelve times she could no longer remember whether they'd done it three or four times the previous day. To begin with, if they'd made love twice in one morning, Lia would think something wrong if they only did it once the next, but then suddenly it no longer mattered – Ben was as crazy about her as she was him, and their love-making had become an expression of that, and not a contest.

They talked about everything and nothing, their stories meandering into each other's, unstructured and without detail: the kind of stories that made for fascinating listening but were largely unrepeatable because of their lack of form. She knew about his first crush, but had no idea who his last girlfriend was. She knew something of his work, but how he supported himself or his travels remained a mystery, and she knew he'd stayed at Les Eglantines, but was no nearer to understanding why.

But she didn't want to be the sort of girlfriend who plagued him with questions until she'd extracted all the facts – she wanted their relationship to grow naturally, for them to discover each other and to reveal themselves at their own pace. Wasn't it more exciting that way, she'd ask herself when the doubts, usually fuelled by Jules, started to grow. Wasn't it better that they'd still be learning about each other in two, five years' time? If he had his secrets, if there *were* things he deliberately chose to hold back, then wouldn't it be all the more rewarding when he *did* tell her?

They were making love in the sitting room one evening when the phone started to ring for the fourth time that day.

'You'd better get that,' Ben told her quietly, reaching for the receiver and handing it to her.

She groaned and said 'hello' curtly, as if to let the caller know they were interrupting something.

There was a brief pause, and then a quiet voice said, 'Lia? You're there at last. I've been trying to get you all day.'

It was Jonathan.

'God, I wasn't expecting you,' she told him, trying to remember what he even looked like.

'I'm not disturbing you, am I?' He sounded broken, only half himself.

'No, of course you're not.' Another man was inside her, she thought, but apart from that, no, not at all. She pulled a face at Ben, to let him know the call would be an awkward one, and he climbed off and disappeared to the bathroom. She tried to pull some clothes around herself.

'It's just, well, how are you?' Jonathan continued. 'How have you been?'

'Fine. The weather's dreadful at the moment, but otherwise I'm fine. How are you?'

'Terrible,' he told her sadly, and she wondered if someone had died, or he'd lost his job. 'I can't do it, Lia, I miss you. I'm sorry, I've tried, I really have, but I can't get you out of my mind.'

Was he crying? Was he drunk, perhaps? She checked her watch – it was only eight o'clock in England. 'I'm sorry,' she said quietly. 'I'm sorry you feel that way.'

'Can I see you? I was thinking, maybe, for Easter? Come on, Lia, we need to talk. I miss you so much.'

'Oh, J.' Her heart sank. She could live with the huffy Jonathan, the Jonathan who forwarded mail without adding a note, but this sad, deserted, Jonathan was much harder to face. 'I don't think it's a good idea.'

'Come on Lia, we can pull through this. I need you. Please. I've been checking flights. I could come out on the Saturday and leave again Monday. They're quite cheap, especially the early morning ones. Please, Lia.'

103

She almost laughed. So he hadn't changed that much, then. Her sympathy dissipated. 'I'm sorry, Jonathan, but to be honest, I've started seeing someone here.'

There, it was out. She hoped Ben hadn't heard. What would be the appropriate way of describing their relationship, anyway? *We've been bonking our brains out all month? It's been pissing down and so we've only left the bedroom to stock up on food and condoms? Or rather, I feel like I've known this man all my life, and now nothing else, and no one else, seems important?*

'You have?' He sounded startled. 'Already?'

'I know, I wasn't expecting it myself.'

'But, it's not serious, surely?'

Why the hell wouldn't it be? she wanted to snap. 'I don't know,' she told him truthfully. 'But I think it could be.'

There was silence, then a quiet choking sound. 'That didn't take long.' He was trying to sound composed, now, back in charge.

Ben had appeared at the door with a blanket, and covered her up. Then he poured a glass of wine and handed it to her, before leaving for the kitchen.

'Oh, God, is he with you now?' Jonathan cried out, sensing his presence.

'He is, actually, but it's OK, he's in the kitchen.'

'How very cosy. Well, I'd better not disturb you any longer.' Bitter, now. Angry and bitter.

'You're not disturbing me, and I'm sorry.'

He sighed. 'Fuck you,' he spat and hung up.

Lia threw the receiver down and tried not to cry, more out of shock than anything.

'You all right?' Ben was there, by her side, his arm protectively around her.

'He just sounded so awful,' she cried, telling him the gist of the conversation. When she mentioned the cheap flights, though, they had to laugh, and she felt better. Her new life, her life with Ben, was suiting her so much better than life with Jonathan ever had, and she knew there was no going back.

'And you?' She felt courageous enough now to ask. 'Is there a girlfriend or an ex-girlfriend somewhere in the background, any unfinished business I should know about?'

He shook his head. 'Of course there isn't. It's a cliché I know, but I really don't have time for relationships. My only free time is spent here, which is why you've been such a lovely surprise. I can't go about getting involved when I don't know how long I'll be anywhere or where I'll be heading next. It just wouldn't work.'

They fell silent for a moment, as if the call had woken them up, breaking the spell which had kept them inseparable for so long.

'I've been thinking how I should contact my agencies again,' he started. 'I've been taking the piss. If I don't do something soon, they'll drop me totally.'

'God, I can't bear the thought of you going away,' she said without thinking. 'I mean, I know you have to, it's just a terrible thought. I'll miss you.'

'That is exactly my problem,' he turned to her. 'That's why I don't get involved. Because I always have to leave at some point, and the other person doesn't get it.'

'I'm sorry, I didn't mean that.' She could have kicked herself. 'I understand. I know you have to go away. I've just been spoiled these last few weeks. I wouldn't hold you back, I promise.'

He smiled, pulled her towards himself and they hugged.

'Maybe it can wait a bit,' he whispered, and with that he pulled her towards him, kissing her hair and her face, and led her upstairs again, where they stayed another week.

Chapter Sixteen

When the rains stopped, Lia emerged from the pink cottage into a whole new world. All around her she found lush greenery – trees which had been bare now filled the winter gaps with their leaves, ironically creating more shade than they had before. Irises peeked out of hedgerows – some their usual deep, vivid purple, others a paler, softer lilac and in one garden there were even sunny yellow ones, replacing the daffodils which were now looking tired and weather-beaten. Everywhere bushes she'd always considered weeds had sprouted beautiful yellow flowers which smelt heavenly, and Lia made a mental note to ask Etienne what exactly they were. An elegant, lilac-coloured cloak of wisteria had draped itself onto the kitchen wall of Peaches' house, whilst on the archway she could see the buds of hundreds of tiny canary roses, waiting to burst out.

The air smelt fresher and there seemed to be a sense of purpose in everything and everyone around her. Maybe everyone else had spent the last few weeks in bed, too, she mused one morning, wandering up to the supermarket. And like them, Lia wanted to do something, to get out and explore this exciting new world.

'Why don't we go on a trip?' she suggested to Ben one

day when she thought they might start getting bedsores. 'Go to the mountains – there's this town I'd really like to see, Barcelonnette. It's famed for all this special produce and could be really useful for the book.'

Ben had just shrugged. 'Sure,' he said, thrilling her with his readiness simply to be with her, and they arranged to go the following week. Their first day out as a couple, Lia thought excitedly, and an important step for the book.

The day before their trip, Lia was heading for the village and admiring a hedge that was now thick with jasmine buds, still red and tightly closed, and wondering how long it would be before they opened, when a familiar voice rang out behind her. 'Haven't seen you for ages.'

She turned round to greet Chloe. 'Hibernating,' she smiled.

'Don't blame you, it's been a nightmare. Have you seen much of Ben lately?'

'A bit of him,' Lia said noncommittally. *Every single bit of him*, she thought to herself, and suddenly it felt wrong not to be with him right now.

'I don't know, I hope we've had the last of that rain,' Chloe chattered on, with Lia paying some fifty per cent of her attention. 'I've been rushed off my feet, I have. Peaches has got me doing her bookings now, and it's taking up so much of my time. She sent out a letter, or rather, I did, to anyone who's been on a retreat before, telling them about the comet and how she's planning on doing something special to welcome it. A sacred circle, or guided meditation, that kind of thing. We've had a few takers.'

'What, so there are going to be people coming?' Lia frowned, hating the idea of her little haven being spoiled.

'Yes, some even next week. Not a full retreat, mind, just a holiday with the comet thrown in. She expects me to sort out all the studios, too, clean them up and change the sheets. I mean, I know I don't pay much rent, but that wasn't what I came here for.'

'How's Etienne?' Lia asked as she drew breath. 'How's the lunar garden going?'

107

'Bit waterlogged. He got ill, poor love, but he's getting better, now. I'm just on my way to the pharmacy, pick up some pills for him. He hates being stuck indoors, you know; it doesn't suit him at all. He was getting really grumpy. It's hard being with someone twenty-four hours a day, isn't it?'

It was pretty easy, really, Lia thought fondly, and now this little break felt hard. She said nothing, just let Chloe go on.

'We have got a bit of a language barrier, I know,' Chloe sighed. 'But we're ever so close, even if we don't always understand what each other's saying. Oh well, must dash, I'll pop in for coffee one of these mornings.'

With that, Chloe darted into the pharmacy, leaving Lia to her shopping. Laden with goods, she wandered back, regretting not having taken the car. But as she once again reached the lane and the smell of the mysterious yellow bushes filled the air, it no longer bothered her that her arms were weighed down with milk and orange juice and wine. As she approached Les Eglantines she heard the roar of a motorbike, and there stood Etienne and a man she didn't know, chatting to a biker wearing his helmet. As she got closer she realised the biker was Ben, and joined them.

Seeing her, he removed the helmet, a boyish smile on his face. 'Like my new toy?' he asked.

'Impressive,' she said, not knowing one bike from another.

'Joseph here is lending it to me,' he added, signalling his friend, and Lia introduced herself. 'He's going away for a month.'

'What fun,' she told him, enjoying the secrecy between them. Did Etienne suspect anything, she wondered? Or Chloe, or even Peaches? They'd never spoken about whether to tell anyone or not, and although Lia knew she'd tire of keeping their relationship quiet soon enough, right now it was more exciting that way. 'I'll see you later,' she told him, gathering up her bags and heading for the entrance, having exchanged the obligatory *ça va*'s with Etienne.

He joined her later, and over supper suggested they took the bike to Barcelonnette instead of the car. She'd had slightly mixed feelings about such a long drive, and although she'd thought it might be good for her, she liked the idea of whizzing there on the back of a motorbike even more. It just meant rethinking her hair and wardrobe, that was all.

They got up early the next morning and had started their journey by eight-thirty. Joseph had lent Ben a second helmet, and Lia wore jeans, some low boots and a denim jacket of Ben's over her fleece, with a small rucksack on her back for any shopping. She sat comfortably, holding onto the bar behind the seat, rather than around Ben's waist, which had always struck her as looking rather clingy. It took her a while to get used to leaning into the bends with him, but as there were so many, and as they never came close to spilling over onto the road, she eventually got the hang of it.

The roads were extraordinary, with tree-covered mountains all around them and higher, more barren ones beyond, with hints of snow still in their crevices. Every now and then they'd spot a tiny village, perched impossibly high up, and marvel at how anyone ever thought of building it there, let alone got on with it.

Eventually they got to their destination, and, wandering around the cobbled streets, Lia kept thinking she could be in Switzerland, because of the mountains, or Mexico, because of the architecture, and the combination both intrigued and delighted her. Strolling in and out of all the speciality shops, she filled her rucksack with mutton sausages, a rose-hip jam, smoked mutton and a selection of cheeses, including one that was covered with honey. Then they sat down to an impromptu picnic of crusty bread filled with thyme-flavoured goat's cheese, before setting off to explore the surrounding countryside.

'It's all about *maquis* and *garrigue*, you know,' Lia told him as they stopped off by the river. 'This terrain. *Maquis* is the collective term for the evergreen shrubs, like rosemary, or those juniper bushes over there. *Garrigue* is the dwarf stuff, the grazing for goats and sheep, like lavender, thyme, grape hyacinth, all that kind of thing.'

Ben nodded, a half-smile on his face, and encouraged, she went on. 'People marvel at how much grows when it's so hot and dry in the summer, and the soil is so full of rocks. But it's the rocks that hold the secret, because they're what improves the drainage.'

'You've been doing your homework,' he smiled, turning away from her.

'I have to, it's my job,' she smiled back, enjoying herself. *I could be in the office, now*, she thought, watching Ben climb down the banks to get a closer look at the water, which flowed from the lake further west. *I could be preparing another* Miracle Mick *episode, or putting together a proposal for yet another nixed show. I could be working my way through a pile of bills, or sorting out a headache in the studio. I could be freezing my arse off in the garden, or I could be rushing to the supermarket for some forgotten but vital ingredient for a show. But I'm not, I'm here*, she thought ecstatically. *I'm here, and I'm with him! And he makes me laugh, and he's special, and he's talented*.

She watched as he peered into the water, looking for fish, and then hurled a couple of stones upstream. As he climbed back up to join her, she instinctively threw her arms around his neck.

'I can't believe how happy I am!' she gushed. 'I can't believe how much my life's been transformed. I just love where I live, I love being here, I love what I do, and I love you so much, too, I really do!'

There, they were out – the words she'd been wanting to say for weeks – they'd finally tumbled out of her mouth like water cascading from a spring. She jumped back, shocked by her own boldness.

He smiled and hugged her, but said nothing. For a moment, she wanted to pull back, urge him to say the same thing, bully him into making the same admission. But she

110

stopped herself, realising that for their relationship to be sincere, she'd just have to wait until he did so without prompting. There was no point in pushing him, because the chances were she'd just push him away. She'd be patient, she told herself, and he'd say the words when he was ready.

And he *would* say them, she told herself, trying to inject more of that Jules-style confidence that so eluded her. She just hoped she wouldn't have to wait too long.

Climbing back on the bike, they noticed threatening clouds gathering overhead, and as they drove back towards Barcelonnette, they became thicker and uglier, descending into a swirling mist which hid anything beyond just a few metres. As they reached the town it started to rain, big isolated splodges at first, which quickly gathered pace, forming torrents of water all around them. Once they'd reached the town centre, Ben pulled off his helmet and suggested they had an early supper somewhere, and wait for the weather to clear.

They chose a little café in the main square and piled in. What must they have looked like? Lia asked herself. She'd only rarely ridden on a bike before, and always thought the impression it gave was a tough one. She'd see girls in tight jeans pulling off their helmets and almost expect them to have a hard edge, to be unapproachable, but now here she was giving exactly that impression, when nothing could have been further from the truth.

They sat down to a meal of ravioli stuffed with walnuts followed by grilled local lamb, washed down by a *pichet* of red wine. As it soaked into their veins, Lia began to regret her earlier outburst, and the spontaneity behind it. She felt foolish, chastened by his refusal to say the same thing back. She found herself resenting everything he *did* say, as if it were nothing but a cover, a distraction for his lack of feelings.

She listened to him without contributing a word, imaginary conversations busily going on in her head. *So, Ben, tell me about your last girlfriend?* she could hear herself

111

spit. *Did you love her? What happened, she left you for your best friend? She dumped you for someone richer, better looking, more sophisticated? Is that why you're holding back now, because you're afraid of getting hurt? Is that it? Is that it?*

Abruptly she excused herself before she could say anything and went to the loo, descending into a mass of anger and resentment – that dark, bitter place she managed to avoid most of the time. She knew the pattern – first would come the love – the glorious, idolisation of someone and the fantasies that life was now somehow complete. Then would come the hurt – their failure, perhaps, to live up to expectations and the feeling that this was perhaps not the big love after all. Next would come resentment, slowly sucking her down into a well of anger, which in turn could only be relieved when some form of regret came to replace it. But to get to that regret there had to be words – bitter, angry words neatly aimed at hurting their recipient. Only then would the anger dissipate, leaving in its wake that regret and shame.

She took deep, pacifying breaths. What had happened to that confident woman who knew to wait and let Ben take his time, who *knew* that he'd eventually proclaim his love? Where had she gone, that sensible girl? Driven out by wine, she thought regrettably, forcing herself to be rational.

She washed her hands, scouring away the anger that was welling up. They were in a lovely town, she kept telling herself, and they'd had a wonderful day. It wasn't his fault that she'd blurted out her feelings – she herself had to take responsibility for them. They had been a mistake – inappropriate and unnecessary – but it was over now; it was time to draw a veil over them.

Taking deep breaths, she rejoined Ben, who was looking slightly worried. On the table was another *pichet* and a platter of cheese.

'More wine?' she asked disapprovingly. 'We've got a long way to go, yet.'

112

He shook his head. 'They reckon the fog's here to stay, so I booked us a room. A standard, not their deluxe suite, admittedly, but it sounds very comfortable.'

'You did?' She sank back into a haze of delighted surprise. A cosy room in the mountains, making love with the man she, well, had feelings for. It sounded perfect, and all the anger and hurt and rejection disappeared as they'd descended – faster than the mountain fog, in any case.

They finished their meal, had a glass each of *Génépy*, the local digestive that was similar to pastis, and made their way to their room, falling into each other's arms and staying warm despite the sinking temperature outside; and Lia felt certain that despite his reticence and her earlier irrationality, Ben really was the man she wanted to spend the rest of her life with.

If only he could feel the same way, though.

Chapter Seventeen

'Oh blimey, the lentil brigade's arrived,' Ben announced
one morning, peering out of the bedroom window.

Squinting through the morning sun, Lia could make out
three women carrying luggage through the garden and
down towards the studios.

'Peaches' disciples – a bunch of losers, loners and
misfits,' he continued dismissively.

'That's a bit rich, coming from you,' she tutted. 'You
went on a retreat, didn't you? So which do you consider
yourself, then, the loser, loner or the misfit?'

'That was different,' he laughed, pulling on some clothes.

'Why?' She hauled herself up onto the pillow. 'Why was
it different for you and not the others?'

'You know, I recognise one of them,' he'd turned back
to the window, ignoring her. 'Glenda, a bit butch. Vegan,
I think, very disapproving of Peaches' dirty little meat-
eating habit. Said it was totally at odds with her spiritual
cleanliness.'

'They've come for the comet,' Lia remembered, sinking
back onto the pillow. 'Chloe told me about it. Peaches is
doing something special, a sacred circle meditation or
something.'

114

'Wouldn't want to miss that,' Ben smirked. 'So what do you want this morning, proper tea, coffee, or rosehip and rabbit droppings?'

'Coffee, strong,' she tried not to smile. 'Out of rebellion. And maybe I should take up smoking while I'm at it. And we could have egg and bacon for breakfast,' she called as he disappeared down the stairs. 'And perhaps a sausage or two.'

They'd fallen into an easy routine now that the rains had stopped and each had remembered they had projects to work on, and weren't just there for the sex. They'd have breakfast together and then separate for the day, only to reunite in the evenings for dinner. Occasionally she would pop down to see him and they'd go through his photos together, and he'd tell her why he wanted one to be included and not another. She could look at them from an emotional angle, she found, but was less good at seeing technically why one was superior to another, or so much better framed.

'Life goes on, that's what this is saying, isn't it?' she'd asked one afternoon looking at a shot of a woman hanging some washing out on a makeshift line which ran from one gutted house to another. 'In spite of all the shit that happens, life goes on. No matter that you don't have a roof, or windows, or walls that are standing up straight, you've still got to do the washing; you've still got to get on with it all.'

Ben nodded. 'There's a better one, though,' he said, searching for it. 'Here. The eyes – caught her eyes this time. In the other one she was squinting, you see?'

'Yes,' she smiled, recognising the difference. 'You're absolutely right. And the corner of that towel is in frame,' she pointed out. 'It was slightly clipped in the other one.'

She felt with every viewing that she was learning more, understanding what he'd gone through in the past, and why, perhaps, he now needed a break. But she still couldn't picture him at one of Peaches' retreats, and certainly not now other former participants were arriving.

Jules remained cynical but grudgingly seemed to accept that her friend was happy. Lia had e-mailed her a few times since their affair had begun, but was quietly ashamed at how little she seemed to be achieving with the book. She had meant to get three chapters off by the spring, and now it was already the last week of May.

She was walking back from the supermarket when she found Chloe with the new arrivals, correcting yoga positions by the pool. Standing slightly apart, Glenda was making odd brushing movements just a few centimetres above her skin.

'She's cleansing her aura,' Chloe informed Lia quietly.

'That's a good thing, is it?' Lia tried to keep a straight face.

'Oh yes, it creates balance and promotes harmony and a sense of well-being,' Chloe trotted out. 'You should try it some time.'

'I think I'll live without.'

'You are so closed!' Chloe scolded her. 'Honestly. I've never known anything like it. If you'd just open yourself out more, you'd get so much out of life.'

'But I don't feel I'm missing anything,' Lia protested. 'I'm very happy, happier than I've ever been. I'm fulfilled in my work and I love living here. I feel balanced, I feel harmonious, I don't need any rituals or meditation to help me.' There was one specific thing making her happy, of course, but she didn't want to admit that just yet.

'That's all very well for now,' Chloe countered, smiling but serious. 'But what if it all goes wrong? What then? Will you be prepared then, I wonder?'

Lia just laughed. 'Thanks for the encouragement.' She started moving off.

'You know what?' Chloe followed her. 'I've just realised something. They say that everyone comes into your life for a reason, and now I know why you came into mine. You came in to show me how far I've developed spiritually. That's your gift to me. A few years ago I would have been like you, all closed and stand-offish, but now

116

here I am, a balanced and centred individual. You've shown me that, so I suppose in a way I should be grateful.'

Lia tried to memorise the exact words Chloe had used, knowing how much Ben would appreciate them. *And you've come into my life to give me funny stories and make me laugh*, she wanted to say back, but refrained.

'Ah, there you are, Lia, dear,' Peaches appeared in a soft pink tracksuit. 'Have you met our tiny group yet: Lucy, Trisha and Glenda? Oh, and would you like to take part in our sacred circle on Saturday night? That's when Levin-Bayes will first appear in the sky. Felix will lead us all in a guided meditation to welcome it, and then we'll each make two wishes: one for ourselves, privately, and the other for the world, and its well-being. We'd love for you to join us.'

'I don't think I can, I'm afraid,' Lia apologised. 'I've already got plans.'

'Oh, that is a pity,' Peaches cried. 'It'll be a most powerful event, you know? But how are you, anyway? I haven't seen you in ages. You must have been terribly busy.'

'Yes, I have rather.' Lia hoped it wasn't obvious she was lying.

'Or Ben, for that matter,' Peaches went on. 'Perhaps we should have a little drink on Sunday or something. The girls here want a day of cleansing and fasting, so there won't be many activities to arrange.'

'I know, why don't we have lunch?' Lia suggested suddenly. 'A comet lunch, something to celebrate its arrival? I feel bad I never did anything for Easter, but then the weather was so awful. So how about it? You, Felix, Chloe, Etienne, and I could always invite Ben,' she added vaguely.

'What a marvellous idea,' Peaches enthused. 'I'd love that – you're such a wonderful cook, and Felix is so terribly fond of you. Now, what would be an appropriate dish for the comet, I wonder?'

117

'How about a nice big leg of lamb,' Lia suggested, knowing she was within Glenda's earshot. 'Nice and pink, and studded with garlic and rosemary? I haven't cooked a roast in ages, and I really need to practise. Consider it research.'

'I shouldn't,' Peaches giggled guiltily, peering anxiously in Glenda's direction. 'Oh, but why not? It sounds marvellous. Sunday, then, I look forward to it.'

Chapter Eighteen

Lia spent most of the next day planning her comet lunch. She would serve chilled avocado soup for starters, she decided, followed by a huge leg of lamb studded with garlic, rosemary and anchovies. On the side she'd make a large pot of ratatouille and a potato and mushroom *galette* with crème fraiche. There would be plenty of cheese, and for pudding she would do a lemon tart with summer berries. These, of course, would have to be frozen, as it was too early for fresh ones, but they would still add colour. She'd also decided to make some basil, tomato and anchovy flavoured butters to have with the bread, which would be decorative as well as tasty.

The day before the lunch, she needed to pick up a few vegetables from the village, and decided to walk up rather than take the car. The countryside was going into overdrive now, she'd noticed, and it was a pleasure just to see it all come alive: lavateras and lilacs were bursting open, geraniums filled every window box and vivid orange nasturtiums had started tumbling down the walls. Even Lia herself had begun to get excited about the comet, and the thought of a big early summer lunch delighted her.

She loved entertaining. There was nothing nicer, she

119

thought, than waking up knowing there was going to be a party, planning a list of things to do and methodically working her way through it. The guests were due to arrive at one, and the lamb was to be pink by one-thirty. Ben, she reckoned, would help her out first thing and then sneak back to his flat, to return with the others later. It was a charade, and they both knew it, but if it made him happy then she was prepared to go along with it.

Approaching the archway which led to the village she passed a boy in his pyjamas carrying two loaves of bread home and a dog splashing about in the spring. Village life, she smiled contentedly, how she'd grown to love it.

She bought her vegetables from the *traiteur*, chatting to the ladies as she did so. She chose the plump round courgettes which had started appearing, thinking it would be fun to have courgette chunks in her ratatouille rather than just slices. When she told them, however, they were most put out, urging her to reconsider, and an animated discussion broke out with several villagers, all of whom clearly disapproved of her plans. Lia held firm, and bought her round courgettes, thinking how the scene would make a nice vignette for the book.

When she emerged, laden with bags, there was a shout and Ben appeared from the bar tabac, offering to help her carry them, and they walked towards Les Eglantines together. She started going through her checklist with him, not sure but not really caring either whether he was listening or not.

'I'm going to make the butters today, and the ratatouille,' she started. 'They'll both last until tomorrow. Though maybe I'll add the herbs and the garlic tomorrow, so that they taste fresh. The pudding, of course, I'll make today, and I think I'll do the potato thing as well. So that means tomorrow I'll just have to take care of the soup, the lamb and the presentation.'

'You're going to a lot of trouble for us lot,' he told her. 'I mean, it *is* only us, isn't it? So that's Peaches and her comet, Chloe's spiritual enlightenment and Etienne's table

120

manners we've got to look forward to. We don't deserve you and your cooking, you know that?'

She was aware of a car behind them, and that it sounded quite fast, but it was only when Ben pulled her to the side of the road that she realised quite how close it had come. It screeched to a halt, an open-top Golf, rented – she could tell by the number plate – and in it sat a woman somewhere in her thirties with dark bobbed hair. She was wearing a tan leather jacket, cream turtle neck and a pair of cream cords. She lifted her huge sunglasses off her eyes with a perfectly manicured hand.

'Ben, darling! I thought it was you. How are you?' she called out in a crisp, clear tone.

'Bella, this is a surprise.'

'I know, last minute thing, decided to come for a few days to see how the house is getting on. Staying in one of the studios – unfortunately, the pink cottage is taken.'

'Yes, it is, by Lia, here, in fact. Lia, this is Bella.'

'The artist? Of course, how are you?' Lia tried to smile yet something was definitely telling her to be wary.

'So you've got my lovely cottage, have you?' Bella cried. 'Well, I just hope you're appreciating it. What are you doing tomorrow, Ben? Let's have lunch somewhere perhaps, up in the mountains, say?'

'I've got plans already, actually, Lia's doing a big lunch,' he told her awkwardly.

'You're very welcome to join us, of course,' Lia heard herself say, dutifully.

'Well I'd love to – what fun, thank you! How very kind. Well, I must go and find Peaches. I'll see you later. Bye, Lia, see you tomorrow.' She drove off at great speed, even though they were only a short distance from Les Eglantines.

'Wow, so that's Bella.' Lia filled the sudden silence.

'That's Bella,' Ben repeated, not altogether happily.

'I had to invite her, didn't I?' She turned to him anxiously. 'I mean, it would have been rude not to. She's not going to do a Glenda on me, though, is she, and go on about having meat?'

'God, no, she's not like that.'

They walked in silence for a second. 'So another of Peaches' disciples, then?' Lia asked.

'She was on the same retreat as me.' His tone was colder now, and he seemed preoccupied.

'Here for the comet?' Lia wondered aloud. 'She really doesn't look the type, does she? She's so, well, put together. She looks like the last sort of person who'd be interested in all that sort of thing.'

'I think she had a tough time during her divorce. I think that was why she came.'

'And I mean, why stay here now? She doesn't look as if she's on a tight budget.'

'Look, does it really matter?' he snapped irritably. 'She's here, we're here, Glenda and the others are here. Do people have to fit into some kind of mould to be here, is that what you think?'

'No, I—' Lia was too shocked to know what to say, and so fell silent. She'd never seen Ben like this before, never imagined he could even have a temper, and she hated this unexpected awkwardness between them. She had no tangible reason for disliking Bella, yet she did, intently, and felt immediately threatened by her.

It was as if the woman had just ripped open a wound – Ben's wound – and Lia was powerless to stitch it together again.

'So, did you know she was coming?' She had to ask something. Ben had become dangerously quiet.

'No, I didn't,' he told her. 'I wish I had,' he added.

'Why?'

'Then I might have gone somewhere else.' It was delivered with a bitter laugh.

'Look, is there anything you need to tell me?' Lia turned to him as they approached the entrance. 'I mean, is there anything between you and her—'

As she said it, she knew there was.

He frowned, as if he'd got a sudden headache. 'Can I come and see you later?' he asked. 'I just need to do some thinking, that's all.'

'OK,' she said with a resigned shrug. She was not to let Ben know that this bothered her, she told herself. So he had a past. Didn't everyone? 'Come up whenever you want – I'm not going anywhere.'

They kissed briefly on the lips and wearily she carried on up to the pink cottage, a nasty feeling that nothing would be the same from now on.

Chapter Nineteen

'We had a brief fling,' Ben told her later, over supper. She'd made tagliatelle with a pack of smoked salmon she'd found on special offer, and was just stirring in some crème fraiche before checking the seasoning. It would need black pepper, she told herself dully, but go easy on the salt. She paused, incapable of deciding whether the tagliatelle was al dente or just plain undercooked, trying to take it all in.

It wasn't as if this had never occurred to her – his reaction earlier on had been obvious enough. But they were just so different it was hard to imagine them together. She tried to picture them – naked, kissing, intimate – Ben and Bella. Any other couple and she'd be laughing, scandalised; she'd probably joke about what a strange and unlikely pair they made. Ben and Bella – even their names sounded wrong together.

She drained the pasta, enjoying the dramatic whoosh the water and steam made and half wishing it was Bella's beautiful head she was drenching, and not just the sink.

It was all in the past, she told herself, again and again, stirring in the salmon. It was all in the past. And what was the point in getting jealous, she reasoned, of something that happened in the past? Hadn't she had other lovers, after all, and wasn't Jonathan equally capable of turning up without warning? How would she feel if Ben got jealous and sulky about that? Wouldn't it make him look childish and petty?

There was no reason to get upset, she told herself, and no reason to feel threatened, because in doing either, she would only make herself look bad.

'It was last year, on the retreat,' Ben continued, and she realised she'd been quiet for too long. 'Odd, really, as we're so different, but there you go. It wasn't anything heavy or serious, it was just a bit of fun.' The last words came out apologetically, and he drained his glass before refilling it immediately.

She put their warmed plates down on the table, feeling horribly like a housewife to Bella's desirable mistress. She could almost see herself in a pinny, hair in rollers, meekly listening to whatever Ben told her– a couple of stone heavier, middle aged and frightened. Dependent on him for her life, her well-being and her welfare. She reminded herself that she was in fact wearing a black turtleneck and jeans, and was smelling of expensive perfume. She was a size twelve, had blonde hair and never went without mascara or lipstick. She was independent, with money of her own and was not afraid to take a risk. She could stand up to the likes of Bella DeVere.

'So it's all over now, isn't it?'

'Of course it's over,' he replied quickly. Almost defensively, she thought, finding herself reading something into his every word.

'Well, we all have a past,' she said, wishing that her own had been more interesting, and began spooning pasta onto his plate. 'It's just a bit tough when it turns up on your doorstep and you invite it in for lunch.'

Lia enjoyed referring to Bella as *it*, as it dehumanised her, making her seem less of a threat.

'I know, I'm sorry,' he sighed awkwardly. 'It'll be fine. She can be good company, you know.'

'Good enough for you to shag her, anyway,' Lia

125

snapped, regretting it instantly. 'I'm sorry,' she sighed, pushing her hair out of her eyes. 'That was uncalled for.'

She stirred her pasta, reluctant to take a bite in case it made her throw up. Then suddenly she realised something that *did* make her want to throw up. 'It was in here, wasn't it? Your fling was here, in the pink cottage?'

'Yes, it was,' he said quietly, putting his fork down. 'I'm sorry, Lia.'

In the background she could hear something that sounded like chanting starting up.

'You were in my bed,' she thought out loud, taking it in, picturing them together: laughing, naked, in *her* bed. Oddly, she almost savoured the moment, relishing the way her insides seemed to implode and her heart quickened, sending an angry flush to her cheeks. He must have thought about Bella, she told herself, climbing into the same bed again; he must have been reminded of her? How many times had his thoughts drifted towards her, whilst Lia lay in his arms? And wouldn't everything in the cottage remind him of that period?

The chanting seemed to grow louder, depressing her, dragging her down into solemnity, and she fought to climb out of it. It was in the past, she told herself; it was before Ben even knew she existed. Jealousy at this point was irrational, pointless and damaging. All Bella had were a few fading memories, but what she had with Ben was tangible, it was real, it was happening in the present. Bella was the one to be jealous, she told herself, not her.

'Look, it's over,' she rallied, determined not to let the woman beat her. 'It lasted, what, a maximum of two weeks, and you've had nothing to do with her since.' *How many days were you together*, her mind raged, *how many times did you do it?* 'So she's turned up here for a few days,' she continued, pushing the questions out of her mind. 'So what? I'm not so insecure as to be threatened by her.' In saying the words, she willed them to be true.

He took her hand. 'Thank you. Some girls would find this hard. I had no idea she was coming, believe me.'

'Did you see her today?' Lia had a healthy mouthful of Côtes du Rhône, and forced herself to seem bright and unconcerned.

'Briefly. She went shopping and then we had a cup of tea. I told her all about you and me.'

'You did?' Lia asked, cheered. There she was – real, tangible and being talked about. She was the threat in this story, not Bella. 'And what was her reaction?'

'A bit disappointed, I think, a bit hurt. I don't think she seriously thought anything would come of us, but I think she would have enjoyed a bit of fun while she's down here.'

Us. The word sent a shiver down Lia's spine, which she chased away with another mouthful of wine. 'How long's she down for?'

'I don't know. They're doing some work on her house and she wants to see how it's going.'

'Does she work? I mean, does she have an office to go to? Does she have to be somewhere at some point?'

'I actually don't know her that well.' He was beginning to sound irritated, and she stopped. Clearly he was tiring of this conversation, but where could they possibly go next?

She was rescued by the sound of applause and cheers, and remembered the comet.

'Oh God, it must be here,' she said, and they moved out onto the terrace. The sky wasn't fully dark yet, but in the distance she could see what looked like a star with a faint trail behind it.

'So that's it, the comet that's changing the world, then?' she found herself whispering almost reverentially.

'That's it,' Ben said without emotion.

'Not sure if I like its revelations so far,' she joked, and he put his arm round her, pulling her in towards his body.

Lia couldn't keep her eyes from wandering eastwards to where Peaches was gathered with her group, and she could just make out one extra head in her count. Bella. Perhaps it was her imagination, but she thought she could see the

127

woman turning to look at her, and then quickly turning back again.

'Well I'm glad you were honest with her,' she said once they were inside again. She was aware that it might sound condescending, but didn't care now. She was on a roll, urging herself to feel victorious. Bella, the glamorous, beautiful and dangerous, was now Bella the thwarted, the loser in love, while she, the homely, earth-mother type was the winner of Ben's heart.

Tomorrow might not be easy, she told herself, getting ready for bed, but at least she would be the hostess, the one in charge. How simply and elegantly she'd show Bella how she could cook and create and cater for a man, making it clear just how much she had to offer. And in the others she had an appreciative audience, who would rub in the point even further. And of course, there was Ben to show how much he appreciated her efforts, and how strongly he cared for her.

He wouldn't let her down, she reassured herself, climbing into bed beside him; he wouldn't let her down now. A vague image of a cold and unresponsive Ben flickered through her mind, a Ben who ignored her, who remained deep in conversation with Bella over the meal, and she pushed it away.

And as she tried to get to sleep, cradled in his arms, she pictured him smiling at her in the midday sunshine, unafraid to show his affection, and held onto the image as hard as she could. Because somehow, for some reason, the walls, the floor and the bed all seemed to have turned against her. Maybe Bella's painting was behind the mutiny, as it had taken on a darker tone now, but together they wanted to mock her, to bring her to her knees and turn her blissful world into something darker and unhappy, and no matter how hard she tried to shrug them off, they kept returning, their laughter growing louder, to haunt her through the night.

Chapter Twenty

Ben left at midday, as she'd expected, to come back later with the others. Lia willed herself into the party spirit, fetching fresh bread and checking her time-plan over and over, making sure she hadn't, or wouldn't, forget anything. More than ever this lunch had become important, and she had the feeling that her every move, word and dish would be scrutinised. She was the one in control of this situation, she kept telling herself, and Bella was just a guest – a last-minute invitation, an extra place setting on the table – nothing more significant than that.

As she'd hoped, the sun came out and by eleven the terrace had become gloriously warm. She studded her lamb with rosemary, slivers of garlic and some mashed-up anchovy, whizzed up some avocados, crème fraiche and stock in the blender and laid seven places on the table. She'd put Bella between Felix and Etienne, she thought, and herself between Felix and Ben. But there would be two women, she realised, poring over her seating plan, so mightn't it be better to put her between Etienne and Chloe? But that way she'd be right opposite Ben, which Lia didn't want. Finally she decided on having Bella as far away as possible, at the end of the table with Chloe and Etienne, with Peaches and Felix between her and Ben. Chloe would barely let her get a word in, and Etienne's table manners would put her nerves nicely on edge.

She'd got to the point when all she had to do was either warm things up or keep them chilled when the first guests arrived – Chloe and Etienne. Happily she got Etienne to open two bottles of sparkling wine and pour them a glass each. As ever, she found the first mouthful the best, bringing with it a sense of drama and expectation. Today was going to be *her* day – the day she'd make her mark, let her rival see what she was up against and pee all over Bella's metaphorical fireworks like a cat marking its territory in a new neighbourhood. Before even realising it she'd drained her glass and got Etienne to top it up again, reminding herself to stay safely in control.

Felix and Peaches came next, gladly accepting their glasses.

'It's not real, I'm afraid,' she admitted.

'No, no, dear, why bother? It's only a name after all, and this is just as good,' Peaches clucked, clearly excited at the prospect of a delicious lunch. 'We had a marvellous night last night – did you?' She began describing the meditation, the chants and the various wishes for world peace they'd enjoyed as Lia put out olives, bread and the flavoured butters.

Where was Ben, she couldn't help but wonder? The ratatouille was fine, bubbling away on the stove, but the lamb? She'd hate for it to be overdone. She did some calculations and took it out of the oven to relax, replacing it with the potato and mushroom *galette*.

She heard more voices and there they were, Ben and Bella, turning up together like a couple. Did the others all know about their past, Lia wondered, kicking herself for not having asked him the previous night. How humiliating, she shuddered, if they did, and were now assuming that they'd got back together. She checked herself in the reflection of the ratatouille pot, which was not a good idea, but the moon face which greeted her had clean and brushed hair, unsmudged make-up and a flattering shade of pink lipstick on. She'd kept her clothes simple with jeans, a T-shirt and a dusky pink jacket, with tan belt and shoes.

Bella, she scrutinised from the kitchen widow, was wearing a black and white floral dress with a neat white jacket perched on her shoulders, and was clutching a posy of pretty white flowers. Lia felt chastened, as if the posy were some kind of olive branch.

'Now where's Lia?' she could hear her saying, as she prepared to say her hello. 'It was so sweet of her to invite me when she doesn't even know me!'

'Bella, hi,' she stepped onto the terrace, trying to sound as confident as the woman now facing her. 'I'm delighted you could come.' She should have become a politician.

'These are for you,' Bella handed her the flowers with a big smile. 'Just to show my appreciation. Ben?' She turned around to face a subdued-looking Ben behind her. 'You've got the wine, haven't you?'

He offered Lia a bag with two bottles, leaning forward to kiss her on either cheek. Etienne, who'd quickly refilled his own glass on their arrival, handed them a glass each.

'I love this cottage,' Bella gazed at it dreamily. 'It has such charm. Are you loving being here?'

'Yes,' Lia said shyly. 'It has a wonderful feel.'

'I was so happy here, even though it was just for a couple of weeks. I painted this marvellous vista, and the view of the willow and the citrus orchard. It was all so inspirational. You're writing a book, aren't you?'

'Yes I am,' Lia said quickly, not wanting to go into it. Already it felt as if Bella was gaining control. Why couldn't she just be a guest and sit down quietly? 'Excuse me for a moment while I check on lunch.'

She'd hoped Ben might follow her into the kitchen. She'd hoped he'd come in and they'd have a conspiratorial chat, or he'd ask if there was something he could do, or even just lend moral support. But instead he stayed outside, chatting, and as Lia caught another glimpse of herself in the reflection of the ratatouille pot, she hated her jeans, the

131

jacket and the flat tan shoes, thinking they made her look boyish and unfeminine. Bella looked softer today, more like her name, and almost as if she needed protecting.

'Is there anything I can do, dear?' Peaches had fluttered in, a vision of orange and gold, a smudge of lipstick on her teeth.

'No, I'm fine, thank you, just wondering whether to serve the first course yet.'

She stirred the ratatouille and checked that the potatoes were warming through. Outside she could hear chairs being drawn up, and frightened that her table plan was about to be ruined, rushed out to check. Chloe and Etienne were dominating the far end, whilst Bella had put herself comfortably close to Ben.

'It's free seating, isn't it?' Chloe asked as Etienne topped both their glasses up.

'Sure, sit where you like,' Lia swallowed, beginning to hate her own party already. 'I'll bring out the first course.'

She found herself sitting at the head of the table, with Felix and Peaches on either side – Ben at the far end between Bella and Etienne, with Chloe opposite – and tried not to sulk. Everyone, Bella in particular, enthused about the chilled soup, which felt so right on a warm spring day. But halfway through the lamb, Bella went for the jugular.

'Tell me about this book you're writing. It's recipes, isn't it?'

'Not just that,' Lia started, remembering her lines. 'It's called *The Sensuous South*, and it's all about the produce of the Mediterranean, and the recipes that go with it.'

'How charming,' Bella countered. 'But what's your angle? I mean, what makes you different from, say, a Claudia Roden, or a Carrier?'

'Well, they're strictly cookery writers, while I'm exploring where the food comes from, and how best to grow the various produce.'

'So who's your market?' Bella looked puzzled. 'Are you targeting the UK, for example, and so explaining how to obtain the right conditions, or soil, or whatever it takes to grow these things, or are you targeting the expat community over here? Though, in terms of sales, I'd have thought that was a pretty small market.'

Lia stopped for a moment – it was a point she'd never considered. In all her plans, all her thoughts and all her conversations and e-mails with Jules, the thought of who actually might want to buy the book, or why, had never actually come up. She felt herself floundering and raced to come up with something that appeared intelligent and well thought out.

'I'm not giving instructions on how to adapt your soil, no, though I do talk about how good drainage is vital, and about how the gravelly condition of Mediterranean soil plays its part. But it's more about rejoicing in style of food down here, and how to cook with the seasons, and make the most of all the produce.'

'So your audience is down here, then?'

'I think it's either. I don't think people will care whether or not they can actually grow aubergines for themselves, but they're still interested in *how* they grow, where they originate from, and how they are used in different countries.'

She hoped she hadn't sounded garbled and unprepared, and took a grateful sip of wine. Bella wasn't finished, though.

'And do you have a publisher?'

'I do, actually, and they're very supportive.' She thought with a shudder back to Jules's last e-mail, asking if she was *ever* going to send her some chapters to go through, and to all her notes, pages and ideas, still refusing to conform to any structure.

'Did you get a wonderful book deal? You hear of people signing for hundreds of thousands, these days, don't you?' This was said to the whole table, whose eyes lit up enthusiastically, as if one day each could be the recipient of such an offer.

'I certainly haven't got hundreds of thousands,' Lia smiled, deciding to leave it at that. She rose and began to

133

offer second helpings. Bella refused, saying the meal was delicious but that she'd had plenty; the others all held their plates out for more slices of meat and the ladles of ratatouille which Ben served.

'So what about you, Bella?' Lia asked after a deep breath. 'What are you doing here? Will you be painting much?'

'Oh, it's just a hobby, but I love it. No, I just wanted to oversee the work on my house, see how they're coming along. You've got to keep an eye on these people. I'm trying to persuade Ben to take some before and after shots for me, as a record.'

'What a good idea,' Lia snarled towards Ben.

'And then I'm determined to get him to do something with all his other shots – he's been cataloguing them since last year. We'll either set up an exhibition somewhere or get the material together for a book, but I can't bear to see another year go by with nothing achieved. And I've got a good eye, haven't I, Ben? You trust my opinion, don't you?'

Ben, who had uncharacteristically said little throughout lunch, just nodded and then reached for his wine. Lia drank more of hers, too, fantasising about spilling it over Bella's pretty floral dress.

She served cheese followed by the lemon tart, which was a great success, and then Peaches and Felix excused themselves to go home for a nap.

'Come on, Ben, I'm sure Lia wants the place to herself again now. Let's go for a walk,' Bella urged him. 'Or why don't we go to the house and take some shots?'

'The light will be terrible,' he said feebly.

'Well in the morning, then. But how about a nice walk to work off Lia's excellent lunch? Come on, before we lose the sun.'

'Let me just help Lia with some of this,' he said, piling together some plates and heading for the kitchen. Quickly Lia grabbed the salt and pepper and some scrunched-up napkins and followed him.

134

'I'm so sorry,' he said. 'I don't know what to say.'

'I get the impression she doesn't give you much of a chance,' Lia said fairly.

'She's like a bulldozer. Look, I'm really sorry Lia. Let me go on this walk and make things clear. She's trying to take over and I won't let her.'

'Tell me about it. Your exhibition, your book? She'll be turning herself into your agent, next.'

'That was a simply marvellous lunch, Lia, a real treat.' Bella was behind them, pulling her jacket on properly. 'I think your book sounds wonderful, and can't wait to read it.' She grasped Lia by the arms and air-kissed both sides of her face.

'I'll see you later,' Ben said reluctantly, kissing her.

She watched them leave together and felt helpless, hopeless. Bella had effused good manners and charm, yet effortlessly ridiculed her book and made her intentions on Ben abundantly clear. Lia felt she had been politely mugged, and that all she cherished had been snatched away from her.

The cottage felt empty without him, and although she could hope he'd come round later on, somehow she knew he wouldn't. Not because he didn't want to, but because he wouldn't be allowed to. She tidied things up in the kitchen, wanting to get the washing up done and relax, but outside at the table, Chloe and Etienne stayed in their seats, and she watched as Etienne, leaning perilously back on his chair, eyed up the three-quarters-full bottle of wine.

She joined them and poured herself a glass, grateful, at least, that Bella had gone. 'Well, that was OK, wasn't it?' It was funny how they suddenly seemed more familiar and trustworthy now that someone new had been introduced.

'It was lovely – you deserve a medal,' said Chloe, holding her glass out for Etienne to refill. He topped up both their glasses and cut himself a thick slice of Brie, before leaning back again, glass in hand. 'But I'd watch Bella if I was you,' Chloe added, and Lia felt herself sitting more upright. 'She's poisonous if you ask me.'

If Chloe was about to start on one of her rants, this was one that Lia actually wanted to hear. 'Why do you say that?'

'She's a manipulative bitch who won't stop until she gets what she wants. I wouldn't trust her further than you could throw her, seriously.'

'Did you know her last year?'

'Yes,' Chloe rolled her eyes. 'A right pain – no one liked her. Everything had to be done her way, and she spoke to everyone in the same politely bitchy way. She's so insincere.'

'She was pretty tough about my book,' Lia drank some more wine, beginning to wonder if Chloe mightn't become a friend after all.

'Lia, can I ask you something?' The look on Chloe's face was part questioning, part knowing smile. 'Were you and Ben, you know . . .?'

Lia had a rush of blood to the head. She no longer cared that Ben wanted to keep things a secret; in fact she found it insulting, and in the wake of Bella's onslaught she knew she needed an ally, and might even have one in Chloe. Without pausing to think she blurted out, 'Well, we only spent the last month in bed, if that's what you mean.'

'I knew it!' Chloe roared and raised her glass. Even Etienne managed an approving smile. 'Good on you, girl, here's to you!'

They both laughed and Lia started to feel as if a weight was lifting, that her secret was finally out.

'I knew something was up – Ben was just never around. I knew he was with you.'

'And now bloody Bella's turned up to ruin everything. She's so obviously after him.'

'As a plaything, that's all. I'm sure she's got some rich bloke in London. She just plays with people. I know they had a bit of a fling last year, but I never thought it meant anything.'

'Was that out in the open?' Lia asked jealously.

'No, not really, but he was caught sneaking out of the

136

pink cottage a couple of times. I think Ben likes his private life to be private. But you want to watch her, you know. You've got a fight on your hands.'

'I've never fought for a man before,' Lia told her. 'I'm not sure I can start now.'

'Then you'll lose him. Ben's too laid back to even realise what she's up to. If you want to hang on to him then you've got to fight her, tooth and nail.'

'I don't know,' Lia sighed. It sounded exhausting. 'If I'm fighting, then aren't I being just as manipulative? I mean, I'd rather he was with me because he wanted to be, and not because I'd forced him to.'

'That's very noble, Lia, but you'll lose him. She'll be on at him to photograph her house, then to sort out his photos, then something else, then something else, and you'll hardly see him. You've got to be tougher than that.'

'I don't know. I'll think about it.'

Suddenly Lia wanted the conversation to be over, for them to leave and for her to be soaking in her hot tub full of aromatic bubbles. She wanted Ben to turn up later with wine and apologies, and for Bella to leave in the night, and go back to wherever it was she came from. She wanted to be alone, to think things through and work out what to do next. She wanted the cottage to be hers again. She wanted to snuggle up on the sofa in Ben's arms – she wanted his warmth, his companionship and his love.

Etienne burped and suggested they opened another bottle.

Chapter Twenty-one

Ben turned up the following morning to find Lia depressed and bad tempered. She'd not slept well in the night, partly because of her alcohol intake but mostly because she'd been busy tormenting herself with images of Ben with Bella together in her flat: laughing, kissing and making love.

She put the kettle on and filled the cafetière with hot, strong coffee. She knew she looked a wreck. She'd done exactly what she always did each morning: a tiny bit of foundation on her nose and cheeks, a little eyeliner on the outer corners of her eyes and plenty of mascara, and had pulled her hair back into a rough knot, and yet where some days the result was cute and girlish, today she just looked plain and drawn.

'So how was your walk?' she asked coolly, not wanting to become the possessive and insecure girlfriend she knew she sounded like.

He sighed. 'I'm really sorry,' he said, and her stomach lurched. 'It was fine. We went for this long walk, then had some tea and before I knew it, it had got really late. I never meant to stay with her all that time, and I'm sorry I didn't come up. I just felt bad, I can't explain it.'

'I knew you weren't going to come,' Lia said evenly,

wondering what they could have talked about for so long. 'And in some ways I was in no mood to see you.'

'I can imagine. You don't deserve to be treated like that, and I'm sorry. Look, I agreed to take those photos, but I told her in no uncertain terms that I'm with you now. I made it quite clear that she's not to come between us.'

She already has, Lia wanted to say. 'Good,' she said instead, feeling little tears of emotion bubbling up in her eyes. 'And was she OK about that?'

He didn't look convincing. 'She was just Bella, you know? She doesn't really show emotion. You could tell her that her house was burnt down and her parents had been killed and she'd say "Yes, well, let's have a little drink and we'll talk about it".'

She knew he was right. She was intrigued, she found to her irritation, and wanted to know more about the woman. How old was she, for example? Bella seemed pretty ageless, so could be anywhere between thirty and forty-five. About thirty-five, Lia guessed, but a mature thirty-five, one who was sophisticated and confident, who had married well and led a grown-up life. It was odd to think they could be about the same age, when they were such worlds apart. She wondered if Bella had ever been young and gauche; if Bella had ever made mistakes or done anything wild.

And then it occurred to her, and she was surprised not to have thought of it before. Perhaps Ben himself was her idea of being wild, letting her hair down?

'So why did you agree to do her house?' she snapped, growing convinced of her theory. 'I mean, isn't she capable of buying a camera and taking some snaps herself? Why does she need a professional?'

'I don't know,' he said patiently. 'Maybe you're right, maybe I shouldn't have agreed to it. But she's still a friend, you know? I'm sorry if that's tough, but she's still a friend. And the one thing I've learnt over the years is how important your friends are. So I'm sorry if you don't like it, but I still want to see her.'

139

Lia nodded, hating this block that was suddenly developing between them. Could things ever be the same again? Some far-off point in the distance, perhaps, but not yet, not as long as Bella was around.

'So, when do you start taking the photos?' she asked eventually.

'When there's good light,' he said. 'Tomorrow morning, perhaps.'

'And what about this house? Where is it?'

'Not far, about a twenty-minute drive.'

She wanted to know all about it, suddenly, to be able to picture it in her mind. Would it be charming, covered in cottage roses and surrounded by olive groves and vineyards, or would it be flashy, set near the coast and reeking of extravagance? What kind of a house would Bella own, she wondered, knowing it would reveal much about her character.

'So what, she inherited it? Bought it?'

'Bought it, I think. With part of the proceeds of her divorce. She was married to someone quite wealthy, an investment banker, I think, and got quite a lot out of him.'

She nodded, taking this in. 'But you know what'll happen, don't you? You'll head off in the morning, take some shots, and then she'll suggest lunch in some delightful little place she knows to thank you. You'll have lunch, then a wander round the village, and before you know it the day'll be gone, and she'll start mentioning a drink, and then perhaps some dinner.'

'Don't be ridiculous,' Ben said defensively. 'I won't let that happen. We'll go, come back and I'll get on with my work. Alone.'

Lia laughed hopelessly, instinctively knowing that her version was the more accurate.

'Well, it's not as if I came to France looking for love or romance, or anything, so if things between you and me don't work out, I'll still be fine.' She made it sound like a joke, but seeing the reaction on his face, tried to backtrack, regretting her words. It was the same pattern all over again, she realised – love, hurt, anger, regret. Would she never be free of it? 'I'm saying I should stop worrying about you and that woman, and get on with my work, that's all,' she said more softly.

'Fine, because I want to carry on seeing you,' he told her, and she felt an immense sense of relief. 'I don't want her coming between us. So I'll come round this evening, if I may.'

'I'd love you to,' Lia smiled. 'I've got tons of leftover lamb and ratatouille to eat up.'

'Excellent.' He'd finished his coffee, and began standing up. 'So I'll see you around sevenish, then.'

'Good,' Lia smiled, and then they hugged, tightly, not wanting to let each other go.

'You always smell so nice,' he whispered, and she giggled. 'Your hair always smells so nice,' he added, pulling it out of its knot and breathing in its scent. 'What were your plans for this morning?'

'Work,' she told him pointedly.

He took her by the hand and began leading her up the stairs. 'That can wait a bit, though, can't it?'

Chapter Twenty-two

They were just finishing breakfast when there was a tap on the window and there stood Bella, smiling at them both sheepishly. She was in crisp, well-fitting jeans with a white shirt and a soft grey cashmere cardigan, and had swept her hair behind both ears.

'I'm sorry to bother you,' she said to Lia before swiftly turning to Ben. 'But look at this light, Ben. Let's go and take some pictures this morning. They're supposed to be starting work on the extension today and I'd hate to miss it.'

'OK,' he agreed, standing up. He looked neither pleased nor irritated. 'I'll just go back to the flat and pick up the camera.'

'Marvellous,' Bella said, clearly delighted. She turned to Lia. 'I hope you don't mind me borrowing him for the morning?'

'Not at all,' Lia smiled back stiffly, certain that resentment was etched all over her face. 'As long as you bring him back the way you found him.'

As she said the words she began to feel threatened again. This would just be the start, she told herself. Before long there would be other trips, more favours and an increasing amount of time spent together, until eventually Bella had control over every aspect of Ben's work and life. She could either do nothing and allow it all to happen, or she could try and make some kind of stand.

Ben kissed her goodbye in front of the waiting Bella, who, Lia noted with some satisfaction, averted her eyes at the point of impact. She told herself off for being paranoid, and for attributing Bella with too much power. As Bella excused herself and followed Ben to the gate, an idea suddenly struck her, and she ran out after them.

'You know something, Bella? Do you mind if I invite myself along, too? Only I hardly ever leave this place. In fact, apart from a romantic trip to Barcelonnette the other day,' she added pointedly, looking at Ben, 'I've hardly left the village since I got here.' The cherry jam she'd been going to make could wait, she told herself. This was far more important. 'I'd love to see your house,' she went on. 'And to have a nice drive in the country. Would you mind?'

She felt the blood rush ironically to her cheeks, as if in response to the cheek itself of her suggestion. Ben looked taken aback and then faintly amused while Bella did her best not to show any reaction. But in her hesitation alone Lia could see she had wrong-footed her.

'Oh, but of course,' she smiled. 'How silly of me not to have thought of that – I just assumed you were so busy with your book and everything. But what fun! Do tag along, by all means.'

They set off about twenty minutes later and drove westwards, towards the perfume town of Grasse. Bella drove fast, like the French, but with confidence and authority, as if she had known the roads all her life. Lia sat in the back, giving Ben more legroom in the front passenger seat. The 'tag along' comment she could have lived without, but still she felt as if she had won a battle – the first of many, no doubt. It excited her, empowered her even, as if the mere act of inviting herself along had sent Bella a direct and unambiguous warning – she was not someone to be trampled over; she was to be treated with respect. Chloe would be proud of her.

They took the left turning down towards Cannes, and quickly entered a tiny hamlet. Bella forked right and swung into a large drive, and there was her house – it *was* a house, Lia decided immediately, and not a cottage or a villa, but a rather elegant and lovely house. Set in a rambling garden full of Californian lilac and sprawling lavender bushes, it was made of cool cream stone with white shutters and a tiled roof. Towering above were several cypress trees, and in various corners of the terrace were terracotta and stone pots full of exhausted-looking geraniums and petunias. As they approached, Lia marvelled at the wild thyme and rosemary in all the beds, the marguerites which peered up at the sun and the young olive trees which scattered their silver green leaves on the ground. It was unkempt, it was unloved, but Lia thought it enchanting.

'Bella, it's wonderful,' she cried in admiration. 'It's such a find.'

'Wait until you see inside,' Bella told her. 'It belonged to an elderly couple, and I'm afraid the décor hasn't changed since they first got married. There's an awful lot of work to be done, even though the structure itself is sound.'

There was no sign of any builders and she tutted, letting herself in through the front door. Inside, Lia could see what she meant about the décor. Each room was done up in a different style of wallpaper, all of which was fading and peeling away from the walls. The paintwork was cracking and the kitchen basic to say the least, with just a sink, a distinctly dangerous-looking gas oven and some bare pipes. The sitting room had one of the ugliest fireplaces she'd seen and the dining room was dark and pokey. Upstairs, two bedrooms were reasonably sized with bare floorboards and painted a cold blue, but the third was no more than a box room. The bathroom, decked out in various shades of pink, was little short of hideous.

144

Ben started to take photos, letting the light dictate which room he worked on first, and Lia found herself alone with Bella.

'Quite a challenge, then,' she tried as they explored.

'Isn't it? I've had plans drawn up to extend the dining room and bedroom above, and I'm going to rip out the bathroom entirely. I rather like the one in the pink cottage, and may do something along those lines. The kitchen, of course, I'll keep fairly traditional, and then decorating in general. And new fireplaces, of course.'

'But it has wonderful potential,' Lia said, looking at the view out of the main bedroom window. 'I mean, it's in such a lovely setting.'

'Yes, it could be quite special,' Bella said with an air of resignation. She knew the house too well, Lia thought, having no doubt visited it with estate agents, surveyors, architects and builders. And perhaps there was an element of sadness to it, she wondered, because it was being paid for by her divorce? Perhaps every wall and every ceiling echoed something that had gone wrong in her marriage? Perhaps the house itself represented, not a new beginning, the turning of a page, but the failure of the past? Until it was finished, until all the cracks had been pasted over and the smell of fresh paint filled the air, all Bella could see were its problems and weaknesses. Lia, on the other hand, was only aware of its loveliness and charm.

Off the main bedroom was a small balcony, cluttered with terracotta pots whose flowers had died months ago. Bella stood there for a moment, watching something below, and Lia joined her. The something was Ben, adjusting the focus before taking some external shots.

'I'm sorry if it looks like I've been trying to take him away from you,' Bella said and Lia almost jumped. She wasn't expecting such directness, and didn't know how to react to it. 'I wasn't really, you know, but he needs a bit of encouragement. The last year's been tough for him. I was determined he was going to shoot this place because I wanted to give him some confidence back.'

145

'I hadn't realised he was lacking it,' Lia replied.

Bella turned to her. It was the closest they'd ever been, and Lia couldn't help but scrutinise her make-up and skin, noting to her surprise the number of open pores she had around her nose, and the foundation she'd used to disguise them. 'Well, you tell me. How many photos has he taken since he's been down here?'

'I don't know,' Lia found herself backing away, uncomfortable at their sudden proximity. 'It's not his type of photography.'

'And all last year? Maybe he hasn't told you, but he found Afghanistan particularly harrowing.' She frowned. 'And he's turned down one or two assignments since. I think he's lost his nerve, rather.'

'But he was in Kosovo up until now,' Lia argued defensively, irritated at how much Bella seemed to know.

'Well, that hardly counts these days,' she was dismissive. 'Hardly in the line of action, is it? Just a few peasants rebuilding their farms.'

Lia was taken aback at Bella's dismissal and smarting that Ben must have taken her into his confidence. 'But he doesn't want to do that kind of thing any more,' she insisted. 'He wants to revisit people, see how they're getting on once the news crews and the press have gone away.'

'Is that how he puts it?' Bella scoffed, a secretive smile on her face.

Lia looked around herself uncomfortably. She couldn't exactly see how photographing an old fireplace was going to help get Ben back into a war zone, but couldn't bring herself to say so. 'Show me where they're extending the dining room,' she asked instead.

Outside she could see the foundations which would give the room another two metres width. There was the sound of a truck in the lane and three workmen arrived, carrying bags of cement and building utensils. Bella rushed to greet them, admonishing them for being late in what sounded like flawless French.

146

With Bella and Ben both occupied, Lia walked round the house, trying to imagine how each room might look when finished. Bella, of course, would know exactly what had brought Ben to the retreat last year, she kept thinking, and it bothered her that he still hadn't confided in her, just as he still hadn't said he loved her. He was deliberately keeping his distance, she realised, and now here was Bella, ready to take advantage.

He joined her in the sitting room. 'A lot of work,' he muttered, extracting a film out of his camera and replacing it with another.

'But think how lovely it'll be.' She watched as he chose his position beside the window, framing the fireplace, and started to click the shutter. 'When did you last use that thing?' she asked casually.

He frowned, puzzled by the question, and tried to remember. 'I don't normally take this sort of photo, you know.'

Bella suddenly entered the room. 'You couldn't take some of the builders for me, could you? They're just mixing some cement and getting ready to lay the first stone.'

He nodded acquiescently and went to join them, Bella at his heels. Awkwardly Lia followed them, tagging along, she thought grimly, feeling like a little sister, forced to accompany her older sibling on a date.

'I'm going to have a conservatory here, from the dining room to the kitchen,' Bella told her. 'It would catch the evening sun beautifully, don't you think?'

'Yes,' Lia agreed, looking up at the cypress trees that surrounded them, and out towards the hills beyond. 'It would, wouldn't it.' She thought about how much she would love to own a place like this, to have the security and comfort it would provide.

As if reading her mind, Bella asked, 'So, how long are you planning on staying at Les Eglantines, then?'

'Indefinitely. Or at least until Peaches decides to throw me out. I don't know if the retreat is still going on this summer or not.'

'Well, we're almost in June now, so you haven't got much time.'

'You went on one, didn't you?' Lia turned to her. She felt she was entitled to match Bella's directness.

'Yes, I did. Last year.' Bella looked slightly embarrassed. 'An awkward divorce following a difficult marriage. I needed ... something. I don't know, a greater level of understanding, a different perspective on life.'

'And did you get it?'

'Yes, you know I did, actually,' Bella replied with a smile. 'There's something very special about those two, Felix and Peaches. You might not have come across it yet, but there really is. Right,' her tone changed dramatically. 'I don't know about you two but I'm famished. How about a baguette and some coffee in the local?'

And as ever, Bella got her way.

Chapter Twenty-three

Bella seemed to keep her distance after that day. She was too occupied with the house, it seemed, to worry about Ben and what he was doing. The evenings were getting longer and warmer, and so Lia and Ben would spend their suppers sitting outside until late. Each night they'd be taken by surprise by the light – *it's nine-thirty already!* – and then watch as darkness would fall to reveal the comet making its way through the universe. It felt mysterious and exciting, and made Lia feel bolder, somehow, freer to ask more questions and so piece together the elements of Ben's life which were still a mystery to her.

'So, you're not answerable to anyone, then?' she asked one evening, as they'd finished supper. 'I mean, an agency or some news organisation?'

He shook his head. 'I'm a freelancer. I work for several agencies. Sometimes I instigate a trip, and other times they send me.'

'It's all a bit uncertain, though, isn't it?' she asked. 'I mean, financially. Isn't it safer to be on someone's books full time?'

'Of course it is,' he told her simply. 'But that's not for me. It would be like having to go to an office every day –

149

I don't want to be so restricted. I want to do what I want to do, go where I want to go. I don't want to be chained down. I mean, I could hardly take all this time out in France if I worked for someone full time, now, could I?'

'Sounds like you're a commitment phobe to me,' she teased, before realising what she'd said, and trying to change the subject. 'But financially, isn't it tough, working the way you do?' *Or don't, as the case may be*, she could have added, but stopped herself.

He smiled sheepishly. 'I survive because I got lucky a few years ago,' he told her. 'But just please don't ask me how.'

'How?' Lia asked, delightedly, knowing the story would be entertaining. 'Go on, Ben, tell me. How?'

He paused, staring into his glass. 'I took a shot that got used all over the world, time and time again. It made me thousands, tens of thousands of pounds, and that's what I live on.'

'Which shot? I mean, would I know it?'

He laughed, embarrassed. 'Knowing you, you probably would.'

'Ben, tell me!' She implored, frustrated at his embarrassment. 'Come on.'

'It was of Princess Diana,' he revealed. 'In London. It was around her birthday in '92, a few months before her separation from Prince Charles was announced. I'd spent the last year in Bosnia and had come back for a break. My dad had told me about a friend of his who had an old Leica he wanted to get rid of. He lived in Clapham, so I went to see it. It's a dream of a camera, the same one I use now, and he'd had it for years without hardly touching it. So I bought it off him, left the house, and had just put some film in it, when I looked up, and there she was, Diana, coming out of the house opposite.' He paused to sip his wine.

'I couldn't believe my eyes,' he continued. 'She was carrying a bunch of white roses, the old-fashioned cottage roses, not from a florist, but some that must have been

150

given to her from the garden, for her birthday, I should think. She was heading back to her car when this old woman shuffled past, a decrepit old thing pulling one of those shopping baskets on wheels stuffed full of Co-op bags. And Diana just smiled at her, said something and offered her the flowers. The old woman looked startled at first, and then broke into this glorious broad grin, and they sort of hugged – and I got the whole bloody lot. Shot after shot.'

'I remember those shots,' Lia said excitedly. 'Hadn't she just been to her psychic or something?'

'I knew you'd know,' Ben laughed, teasing her. 'I knew it was your kind of thing. Daphne Simpson – Diana used to see her a lot, apparently. So the press went into over-drive about what she might have told her. And then of course months later the separation was announced and all those shots came out again.'

'They fell out a couple of years later,' Lia remembered. 'Because Daphne wrote a book about her.'

'Which was serialised in a paper, and they ran my shots again.'

'God, I totally remember all this. I can't believe that was you,' Lia said admiringly. 'As her marriage was breaking up, they kind of spoke up for the person she was – you know, kind and spontaneous and fun. And they ran them again when she died, didn't they, as a kind of testimony.'

'Earned me a fortune,' Ben smiled wryly. 'My agent thought all his Christmases had come together. He set up deals all over the world. It was bizarre. I mean, I'd been a jobbing photographer for almost five years by then, barely scraping by, working all over the place, and then suddenly I struck lucky on some totally fluke shots.'

Lia paused for a second. 'Do you think she knew you were there?' she asked.

'Now, that would be cynical,' he smiled. 'But no, I don't think so. She saw me at the end, as she was opening her car door, and looked surprised, so I just nodded. In retrospect, I hated how she must have thought I was just

151

another sleazy opportunist, and I kind of wanted her to know what I really did, that there was actually a little bit of honour to it.'

Lia tried to remember. 'You know, I'm sure when she died, and everyone who knew her was giving interviews, that someone said how that had been one of her favourite shots. She'd loved the spontaneity in it, and the look on the old woman's face. I'm sure I read that somewhere.'

'Really?' Ben looked surprised. 'Well, if that's true, it makes me feel a bit better,' he smiled, topping up their glasses. 'Because I always felt guilty, like I'd taken advantage, you know, exploited her.'

'But like you say, it's funded your work for years after. And you've gone on to take exactly the kind of shots that she would have approved of – like in Rwanda, or landmine stuff in Bosnia ...' her voice trailed off uncertainly, not sure of the facts.

It was funny how she could remember all the trivial things in life, she chastised herself, like the story of Diana's psychic, whilst the important events remained frustratingly elusive. If only there were some kind of signal in life, she thought, that let you know when something might be relevant in the future. Her life seemed full of missed lessons and conversations she couldn't join in, and she wished she'd followed Jonathan's lead by reading the broadsheets rather than the *Daily Mail*.

'That's a nice way to look at things.' He smiled, rescuing her. 'But I'd like to get recognition for some of my harder-hitting stuff. I mean, it was ridiculous. I'd spent a year taking shots in Bosnia that no one was that bothered about, and then made a fortune out of a princess hugging a pensioner. And at no risk to myself – no danger, no nothing.'

'Have you seriously been in danger often?' Lia asked, thinking how at last she might be getting towards the truth about the retreat. 'I mean, has there ever been a moment when you've really thought, "That's it"?'

'Yes, once,' he told her. 'I mean, there's an element of

danger all the time, but yes, there was one day when I really thought the game was up.'

'What happened?' she asked quietly.

He took a deep breath. 'I've actually spent the last year or so trying to forget about it,' he smiled sadly.

'I'm sorry, don't tell me then,' she replied, sure that both Peaches and Bella would know, and trying not to resent the fact that she still did not.

He paused, looking deeply into his glass. 'It was in Afghanistan, almost two years ago. There was me, an Italian photographer, Giancarlo, and a driver, heading out towards the hills south-east of Jalalabad, to find these heroin laboratories we'd been told were there.' He paused again, his eyes quickly leaping from his empty glass to the no less empty bottle on the table. 'Look, can I open another?' he asked, jumping up to the spares left on top of the fridge and opening one quickly.

'The area was pretty unstable, lawless even, with recent assassination attempts, drug-related feuds, bombings – all that good stuff.' He took a large sip of wine. 'So we knew the risks,' he continued. 'But we went anyway. Basically we were ambushed. Don't think they wanted us snooping around. There were four of them. This guy just pulled a gun on us.'

'Was anyone hurt?' she asked quietly.

'Giancarlo, killed instantly.' He took another swig of his glass, and she could see the tears of shock in his eyes as if it were happening all over again. She reached across the table and held his hand. 'This bloke shot him straight in the chest. One minute he was sitting beside me, complaining about some stomach bug he'd picked up, and the next he was dead, his blood splattered all over my shirt. Just like that. I don't know why the guy chose him first – I mean, it could just as easily have been me.' He broke off abruptly, taking another deep breath. 'So then he *did* point the gun at me.'

'And?'

'Fucking thing jammed.' He laughed, shaking his head.

153

'It just jammed, can you believe that? He couldn't, the bloke – he saw it as some sign from Allah that I should be spared. Let me and the driver go.'

'Oh my God,' Lia exclaimed, trying to find the right words. 'How do you get over something like that?'

'You tell me. I just went back to the UK. Had a nervous breakdown.' The last comment was accompanied by a cynical laugh.

'So that's how you came to Les Eglantines?'

He nodded. 'I couldn't stop asking myself why I'd been spared and not Giancarlo. It didn't make sense. He was married with two kids, you know, and there was me, no dependants, no nothing, and yet I was the one who survived. I went to his funeral in Rome, sat with his devastated family, and I just felt guilty. I felt as if I'd taken something away from him.'

'And it helped, did it? Coming here?'

'It did, actually. Not just for all Peaches' mystical nonsense, but I think this place, the whole atmosphere – it all helped. Meeting completely different people.'

'Like Bella.' She couldn't help herself. It was out before she could stop and she bit her tongue in anger. 'I'm sorry, you didn't need that.'

'Thing is, I've tried to work again,' Ben continued as if he hadn't even noticed. 'I could have gone to Iraq but I turned it down. I was offered Afghanistan again but I couldn't face it. I'm getting there, and I *will* go back, but it was too soon; I'd lost my nerve. So I hung around in London, wasting money, and eventually went back to Kosovo. I revisited some of the camps, followed up some of the old stories. But of course, no one's interested any more, it's old news.'

'Which is why you've got to get your book together,' Lia told him. 'To make them interested.'

He laughed. 'Sometimes I think it's all a waste of time. I mean, what good is yet another photography book or exhibition? People don't want these things in their homes – they're too busy trying to forget them. What's the point?'

'Come on, Ben, you're being too defeatist here. You'd be putting forward a positive aspect, remember? It's only human to have doubts about what you're doing, but it shouldn't stop you from doing it. I mean, even in my limited capacity, you don't think I sometimes think like that?'

It might have been the wine that was talking, but Lia suddenly felt passionate, tearful. She could see herself mirrored in Ben: her doubts, her fears, her insecurities. In encouraging him, she would be encouraging herself, talking her own project up, ridding herself of the demons which regularly came to mock her.

'You don't think there are days when I wonder what on earth I'm doing?' she continued. 'I'm not known, I never had my own TV series, I've never cooked or gardened professionally, so what the hell have I got to offer? What makes me think I can write this stupid book? You don't think I've ever woken up in the middle of the night, terrified that I'm going to run out of money and find myself back in London with no job, no flat and no nothing? You don't think I go through that? But you and I are different – we have to push ourselves. We'll succeed because we had the guts. Don't ever stop believing that.'

He took her hand. 'You're very sweet,' he said, which she could have lived without. It made her feel like that nine-year-old sister again, tagging along after him. 'And compelling. I *am* going to do it, you know – it's getting closer. But I need to get out there again. I need to take more shots, prove to myself that I still can. I can't stay here for ever, lovely as it is.'

As he said the last words, he pulled Lia into his arms and held her tight.

'Well, go,' she told him simply. 'Go, and take care of yourself. And when you come back, I'll still be here for you.'

She had the feeling that there was something he wanted to say, but he just breathed heavily and held her, and suddenly she wanted to be everything for him – his love,

155

his inspiration, his muse – and she wished that Bella was out of his life, had never been in it, even, and that she could just get a glimpse into the future, and check that they were still together, and happy.

Chapter Twenty-four

Lia worked hard over the next few days, probably, she realised, as a reaction to Bella's comments, and finally posted Jules the first three chapters and synopsis. She would prove that she had a valid product for which there was a valid market, and this was just the first step. And if Jules didn't like it, she told herself, she would simply send it to another publisher, and then another, and another – to as many as it took, in fact.

She felt clearer now that she knew how Ben supported himself and what had first drawn him to Les Eglantines – there were no more secrets, she thought, and no more mysteries. All the doubts that Jules had raised were now accounted for, and Lia thought that even she, finally, would have to approve.

It occurred to her, though, as she left the post office, that her life seemed somehow to be in Jules's hands – she'd found her a place to stay, after all, and was now in control of her work – and that feeling disarmed Lia. Jules had often complained that she was too passive, and here she was, practically laying herself at the feet of her younger friend.

She had to accept, she told herself on her way home,

that Jules might not like everything she'd written. She had to accept that there'd be changes, suggestions and criticism, and that she was to take them all in a positive light. How would it change their friendship, though, she asked herself, to turn Jules into what was effectively her boss? Would she be gaining a book deal and losing a friend? Or worse still, if Jules were to reject the project totally, would she be losing a book deal as well as a friend? Or would it be possible, somehow, for it all to work out, and to balance the two?

Jules would never think like this, she admonished herself. Jules would be far more focused on the work itself. If something needed fixing, she'd just fix it. If something wasn't good enough, she'd just reject it. It was up to Lia herself to ensure that what she'd sent in was of a high enough standard for that not to happen, though. And she thought she had. She really thought, after all this time, that she had.

It was Etienne's birthday that weekend, and she'd offered to throw a dinner party for him. She'd invite everyone, including Bella, and make an effort to like the woman. Now she'd laid off Ben it almost seemed possible. Inspired by all the vegetables on sale in the village, she decided on a *soupe au pistou* followed by chicken fricassée with cherry tomatoes and rosemary, with perhaps a mushroom risotto and a salad on the side.

Felix and Peaches were the first to arrive, followed closely by Ben, Chloe and the birthday boy himself, but no sign of Bella.

'You have Venus in Taurus, if I remember rightly,' Peaches giggled, accepting a glass of sparkling wine. 'Which gives you a love of good food and wine, so you're in the right place tonight, aren't you? I remember being a little worried about Saturn in your ninth house, but your health doesn't seem to be bothering you much, does it?'

Lia started them on olives marinating in garlic and parsley, and a courgette dip with warmed pitta bread as they waited for Bella to arrive. She held no threat these days, Lia told herself – in fact, she had almost begun to feel sorry for the woman. From what she could glean from Chloe, Bella had once worked as a secretary and married her boss, and some fifteen childless years later found herself being dumped for a younger model. She'd made a lot through the divorce, but clearly still lacked substance in her life, and so had been reduced to chasing after the likes of Ben, and persuading herself that she was still young and vital.

Where was Bella? She'd invited her for 7.30 and it was 8.15 already. Irritated, Lia decided to start, ladling soup into everyone's bowl. In front of them all she'd filled tiny butter dishes with individual portions of pesto to swirl in amongst the vegetables, adding a heavenly basil and garlic flavour.

They were halfway through when Bella arrived, full of apologies and gifts – a bottle of wine, a cellophane-wrapped bunch of roses – and a sheath of papers under one arm.

'Felix, I don't want to bother you, but I've just had the most extraordinary experience,' she started, handing him the sheets. 'I've been trying out the automatic script you taught us last year, with absolutely no joy, for the last few weeks. And then this afternoon, something happened. A lot of it's garbled nonsense, I know, but there are pieces there, kind of warnings and guidance, things that are really quite remarkable.'

Lia offered Bella some soup, irritated that instead of just apologising and waiting for an appropriate moment to join in the existing conversation, Bella had simply begun a new one of her own. It was typical of the woman, but something that Lia could never do. She'd tried it, from time to time with Jonathan, arriving late and full of a funny story, but her voice would be drowned out by the continuing conversation, and she'd slump quietly into her seat, with all the charisma of a rag doll with half its stuffing missing.

'This is quite interesting,' Felix peered through his glasses at what looked like strange lines with the occasional indecipherable word thrown in. Lia hoped to see scepticism etched at least on Ben's face, if not Chloe and Etienne's, but all she saw was intrigue. Felix had perched his glasses on his nose and began leafing through the sheets, and as he did she could see how the aimless lines became fewer and the words increased.

'In the sun, where the roses grow, joy will be regained,' he read out.

'How thrilling – roses – that must mean here!' Peaches cried excitedly.

Little attention was being paid to her soup, Lia noticed, and she pointedly offered them all more. Only Ben and Etienne accepted.

'A freshness of heart and spirit will learn to grow old,' Felix continued. 'Her time is not yet come.'

'What is that supposed to mean?' Lia laughed, willing them all to start ridiculing Bella's notes.

'As the soil dries and the water becomes warm, love will return to its rightful home.'

'Has everybody finished?' Lia jumped up. 'Shall I start clearing the dishes?'

Ben helped her, carrying the soup tureen into the kitchen.

'I might have expected Bella to hijack my evening, but not some fucking spirit,' Lia hissed at him. 'What's she playing at?' She returned to the table with the chicken and risotto.

'Ben, this has to be you,' Peaches was saying. 'Listen to this.'

'He who has seen war and famine and loss, the happiness can come, if he so chooses.'

'Wow, Ben, so now you know.' Lia began serving the chicken, willing the farce to be over.

'So near death, so thirsty for life, he must lie with the goat to share joy.'

'I'm sorry?' Lia was getting seriously irritated now, and wished they'd all just concentrate on her food. 'Is this Ben again? So to get happy he's got to shag goats, is that what

160

it's saying? Come on, everybody, this is ridiculous, and your food's getting cold.'

'Don't be such a cynic,' Bella cried. 'Open your mind for once. You're such a practical girl, Lia, you have to develop your spiritual side.'

'How, by listening to this? I'm sorry Bella. I don't mean to belittle the spiritual experience you just had. But if you mean to tell me that some spirit up there has taken the time out to tell you to tell Ben to start shagging goats then I'd say it's a type of spirituality I can seriously live without.'

'Not goats, dear,' Peaches touched her arm. 'Capricorn. That's what it's saying.'

Lia rolled her eyes and looked towards Ben, who was clearly embarrassed. 'Risotto?' she offered, wishing someone, somewhere on the table, would have the good manners at least to compliment her on the food and change the subject.

'I'm a Capricorn,' Bella said quietly, and the table fell to a hush.

Lia put down her knife and fork. She felt she was alone against everyone, the only sane one in the room, the tee-totaller amongst drunks. Quietly and calmly she said, 'So this spirit's telling Ben via you that he'll only find happiness with you, is that right?'

'There's no need to be defensive, Lia,' Bella laughed, nervously. 'I can't help what came to me. I didn't actually write it, after all.'

'And Felix? In your experience, is it normal for spirits to advise people on who they sleep with?'

Felix said nothing, but put the papers down.

'That was just one of several messages, dear,' Peaches tried soothingly. 'You can't just take each one separately – they need to be put into context.'

'This chicken's delicious,' Chloe said brightly. 'Hmmm, and the risotto. You enjoying it, Babe?' This was directed at Etienne, who was loudly sucking a piece of chicken off the bone.

It was the last time, Lia told herself angrily. It was the

161

last time she'd ever invite them all around. It was too much work, too much expense and it always seemed to result in unhappiness. Why was she putting herself out for these people, she wondered, when all they did in return was insult and humiliate her? She felt tears of indignation pricking in her eyes. She wished the phone would ring, and that she could excuse herself, and that they'd hear the sound of her laughter and joking from the other room. She wished Jules could ring with a major book deal and a spin-off television series – a dramatic announcement she could make on her return, something they'd be envious of, that they'd admire her for.

'Well, I don't know about finding happiness,' Ben said lightly. 'But it looks like I'm off to Afghanistan in a couple of weeks.'

The table erupted into excited coos and Lia was grateful for the distraction. He'd told her about the offer earlier that day, so at least that didn't come as a shock. But without him she had nothing there, she realised. She would find another place, rent a cottage somewhere else, meet new people, get away from this lot. Their company was stifling, she told herself; she needed a new crowd. She would go to the estate agents tomorrow, she thought, have a look around.

Whatever it was, she had to do something, she decided. This place was verging on the ridiculous.

Chapter Twenty-five

She didn't make it to the estate agents. A large e-mail arrived from Jules instead offering no end of thoughts, ideas, recipes and practical advice before she would take the project a stage further. Lia's stomach churned nervously as she scrolled through it all before printing it out and collating it. At first she felt – what exactly was it? – betrayed, perhaps, by her friend. She'd have liked Jules to have loved everything she'd done, to be full of praise and congratulations, not to mention the offer of a book deal. Instead she'd become involved, taking up clearly much of her own time to research the subject. But once Lia had read everything through, slept on it and finished smarting, she realised how valuable her friend's input had been, and was grateful. And, strangely, she got quite a high out of that feeling, as if she realised she'd turned a corner, and could now take criticism constructively, turn a negative into a positive. It felt like a part of a maturing process, and she felt she'd entered a new level of self-awareness.

She'd made her laugh about Bella's scripts, too, which was a relief. *I admit I was wrong about Ben but I still don't condone his reactions*, she'd written, *and I think he sounds pretty weak around her. But look how ridiculous Bella's being – it just shows how insecure she is about you. Don't let her get to you – she sounds like a fruitcake, and not the sort to be taken seriously.*

Jules was right, it made the woman look ridiculous, Lia thought, as well as vain and stupid. If she seriously thought those messages meant anything then she needed her head examining. So now Lia had risen above all that anger, she decided, and on to a plateau of laughter and something closer to pity. She, at least, had a valid project to work on and was open to new ideas and interpretations. What did Bella have but an empty house and some mumbo jumbo to fill her days?

But then, one afternoon, Ben appeared on the terrace. 'Look, Lia,' he started. 'I hate to do this to you, but do you mind if I don't come up this evening?'

'Mind?' She bristled. 'No, of course not, but, what's happening?'

'You're not going to like it,' he said the words quickly, as if wanting to get them over with. 'Bella's asked me to have dinner with her. Insisted, really.'

'She has?' Lia tried hard not to react. There was nothing that bound them together, after all, and he was free to do as he liked. And hadn't she even told Chloe once about how she'd rather Ben was with her because he wanted to be, and not because he felt he should be?

He sighed. 'She's had more messages, and wants to go through them with me.'

'Oh Ben,' she laughed out loud. 'Don't tell me you're taking them seriously?'

He shook his head, confused. 'What if there is something? I don't know, I know it sounds stupid, but apparently it goes on about, you know, Afghanistan, and what happened.'

'Oh, please don't fall for this,' Lia heard herself implore. Bella's messages seemed suddenly less of a joke and something more sinister and manipulative. 'I know it's a subject that's painful for you, and I know it's something that changed your life, but please don't get yourself involved in this nonsense.'

164

'But what if it isn't nonsense? What if it's, I don't know, something from Giancarlo, the other photographer? I can't just ignore it.'

'And what if she's just making it all up? Have you thought of that?'

'Why would she—'

'Because she knows that's where you're vulnerable,' she snapped impatiently. 'She knows this is how to reach you. Think about it, Ben. How do you know that she just hasn't made this all up herself? Huh?'

'I knew you'd be like this,' Ben said defensively.

'Like what, sensible? Practical? Clear headed?'

'Anti Bella. You're threatened by her and so you're suspicious. But maybe she's got my interests at heart. She made it sound important. It's only a dinner, after all. It's only a pizza up the road.'

'It's not only a dinner,' she snapped again, hating herself for her anger. 'It's a trap. She's luring you. What about all that bollocks about you only finding happiness if you slept with her, I mean, for God's sake!'

'You think this is what it's all about?' His voice had grown cold, now. 'You think it's all about Bella wanting to sleep with me? Is that it?'

'Frankly, yes, I do. She's the type who can't be without a man. You're not for her, any old fool can see that, but she can't bear to be alone. She wants to feel attractive, she wants to feel wanted. She's out here, supervising her house and she's got no interesting distractions, no one to have dinner with, no one to flirt with. It *is* a lonely place on your own, here, of course it is.' She lowered her voice, trying to sound more sympathetic and even. 'She's stuck in a tiny flat when she was expecting the cottage, and she's without you when she thought you'd be here for company. And sex. And look at me – I've got everything, and now she's determined to get you back. If it's not through persuading you to take shots of her house, it's through exploiting the one weakness she knows you have. It's despicable, really. Manipulative and despicable.'

165

'Look, I don't know what to think,' Ben tried fairly.
'And I won't know unless I hear her out.'

'And that has to be over dinner, of course – she could-n't have just popped round for coffee, now, could she?'

'Why not for dinner?' He was raising his voice now. 'I mean, what's wrong with that? We're not married or anything, you and me. I *am* a free agent.'

The words stung her, just as his lack of *I love you*'s had. 'Of course you are,' she said quietly.

'So I'm going to go, all right? I don't want to hurt you, that's the last thing I want to do, but I feel I should give her a fair hearing.'

'Fine.' Lia turned away, so that he wouldn't see the tears of indignation and frustration welling in her eyes.

'And I'll see you tomorrow.'

'Yeah, whatever.'

'Lia – please don't be like this.'

'Like fucking what?' she snarled. 'Possessive? Protective? That practical girl who doesn't have a spiritual bone in her body?' She put her head in her hands, frustrated that he didn't understand. 'We have such a nice time together, Ben. We're such great friends, we have such great sex, we're so good for each other. I can talk to you about anything and I think you feel the same about me. We help each other's work, we never row. But there's just one major fucking cloud that keeps passing over us, and her name's Bella. And you don't seem to see that.' She'd started crying now, the tears streaming down her cheeks. 'You forgive her everything, you defend her, you protect her, almost. And that *hurts*.'

'I don't know what to say.' He looked awkwardly down at his feet. 'I'm sorry. Things can't be perfect all the time. She won't be around for ever, and God knows, I won't, either. Just let me do this, just let me hear her out. It won't do any harm.'

If he'd have approached her right then, taken her by the hand, brushed a tear from her cheek, looked up at her imploringly and told her how much she meant to him, how much he loved her, Lia would have acquiesced. She'd have broken, put his need before her pain, and lived with it. Instead he stood by the table, looking as if he wanted to get as far away as possible. And that hurt.

'You know something, Ben? Just go. Go and have a nice evening. Go and be told your future lies with her and that I'm wasting your time. Go and share Bella's mystical experience. But just don't come back. I don't want to hear about it, I don't want to know about it, and I don't want to see you again. I've had enough. If you don't feel as strongly for me as I do you, then I don't want you around. And if you can be so disrespectful of me, and of our relationship, then clearly you don't. So go. Now. Go and have fun. Good luck in Afghanistan. I'll always care about you, but it just hurts too fucking much.'

She turned away, the tears now coursing down her cheeks. All she could hear was the creak of the gate, and when she turned around, he was gone.

Chapter Twenty-six

The next time she saw him, it was to say goodbye. Ben was heading back to London, and from there on to Kabul. Lia tried to be pleased for him. She knew this was a hugely significant trip, and how in many ways it would release him from his demons. Yet somehow she just felt numb, as if she'd blanked out all memory of how close they'd been. She'd cried more than she could ever remember crying, incapable of getting out of bed yet resenting the memories it brought. She couldn't remember ever feeling so low, or so lonely, before.

But whilst he'd been there, at Les Eglantines, she realised, at least there'd been a chance. There was the chance that he'd wake up, in Bella's bed, she presumed, and realise what a fool he'd been. Whilst he was there, there was the chance of a surprise meeting at the supermarket, or along the lane, or even just on the path amongst the citrus trees.

Now he was going there was nothing. Her only consolation was that Bella would be feeling his emptiness, too; waking up with nothing but the sunshine and the twittering of birds for company. But at least she might hear from him; she might get the odd message, or e-mail, or phone call. Lia felt cast aside, worthless.

And yet they'd been so close, she kept thinking, as if they'd known each other all their lives. It had seemed perfectly normal to see each other every evening, to wake up together every morning, and for him to disappear after breakfast and return again as night fell. There had been no rows, no disagreements and no disputes. To all intents and purposes, they'd had a perfect relationship, and now, unbelievably, it was over.

She found it hard to imagine that he was happy with that, but the fact that he'd made no attempt to see her again seemed to testify to it. For days after their break-up she'd hoped, prayed and fantasised that he'd come back, shamefaced and clutching some flowers from the supermarket. He'd admit he'd been wrong, and that Bella's messages were all nonsense, and tell her how wretched he'd been since he'd last seen her.

But this didn't happen. He never came. She'd listen out for the slightest noise, a hint that he might be on his way, but he never came.

She was careful to avoid the flats, walking the longer way round to the village for fear of bumping into Bella, or worse still, him and Bella together, laughing together like lovers, smiling over secret jokes that no one else would understand. So it was strange, one morning, catching sight of him through the window like that. She'd leapt out of her chair, smiling with relief and trying to act like a delighted neighbour and not the demented ex-girlfriend she felt like.

'How are you doing?' he asked, after the obligatory peck on both cheeks.

'Fine. You?' she answered breathlessly.

'Fine.' He didn't particularly look it, she thought, but then neither, most probably, did she.

'I just wanted you to know that I'm leaving tomorrow. I'll be gone a few weeks.'

'Great, great,' she said awkwardly. 'I know this is a big one for you. I hope it all goes well.'

But she couldn't begin to imagine what he'd be doing

169

there, or where he'd be living, or the experiences he'd be faced with. Those images refused to come. She felt distanced from him, distanced from his background and now, sadly, from his future, too – it was all a blank, a mystery, the unknown. And, she realised, it was no longer her place to know these things, either; no longer her business.

'Look, I'm sorry,' he began, looking down at his shoes. 'I'm sorry it didn't work out. I really am.'

She almost cried. She'd thought it wasn't possible, that there could be no more tears left inside her, but she almost started again. *It hadn't worked out* – he had come right out and told her so. She was now the ex, due one final piece of respect before entering oblivion. 'Me, too,' she agreed quietly.

'Have you been OK?'

'Yeah,' she shrugged. It was a stupid question. What was she to tell him – that she'd had to drink herself to sleep every night, that she couldn't cook, couldn't eat, how she'd found it impossible to do any work and had felt so low she'd even considered giving it all up and going back to London? 'I've been fine. You?'

He frowned and then shrugged. 'Not bad.'

Not bad. The words stung a bit. Better than her, then. He was still waking up with a warm body beside him, after all; he was still sharing his meals with someone else.

'Well, I'd better get on with my packing.' He began to leave and she panicked. She wished he'd just hug her, tell her it had all been a mistake, tell her he loved her and mean it. But real life refused to play itself out as she wanted, and Lia watched as he made for the gate.

'Ben,' she called out, following him. 'Take care. Be careful, won't you?' She put her arms round his neck and pulled him in to herself, hugging him closely, breathing in the smell of his neck, remembering the shape of his body, enjoying his familiar warmth.

'Of course I will,' he said quietly, holding her. Gradually they pulled away. He looked close to tears

170

himself, she thought, wondering about all those unspoken words and unexpressed feelings. Did he still care?

He turned, and Lia realised that she'd never know. As she watched him disappear through the orchard, growing smaller and increasingly blurred by her tears, Lia tried to work out how they could have come to this, and what she could have done to prevent it. Was it all her fault, she kept asking herself? Had she driven him to this? But there were no answers, she realised, just more and more questions; and although a part of her wanted to follow him – to shout and yell and rant and make a scene – she knew inside that by keeping quiet, she was drawing on the one thing that neither he nor Bella couldn't take away.

Her dignity.

Chapter Twenty-seven

Lia was sitting on the terrace, sipping some strawberry and rosehip tea, when Peaches appeared one morning, clutching a large brown envelope.

'This came for you, dear,' she said, handing it over.

Irrationally Lia thought it might be from Ben, and jumped up to take it, but the London postmark and familiar writing on the address label deflated her momentary excitement.

'It's from my friend Jules,' she said dully. 'She promised to send me some cuttings and things from the Sunday supplements.'

She opened the envelope and watched in dismay as the papers slid out – bright, glorious Mediterranean recipes she no longer had the energy, or desire, to try out.

'How very thoughtful of her.' Peaches sat down. 'What a help that'll be.'

Lia smiled disinterestedly. 'I don't know, Peaches,' she sighed. 'I'm beginning to think it's all a waste of time. That maybe I should just let it go.'

'But Amelia, no!' Peaches rarely used her full name, and it felt like an admonition. 'How can you say that?'

'Because.' She hadn't the energy even to justify it. She

hadn't the energy for anything. She just sat there, wanting to be left alone.

'Amelia,' Peaches started firmly. 'I know you're in a difficult place right now. I know you feel betrayed and hurt. But you can't give up. You mustn't.'

'Peaches, I don't have anything. I don't even have a deal, although I don't think Jules would be doing all this if she didn't think one might come through. But I don't care any more. I don't feel up to it. Let's face it, I'm nothing. I'm not a cook, I'm not a gardener, I'm not even a writer. So who the hell do I think I am?'

'You're someone who's hurt and feeling a little bit sorry for herself,' Peaches said gently. 'Which is fine, you're allowed to, up to a point. But then you have to pick yourself up. There was a life before him, remember?'

Lia smiled. 'Yes, I remember,' she said quietly, willing herself not to cry again. So Peaches had always known, she thought. Of *course* she had. But in her own sweet subtle way she'd said nothing. And now, strangely, it felt natural to be talking about Ben, as if there'd never been any pretence of secrecy.

'There was a determined woman called Lia Scott who knew she had a good idea,' Peaches continued. 'And had the courage to give it a go. Now don't tell me that determined woman has shrivelled up and become a frightened little girl again, and all because of a man!'

'I'm sorry, Peaches, I don't mean to be rude, but I'm really not in the mood right now—'

'Of course you're not, dear, of course you're not. You're trapped in that dark, lonely space and you don't see a way out of it. And while you're there, you can't even see that there are far darker spaces you could be in, far worse positions, and that people do overcome them. And sitting around, contemplating your pain, is not going to help you to do that.'

'I know all that, Peaches,' Lia cried, exasperated. 'I know that. I've tried. I've tried working, and I just can't get it together. I've tried reading books, but I can't concentrate.

173

I've tried cooking, but I fall at the first clove of garlic I've got to chop. So now I'm trying immersion therapy. I figure if I just immerse myself in this pain for long enough, I might actually start to get bored by it. And *that* would be a wonderful feeling.'

'You've gone through this before, though, haven't you? Remember how badly you felt? And how do you feel about those men now, hmmm? Those heartbreakers? I bet they mean nothing to you. What I'm trying to say is this will pass, you will come through it.'

Lia laughed. 'Actually, I haven't gone through it before. I've had wall-to-wall boyfriends and I was always the one who gave *them* up. It was always me.'

'How interesting.' Peaches looked contemplative. 'So you were long overdue this experience.'

'Thanks. That doesn't make it any easier.'

'That's because you're poorly equipped to deal with it. It was an experience you had to have some time – we all do. I'm sorry it came so late, and so it's such a shock, but most people have gone through this two or three times by the time they're your age. Believe me, there are worse pains. You're just at the beginner stage.' She laughed, and Lia wondered just how much she herself had experienced.

'I know, I'm being indulgent. It's just that we saw each other so much, it's hard to believe he's gone. It's like a death, of sorts, though almost worse, because he hasn't just gone, he's gone to another bloody woman!'

There was a pause. 'Work is the best therapy,' Peaches said simply. 'You're right about the immersion therapy, but it's work you should be immersing yourself in, not pity. I believe this parcel has come at the perfect time. Go through it, learn from it, catalogue it, glean what you can from it, but don't waste it. It's a gift, sent to help you through all this.'

'Peaches, it's just a few cuttings,' Lia laughed, realising how good it felt to smile again, to feel her lips curl up, the lines around her eyes to fan out and the dimple in her cheek to put in a long overdue appearance.

174

'I think you know what I'm saying. Work is the best tonic. Fulfilment. It's like when I took up astrology. I felt I had nothing. No self-respect, certainly, and little confidence. And then I started studying, and as I did I grew.'

Lia looked at her companion intently. She'd never taken Peaches terribly seriously before, she realised; she'd simply been a picture of fun – a caricature, almost. And now she began to wonder what the younger Peaches must have been like, and what had led her to become the person she was now. 'How did you come to study it, exactly?'

Peaches sighed. 'I'd gone through a hard time – worse than yours, if you can believe that – and felt my life was worthless. I couldn't be trusted with anything and I had no positive role to play anywhere. Then a friend bought me a book on astrology, something to lift me out of myself, she thought. I started to study, and found I had quite an affinity for it, which was exciting, as I'd never particularly had any affinity for anything before.'

'You were married to Felix by then?'

'No, no, dear, that came later. The same friend then suggested I went along to a talk with her, held at a New Age centre near my home in San Diego, and so I went along. It was Felix giving the talk.' She smiled fondly. 'About death, the spirit world and reincarnation. I was entranced, not just by what he was saying, but by the man himself. He was so tall, so handsome, and with that divine British accent. I quite fell in love!' She giggled at the memory. 'After the talk there was an informal question and answer session over coffee and poppy seed cake, and our eyes kept catching each other's – we were drawn to each other, just like that. I asked if I could see him privately, for some spiritual counselling, and he agreed. He saw me through the darkest point in my life, and I can never thank him enough. We became lovers, of course, and then married, in a simple ceremony on the beach. I was divorced already, you see, and he'd never married.'

'Did you have children?'

Lia thought she saw Peaches' face cloud slightly. 'I have

175

a daughter, yes, by my first husband. But not with Felix, no – we were too old for that. He was about to inherit this place, you know. His parents had retired down here for the sun, and were getting too old to cope. So we had the idea to build the studios, expand the pink cottage, and set up a marvellous retreat, where people could escape to the sun, and nurture themselves spiritually, if they so wished. And so here we are, some twelve years later, still blissfully happy.'

'It's a lovely story.'

'So you see?' Peaches began standing up. 'Out of my darkness there came light. There is always a future, never forget that. Life is constantly moving, it doesn't stand still. But you have to help yourself, and be open to help. I need not have picked up that book, or gone to that talk – I remember resisting both at first, believe me. But you have to be open to the signs, and this –' she indicated the package on the table '– is another of them.' She began to get up. 'I'm glad we had our little chat.'

She began trotting down the terrace towards the gate. 'Hello James,' Lia heard her call out. 'I wondered where you'd gotten to. Come along, now, it must be time for lunch.'

Lia smiled, touched by Peaches' story, and grateful for it. Slowly she went through the contents of Jules's package, and began to collate her ideas.

Chapter Twenty-eight

June had been the worst month, Lia decided. Bella had arrived at the end of May, and Ben had left about a month later; in that time Lia had been more stressed and depressed than she could ever remember. But with the new month, Lia felt perhaps it was time for a new start.

It had become so hot she found it hard to believe that she had ever lived in thick jumpers and a fleece, yelping with the cold as she pulled them on in the mornings; or that she had shivered in her bed under the thickest of duvets and rushed to turn the heater on the minute the sun had set. It was hard to imagine that by five-thirty she'd have pulled the shutters to, as if to hide from the pitch darkness outside, while she was now free to sit on the terrace all night, with the comet and a few fireflies, miniature shooting stars themselves, for company.

This should have been the best time of year, she kept telling herself, the time when her book really came to life, but all Lia could feel was an empty flatness. Putting her even more on edge was the stream of visitors, former participants of the retreat, whom she'd find languishing by the pool or bump into while heading through the citrus orchard. She had no interest in talking to anyone, and so instead of swimming, which she would have enjoyed, she'd stay on her terrace, moving only occasionally to join Etienne in the lunar garden. He'd present her with aubergines and courgettes and the odd pepper or two, and as she cooked and then tried them, she'd persuade herself that they tasted far better than anything she'd found in the shops. In reality, though, she couldn't actually tell much difference, and had usually lost interest in eating after just a couple of mouthfuls.

She studied gardens and roadsides, making note of all the flowers which were springing up, and decided to weave them into each chapter, and one by one the chapters grew like the bindweed she'd watch progressing down old stone walls, or the happy snow-in-summer which would tumble out of rock crevices. How cruel that everything seemed to be so cheerful, when she herself was so down.

Bella had returned to England, which was a relief. Lia had grown tired of worrying about meeting her on the pathway or in the supermarket. She wouldn't know what to say – whether to pretend that nothing had happened or to spurn her like the angry ex-girlfriend she was trying not to be. But one thing was clear – how could they possibly have a normal conversation ever again? It was not a position she wanted to find herself in, and so she sloped carefully about Les Eglantines and the village like a convict on the run whose face was on posters all around. Then one day Chloe told her she'd gone, and Lia felt an odd mix of relief and disappointment, as if a game had finished and life had become rather dull without it.

Chloe would pop up from time to time to invite her to a yoga class or suggest a pizza in the village. At first Lia was reluctant to say yes, but she started persuading herself that she should get out more – that if she wanted to stay in the region, which she did, then she had to circulate and meet more people. It was the only way. No one was going to come and find her, after all, and hadn't Peaches encouraged her to help herself? She doubted that Chloe and

Etienne might lead her to anyone she wanted to meet, however, but it felt like a start.

One evening Chloe suggested she joined them for dinner with Etienne's family. Theirs was a deceptively large house at the mouth of the village, built on three floors and housing all three existing generations – Etienne's sister and younger brother, his parents and his grandmother. Lia had no idea what to expect, but had thought a nice family meal might be fun, and a good source of stories for her book. She imagined discussing seasoning techniques with his mother, hearing about recipes which had been handed down through generations and finding more neat little anecdotes with which to start each chapter off.

But as they arrived Lia's heart sank – Etienne's parents were away visiting relatives and so his brother and sister had decided to party. They were greeted by the strains of overloud French pop music and a glass of cheap red wine. Lia sat near Chloe in a tatty armchair and watched as an army of twenty-somethings paraded in, giggling and shrieking together in colloquial French. The scene was about as appealing as an end-of-term sixth-form disco, and Lia longed to escape, wander back to her pink cottage, pour herself a decent glass of wine and curl up with a book.

Chloe seemed oblivious of the age gap and settled down comfortably with the group, some of whom, it appeared, took part in her yoga classes. She chatted enthusiastically, in pretty terrible French, laughed at their juvenile jokes and enthused about their high street clothes and trinkets. Lia felt uncomfortable, old and alone. Etienne set about supervising the meal, which was to be a ragout of pork in apples and cider, and unfortunately, from what Lia could make out, still quite a long way off.

She tried chatting to a friend of Etienne's brother; a quiet boy with droopy hair and spots around his nose and chin. He'd just finished school, she learnt, and was entering the building trade with his father. There wasn't much Lia could think of to talk with him about, so they fell

179

silent, and she couldn't help imagining what would happen if Ben were to walk in right now. He'd laugh at her discomfort, she thought fondly, and hopefully steal her away somewhere. But there was no more Ben, she reminded herself with a shiver. *Her* Ben was long gone, to be replaced with one who'd betrayed and hurt her. He was now somewhere she couldn't even picture and probably hadn't given her a thought for weeks. He was no more a reality in her life than the character of a novel, someone she'd felt close to for a while but whose memory had faded once she'd turned the last page. Her reality was here, now, surrounded by these kids and Chloe, the eternal kid, waiting for a long evening to draw to a close.

The door opened and a heavily jewelled woman appeared. At first Lia assumed she was Etienne's mother, or aunt, but as she chatted and laughed, admonishing them for the mess they were making and criticising their plans for the pork, she realised she was of a different generation altogether, and so had to be the grandmother. Her long wavy air was dyed a dark red, her fingers were covered in rings and her orange lipstick clashed with her long, pink nails. She was wearing slacks with an open-necked black shirt on which three heavy gold chains bumped up and down against her bosom. Lia could barely understand a word she said, but she was evidently quite a character.

After a few minutes of excitable but incomprehensible shouting, a friend of hers appeared. She had dyed blonde hair, matching orange lipstick and nails and wore black slacks and a gold shirt. She lacked the jewellery but Lia suspected she'd had a facelift instead. She was shyer than Grannie, but still joined in the conversation which seemed to focus on what temperature the oven should be for the pork.

Eventually they left, apparently for an evening of dancing and gambling on the coast. Grannie, Etienne told her, loved nothing better than dancing and gambling on a weekend. It kept her young, he said.

Lia sipped her red wine unhappily, wishing she could come up with a reason to leave. It wasn't as if she was contributing anything to the conversation, after all. They might complain, but would anyone actually miss her presence? But she couldn't do it. She'd been invited and was being catered for, so she had to get on with it. It wasn't in her nature to duck out of something. She spoke to a pretty girl who wanted to become a nurse, and to Marie-Claude, Etienne's sister, who had just started as an office junior. She befriended the family labrador and the neighbour's cat, which popped in to sniff around the dog's food. She tried not to think about Ben, or about Bella, or about what contact they might have had. She tried not to think about the novel she was reading, or the supper she'd have eaten by now, or the comforting thought of climbing under her duvet knowing that tomorrow would be another day.

By quarter to ten the food was served up. It was perfectly nice – chunks of pork and apples floating in a sauce of cider and cream – and it gave her a welcome break from trying to think of things to say. She turned down the offer of seconds, and of more wine, and by ten-thirty was excusing herself. No one tried to persuade her to stay, and gratefully she found the front door, felt the warm July air against her skin, and under the watchful gaze of the comet, wandered out of the village and back to Les Eglantines.

She took the less direct route, which was better lit and passed by Peaches' and Felix's house. As she arrived at the entrance, she heard Peaches calling out for one of the cats.

'Is that you, dear?' She peered into the shadows. 'I can't get Timothy in. He's not supposed to stay out all night, you know – there are foxes around. Oh, just look at Levin-Bayes – you can just feel its power and significance, can't you? I've been taking a look at him every evening, just soaking up his energy, haven't you?'

'No,' Lia said firmly. 'I don't like your comet, Peaches. I was very happy before it turned up.'

'You just wait,' Peaches giggled. 'All around the world there'll be sweeping changes, I'm sure – positive, dramatic changes. Did you have a nice evening?'

181

'It was fine,' Lia told her noncommittally. 'I met Etienne's family.'

'Oh, did you? Yes, well, they're perfectly nice people. A beautiful sister, if I remember rightly. Ah, there you are, you naughty boy,' she added as the tabby appeared from over a wall. She allowed him in and turned back to Lia. 'Well, dear, how about a nightcap? I was about to pour myself a little brandy.'

'Oh, I don't know,' Lia started doubtfully, thinking about her duvet.

'Oh, do join me. Felix is meditating tonight and so I've been all alone. Just a quick one.'

Lia wondered if Peaches hadn't perhaps had a couple already, but accepted, thinking her friend's company might cheer her up. Peaches poured them both a large glass each and indicated that Lia should sit down. She twittered on merrily about the comet, an interesting planetary alignment that was coming up and how Friday, with the moon in the ascendant, was the perfect day to sow beans and corn; Lia began to wonder whether she shouldn't just have gone straight to bed after all.

Then her mood changed. 'How are you getting on now, dear?' she asked, and Lia knew she meant more than work.

'I'm fine, really, I'm OK. A bit dead inside, perhaps, but I'm fine.'

'Dead inside,' Peaches shivered. 'I'm not sure I like the sound of that.'

'I just didn't enjoy this evening. It's funny, isn't it? I mean, it was very sweet of Chloe to invite me, so I don't want to seem ungrateful, but she did it because she didn't want me to be lonely, and all it did was make me feel just that.'

'Maybe it was a message? That actually your own life is just fine right now, and that you don't need any help from anyone.'

Lia smiled. 'You see messages in everything, don't you?' she asked. 'I wish I had your optimism.' She paused. 'Peaches, can I ask you something?' Fortified by cheap

wine and the brandy, Lia felt she could. She felt they'd
become closer now, and could be more open. 'Do you
honestly believe that Bella was receiving messages from
spirits, or do you think she was just making it all up?'

Peaches chuckled. 'Eats you up, doesn't it? The
unknown? I believe you need to open yourself out more,
become more accepting. You're very closed; I can feel it
in you right now.' She took a sip of brandy. 'Do I think
she made it up? Possibly, dear, knowing her. Her Uranus
is sextile with Neptune, which makes her a little delusion-
ary, I'm afraid. Ben's not for her, of course. She wants a
man of high standing, someone who'll elevate her position
in society – all Capricorns do. And Ben's not that man.'

'But right now she wants him, and has done everything
she can to get him. What I don't understand is why he was
so willing to believe it.'

'He wanted reassurance, dear, there's nothing sinister
about that. And maybe she gave him the messages he
needed to hear, even if they weren't authentic.'

'Peaches, she was telling him to sleep with her! Lie with
the goat, remember?'

'Oh, that's true, isn't it, I'd forgotten that,' she agreed,
a look of embarrassment spreading on her face. 'But there
were other things, too, weren't there? Maybe some of the
other messages are what gave him the confidence to go
back, you know, to work again? Maybe she did that much
for him.'

Lia could feel tears welling in her eyes, tiny tears of
jealousy and hurt at the thought that Bella may have
achieved something she hadn't, and in a way she'd never
have dreamt. Peaches, seeing her discomfort, jumped up
and refilled her glass. 'Wait here, dear,' she said before
disappearing off to the back of the house. She appeared
again clutching a tiny photo in a silver frame.

'I'm going to tell you something I've never told anyone
– not Chloe, not Bella, not anyone. I don't know why,
maybe it's just the brandy, but I feel you won't let me
down, and that you'll appreciate why I'm saying it.' She

handed Lia the frame – the photo was of a three-year-old girl with blonde curly hair and a huge, gleeful smile on her face.

'Peaches, she's lovely. Is this your granddaughter?'

'Was, dear, was. Lily. Such a pretty girl, so full of joy, always laughing.'

'What happened to her?' Lia asked carefully.

'There was an accident,' Peaches' face darkened. 'It was my fault, all my fault.' She took a deep breath. 'She used to come and see me at home, in San Diego. She loved it – the garden, the pool, and all the birds. She especially loved robins. They were her favourites and she'd talk to them as if they were her friends. I'd look after her sometimes while her mother was at work – she was a single mother, you see. Well, one afternoon, we were out there as usual, near the pool, taking a walk. There was this song she kept singing, something from a children's show she loved.' She took a deep breath and steadied herself. 'There was a commotion – the neighbour's cat, a big bully brute of a thing, was attacking my Portia, my beautiful Siamese. She's dead now, sadly – she died of old age a few years ago. But he was always doing it, you know – she'd had to have operations, he'd hurt her eye—' Her voice started to break. 'I was only gone for a second, a second or two I swear, but when I got back—' She stopped to wipe the tears from her eyes.

'Not the pool?' Lia's voice was hushed.

Peaches nodded. 'She was face down, limp, like a little rag doll. I pulled her out and tried giving her the kiss of life, but she was gone and I knew it. I'd lost her.'

'Oh Peaches, I'm so very sorry.'

Peaches blew her nose, composing herself. 'The day after her funeral, I woke up and turned the radio on. Can you imagine what was playing? That song, the very song she'd been singing, minutes before. And then I looked out of the window, and there, on the bird table, were two little robins, just looking up at me. And I knew then that she had passed through safely, and was trying to let me know. The

184

dead do communicate, you know, I'm quite sure of that. And yes, I can hear you thinking – hardly conclusive evidence, is it? It was just a coincidence, the two events meant nothing. Well I don't care if that *is* the case – to me they meant everything. To me they meant the difference between falling apart or rebuilding my life. To me they *were* my life.'

Lia sat quietly, not knowing what to say. Somewhere, deep inside her, she felt the story sounded familiar, but she couldn't place how. She said nothing, feeling that it was better just to let Peaches get it all out of her system.

'So you see, Bella might not really have received those messages, but if they meant enough to Ben, if they gave him the strength to carry on, then they served their purpose. I don't care about science or facts or logic, they aren't important to me. What I care about is having the strength to go on.'

'This was the time you were telling me about, wasn't it? When you met Felix, and started to study? This was the terrible hurt you spoke of?' Lia felt formal all of a sudden, as if common language was too flippant, too trivial, for such a terrible story.

'It's exactly that. There are some great hurts we have to endure in this life, and I believe they are sent to test us. Are we capable of overcoming them ourselves, without resorting to drugs or drink or whatever props we come to rely on? It's these challenges that make life, that create the whole point of life. You've picked yourself up, dear, or are in the process of doing so, anyway, and soon I've no doubt you'll be rewarded. I even took a peek at your chart the other day, and I can see that love is on its way.'

'Oh Peaches!' Lia laughed. 'I'm not ready for that. I need a break, and I need to work.' She started to get up. 'Thank you,' she said, holding her friend's hand warmly. 'Thank you for sharing that. I can only imagine how tough it must have been. I won't tell a soul, don't worry. You know you can trust me.'

'Thank you, dear,' Peaches smiled. 'I know I can.'

Lia started to leave, and then remembered something. 'Your daughter?' she asked. 'Where is she now?'

Peaches' face fell again. 'I don't know. She abandoned me after that. I can hardly blame her, can I? She moved to another state, left no forwarding address, rebuilt her life. Or I hope that's what she's done, at least.'

'I'm sorry. How awful for you.'

'It's been years, now. I don't expect her ever to be close to me again – I understand that. But I would just like to know that she's still alive, that she's all right.'

'And you have no way of knowing that?'

Peaches shook her head. 'None.'

'She's not been in touch with anyone else – a relative?'

'No one. She's divorced herself totally.'

'I'm so sorry. How very hurtful.'

'Creating Les Eglantines was a godsend,' Peaches whispered. 'My pupils became my children. I felt maternal, protective of every one of them, as I do you.'

Lia smiled, again not knowing how to respond to that. 'You've certainly made the transition for me here so easy and nice,' she said in the end. 'Your warmth and care. Really, I never felt alone, right from the beginning.'

She hugged Peaches, slightly awkwardly as it wasn't a gesture she was used to, but felt that her friend needed the hug, and would appreciate it.

'And you know something?' Peaches' eyes were glistening, partly from tears, and partly with excitement. 'Ben'll be back, I'm sure of it.'

'He's the big love?' Lia laughed. 'Second-hand goods, now,' she added with a smile. 'There'll be someone else,' she added. 'I can wait.'

Chapter Twenty-nine

A few days later, Lia received an e-mail from Jules saying that she was ready to pitch the book to the editorial team, and would Lia send her a detailed biography to add to the revised chapters and synopsis they'd been working on. Suddenly the words on the screen took on an incredible importance, as if the most minor of mistakes might ruin the project entirely. She wrote and rewrote, unsure of how much or how little information to include, and then cringed as she hit the send button, convinced that she'd remember something significant to add about half an hour later.

After a break for lunch she decided to start on the summer chapters. This was by far the weightiest section of her book, with salads, grilled fresh fish and fabulous fruit puddings. She would buy chunks of mozzarella and slice them with tomatoes and basil, drizzled with olive oil; she'd make jams out of the figs, plums and apricots that so added colour to the *traiteur*'s window display in the village, and she'd buy summer fruits to serve with a fragrant geranium cream. She'd make goats' cheese salads, grill fresh vegetables to dip into a yoghurt pesto mix and slice melons and figs and arrange them with wafer-thin slivers of Parma ham.

Everywhere she looked there was an air of lazy, midsummer hedonism. The fragile-looking heliotrope Peaches had planted in the winter was now double its original size and bursting with pretty lilac-coloured flowers; petunias in all colours tumbled out of pots surrounding Peaches' kitchen; and the wall of lavender smelt divine. All around her, the air felt heady, as if everything was revelling in the summer and its lazy warmth. Lia herself was beginning to share that feeling – the clouds that had hovered over her were passing now and she felt focused again, knowing there was a good chance she'd get her deal.

But as she logged on again, her PC did something she'd never come across before. It started running a scan and after several minutes announced that she had bad clusters, and what did she want to do with them? She wasn't sure, but followed what seemed to be its suggestions, watching anxiously as each bad cluster was then discovered and isolated. She made some peach and apple tea, which tasted vile, and tried to study some recipes, casting a glance at the screen every now and then. One particular cluster was taking ages, she noticed, and she knew something wasn't right. After fifteen minutes of waiting, she exited the system and logged off, hoping that the problem might disappear overnight.

The next morning it was back again. She logged on and instead of her normal, reassuring background the scan popped up, and began to find clusters again. She watched with a sense of dread until it stumbled on the cluster which refused to be isolated, and moved no further.

'Please don't do this to me,' she whispered, willing the problem to go away. 'Please don't, not now.'

She exited the scan and logged off, wondering what to do next. There had to be someone around who'd know how to fix it. Peaches, she thought, might know someone who was computer literate, or even Chloe. She'd go to the village, pick up some more ingredients and try to find either of them on her way back. Then at least whilst she waited she could try out more recipes, do something productive. She hated being cut off from e-mail, especially as there could be something from Jules any time now. She'd call her later that afternoon, she decided, and let her know the problem. Maybe even she'd know someone who could guide her through it over the phone.

Ahead of her in the lane she saw Peaches, who was carrying a large basket and wore a floppy straw hat and some voluminous purple trousers. She ran to catch up with her.

'What a nightmare, dear,' Peaches gasped on hearing the news. 'I don't know anyone, truly I don't. Oh no, what a shame. You work won't all be lost, will it?'

'I certainly hope not,' Lia said, getting increasingly worried.

'Is it a virus, do you think? You hear about them all the time on the news.'

'I don't think so,' Lia replied. 'Because for a virus to get in your system you have to open an attachment, which I haven't done. I rarely get sent any, and nor do I download things.'

'I don't know anything about computers,' Peaches laughed. 'It's all double Dutch to me. I have my astrology programme, of course, but I certainly wouldn't know what to do if anything went wrong. Felix is a bit more clued up, but not that much. He did talk to someone about a website once, though – I wonder if they could help?'

'Well, they might,' Lia began to feel encouraged. 'Could you get in touch with them?'

Peaches had suddenly lost interest. 'Well, hello you,' she paused to stroke a little tabby which had appeared on the lane. 'Are you hungry?' She opened her bag and rustled around inside it, producing a plastic bag full of cat biscuits. 'There you are, good kitty,' she said, putting a handful down for the animal to eat.

'I can't believe you do this,' Lia laughed. 'You walk around carrying cat food?'

'Why, certainly, I do,' Peaches looked almost affronted. 'They wouldn't survive otherwise. Now, what were we talking about?'

189

'Some contacts of Felix's, who might be able to help?'

'Oh, that's right, dear, but they're in San Francisco, so I'll have to work out what time to call.'

Lia's heart sank. 'Don't worry, I'm sure I'll find someone else. You never know, Chloe might know someone.'

'I wish I could be more help,' Peaches laughed apologetically. 'I lead such a sheltered life these days.' Then she stopped, peering forward, and gasped. 'Oh – my – dear! Help is at hand.' They had reached the mouth of the village by now and Peaches' eyes were firmly set on a figure sitting at the bar tabac. 'Is that really you?' she cried with an excited giggle.

Lia followed her gaze to see a well-groomed man in his early forties, having a beer and reading the *Nice-Matin*. He was well built with enough muscle definition to have worked out, but not so much as to be obsessive about it. He had a strong jaw and dark features, from what she could make out beneath the sunglasses he wore. His hair was thick and dark but going slightly grey at the temples. He wore some immaculately pressed chinos and a neat white shirt with the collar open, a satisfying glimpse of dark hair peeking out. On seeing Peaches he let drop his paper and his face broke into a warm and welcoming smile.

'Peaches, what a pleasure!' he said in a neutral American accent Lia found impossible to place. 'How are you?' He jumped up to greet her, kissing her on each cheek.

'What are you doing here? Are you on vacation? How perfect!' Peaches gushed like a teenager. 'We were just discussing Lia's problems, and you're the perfect solution!'

He laughed, amused, and Lia hung back, feeling like a problem friend who needed psychotherapy and a good shag. Warily she looked on, not wanting to intrude on their obvious affection for one another. She didn't need to be introduced anyway. She knew straight away who the man was, and her stomach began tying itself in knots.

190

'Lia, this is Nick Delaney,' Peaches announced proudly as Nick whipped off his sunglasses to reveal dark, welcoming, chocolate-coloured eyes which crinkled at the edges as he smiled. Reluctantly she held out her hand, and he shook it warmly, smiling and looking straight into her eyes.

'Now, dear, tell Nick about your problems, because you know I don't really understand. It's her computer,' she added knowingly. 'It has bad blisters or something.'

'Clusters,' Lia corrected her. 'But, you know, I'm sure they're nothing.'

'Well, the system's designed to deal with them itself. Isn't it doing that?' He had that rich, confident, sexy voice that only Americans are capable of, Lia noticed, appalled at how attractive she found it. It implied power, control and authority, but instead of being intimidating, it was still approachable and warm.

'Yes, it does, but then it gets stuck on one, I mean for ages, until I hit the escape button.'

He frowned. 'Which drive are they on?' he asked.

'I have no idea,' Lia said apologetically, wishing she could explain the problem more clearly, but better still, just deal with it herself.

'Well, look, give me a call,' Nick said, reaching in his pocket for a wallet. 'Here's my card. Let me give you my number.' He pulled out an expensive-looking pen and scribbled a number on the back. Lia accepted it awkwardly, as if taking a gift from the devil.

'Call me later, when you've got your machine switched on, and we'll see if we can figure this thing out together.'

'Do call him, won't you dear?' Peaches was wittering in the background. 'Nick's a computer expert, aren't you, Nick? A dotcom millionaire.'

At this he laughed. 'I design software systems,' he corrected her. 'I'm more on the business side these days, but I should still be able to help you out.'

He seemed modest, Lia thought, as she excused herself and made for the supermarket. Quite modest, really, for someone who'd beaten his wife and made her so miserable

191

she'd killed herself. And good looking, too – dangerously so. Not to mention friendly and helpful. The sort of man she'd always wanted, really. Sophisticated yet warm, successful but unassuming and effortlessly, effortlessly sexy.

So why, then, was her stomach in knots and she felt she wanted to cry? Why did she feel guilty passing the time of day with him? If his wife were buried in the cemetery at the top of the hill, she thought melodramatically, she'd pay her a visit and apologise. Explain what had happened, beg her forgiveness and pray for her soul.

But what really terrified her, the thought that nagged at her all evening and kept her awake for most of that night, was that right now she needed him. With Jules about to pitch the book and a major chapter to write, she needed him, and his help, more than anyone or anything else in the world.

Chapter Thirty

'I've got some good news and some bad news for you,' Jules was on the phone the following morning. 'The good news is, they really like the concept, the way you write and the recipes you've put in so far. They love how your personality comes through with each introduction, and the warmth and passion you show about what you're doing. I told them all about you and they think you sound marketable and promotable.'

'And the bad news?'

'They think the structure's a bit messy. You've got three things going on, what with the seasons, the gardening part and the cooking, and they think it's hard to follow. So they suggest ditching the gardening bit, and turning it into a straightforward Mediterranean cook book.'

'But that defeats the whole object,' Lia moaned. 'I wanted to look at it as a whole, the produce as well as the end result. I don't want to do another Mediterranean cook book – there are plenty of them around already. I want this to be different.'

'I know, I know you did, but it *is* a bit confusing. Let's face it, you've spent months fretting over whether to include anchovies in the winter pastas or the summer anchovy butter. You still haven't really figured out whether aubergines count as summer or winter, as they appear in the shops year round. Think about it, Lia. It'll be difficult for readers to follow. I mean, you're assuming they'll follow you season by season, which they might, but what about the ones who just want to look up nice recipes? They won't know where to find them.'

Lia hummed. Jules had a point, and it was one she'd rather hoped would have somehow resolved itself by now. She felt irritated, at first with Jules for having raised it, but then, she realised, it was with herself, for not yet having tackled the problem. 'So what happens now?' she asked tetchily. 'I have to kill off the gardening element?'

'I bought you a bit more time,' came the voice at the end of the line. Jules sounded like God, Lia thought again, before reminding herself that she was in fact only cross with herself. 'I suggested we give you a bit more time to work something out before abandoning that part altogether.'

'Thank you,' Lia said, beginning to feel humbled.

'One more thing,' Jules added, and Lia's heart sank. 'And on this they're not negotiable. Ditch all the Middle Eastern stuff, and the Spanish and Italian recipes as well, and focus just on France.'

'Oh no,' Lia groaned. 'I wanted it to be all the Mediterranean, not just one country.'

'I know you did,' Jules countered. 'But it doesn't work. I'd had my doubts but the senior editor was adamant. To do the other countries justice you're going to have to produce a colossal book, and that's not what we're about. And anyway,' she added impatiently, 'think sequel, Li. If this goes down well you could get another commission. So this could be *The Sensuous South part one: France*. Get it?'

'Wow!' Lia was stunned. 'You really think they could go for that?'

'Yes, I really do. They think you're on to something good, but it needs to be more accessible. It's all positive, Li, believe me it is, and it could well turn into something long

194

term.' She paused. 'How's it all been going, anyway?'

It was the first time Jules had sounded concerned about her.

'Fine,' Lia started, knowing it had been anything but.

'Come on, Li, he's not worth it. I always had suspicions about him as you know,' she went on. 'You're better off without him, you know, you deserve so much more.'

'Yes, thanks Jules,' Lia said irritably. 'Suddenly I feel so much better. I mean, now you've said that, I wonder what I ever saw in him. So I'll just switch off all my feelings then, just like that.' She snapped her fingers. 'There, gone.' She heard an impatient sigh down the other end. 'Anyway,' she added huffily. 'We were talking about the future, and other versions?'

It was safer to stick to work.

'Well, get the format sorted first, and have a serious think about ditching the gardening stuff. But by all means come up with an outline for further books and their time-lines – that would be a great help.'

'Yes, I will,' Lia said doubtfully. 'The trouble is, my PC's buggered right now.' She explained the problem.

'D'you know anyone who can fix it?' Jules asked.

Lia explained that problem, too.

'Bloody hell,' Jules whistled. 'So what are you going to do?'

'I don't know,' Lia said despondently. 'I don't see that I've got an option. I'm just going to have to call the killer. Maybe he can talk me through it on the phone, so we won't even need to meet and he won't be tempted to beat me up. Or maybe I'll tell Peaches and she can chaperone me. She fancies him like mad. He *is* bloody good looking, I must say.'

'Is he? Well, things could be worse.'

'Not tempted,' Lia said firmly. 'After the Ben fiasco, the last thing I need right now is another doomed fling. I have work to do, and that comes first.'

She braced herself, switched on her computer and as she swished a lemon and cinnamon teabag round in her mug, prayed that all would have returned to normal. But as she reached the dining table her heart sank. There was the scan, and there were the bad clusters again.

She took a deep breath, reached for his card, picked up the phone and called Nick Delaney.

'They're on my C-drive,' she told him, talking through everything she could read on the screen.

'OK, this is what I need you to do,' he said calmly and with authority, making her feel oddly reassured.

He guided her through a series of checks using simple and clear language she could understand, being neither patronising nor complicated. She could tell he was sipping coffee as he did so, and she caught herself wondering how he was looking, whether he was fully dressed yet or sitting there in a towelling robe, fresh from the shower. She wondered were he might be – in a study or a kitchen, perhaps, or maybe he had a conservatory which caught the morning sun, and he was sitting there?

His voice was seductive even though he was just telling her how to get into the system in safe mode or how many kilobytes made up a megabyte; and she had to keep reminding herself of his history, and that he was neither a potential lover nor even friend.

'OK, it sounds like we have a problem here. It sounds like the clusters are located on your hard drive, in the exact spot where the operating system has been stored. I need to see it for myself, though, and try a couple of things I can't describe over the phone. If that's the case, though, you could do one of three things. You contact the manufacturer and get them to replace the hard drive, at their cost if you're under warranty, your own if you're not. Or, we just switch off the scan and you live with the fault, but it'll always be there, like a time bomb waiting to go off. Then there's one other thing we could try. You could save all your information, and I mean everything, onto disk, and we can reboot your machine. With luck it'll store the oper- ating system someplace away from the bad clusters, and your problem goes away.'

196

Lia tried to take it all in. 'I don't think it's under warranty any more, and I'm not in a position to pay or lose my machine for a while—'

'Let me come over,' Nick broke in. 'I'll try a couple of things, and if they don't work, we can reboot.'

'Is that complicated?'

'Not at all. You just need to save everything onto disk – all your files, everything you want to keep, because if you don't, you'll lose the lot.'

He told her how to switch off the scan and access all her files, and promised to come round that afternoon.

Lia spent the next few hours saving everything onto disk, methodically and carefully, terrified she might miss something. She couldn't quite believe that Nick Delaney, *the* Nick Delaney, was coming to her house, to her home, to work on her computer. She was at once flattered and terrified. Would she make tea, or would he prefer coffee? Should she change into something more presentable, or was it better to look like a struggling writer, and one who wasn't remotely bothered by his presence? Irrationally she worried about making the right impression, and not angering him or getting on his wrong side. What if she scalded him with hot coffee by mistake? What if she said the wrong thing, at precisely the wrong time, and interrupted his train of thought? Would he lash out at her? Would that handsome face turn vicious? Would he raise his hand to strike her, or yell, or reduce her to tears?

By the time he arrived, promptly at three o'clock she'd wound herself up as tight as a spring, and was surprised to feel herself relax the minute she saw him. This time he wore jeans and a clean white shirt, and had a five o'clock shadow she found rather attractive. He carried a soft leather briefcase which looked like it had been around the world and back. They shook hands.

'Here's the offending machine,' she pointed to the laptop sitting on the desk. 'May I get you anything?'

'No, thanks,' he shook his head, smiling, before pushing up his sleeves as he sat down. 'OK, let's see what we can do.'

197

Awkwardly she stood beside him, watching as he turned the machine off and then on again, before hitting a couple of keys she'd never used before and waiting patiently. The screen took on an unfamiliar layout, a pale blue with an intimidating white font, and showed a range of commands she couldn't understand. It felt like her machine, her constant companion over the last few months, had become something altogether different. It was as if Nick were a surgeon, and had opened up its very heart and was now exploring its inner workings, looking for clues as to its current ailment.

She watched as his fingers tapped in commands and then snapped back replies to the machine's queries. They were speaking a language together, and one that was as alien to Lia as Arabic. She felt like an outsider, an eavesdropper, and shuffled off towards the kitchen. What to do next? It hadn't occurred to her to lay on something to occupy herself with whilst he worked, rather than just hang around limply as she was. She should have arranged to have left some filing, or better still, to be cooking something tasty in the kitchen, or having an important-sounding conversation on the phone.

'Would you like some tea?' she asked hopefully from the kitchen door.

He shook his head. 'Water, maybe.' He frowned at the screen, and she didn't like to ask if he preferred fizzy or still, bottled or tap.

She put the kettle on and poured him some still bottled, which felt like a good compromise. She could hear him muttering and retorting, 'So try this, then, buddy' and 'If that's the way you want it', and brought the water out with a smile.

'Is it playing up?'

He smiled back. He had such even, white teeth, she noticed, and were his eyes green? 'It's fine, but I think you have a problem. We'll have to reboot.'

'How exciting, I feel like I'm in *Star Trek*,' she laughed.

He smiled, raising one eyebrow. It was a strong, well-defined eyebrow, and she suddenly wondered what it would feel like to stroke it, to hold his face in her hand, to brush against his stubble and to draw her lips towards his.

'You saved everything?' he asked, bringing her back to real life.

'Everything.' She could feel herself blush.

'Sure?'

'Affirmative.'

'Good girl. OK, I'm going in.' He rolled up his shirt sleeves again, blew a faint whistle and tapped on the keyboard.

'Boldly going,' Lia continued, admiring the shape of his hands, and the tufts of dark hair on his knuckles. He had even, neat fingernails, she noticed, and wore no jewellery.

Then, shocked, she turned away, imagining those hands clenching up into fists, imagining them beating into her face, her mouth, her teeth imploding under the pressure, her mouth full of blood. Was that how it happened? Was that what he'd done?

'One hundred per cent sure you saved everything?' he asked again.

'Yes,' she told him, exasperated, but with a tinge of fear. She turned back into the kitchen, and poured herself some calming camomile tea. She heard him tapping away and after a few minutes he declared that all programmes had now been irreversibly deleted. Then he loaded a disk and began to reinstall the system.

'OK, sit beside me,' he beckoned, and she obeyed. 'What's that?' He wrinkled his nose.

'I keep trying these different teas,' she told him. 'None of which I like much.'

'Stick to wine,' he tutted. 'It's probably cheaper. OK, now, I need to run through a few things. You want an English keyboard, right? Day and time, European standard.'

He started inputting all the basics into her machine, checking that they were exactly as she wanted, and occasionally stopping to show her a shortcut, or to explain a different technique.

'I think we're done, here. Let's just run through the scan one more time.'

He set it up and sat back, watching the screen and sipping water, pleased with his work. Silently she sat beside him, watching the dreaded scan, feeling reassured yet on edge, attracted yet repulsed.

'Excellent, see? No clusters. At least, they're still there, but they're not going to affect your operating system. So you lucked out. All you have to do now is restore your old files.'

'I can't tell you how grateful I am.'

'Not at all. Anything I can do to help.' He started rising, gathering his belongings and picking up the car keys he'd slung onto the table. She felt strangely panicky, as if she didn't want him to leave just yet.

'You feel like a drink later?' he asked her suddenly. 'In the village or someplace?'

'Oh, I don't know,' she said quickly, flushing.

'Why ever not?' he asked, surprised. 'You have other plans?'

'No.' Her mind raced. A part of her wanted nothing more than to sit in the evening sun drinking a chilled glass of rosé with him, whilst the other part was yelling at her to stay away, keep her distance, run a mile. 'It's just, well, I'm a bit behind on my work now, that's all.'

He raised an eyebrow, teasing her. 'So you mean to tell me that I just used up a big chunk of my day helping you and you don't even grant me the privilege of buying you a drink later?'

She cringed. 'I'm sorry. I don't want to seem rude. I'd love to have a drink. But it's on me, I insist.'

'You've got a deal.' He smiled that big, warm smile of his, and she wondered whether he'd had his teeth capped. 'Bar tabac, seven o'clock?'

'That would be great. And thank you so much,' she added breathlessly.

'It was my pleasure,' he told her quietly. 'Let me know if you have any other problems.'

200

Like needing sex? she thought quickly to her horror. 'I will,' she told him and he leant forward and kissed her on the cheek. She thought she might faint, and gulped hard. 'See you later, then.'

Chapter Thirty-one

It was five to seven. Lia quickened her pace as she headed towards the village. It had taken her a ridiculously long time to get ready. She'd showered and washed her hair, fussing over how it dried, and the way it fell at her shoulders. She'd taken more care than she could remember with her make-up, trying out a new pink lipstick she'd bought and promptly forgotten about. And then she'd spent an age staring in front of her wardrobe, wondering what would be an appropriate thing to wear. She settled finally on a floaty skirt, strappy sandals and little white T-shirt, with a silk wrap in case the temperature fell. A little overdone for the bar tabac, perhaps, but she so rarely got to dress up these days that it didn't bother her.

He was waiting for her at an outside table, wearing a baggy linen suit, and she wondered whether he'd gone to as much trouble as she had? And did she even like the idea of him going to any trouble, or would she have preferred him to act as if this were nothing but a courteous thank you drink? He stood up to greet her. In front of him was a pitcher of rosé wine and two glasses, and she felt thankful not to have to make any more decisions.

'How's the machine going?' he asked her.

'Fantastic, thanks. I spent the rest of the afternoon catching up on my e-mails.' *About him*, she could have added – they'd been all about him. Telling Jules what had happened and what was about to happen, receiving her scathing reply about a half an hour later and then spending the next half an hour trying to justify herself. 'How about you?'

'Bit of business, a few calls, yelled at my builder.'

'Yelled?' Lia took a swift gulp of wine.

'I asked for an outdoor kitchen six months ago. You know, just somewhere for a fridge and basic cooking facilities. We discussed plans, I approved them, and then I get back here to find nothing's happened.'

'How frustrating.'

'Tell me about it. But that's boring. Tell me about your book.'

Lia was getting tired of telling people about her book. She was tired of explaining the concept, of watching eyes glaze over as if disappointed that she wasn't writing a torrid bonk-busting romance set on the Riviera. Patiently she explained it to him, but instead of glazing over, his eyes remained alert and interested.

'What a great idea,' he told her. 'I'd love to have something like that. I'm not much of a cook, I've got to admit, or gardener for that matter, but one day I could see myself growing zucchini and aubergines and then wondering what the hell to do with them. I think it sounds terrific.'

'You do? I've had a mixed response. Do you know Bella, Bella DeVere?' She tried to keep her voice as casual as possible. He shook his head as if Bella were no one he'd like to know, either, and Lia felt quietly thrilled, grateful that he wasn't already in the woman's clutches. 'She's stayed at Les Eglantines in the past,' she told him. 'Funny woman. But she questioned who the market would be, and who'd want to buy something like that. Made me feel like it was a waste of time.'

'A lot of people have no imagination,' he told her. 'It's only the few who've got the guts to try something new who

203

make a difference. If you think it's a good idea, don't let anyone else deter you.'

'You're right,' Lia smiled, cheered. He couldn't have said something more appropriate if he'd tried. And now he'd got the impression that Bella was unadventurous and negative, which would cloud his judgement nicely if he ever met her. 'My publisher, after all, thinks I'm on to something.' She said the words proudly. *My publisher.* They felt good, even if they weren't strictly true.

'So what are you worrying about?'

She told him about her problems with the format, and he listened carefully, nodding. 'I'm sorry,' she laughed, interrupting herself. 'I can't believe you're really interested in all this.'

'I'm interested in anyone who's got guts. What were you doing before, anyway?'

She told him about her London life and the job that had diminished as the years went on. 'I had this awful boss,' she continued, as he'd ordered a replacement *pichet* of wine. 'Rebecca. No one liked her. She made me see what I didn't want to become – forty-something has-been whose highlight of the day was to buy some crappy American talk show for her channel and ridicule a colleague for trying to come up with something new.' Then she remembered herself. 'Oh, I'm sorry,' she added guiltily. 'Not all American talk shows are crappy, of course. But this one seemed particularly odious. I don't understand the mentality of someone who can go on air and reveal their deepest secrets, or family tragedies, or whatever.'

Her voice trailed off. What exactly *had* she seen on that show? And why was it shouting out to her now? A woman with badly dyed blonde hair who hadn't spoken to her mother for years. *Who hadn't spoken to her mother.*

'Everyone has some weakness,' Nick said evenly. 'I wouldn't go on air to discuss mine, either, but I guess some people find it cathartic.'

Lia was half aware of what he'd said, but was too busy trying to remember the exact details of the woman's confession. Her daughter had died, she'd said, in a pool accident. It was the grandmother's fault, wasn't that it? *It had been the grandmother's fault.*

'Do you want to get something to eat?' Nick was asking her, snapping her back into the present.

'Oh, I'm sorry, I was just thinking of something.' It was too much of a coincidence, surely? But the story seemed to tally perfectly with Peaches' own.

'Is anything wrong?' He looked concerned.

'No, no, I'm sorry, forgive me.' She had to stop thinking about it. She'd been sworn to secrecy, after all. It was hardly the kind of thing she could share with Nick Delaney.

'Well? Dinner?'

'Yes, I'm sorry. I'd love to.'

All afternoon she'd been telling herself not to have dinner with him, if he asked. A quick drink, that was all she was to have. But sitting there, outside the bar in the fading sunlight, chatting with someone who seemed genuinely interested in what she'd done, made such a refreshing change from sitting on her own reading a magazine, that she could feel her willpower shrinking away.

'A pizza in the village, or would you like to try something else?'

'I don't really know anywhere else,' she admitted. 'So the pizza place is fine. It's expanded now and they've got tables outside, so it sounds quite fun. I haven't been for a while.' An image of Ben sitting opposite her flashed through her mind and she pushed it sharply away. It had been four weeks and two days since he'd left for Kabul, and so five weeks and three days since they broke up. Not that she was counting any more, she reminded herself.

'You know something?' He looked at his watch, 'Let's skip the pizza. You, my dear, are in for a treat.'

He escorted her to his car, a sporty black Mercedes, which he'd left outside the supermarket.

'Where are we going?' she asked excitedly, and he smiled, before starting the engine and heading off towards the neighbouring village. 'I've led such a sheltered life here,' she continued, feeling like an indulged schoolgirl. 'I rarely leave the pink cottage.'

He sped along the narrow winding lanes, fast but in control, expertly guiding the car up and down hills, past olive groves and lemon trees, dogs barking wildly through their gates and children playing football on a patch of grass. The world seemed intoxicating, suddenly, and Lia felt as if she'd been released from a self-imposed exile and was seeing everything with new eyes. They arrived at a large open square, full of restaurants, bars and speciality shops, and he parked.

Climbing out of the car, she wished she'd put on something more glamorous. Her skirt was only cheap after all, and her sandals a bit scuffed. She'd forgotten to wear any jewellery, too, and as a woman wearing gold against a deep tan walked by, Lia wished she looked more like that and less like a bumpkin who rarely left the kitchen.

Nick escorted her through the square, guiding her gently towards a restaurant hidden among the labyrinthine streets beyond. He was welcomed warmly, like a regular, and they were shown to a good table. The restaurant itself was unprepossessing and simple, with creamy walls covered in old black and white photos of the region, beige and cream tablecloths and expensive wine glasses.

She was just taking it all in when two glasses of champagne arrived, which he must have ordered without her hearing as they'd arrived. He toasted her future success and they settled down to study the menu. Lia couldn't decide between poached asparagus with tapenade or ravioli with herbs and *cepes*, but with Nick's encouragement opted for the latter. Then she chose the pan-fried sea bass with a saffron ratatouille sauce to his warm *gesier* salad followed by rabbit in basil. To go with the food he chose a Sancerre, chatting easily to the *maître d'* in a French that might not have been perfect, but was certainly competent and confident.

'What made you come to this area?' she asked when their orders had been taken.

'My wife was French,' he told her simply and she felt herself straighten, scrutinising him for clues. 'Her family comes from down here. We had an apartment in Paris but she wanted a place in the sun. This came up and we fell in love with the location and the views.'

'And you're divorced now?' she asked carefully, feeling it would seem odd not to ask.

'She died.' His voice was softer now, with a discernible trace of regret.

'I'm so sorry, I had no idea,' she said guiltily.

'It's been five years now. You reach a place of acceptance. It's just tough when people ask, as they inevitably do.'

'I'm sorry,' Lia said quickly. 'I certainly didn't mean to—'

'It's OK,' he said warmly. 'You weren't to know. I've learned to get used to it, and I can talk fairly openly by now – it's the people around me who find it hard. I don't mean for you to feel uncomfortable, that's the last thing I want.'

Lia nodded, understanding. A part of her would have liked to have pressed him – to find out how she'd died – but she decided against it. 'And so you still live in Paris?'

He shook his head. 'I quit, which makes it all the more of a treat coming down here. I divide my time between New York, Asia and London.'

'And what exactly is it you do, again?'

'We produce and sell enterprise software,' he began. 'Which in theory means everything from easy-to-use programs for small companies to complex solutions for larger ones, though in practice we're currently over-reliant on two multinationals, and it's become my job to change that.'

'You mean, to create a larger client base?' she asked, feeling very corporate all of a sudden.

'That's right, along with maintaining relations with our existing clients, hence my charging around the world the whole time.'

207

She paused as a plate of ravioli was placed in front of her. 'Why does Peaches think you're a dotcom millionaire?' she asked.

'Because Peaches wouldn't know a dotcom if it bit her on the butt.' He laughed. 'No, that's not strictly fair – we invested in two dotcoms, one at the start of the boom, which we sold at just the right time, and the other halfway through the boom which cost us big time. So lessons were learned, and now we're focused on what we do best.'

'And so, is your client base expanding?' Lia asked awkwardly, wishing she could talk more intelligently about the high-tech industry.

'Not as fast as I'd like. Until the economy in general picks up companies aren't in a position to expand – they'll make do with what they've got. But we just got another big contract with one of our existing clients, so I guess we'll keep the wolves from the door a while longer. How's your pasta?'

'Try some for yourself.' She scooped a square up and dropped it on his plate. As she did, she imagined for a second dropping it onto his immaculate trousers, and him leaping up, grabbing her by the throat and smashing her head against the wall.

But he never did grab her by the throat, and by the end of the evening she stopped imagining that he might. He laughed off her offers to pay, or even contribute to the meal, and drove her home, dropping her off at the entrance. And there, relaxed by the excellent food and wine and his company, Lia reluctantly pulled herself out of his car, and forced herself to be satisfied with just a peck on each cheek.

But how she wanted more, she thought to herself in horror. Oh God, how she wanted more.

Chapter Thirty-two

The phone had rung three times before Lia could answer it, her morning cup of Earl Grey still in her hand. It had been two days since her evening with Nick, and she had managed to think of little else.

'I have the solution to all your problems.'

She broke into a beaming smile, thrilled that he should be calling and awed by the easy confidence with which he did away with the usual introductions and how-are-you's. Had it been someone she hadn't warmed to, she thought, that familiarity would have repelled her, but coming from him she took it as a sign of friendship, and was delighted.

'I can't wait to hear,' she told him.

'I was taking a shower this morning, and it came to me. Your book. Split it in two. Start with the seasons, with all the stuff that goes on, and at the end of each part, you index each recipe that includes any of your aforementioned ingredients. And then in the other half you go into your traditional recipe book format – starters, entrées, all that stuff, so that readers can find them easily.'

She thought for a second, trying to picture it, repeating his words. It was such a simple, obvious idea, but one that had somehow eluded her for months. She could hardly believe it was coming from him. 'I can't find a fault with that,' she told him, 'I really can't.'

'Well, thank you so much, neither could I.'

'I mean, it covers everything. I get to explore the produce as a whole and the readers get to find their recipes just as normal. I really can't find a flaw.'

'You can't find a flaw,' he repeated, an edge of sarcasm in his voice. 'Well, thank you for your enthusiasm. It's not as if I was expecting anything along the lines of "Thank you Nick, for coming up with the answer and saving my skin with my publisher",' he teased. 'I'm so grateful you must let me buy you lunch, say, how about today, around twelve-thirty?'

She laughed, appalled at the impression she'd given. 'I'm sorry,' she tried. 'Forgive me. You're right, you *have* saved my skin, and I'm actually very grateful. I didn't mean to be rude.'

But lunch? With the new format she could slot her book into place in a day, and have e-mailed it off to Jules by the evening. She wanted to get started now, without even bothering to get dressed, and know that it was done, all neat and tidy, and that all she had to do from now on was add to it.

'So twelve-thirty, then,' he was saying.

'Oh Nick, now I've got so much to do, I can't break for lunch! How about tomorrow?'

'Tomorrow? Is that all the gratitude I get? I could have been thinking about my business, about future plans, relocating the office, but oh no, I was standing there, under the shower, thinking about you and your book, and now you don't even have the grace to agree to see me?'

She could hear the smile in his voice, wondered how he might have looked in that shower, and felt herself weaken. 'You're absolutely right, I'm a cow, yet again, please forgive me. And lunch will be on me, OK?'

A pizza in the village, she told herself, two hours at most. She could get much of the format done in the morning, then check and e-mail it to Jules when she got back.

'Anything you say. I'll pick you up at twelve-thirty.' He hung up again with that breathtaking confidence that didn't need to say goodbye, and she clutched the receiver for a minute, not wanting to let go.

Then she pulled up a chair, turned on her computer and got to work, allowing herself until eleven forty-five to get as much done as possible. And as she'd thought, it came easily once she'd created her new folders and cut and pasted all their relevant contents. By eleven-thirty she was e-mailing Jules with the revised breakdown, and by eleven forty-five she'd headed for the shower.

Again, it took her a long time to get ready. She ended up with a floaty knee-length silver skirt, a white T-shirt and pale-blue light cardigan, and finished it all off with some pale blue mules and a matching bag. She sprayed perfume behind her ears and through her hair, as she'd once read Joan Collins did. She kept her make-up light and fresh, and jewellery minimal.

As she headed out towards the entrance, she ran into Peaches, deadheading her lavender bushes. She looked at her admiringly.

'My, you look lovely, dear. Do you have a date?'

She smiled. 'Nothing special, it's just such a beautiful day, isn't it?' She carried on walking, not wanting to reveal where she was going, or with whom. Peaches would only get over-excited, she thought, and tell the likes of Chloe, who'd be sure to challenge her.

She'd just arrived in the lane when Nick's Mercedes arrived, and her heart leapt. He looked freshly shaved and wore a white shirt and fawn chinos. Getting in, she noticed his watch for the first time – it was silver and gold, elegant, expensive, and it sat neatly on his wrist. He leant forward and kissed her on either cheek – he smelt clean but without a trace of aftershave or cologne – and as their skin touched a pleasant shiver ran through her body.

'So, you got everything done?' he asked, smoothly turning the car around.

'Most of it – it was just a case of slotting it in. I just

211

can't believe I hadn't thought of it before, you know? I'll have to give you a dedication.'

'I want the entire thing dedicated to me,' he corrected her. '"To Nick, without whose brilliance this book would never have been possible", and then you can name your firstborn after me.'

'I sent the new breakdown off to the publisher,' she carried on, laughing. 'I can't wait to hear their reaction.' *And tell Jules about this lunch*, she thought, and about how totally bloody gorgeous Nick was.

'So, where are you taking me?' he asked, driving away from the village and down towards the coast.

She laughed nervously, feeling totally out of control and rather enjoying it. It was strange to think how uncomfortable she'd felt about Nick before, and how now she couldn't think of anyone she'd rather be with. He made her feel attractive and special, and right now that ego boost was just what she needed. 'You got any good ideas?'

'Yes, I do, as a matter of fact,' he admitted, and she knew better than to question him.

They wound down the old road towards the coast, where they turned eastwards through Nice along the Promenade des Anglaises. Lia could feel the admiring glances from other drivers, and was proud to be sitting there, in an immaculate Mercedes, the Riviera's most exciting man by her side. She had no idea where they were heading, but it didn't matter. He could take her to the swankiest restaurant in the Côte d'Azure and run up an enormous bill at her expense, or he could take her to the beach and present her with a dried-up sandwich; either way it would still be special.

Out of the traffic now, they headed up above the sea along the Grande Corniche, winding around the kind of roads James Bond would race in – a Riviera she hadn't yet experienced, the glamorous, showy part, and as far removed from her rural village as was possible. They laughed at some terrible driving, cursing as people failed to indicate or overtook on blind bends, and Lia gazed in awe at the loveliness of the sea and its surrounds. Finally they came to an imperious-looking building perched on a cliff, with formal but pretty gardens towards the back.

He escorted her through the entrance, where he'd reserved a table on the terrace overlooking the sea, surrounded by terracotta pots filled with citrus trees, geraniums and petunias. One wall was covered in deep pink bougainvillaea and on another a sea of nasturtiums cascaded down. A miniature pink rose decorated every table.

'This place is beautiful,' she cooed. 'I've never seen anything like it.'

'It's special, isn't it? But, then, we are celebrating.' The waiter arrived with two glasses of Kir Royale. 'To your book – what is it? *The Sensuous South*, and to your future success,' he toasted her.

She clinked her glass against his, looking firmly into his dark eyes, and felt herself falling, almost, falling headlong down against the cliff and into the turquoise sea below. 'Thank you,' she smiled, resisting the urge to get up, lean across the table and kiss him firmly on the lips.

How could he be the monster Chloe described? It just didn't seem possible. A part of her wanted to keep her distance, to refuse to succumb to his charm and his generosity, whilst the other part wanted nothing more than to call this man her own. If there had been a sign, *any sign*, that he was dangerous, or violent or difficult in any way, she would have walked away without looking back. But there were no signs, and everything seemed to indicate that this was just another of Chloe's stories.

And wasn't it preferable to be sitting here now, with this man, than crying over Ben's betrayal?

The menu was fabulous, far more complex and involved than anything she'd include in her book. Her recipes had to be good, solid and simple, she told herself, the sort of thing you could cook after a day at the office – this was a different kind of cuisine altogether. She chose the scallop, artichoke and spinach salad in an orange dressing followed

213

by pan-fried sea bass with a 'fruits of Provence' sauce, whilst he ordered a fish soup and the supreme of red mullet niçoise, along with a bottle of Pouilly-Fuissé and some lightly sparkling water.

They chatted easily, now like friends, talking about everything from food to holidays and their various travels. He'd been in a different league to her for several years, having explored South America and travelled extensively throughout Asia, but he still spoke fondly of the simple grilled seafood he'd eaten years before on a beach in Greece, and of the curries he'd enjoyed on a visit to Goa.

As the meal came to an end, he again laughed off her attempts to pay for at least a share of the bill, and sped her safely back towards Les Eglantines. He hadn't drunk much, she noticed, and so was perfectly capable of driving while she, loosened up by the wine, chatted away happily. As they left the coast and headed back towards the hills she realised she didn't want to go home yet, didn't want the magic to end – but would have liked to have continued along the coast, perhaps gone for a drink in Antibes, and had a look at all the yachts in the evening sun. Something held her back from suggesting it, however, as if she didn't feel quite as relaxed with him as she might.

By the time they'd arrived at Les Eglantines she was wishing he was less responsible. She caught herself thinking back to her night in the mountains with Ben, and the wonderful surprise she'd felt when he'd booked the room for them there. If only Nick had done the same thing, she kept thinking, and she could look forward to tumbling into a big warm bed with him instead of returning to an empty cottage with no one to talk to but Peaches' cats.

As they said goodbye she wanted more than anything for him to kiss her, to let her know that this had been more than just a lunch between friends, but he offered no more than the usual peck on both cheeks.

'You've been a very bad, but very welcome distraction,' she told him. 'Let me cook for you soon, eh? And I'll let you know what the publisher thinks.'

214

'You do that.' He smiled affectionately as he turned the car around and headed down the lane. She watched until it disappeared from view, and then reluctantly made her way home.

Chapter Thirty-three

'This was the wife-killer's idea?' Jules's voice on the phone sounded incredulous.

Lia cringed. 'Don't. It's not true. Anyway, it can't be. If you met him you'd know what I mean.' She paused nervously. 'So, what do you think?'

'It's great, it all works,' Jules said casually as if she'd been expecting nothing less. 'I've got a meeting with the senior editor in the morning, so I'll run it by her then. But I think this could do it, you know? I really do.'

'You mean that?' Lia was thrilled. 'Well, if it does get published I have to dedicate it to him and then name my firstborn after him.' She talked excitedly about Nick and the lunch she'd just had. She wanted to do nothing *but* talk about him, because if she couldn't actually be seeing him for real, it was the next best thing.

'Oh my God, you're falling for him, aren't you?'

'Jules, it's hard not to. I've never been so looked after by a man before, you know, so spoilt.'

'But what about that nasty little habit of his? You think that's all lies now?'

'Yes, I do, I really do. I mean, it's just so hard to believe when you're with him. I've been watching out for signs, believe me, and I can't find any. He could have lost his temper with my laptop, but he didn't. On the road, all these other drivers were cutting him up all over the place, but he just laughed them off. I just can't link the man I heard about to the man I've now met.'

'So he's either the victim of a slur campaign, or he's had serious therapy?'

Lia smiled. It was hard to imagine Nick lying on a shrink's couch. 'The former, I think. None of it rings true when I'm with him. And let's face it, Chloe's hardly that reliable. But I suppose there's still this nagging doubt, you know, that I could be wrong. That there's some major problem with him, and I'm about to uncover something nasty.'

'Which in some ways makes him all the more sexy, of course,' Jules suggested, to Lia's shock. All the more shocking though, was the realisation that her friend might have a point. Was there something inherently exciting about the danger she might be in?

'So has he said any more about his wife?' Jules asked.

'No, but why should he?' Lia answered defensively, still reeling. 'I haven't asked, and it's not the sort of thing you just bring up.'

'Who knows, so maybe she died of some illness? Or in a car crash? And you know what villagers are like – they'll make anything up if they want to. He's not around much, after all, so he's an easy target. What if someone took a dislike to him and thought they'd cause trouble? Village people do that sort of thing all the time, don't they?'

'Yeah, I think they do.' Lia found this thought comforting. It could all so easily be lies, she told herself: a vendetta, a quarrel over land or right of way or whatever people quarrelled about in the countryside. 'But Chloe used to massage Elodie, though,' she remembered. 'The ex-girlfriend. She claims she saw bruises.'

'Ah, the missing ex-girlfriend,' Jules said as if this were a hugely significant factor, before adding tartly. 'She might have just bumped herself, you know, it does happen. Oh shit, I've got another call coming, hang on a second.'

Lia found herself hanging resentfully in mid-air. How she hated call waiting, and wished the other caller could just have been sent to an answering machine instead. Now the chances were that Jules would only come back to tell her that she'd have to take this more important of calls. No sense of manners, the phone people who devised all these systems; no sense of the inconvenience they caused, not to mention the loss of self-esteem suffered by those whose calls were deemed to be less interesting.

'OK, I'd better go,' Jules came back on the line. 'I'll call you later, OK?'

Lia tried not to feel too irritated. She made herself a cup of strawberry and vanilla tea, which was just as sickly as she'd expected, and went on-line in a deliberate act of rebellion in case Jules *did* call. Let her be inconvenienced for once, she thought crossly, before reminding herself that it was silly to resent someone purely because they were busy, not to mention the fact that they had found her a place to live and were now in the process of getting her a book deal.

As she skimmed the newspapers and the gossip columns, all she could think about was Nick. Now wouldn't Jules be jealous of the day she'd just had? Didn't Jules ever sit in her grey office resenting Lia and her cottage and her ambition? There was no race between them, she told herself, and she could no more do Jules's job than Jules would want hers. So why this silly resentment?

Jules had always been the organiser, the person who could fix things and make them happen, whilst Lia was the more creative of the two, the ideas person. And although Lia envied Jules the fact that she always seemed to know where she was going in life, she didn't necessarily envy her destination. She could no more sit in an office striking deals with authors, photographers and designers than she could head off to Afghanistan to take photos.

Now where did that thought come from, she asked herself? She had managed not to think of Ben for a good couple of days, now. Nick was making it easier to forget him, and that in itself was a bonus. She sat back, remembering how wonderful Nick had been and envisioning a summer romance full of champagne and laughter, trips down to the coast and up to the mountains. Then the glamorous Riviera wedding followed by regular visits to Hong Kong and New York.

I could become this person, she thought, the kind of glamorous but understated woman she'd often admired at airports, effortlessly chic and unfazed by international travel. She could become a full-time food writer, perhaps basing her books on their travels, whilst his business would grow and become ever more successful. They'd have children – two – and eventually settle in his house above the pink cottage. She could picture family Sundays by the pool and barbecues in the evening. They'd invite Felix and Peaches for the occasional dinner, and be amused by their eccentricities and stories.

Peaches, she remembered suddenly. What to do about Peaches? If the woman on the tape was her daughter, then didn't Peaches have a right to know? All she'd wanted, after all, was the reassurance that she was still alive. Lia tapped out an e-mail to one of the librarians at her old channel, a chap called Clive, and someone she'd have the occasional drink with after work. *Are you still running the American show, Share It With Sara? she wrote. And if you are, do you have an episode called* I'll Never Forgive You? *I hate to ask, but if you do, any chance of a VHS?*

It was the least she could do. She'd have to look through it herself first, of course – be confident that the woman really could be Peaches' daughter. Nick would probably have a video, she thought, picturing herself inside the large, glamorous house that could one day be her own.

Lia Delaney – she wanted to shout it from the terraces – *Amelia Delaney*.

But what to do next, how to move things along a bit? She should invite him to dinner, she decided, cook something special. She sat back, her mind swirling with recipes

219

and ideas and table decorations and which music to play and how to create the right impression.

There was just one important issue left, though, she told herself, her heart beating increasingly faster. How long to leave it before calling him?

She didn't wait long. It occurred to her in the night that Nick was only on holiday after all, and so might not be around for much longer. There was no time to lose. She called him the next morning, after breakfast, and to her disappointment got his answering machine.

'Nick, it's Lia. Just calling to say a huge thank you for yesterday, which was wonderful. I'd like to repay you, if I may, and do that supper for you some time. How about tomorrow evening? And let me know if there's anything you can't eat.'

She flung the receiver down, grateful to have got through the message without stumbling over her words. She'd never felt so excited about anyone before, so dizzy and nervous. How long would this feeling last, she wondered, and more importantly, how long before he'd call back? She tried to get on with some work, but didn't achieve much. She didn't like to go on-line in case he tried calling, and so spent the morning in a state of limbo, not wanting even to go to the loo in case the phone rang.

Finally, just before twelve-thirty, it did.

'I cannot stand Brussels sprouts,' his voice came on the line, that confident, dreamy voice of his, and she laughed in relief. 'And I can live without tripe, ox testicles and lambs' tongues. But tomorrow evening would be perfect. What time do you want me?'

Now, now, now! she thought. 'Seven-thirty?' she suggested as calmly as she could.

'I'll be there. It'll be a pleasure.'

As she put the phone down, it rang immediately, and Jules's voice came on the line.

'Sorry I didn't get back to you yesterday,' she started.

'No matter,' Lia told her, long over her irritation of the

previous day. She told Jules about her dinner plans for Nick.

'Great – just keep a knife to hand to be on the safe side,' she joked. 'Anyway, the reason I'm calling is – get yourself some champagne – I'll be e-mailing you a deal memo later. Just waiting on some picky things from the legal department, but I should get it done by last thing today.'

Jules went through the terms to Lia. It wasn't the most lucrative deal she'd ever heard of, but it was there, she'd achieved that much, and Lia was thrilled.

She selected some recipes, wrote numerous lists and headed for the supermarket that afternoon. She was going to do red mullet fillets in a creamy saffron sauce, followed by saddle of lamb *à l'Arlésienne*, with garlic, rosemary and thyme, roasted on a bed of courgettes and tomatoes. She'd buy a selection of cheese and then finish the meal off with honey and lavender ice cream, if either of them got that far.

She'd buy some good red wine, she thought, although she had little doubt that he'd bring something excellent with him; and a bottle of champagne to start with, with perhaps some pistachios to nibble.

She needed candles for the table and some flowers. Then what to wear? A skirt, definitely, and high heels. She'd have to get the cooking finished before he arrived, so that she could change quickly and look elegant and relaxed. AND SHE HAD A DEAL! In all her excitement she kept forgetting the most important moment of her life. She rang her mother, e-mailed a few friends and popped in on Peaches on her way to the shops.

'My dear, I always knew you'd do it!' she shrieked, rushing to kiss Lia on both cheeks. 'It's Amelia, she has a deal,' she called out to Felix, who was inside in his armchair, half asleep. 'We must celebrate. Felix is busy tonight, but how about a drink tomorrow evening?'

'Oh Peaches, that's so sweet, but I have plans tomorrow.'

'Plans? Amelia, is there anything you're hiding from me?' Peaches teased.

'I'm having Nick Delaney to dinner,' Lia said as casually as she could. 'To thank him for all the work he did on my PC.'

'My dear, that's marvellous! Felix, did you hear that?'

Lia went to quieten her. 'Don't, please, it's really nothing, I mean, it doesn't mean anything.'

'Really, dear?' Peaches cocked an eyebrow teasingly. 'Well, if that's the way you want it. But Nick Delaney, my goodness, how lucky you are – there are very few like him. I don't know what happened to Elodie, I really don't. Such an attractive girl, but well, her loss may be your gain!'

'It's a dinner, Peaches, nothing more than that. Just to say thank you.'

'I did his chart, once, you know,' Peaches started. 'It was a little vague, as I don't know his exact time of birth, but I could try and do a compatibility chart for the both of you if you like!'

Lia tried not to laugh. 'That's very kind but there's really no need. It's just dinner.'

'Just dinner – what nonsense,' Peaches mocked. 'And where were you going yesterday, looking so pretty and dressed up? You can't tell me you were off to the supermarket? And wasn't that his car I saw in the lane later on?'

Lia laughed, enjoying the game. 'Nothing gets past you, now, does it? But seriously, I would prefer to keep this quiet, if that's all right. I don't really want Chloe or Etienne knowing, for example.'

'Of course, dear. I understand perfectly. But how very exciting. After everything you've gone through, this is wonderful news. I haven't seen you look this happy in a long time.'

Lia softened. 'Would you like to join us for a drink early on?'

Peaches looked tempted, but held back. 'No, dear, it's your evening. I'd only spoil things. You two have a wonderful time, and don't forget to tell me *all* about it. And I mean, all,' she added with a wink and a giggle.

Lia found herself chuckling all the way along the lane.

It was hard not to be fond of Peaches, and she hoped they'd always stay friends. She was worried about the tape, though, and how to handle it if the woman on the show really did turn out to be her missing daughter. All she could do was show it to her, she kept telling herself, and hope that she wasn't opening too many old wounds.

The following morning, as Lia began her preparations, Peaches appeared at the window, a worried look on her face. 'I'm so sorry to trouble you on your big day,' she began. 'But I have a terrible favour to ask. I feel so bad, really I do. I should have mentioned this much, much earlier, but I guess I hadn't taken things seriously enough.'

'What is it, Peaches? What's the matter?'

'I have a booking, a group who want to do a retreat for the last two weeks of August. They requested it months ago, and I kind of thought it might go away, but then the other day they e-mailed me a confirmation.'

'The other day?'

'I know, I know, I should check that thing more often, but I forget. I only looked at it last night while Felix was practising his crystal therapy.'

'So what exactly are you saying?' Lia wished she'd just get on with it.

'Would you mind – oh, it's such an imposition I know, but, would you mind vacating the pink cottage for that period?'

'Oh, gosh,' Lia was stunned. 'I had a nasty feeling that was what you wanted.'

'I'm so sorry, I don't know what to say. I wasn't really prepared for any more groups, but now this has happened.'

Lia looked around at the cottage that had become her home, resenting even the thought of having to leave. 'Well, I've got no choice, have I?'

'I'll make it up to you, I promise.'

'I always knew I might have to leave in the summer, but well, it's August already and as you hadn't mentioned anything, I just thought it had gone away.'

'So did I, dear, so did I. I'm not sure I even want any

more groups – it's so much work. I feel so very silly – I should have just turned them away from the beginning.'

'Wasn't Chloe supposed to be doing all this for you?' Lia asked. 'I thought she was taking bookings and doing the changeovers?'

'Well, she was, but I guess she thought I'd already spoken to you. I'm in such a muddle about the whole thing, to tell you the truth. She does some things and then leaves others—'

'Well, there are hotels around here, aren't there?' Lia interrupted, not wanting to hear about how the two of them worked together. Perversely, she wanted Peaches to know how disruptive this would be, make her feel guilty. 'Or I could go back to the UK. I might need to meet with the publisher, after all. Of course, at such late notice I'm going to get a lousy deal on flights.'

'I'm so sorry, dear,' Peaches was close to tears, now, and Lia started feeling guilty herself.

'It's only for two weeks. It'll be OK,' she said calmly. 'But will there be other groups? In September, for example?'

Peaches looked awkward. 'There may be,' she said quietly. 'But I've got nothing confirmed so far.'

'Well, will you just tell me?' Lia was getting irritated now. 'Don't just pretend they might go away. Just give me the dates as far in advance as you can and I can make alternative arrangements. But please don't just tell me at the last minute. A hotel's going to be expensive, you know.'

'You know, Binkie Hardcastle might just have a spare room. I could ask her if you like? She has a darling little house by the river. It doesn't get as much sun as this does, of course, but it has a charm all of its own.'

'I don't think I want a room somewhere, thank you, Peaches. I'm too independent for that. I'll sort something out for myself, don't worry. It just doesn't leave me much time.'

'I know,' Peaches agreed sadly. Then her eyes lit up. 'I'll let you have the cottage at a discount next winter, I promise.'

Lia softened. 'I'll keep you to that,' she smiled. 'Just give me the exact dates you need me out. And I've got a lot of stuff to store away.'

'Oh, I can help you there, dear. I have storage space.'

Lia tried to control her irritation. The more she thought about it, the more disruptive Peaches' favour was becoming. Peaches would be making good money from the rental, whilst she would only have to pay for flights or hotels, and all at highly inflated rates.

She tried not to huff as she started preparations for dinner, imagining packing up all her precious herbs and spices from the kitchen, clearing away all her papers from the dining room, all her books and research. How would the garden survive? she asked herself. Would anyone remember to water it?

She tried to calm down, and not to let her irritation spoil the evening. It was only for two weeks, after all, she kept telling herself. It wasn't the end of the world.

Chapter Thirty-four

At seven-forty Nick arrived, clutching a bottle of Crozes Hermitage and an immaculate bunch of summer flowers, all white and elegantly wrapped.

'How are you?' He kissed her on both cheeks. He was wearing black trousers and a black jacket over a white T-shirt, and he smelt clean and newly shaved.

'Good, good, thanks.' She accepted his offerings and went in search of a suitable vase. 'There's some champagne in the fridge,' she called out. 'Would you do the honours?'

She'd laid the table outside and on one side placed two champagne glasses beside a bowl of pistachios. He followed her inside for a teatowel, and then expertly and efficiently popped open the cork.

'Are we celebrating something?'

'Yes, we are.' She carried the vase out to the table. 'My book deal. It finally came through.'

His face lit up. 'Congratulations,' he told her. 'I knew you could do it.'

'With your help.' She laughed. 'Let's not forget that, now.'

They clinked glasses, looking into each other's eyes. She

didn't like to remind him that not making eye contact meant seven years' bad sex, or so she'd heard, but had no need to anyway. Perhaps he'd heard that already? Or, more likely, he was just one of those people who simply knew all the right things to do; the sort she could take anywhere, introduce to anyone.

'I never get tired of this view, you know?' she told him as they stared out across the horizon. 'The lushness, the greenery. It's funny how when you walk down the lane a bit all these secret houses pop out from behind the hills. The view changes from wherever you are.'

'Mine is rather dominated by your cottage,' he admonished her, although she knew this wasn't strictly true. He'd have to walk to the edge of his garden before he felt remotely dominated. 'And, of course, your delightful kitchen garden.'

'Not to mention the washing line!' Lia laughed.

'Yeah, right, were they your bloomers I saw hanging out there the other day?' He turned to her. 'The voluminous pink ones?'

She giggled, enjoying how he teased her. His was a boyish sense of humour, she thought, which made him seem all the more approachable and all the less a wife-beater. So why hadn't he been snapped up yet, she wondered? What was he doing on holiday alone? Was it the pressures of work that kept him single, perhaps, as well as all that travelling?

The bottle almost finished, Lia returned to the kitchen, where she checked on the lamb and the red mullet fillets in their gently bubbling sauce. Satisfied that everything was ready, she served the first course as Nick lit candles and a mosquito coil. He was so appreciative, she thought, taking a real interest in everything from her book deal to the ingredients in her starter, acting as if everything she said was the most interesting thing he'd ever heard. How could this man be free, she kept asking herself, wondering if there mightn't be girls in Hong Kong, London and New York who all felt as unique and as special as she did now.

227

They'd finished the first course and Lia was just wrestling with the lamb when the phone rang. Without a word, Nick picked it up. 'Lia Scott's residence,' he answered, a wry smile on his face. 'Ah, Mrs Scott, how do you do? This is Nick Delaney here, and your daughter is in the process of cooking me a fabulous dinner. I believe she inherited her cooking skills from you?' With that, he'd taken the phone onto the terrace and continued the conversation out of earshot.

Lia had to laugh, knowing that her mother would be totally charmed, and probably have turned as pink as the lamb by now. She carried the dish out to the dining table and retrieved the phone.

'Mum, can I call you back tomorrow?' she asked quickly before hanging up, a look of mock irritation on her face. 'And she isn't Mrs Scott anyway, she's Mrs Fordham.'

He looked puzzled. 'How does that work out?'

'She remarried,' Lia said pointedly, as if he were being truly thick.

'And your dad, what happened to him?' Nick took over the carving, leaving Lia to pour out the wine and serve the vegetables.

'He left when I was eight. He was a pilot, and had been bonking stewardesses for years. Couldn't handle family life; wasn't particularly interested in his kids. He got a transfer to Dubai, and we didn't see him for ages.'

'Must have been tough.'

Lia shrugged. 'For my mother, certainly. But my brother and I, well, we just kind of adapted. I went through periods of really hating him, and then there were times when I thought he was pretty cool. He was an adventurer, you know, a bit of a daredevil. We'd get cards from the Rocky Mountains, or the Grand Canyon, or India – all these exotic places no one else's parents went to. He loved to travel more than anything. He never remarried – he'd just work and then take off somewhere. A true free spirit.'

'You still see him?'

228

She shook her head. 'He got interested in us again when I was about fourteen. I think he liked it that we were no longer kids, but could converse and were aware of things. I used to see him in London, and he'd take me to a show, and then somewhere nice for dinner. And then just as we were getting close again, the silly old bugger went and died on us. Had a massive heart attack.'

'I'm sorry.'

She sighed. 'It's a long time ago.'

'And your mother? When did she remarry?' He'd finished the carving now and was arranging the lamb on their plates.

'Are you really interested in all this?' She laughed, embarrassed to be talking about herself so much.

'Sure I am,' he told her. 'Because it's you. All this has made you the person you are.'

She smiled. 'She remarried a few years later. She was taking evening classes in small business management and Brian was the lecturer.'

'And he's a good guy?'

'Oh yes,' she said quickly. 'Not going to set the world on fire, but he's a great guy. Solid, dependable, utterly trustworthy and totally devoted. Just what she needed after my dad.'

'But you're not a hundred per cent?'

She had to admire his perception. 'He's just not the sort I'd want to end up with myself. I nearly did, once, with my ex in London, and that's what spurred me to come here. It's a terrible thing to say but I think I'm attracted to my dad's wild side, his lust for life, his refusal to sit still. It feels disloyal to my mum, but I can kind of understand why he had to go.'

As she said it, she remembered Jules's suggestion that it was Nick's wild side that attracted her; the very thought that he *could* be dangerous, or that he *might* turn on her.

'You have a wild side,' he was saying as she struggled with that thought. 'Of course you smother it with your

229

cooking and your kitchen garden and your gentle approach to life here, but I'm sure it's all there.'

'I have a fear of settling down, if that's what you mean,' she told him. 'A fear of convention, perhaps, of getting trapped with a mortgage and a husband and kids, and waking up one morning and thinking *where the hell am I?* That scares me. But I can't say living here feels particularly wild.' As she said it, she remembered Peaches' news. 'Actually, that's a bit of a sore subject at the moment,' she frowned, telling him about the impending retreat.

'You're kidding?' He looked aghast. 'Can she do that?'

'It was always a flexible arrangement here,' Lia shrugged. 'I mean, there's no contract or anything. I pay cash, and I believe I'm getting a good rate. It was always understood that I might have to leave in the summer, but as she hadn't said anything, I'd just thought I'd got away with it.'

'Take my place,' Nick suggested suddenly. 'I mean, I won't be there. I'm in New York next week, then Hong Kong. Then I figure I'll be back in New York before spending some time in London. The house'll be empty. I'd actually like a caretaker there – I'd feel more comfortable that way.'

'Nick, I don't know what to say.'

'Yes would suffice.'

'But, your house, I mean, are you sure?'

'Sure I'm sure. There's plenty of room, and a pool, and of course that way you get to keep an eye on whoever takes over your place – check they're watering the garden properly. You can use the car, too.'

'God, I wouldn't do that,' she said quickly. 'I'd be terrified of scratching it. But if you're sure about the house, then, wow, that's incredible.' Lia felt heady, giddy with delight. 'I'd love just to see it. I mean, I love it already from the outside.'

'Well, come up and see it tomorrow, and I'll show you around. I'm leaving Sunday.'

They clinked glasses again, their eyes looking firmly

into each other's, and this time Lia couldn't stop herself from leaning across the table and planting a kiss on his mouth. His hand reached up and stroked her cheek, and then her hair, pulling her towards him, kissing her firmly but tenderly, his other hand pulling her in towards him. Awkwardly she perched on the edge of her none-too-stable chair, not quite believing she'd started this.

'Tell you what, let's skip dessert,' he whispered, moving in towards her, stroking her hair, looking at her deeply with those dark and sexy eyes of his, catching her free hand with his own.

'Good idea,' she whispered, and they rose.

She felt giddy yet calm, excited but terrified, and he seemed to sense this, giving her that open, relaxed smile of his that released all her tension and forced her to smile back. Calmly she led him upstairs to the bedroom, defying the echoes in her mind urging her to be cautious, to keep her distance and not to become involved, and as they fell onto the bed together, she knew she was lost.

Chapter Thirty-five

The sun was suddenly streaming into her eyes, and Lia squinted through her fingers at the window to see Nick, fully dressed, pulling back the curtains.

'Get up, get up, it's a beautiful day.' He smiled at her. 'And too good to waste in bed.' He came over and kissed her gently, pushing the hair out of her eyes.

'I think I'd quite like to waste it in bed, actually,' she smiled lazily, remembering the previous night.

'Come on, come on, get up! Let's go to my house, we can pick up breakfast on the way. Then how about lunch in the mountains?'

'Oh Nick, what's the rush?' She wished he'd just climb back under the covers and hold her, but he was clearly impatient to get on. She groaned, climbing out of bed, but he was already out of the room, and she could hear the sound of plates being cleared away and water running from the kitchen tap. It was just eight o'clock. She pulled on some clothes, wishing he weren't quite so wide awake.

'Coffee?' He greeted her with a steaming mug as she entered the kitchen. She would have preferred tea, but didn't like to deflate his enthusiasm. 'Let me finish up here and then we can go to my house. I have a couple of calls to make and after we can take a drive to the mountains, if you like.'

'Sounds great,' she said weakly, watching as he washed up the dinner things from last night.

'You sit on the terrace,' he told her. 'The sun'll do you good. Juice?'

She nodded meekly and he brought some out to her. She felt as if her life, her routine, was suddenly being snatched away from her, and that perversely, she was rather enjoying it. He could make all the decisions, she thought lazily, and all she'd have to do was turn up. She finished her coffee and went upstairs to wash and put on some make-up, and by the time she'd returned, the kitchen was clean and tidy.

'Ready to go?' He beamed at her, clearly proud of his efforts and she smiled. Just over a week ago she'd tried to imagine him as they chatted on the phone, whether he would be dressed or not, shaved or stubbly, drinking coffee or tea. Now she knew he was a coffee man, and would almost certainly have been up and dressed for hours. You didn't get rich lazing around in bed, she told herself crossly, as if she herself should have been up at six every morning and at work by half past.

They sped off down the lane towards the village, stopping off to buy a *banette* and some croissants, before turning into the parallel lane above hers and driving along to his house. The view was familiar yet different, being several metres higher, and she looked out between the trees for a sign of Les Eglantines. Then he pulled over to the right and an electric gate opened; he swung into the gravel drive fringed with terracotta pots.

'It's lovely,' she whispered admiringly. 'It's such a beautiful house.'

He unlocked the front door, which led into a spacious entrance hall with pale terracotta tiles and soothing grey washed walls. It was decorated sparsely with two oil paintings and an antique sideboard, on which stood two candlesticks. The hall led through to the drawing room, which was large and white, with a cream marbled floor, high arched ceilings and a large alcove in which two white sofas and some easy chairs waited to be filled. On the floor lay three battered rugs, and a fourth hung on one wall. Otherwise, the walls were decorated not with paintings, but with Moroccan-style plates. It was large, beautiful and untouched, and Lia couldn't help but feel she was more in a gallery than a home.

'Elodie, my ex, had a thing for Morocco,' Nick explained.

To the left was a dining area in a soft apricot-coloured wash, with richly coloured silk cushions scattered on antique French chairs in each corner. A large rectangular table dominated the room, with eight chairs tucked in underneath.

'As you can imagine I use this room all the time,' he laughed, and she got the impression he didn't like it at all. 'Come see the kitchen.'

Through an archway on one side was another large white space with arch-shaped alcoves full of wooden platters and presumably Moroccan artefacts. Instead of being fitted, the kitchen was more random, with open white stone cupboards full of utensils, a large white sink, mosaic tiled table, an American-sized fridge and a cavernous Aga-like oven.

'It's beautiful,' Lia told him. But was it practical, she wondered.

'She had a good eye,' he agreed, spooning coffee into a machine and pouring in some water.

He led her upstairs to his study, which had clearly become the room he used the most. Dominated by an oversized desk which was comfortably cluttered with papers, files, a laptop and a printer, the room had clearly escaped Elodie's determined eye. An enormous battered leather armchair she would surely never have approved of was pointed at a wide-screen TV and video unit, and Lia imagined that it was here that Nick spent his evenings, studiously ignoring the splendours below.

234

'I've got a couple of calls to make, so why don't you explore? The bedrooms are through there,' he said, nodding in their direction, 'and there are a couple of bathrooms.'

Lia left him, not wanting to eavesdrop or get in the way. There were three bedrooms – the first, which had twin beds, had pale-cream walls and a rush matting floor cover. It was bare apart from a rattan chair on which were two cream cushions. Clearly it was unfinished, as if all work had been disrupted when Elodie left, and Lia couldn't help but wonder if she hadn't walked out of Nick's life abruptly, and why. The second room was smaller, and it, too, looked bare and unfinished, with one small bed and a chair in it.

The rooms shared a single bathroom, with a loo, bidet, basin and stand-up, glass-fronted shower. She noticed Nick's shaving things and washing products, and they felt oddly intimate.

Next she came to the master bedroom, which overlooked the garden and the hills leading down to the sea, and was still in that warm soothing cream, with the rush matting floor. His bed was large, and covered in beige and cream bed linen, and on either side were two tall bedside tables each with its own lamp. No photos, she noticed, no personal touches, and little warmth.

One wall was made up of fitted wardrobes, and Lia was relieved to see how his clothes were hanging messily off their hangers, and how some had fallen off altogether. It was a comforting reassurance that someone did live there occasionally, and that the house wasn't altogether unloved.

To one side was another bathroom, which had two bowl-like basins standing upon a stone frame, each with its own tap and Moroccan-looking mirror. Between them stood an empty vase, waiting for the woman's touch that had long left this house. A thick piece of material hung down from the frame, and Lia couldn't resist peeking behind it, but instead of the perfumes and bath oils and womanly things she half-expected to see, all she found were clean-ing products.

235

It was as if they had been exorcised from his life, his late wife and Elodie. Carefully and methodically removed, so that not a trace was left behind.

'So, how are you doing?' His voice called out behind her and she jumped, taking in the immaculate white bath in one corner with a generous surround for all the bath products that had been purged out of sight. 'I prefer the shower,' he told her, as if reading her mind.

'Why do I get the feeling that women have designed this house for you and then left you to get on with it by yourself?' Lia asked.

'That obvious is it? Come on, the coffee must be ready by now.'

He led her back down the stairs to the kitchen, where the smell of fresh coffee was intoxicating, emptied the bag of croissants into a wicker basket and prepared a tray with mugs, plates and milk. Through the kitchen door they entered his garden with its elegant lawn studded with the occasional cypress and palm trees. To the west was a swimming pool surrounded by teak sunbeds. They sat in the shade of an olive tree at another mosaic table. To one side he'd cleared the stiff metal chairs which had presumably accompanied it, and had replaced them instead with comfier teak ones.

'It's a beautiful house,' Lia repeated. Beautiful, but unloved.

'Needs more work, but we're getting there.' He poured her some coffee and she broke into a croissant, enjoying the rich flakiness of the pastry.

'What happened to Elodie?' she asked, persuading herself that having slept with him now, she did have a right to know.

'We broke up last year. I was travelling all the time and we started seeing less and less of each other. It was tough.'

'So where is she now?'

'Paris, I think,' he said doubtfully. 'So what about you?' He changed the subject. 'I know you left someone in the UK, but has there been no one since?'

'No, there was someone,' she started, and he shifted in his seat. 'A guy called Ben. A photo journalist, he stays at Les Eglantines from time to time.'

'Another of Peaches' disciples?'

She smiled. 'That was the expression he used. He'd been through some difficult experiences, as you can imagine. We had a – fling, I suppose you'd call it. Just a couple of months.' Eleven weeks and four days, she thought, but who was counting?

'And how did that end?'

'He started seeing someone else down here. An old flame.'

They fell silent for a moment, and in that silence Lia could remember being with Ben, and the easy silences they shared – the ready laughter, the happy times, and a part of her felt immensely sad. How she would have enjoyed spending the summer with him, she thought, a little guiltily. How much she'd looked forward to a proper future together.

'So, do we go to the mountains?' Nick asked, brushing croissant crumbs off his shirt.

'I'd love to.' Out of habit, she checked quickly inside her bag. 'Damn,' she tutted. 'I've forgotten my sunglasses – how stupid of me.'

'Do you want us to stop off and pick them up?'

'I can't believe I did that,' she said laughing. 'It's still too early for me.' She peered down the hill from the garden which overshadowed her own. 'I wonder if I can take a short cut?'

'Let's give it a try.' He leapt up, throwing his napkin onto the table, before leading her through the garden, past the pool and some pine trees to an overgrown border which apparently belonged to no one, and from where she could see her own kitchen garden. There was a steep decline covered in boulders and weeds, and he led her by the hand, guiding her on where to place her feet next, easing her down the tougher slopes. Laughing, giggling, she followed him, feeling like an intruder, all the time hoping not to

237

disturb anything sinister in the long grass, which he beat with a stick he'd found along the way. Halfway down they rested under a gnarled olive tree, her own cottage tantalisingly close.

'You OK?' he asked her.

'Of course I am.' She laughed, and he leant forward and kissed her. It was the only reminder she'd had yet of their night together, and it came as a relief to be touched again.

They carried on their descent until they were at the fence backing onto Peaches' land, and Nick eased open some loose slatting until Lia could squeeze through and was inside her own garden. It felt strange to be approaching the pink cottage from that angle – she felt as if she didn't belong there and was seeing the place for the first time.

She opened the door and retrieved her sunglasses from the dining-room table. Then she locked up again and joined him at the fence, laughing nervously, as if she were doing something wrong. As they began their ascent, he'd climb ahead and turn to help her up a particularly steep part; gradually, after a few slips and much laughter, they made it.

Having cleared away the breakfast things they climbed into his car and drove off, through the surrounding winding lanes until they turned into the Route de Napoleon and started to climb, higher and higher, where the terrain changed and instead of oleander bushes and geraniums, the air was filled with the scent of heather and wild rosemary, juniper and thyme. They passed villages and small towns, and even signs pointing towards ski slopes, and Lia sat back, enjoying her mystery tour of a different Provence altogether from the one she knew.

'You happy?' he asked as they came to the magnificent Gorge du Verdun, and got out to admire the view.

'Yes, I am,' she beamed. Happy and terrified and thrilled and anxious all in one, she realised. But was she entirely relaxed, at ease, comfortable in his company?

Now that was a different question altogether.

Chapter Thirty-six

Nick left for New York the following day. Lia had to be out of the pink cottage by the end of the week, and so spent much of the time concentrating on what she needed to take and what could be stored in Peaches' cellar. He'd left her a key to his house and self-consciously she visited it a few times, trying to judge how much of her household belongings she needed to take. The kitchen was well stocked with herbs and spices, she noted, and a few basic supplies, not to mention all kinds of tins and packets that were now well past their sell-by date.

She couldn't help but wonder, going through it all, what kind of woman Elodie must have been. An interior designer with a passion for Morocco – a bit precious, perhaps, leaning towards the neurotic? Inclined to exaggerate, possibly, a bit of a fantasist, like Chloe? How much easier it was, she thought guiltily, to implicate her rather than believe the worst of Nick.

In London she used to build mental pictures of her fellow supermarket shoppers from the goods they had chosen, working out whether they were single or married, planning a dinner party or a quiet supper, or whether they were having the grandchildren round for the weekend.

Each basket and trolley told a story, she'd find, sometimes wondering what on earth her own implied. Now she found herself doing the same thing with the products gathering dust in Nick's kitchen, and wondering if they might hold the key to Elodie's personality.

There were couscous packets, bulghur wheat, basmati rice and lentils, tins of tomatoes and flageolet beans, and bottles of all kinds of flavoured olive oils. So had she been a great cook? A health-conscious one, by the looks of things, with a fascination for the East, but perhaps she'd been a bit obsessive. All over the house Lia looked for clues, trying to find another reason for Elodie's downfall other than the one she most feared. She was tempted to go through the files and drawers in Nick's study in the hope of finding a photo, but resisted that – it was one thing to build up an intuitive picture from a packet of couscous, quite another to go snooping into his personal things.

She was temporarily distracted one morning by an e-mail from Clive, her librarian friend, telling her he'd found the tape she was after, and was thrown into doubt once again about the wisdom of pursuing her hunch. The last thing she wanted was to upset Peaches, and she told herself that just because she had the tape, it didn't mean she actually had to show it to her. And it might not even be her daughter, she kept thinking; it could just be a cruel coincidence. She would have to be sure, of course, as she couldn't put Peaches through all that for nothing. There would have to be something that assured her – a resemblance or some mannerism she recognised – before she'd ever consider showing her the tape.

The day before she was due to move out, Lia was packing up the last items in her kitchen when Chloe appeared for a chat.

'So where are you staying then, for the next couple of weeks?' Chloe asked, blowing hard on her coffee.

'At a friend's,' Lia told her uncomfortably. 'Not far away. What about you? Do you get to stay on?'

'No, she's kicking us out and all, and I'm even taking

some of the classes. We'll stay at Etienne's.'

'So how's it all going, then? Has Peaches got a good timetable organised for the group?'

'Yeah, the usual stuff.' Chloe sounded bored by it all. 'Dawn meditation followed by an hour's yoga, then poolside breakfast, followed by dream analysis and classes with Peaches. Mondays and Wednesdays it's astrology, Tuesdays and Thursdays reincarnation and exploring the soul, Fridays – I forget what it is on Friday, crystal healing or something. Then a salad lunch followed by either past life regression with Felix or massage with me, or otherwise they're free to do whatever they want.'

'So you'll be doing massages, will you?' she asked, wondering if she dared delve any more into Elodie's past. It was becoming an obsession with her, this need to disprove Chloe. 'You know I've been thinking about what you said about Elodie, Nick Delaney's ex-girlfriend.'

'You met him, didn't you?' Chloe interrupted her. 'Peaches told me.'

'Yes I did, he helped me out with my laptop. He seemed like a nice person, and not the sort to do something like that.'

'I wouldn't trust him as far as I could throw him, myself,' Chloe insisted.

'But what I'm thinking –' to her relief Lia had suddenly thought of a point – 'is that if she was covered in bruises, then surely the last thing she'd want was to be massaged. I mean, wouldn't that be painful?'

Chloe's expression changed. 'You're seeing him, aren't you?'

'No,' Lia turned away, ashamed. She was beginning to regret having started the conversation, but was on a downhill slope now and couldn't stop herself.

'You are, too, aren't you? I can tell. Lia! For God's sake be careful.'

'I know, I know, I'm sorry. Believe me, I'm haunted by what you said. I just can't reconcile the man you spoke about with the one I now know, that's all.'

241

'He's creepy, that's what he is,' Chloe shivered. 'So smooth.' Her tone changed. 'You haven't, you know, have you?'

'*Chloe!*' Lia tried to look shocked.

'Just watch yourself with that one, that's all. He's got a temper, I know he has. I saw the bruises.'

'But are you sure? I mean, why would she want to advertise them? Maybe she just fell over or something?'

'No,' Chloe sounded definite on that point. 'She never fell. He punched her and he kicked her, but she never fell. I think her coming to me was like a cry for help. A lot of people look to me that way – they tell me all sorts. We used to talk about what she should do. She was terrified of him by the end.' The tears started welling in Lia's eyes, and Chloe softened. 'Look, I know you don't want to hear this,' she continued. 'And I know you've had a hard time, what with Ben and all that, but please don't get involved. Not with him. Please don't.'

'What if he's changed?' Lia said desperately, feeling an idiot the minute she'd said the words.

Chloe laughed. 'He won't change. He started taking therapy, Elodie told me, somewhere in Cannes, but it didn't do much good.'

'I don't know what to believe,' Lia told her. 'With me he's been nothing but lovely and supportive. He's warm, he's considerate, he makes me laugh. It's hard to turn someone like that away.'

'That's exactly what Elodie used to say.'

Lia sighed. She'd been hoping for Chloe to have her doubts, to say something she could immediately disprove, but all the conversation did was confuse her. 'What was she like, Elodie?'

'Mid thirties, attractive, long dark hair, stylish – she was an interior designer, went to Morocco a lot, and India.'

'Do you know how they met?'

'Not really, it was a couple of years after his wife died. I think they were introduced through friends.'

242

'She had a big hand in putting his house together, didn't she?'

'Yeah, I think she did. I never saw it, but I can imagine it's beautiful. That's where you're staying, isn't it?' Chloe turned on her again. 'Lia, you're mad.'

'He won't even be there; he's just letting me use it for a couple of weeks. Then I'll move back into the pink cottage and everything will be the same again.'

'Look, I can't live your life for you, but all I can say is keep your distance.'

Lia laughed miserably. It was a bit late for that. 'Any word from Bella?' she asked, just to torture herself even more.

'I think she's due back in September, when they start working on her house again. I think she'll just stay here until she can move in. And I've got a feeling Ben's been in touch,' she added quietly. 'I think he wants to spend a week or two here, if Peaches doesn't have any other guests.'

'Good,' Lia felt flattened and demoralised.

The phone started ringing, and Chloe excused herself, dumping her half-finished coffee onto the dining table. Lia picked up the receiver.

'You didn't move in, yet then?' It was that velvety smooth voice.

'Not yet – tomorrow,' she answered breathlessly. 'Where are you calling from?'

'My hotel room, Manhattan.'

'It must be awfully early.' Lia looked at her watch.

'It is, I couldn't sleep. I kept thinking of you, and whether you were lying in my bed right now.'

'Afraid not,' she laughed awkwardly. 'Just packing up the kitchen.'

'I wish I was there, helping you,' he said softly and her knees almost gave way.

'I wish you were, too,' she told him, realising how much she meant it, and how much she wanted Chloe's warning to disappear from her mind.

She leaned against the doorway as he spoke, telling her about his meetings and the restaurants he'd been to, and she thought of how she could listen to that voice all day, and how much she wanted to be with him right now; how she wanted to hear that Elodie had been difficult, and that someone in the village had had a vendetta against him, and how much she wanted to be certain that he was the kind, considerate, loving man she felt he was, and not the monster she feared him to be.

Because in their every conversation that fear stayed inert, refusing to budge, and all she could hope was that somewhere, in that beautiful house of his, she might just find the clue she was so desperately looking for.

Chapter Thirty-seven

She moved in that weekend, her bags of familiar items uncomfortably cluttering up the beautiful space Elodie had left behind. Most of her belongings were in Peaches' care, and before moving out they'd changed the bedclothes together, and Lia made sure that the bathroom and kitchen were clean.

'I can't tell you how embarrassed I am to do this to you,' Peaches kept saying as she tucked in the sheets. 'It won't happen again, I promise. And I'll make it up to you somehow.' Her eyes lit up. 'I know, how about a ten per cent discount for next month?'

'Fine, Peaches, I really don't mind,' Lia replied, thinking how ten per cent would hardly begin to cover the inconvenience. 'Actually, there is one thing,' she remembered. 'Could you call me if there's any post? Only I'm expecting a package.'

'Why of course, dear,' Peaches smiled. 'If I weren't so busy with the class I'd bring it up myself and have a good snoop around,' she giggled.

Lia packed up the car and drove to Nick's house, where she found a man cleaning the pool. Nick had warned her that, as well as the cleaning lady, a man called Bernard came twice a week for the pool and garden, so she introduced herself, wondering how long it would take for word to get round that Nick had a pretty blonde English girl staying.

He'd told her to sleep in his room, and she unpacked her clothes, finding space for them in his wardrobe. Then she laid out her toiletries in the bathroom, filling the empty shelves and the bath surround with her most luxurious of products – jasmine oil, lavender and rose bubble baths and some camomile-scented hair products.

Not liking to invade the privacy of Nick's study, she set her laptop up in his dining room. It looked onto the west side of the garden, and in the afternoons she'd open the windows and enjoy the light flooding in. At night she'd have supper under the olive tree, noting with dismay how much darker it was getting. In a couple of months the clocks would be going back and before long it would be winter again. She'd have gone full circle in so many ways, she thought, most certainly emotionally. Could she ever recapture that sense of bliss she'd had when she first arrived, she wondered, or had that gone for ever?

At night she'd slink into Nick's bed and read for a while. She'd already peeped into either bedside table drawer, looking for clues. There had to be photos, surely? Wouldn't he have kept something? But all she'd found were a few coins and a paperback. Then she'd turn off the light and try to sleep, all the time listening out for a sound – a key in the lock, perhaps, or his footsteps on the stairs. Again, she didn't know whether to be excited or terrified.

A few days into her stay Peaches rang. 'I have that package for you, dear. I could bring it round later, if you like? We've given ourselves the afternoon off, and the girls have all gone to Nice, shopping.'

She arrived after lunch carrying a jiffy bag which, Lia recognised, contained the tape she'd requested. She left it on the dining table, wondering how Peaches would feel if she only knew its contents.

246

'Oh my, isn't this place fabulous?' Peaches clucked, exploring every alcove and every piece of Moroccan earthenware.

'A bit unloved, though, don't you think? It was Elodie who put it together, and I don't think he likes it very much.' This didn't deter Peaches, who continued scuttling from one room to another, picking pieces up admiringly and exclaiming softly to herself. 'Did you know Elodie, or his wife?' Lia asked carefully.

'Not his wife, dear, no, she died before I even knew Nick. But I met Elodie several times, very charming girl, very attractive. Not as much as you, of course,' she added hurriedly.

'You don't have to say that.' Lia laughed. 'That's not why I was asking. No, I just wondered what she was like, that's all. I mean, it's odd being here, in what was effectively her house, without ever having met the woman.'

'Well, she didn't live here all the time – she spent most of it in Paris. They had to gut this place first, and then rebuild it. And they did a marvellous job, didn't they? I mean, look at this magnificent space.'

'Do you think they were happy?' Lia tried.

'Happy, dear? Why, I think so, but you never know, do you, what goes on behind closed doors?'

Lia flinched. That was exactly the kind of answer she'd been afraid of.

'Oh my, is that the time?' Peaches gasped. 'I have to go back and prepare for tomorrow's numerology class. It's such a nice group, you know. Very intuitive, very open to our teachings. Totally committed.'

Lia imagined Peaches' students filling their shopping bags in Nice and wondered how true that really was.

Once Peaches had left she made some wild berry tea and took the package from *Staying Alive* up to Nick's study. Carefully she studied the remote controls of his TV and video, not wanting to disturb any of the settings, and eventually she got both machines working. She slotted the video in, and pressed play, and then fast forwarded through the

station clock and opening titles, stopping at the beginning
of the show.

'Today we're meeting women who can't forgive,' Sara
started earnestly. 'Have you been wronged, betrayed, hurt,
and find it hard to forget? Let's meet our studio guests.'

Lia forwarded through, remembering that the woman
she believed to be Peaches' daughter was a member of the
audience. She tried to picture her, but could just remember
the badly dyed hair. Didn't she have thin lips, and bags
under her eyes? What had she been wearing – brown,
beige?

She paused the tape as the attention was given to
members of the audience: a black woman wanting to ask
one of the guests a question, a grandmother offering
support to another, and then a woman stood up, carefully
taking the microphone, and began to talk. Could that be
her? It was strange how differently Lia had remembered
her, how false her memory had become. She had orange
gold hair that had been layered around her face, but which
had grown out, and needed a trim. Her eyes looked green
and certainly had bags under them, but she was wearing a
pink top, which was at odds with her hair, and wore a long
string of beads around her neck.

But the cheekbones, she'd forgotten all about her cheekbones – they were Peaches' all right. And there was
something about her mouth, the way it set when she wasn't
talking that reminded her of her friend, too. She watched,
appalled, as the woman – who *had to* be her – explained
what had happened to her daughter, watched as the camera
cut to the reactions of members of the audience – a woman
brushing a tear here, someone else covering her mouth in
shock there. Once she'd finished her story, Sara asked,
'Do you still have any kind of relationship with your
mother?'

'Absolutely not,' she replied. 'I changed jobs, moved
state, found a new life, and I will *never* see that woman
again.'

'And how long ago did all of this happen?'

248

'Almost twelve years now.' Lia paused the tape, calculating, before realising that the show was probably a couple of years old.

There was a collective intake of breath from the audience. 'Twelve years,' Sara repeated, looking around the studio. 'Twelve years with no contact whatever? And how do you think your mother feels about that?'

'I don't know – bad, I should imagine. But I can't do anything about that.'

A woman in the audience shot up her hand: 'You don't think your mother's been to hell and back enough with all this?' Others applauded quietly in agreement. 'You don't think she at least has a right to know where you are?'

'Maybe she does, but, don't forget, because of that woman my daughter died. I can't forgive her for that.'

Sara took over again. 'Would you ever consider writing to your mother, at least letting her know you're still alive?'

'I don't know. I could, I guess, but—'

'Can you not, somewhere deep in your heart, find some sympathy for her?' Sara tried. 'It was an accident, after all, and one she must have paid for terribly over the years.'

'Yes I do have sympathy,' the tears had started rolling down the woman's cheeks. 'I do care about her, I do. But I've moved on with my life now, and seeing her would just make me think about the past all over again.'

There was a hushed understanding from the audience and calmly Sara turned to the camera and said, 'We're speaking to women who can't forgive. We'll be right back after these messages.'

Lia fast forwarded through the rest of the tape but the woman said nothing else, and her plight wasn't referred to again. She knew at once she had to show the tape to Peaches. Although much of what she'd said was painful, at least she admitted to still caring about her mother. That much, along with the very fact that she was still alive, or at least was a couple of years ago, would surely bring Peaches some comfort.

But how to approach her? She'd wait until the group had

249

left, of course, and then delicately explain what had happened, how she'd remembered a snatch of the programme, got hold of the tape. Would she watch it with Peaches or leave her alone? No, that would be cruel – surely she'd have to stay. Did Peaches even have a video? She tried to picture the room, tried to place where the TV was, whether she'd ever noticed any videos lying around.

Lia sipped her tea thoughtfully. The tape brought back so many memories – of her working life and her times with Jonathan. How was he doing these days, she wondered, and was he seeing anyone? To think all this had been nothing but a pipe dream once, and now here she was, having just been offered a book deal and staying in a luxury villa in the south of France. She'd had two lovers and made some interesting, if somewhat strange, new friends.

Suddenly she felt like a glass of wine, and went down to the kitchen to Nick's enormous fridge, in which there were about twelve bottles of rosé. He'd told her to help herself so she opened one and poured herself a glass, and then spent half an hour exploring the garden in the evening sun, pausing to dip her hand in the pool and to admire a beautiful white rose bush.

She made a quick bowl of pasta with pesto sauce and finished a second glass. She felt like talking to someone, to be cooking dinner for them and to chat and carry on drinking all evening. She couldn't concentrate on work now, or even on reading a book. She considered going online but didn't even feel like that. If only Nick were there, she thought, and they were working their way through a four-course meal, or he was suggesting supper out, and she could concentrate on dressing up and getting ready.

It was funny that it was only now that she'd had some company that she realised how much she'd been missing it. The house suddenly seemed huge and impersonal, and she felt like a little girl in her mother's shoes, awkward and out of place. Restlessly she picked up the phone and dialled Jules's number.

'There you are!' Her friend sounded exasperated. 'Didn't you get my e-mails?'

'No, I haven't been on-line today,' Lia admitted.

'God, you can be frustrating!' Jules laughed. 'Only I've booked a flight to come over – found a great last-minute deal. I wanted to see this bloke's fabulous villa for myself; couldn't stand the thought of you enjoying it there all by yourself. So I arrive tomorrow evening.' She gave Lia the details.

Lia was thrilled – this was just what she needed. With Jules she could discuss Nick and Peaches' tape ad infinitum. They'd have lots of day trips, Lia began to think, and visit more places that would be useful for her book. Jules had become a kind of boss, now, after all – that thought alone was quite odd – and so she mustn't be seen to be slacking. Now was a busy time. There were the lavender fields of the Valensole plateau to visit and the almond trees of Aix-en-Provence; the citrus fruits of Menton and the honey of the Massif des Maures – still so much research to be done, and how much more fun with a friend!

Suddenly lifted, Lia returned to her dining table work space and began making a list.

Chapter Thirty-eight

Lia picked Jules up at the airport and drove her to the village, pointing out places of interest in between the numerous phone calls.

'No, I'm in France, back Tuesday ... no I can't make Thursday, how about the week after?' Jules chattered into her mobile, ignoring the scenery outside, and Lia just wished she'd switch the thing off.

'You know you're here to relax,' she scolded her after the third call.

'I know, but I'm waiting for this guy to get in touch. I met him a couple of weeks ago, and the bastard hasn't returned any of my calls.' Jules started bashing out a text message.

'Look at that lovely hilltop village over there,' Lia said pointedly. 'They have their own vineyard, one of the last remaining independents around here. Who are you messaging now?'

'Him, just to let him know I'm here.'

'So, who is he, anyway?' Lia asked, turning off the main road towards the village.

'Someone I met at a club – bloody good looking. A lawyer. We got really pissed and ended up snogging outside the loos. Juvenile, I know, but he was gorgeous. He promised he'd call, he *promised*, but I haven't heard anything since. It's not fair, I mean, I've rung him a few times and left messages, but I never get anything back.'

'Isn't it time you just gave up?' Lia suggested, not believing she was hearing this. She could no longer imagine herself in a club, let alone kissing a stranger. 'Maybe he's got a girlfriend? Maybe he was a bit drunk and forgot himself? The last thing he wants is to be bombarded by phone calls – it makes you look desperate. Look, that's the village over there.' She pointed. 'And there's the turn-off to Les Eglantines. And now, this,' she said, turning left, 'is Nick's lane.'

'No chance of a drink anywhere, is there?'

'Too late, everything'll be closed by now, but there's plenty of wine in the house.'

Lia turned into Nick's drive and parked, before opening the front door and turning on the lights. If she was hoping to impress her friend, she couldn't have done so more easily.

'Talk about landing on your feet, girl,' Jules exclaimed on seeing the main room. 'This is incredible. I was expecting something more kitsch, you know – Greek-style pillars and marble flooring and big air con units all over the place, but this is beautiful.'

She rushed ahead, taking in the large drawing room. Lia could see her properly now. She looked as if she hadn't seen the sun in months and was wearing a floaty green skirt, chunky black high heels and a see-through hippy top. Her hair was pulled back into a loose knot from which several thick strands were escaping, and her nails were painted blue. The look was intrinsically London.

'I told you it was stunning.' Lia was enjoying her friend's admiration. 'Let me give you a tour.'

Jules's phone started ringing again and Lia had to wait a few minutes until she'd explained why she couldn't meet up later that night. She opened a bottle of wine and poured them both a glass.

'You only get this if you turn that damned thing off,' she said, holding Jules's glass back. 'It's annoying and disruptive, and you're here to get away from it all.' She was surprised first by the force of her own voice, and then by Jules's meek acceptance.

They took a tour around the dining room and kitchen, and then went upstairs to the bedrooms, where Jules deposited her belongings in the larger of the two guest rooms. Lia felt somewhat prim in her company – her clothes felt too sensible and her bare nails seemed to miss an opportunity – but although she admired Jules's boho-chic look, or whatever it was called, Lia knew it wasn't for her.

'You can tell which room he likes best.' She pointed out Nick's study.

'God, this is such a man's room, totally different from the rest of the house,' Jules observed, moving towards his desk. 'So where is he now?' Idly, she picked up a file and started flicking through it.

'Somewhere between New York and London, I think; his plans change all the time.' Lia watched her warily.

As if unimpressed, Jules replaced that file and picked up another. 'So, tell me what he does again?' Lia tried to explain but could see Jules wasn't listening. 'Shit,' she whistled. 'Have you seen these bank statements?'

'Will you stop that!' Lia wrestled the file from her hands and replaced it on the desk. 'Who the fuck do you think you are? You're a guest in his house, for Christ's sake!'

'He left them lying around, didn't he? So that means he's got nothing to hide.'

'No, it means he trusts me. How *dare* you?'

'I'm sorry,' Jules said huffily. 'I didn't mean any harm.' She followed Lia downstairs. 'Oh well,' she joked, 'they say you're only seriously rich when you owe your first million.'

Lia didn't react. She was too busy feeling angry – irrationally, she knew because Jules had just learnt something about Nick that she herself hadn't known. She watched as

254

her friend sprawled herself out on to a sofa and lit a cigarette, and willed her not to spill any wine or ash on the
cushions.

'So, if he didn't have all this –' Jules waved her arm
around wildly '– this house and the car, would you still like
him?' she asked.

'Of course I would,' Lia told her. 'Though I admit the
trappings are a nice bonus. But he himself is much more
than a house and some nice furnishings.'

'So, there's no way it's a rebound thing?'

'Rebound? No, of course not. I was getting over Ben,
you know.'

'You were? I once dated someone for three months and
it took me about four years to get over him.' Jules drew on
her cigarette, and Lia realised she must have already drunk
quite a bit on the plane.

'Perhaps having met Nick so soon after Ben has helped,'
she conceded. 'But I do still think of him a bit. He's due
back, actually, sometime soon – with Bella, no doubt. But
it doesn't bother me as much as I thought it would. So, you
see? I'm moving on.'

'Well, you're better off with this one, aren't you? I
mean, he's not about to get himself killed *and* he's got a
fuck-off house. What did Ben ever have?'

'Oh, he had a lot,' she countered, and in remembering
Ben's qualities, Lia began to realise that perhaps she was
still far from being over him. 'But he let me down,' she
finished. 'He really let me down.'

'Do you ever wonder –' Jules started, her eyes gleam-
ing, as if trying to catch her friend out '– whether Nick
was violent in the past, but is a changed man now because
of you? You know, that you've got something over the
others?'

'No, no, I don't,' Lia said indignantly, although she
could see what Jules meant.

'Nice thought though, that you could have tamed him. I
don't know, maybe I'm just getting desperate,' Jules
continued, finishing her glass. 'I can't believe he didn't

call me,' she added crossly. 'I can't believe I don't have a boyfriend. I mean, you came here for some peace and quiet and time to write, and you end up meeting two distinctly shaggable men; whilst I, who live in one of the world's greatest metropolises, can't get laid for love or money. How does that work out?'

'Maybe you should stop trying so hard?' Lia took their glasses to the kitchen, still reeling at the idea that perhaps she *did* think she could change Nick. 'Maybe you should stop fretting about it, and concentrate on having a nice weekend in the sun, instead? Let's get some sleep, then tomorrow we'll walk to the baker's and have a swim before breakfast. And then we could explore some of the neighbouring villages, if you like. There should be a market on.'

'Bloody quiet here, isn't it?' Jules stumbled up the stairs towards her room. 'Don't know if I'll be able to sleep all right. Any night clubs, discos locally, then?'

'Just the bar tabac,' Lia told her. 'We can go and flirt with the old boys, if you like. Find a couple that have still got their own teeth.'

'That's the only kind of man who'll have me at the moment,' Jules yawned lazily, tumbling into her bedroom. 'I love your wife-killer's house,' she cried out, closing the door behind her. 'And don't worry if he does turn bad – it's a miracle what you can do with make-up these days.'

Lia laughed, shutting the door behind her, but Jules had hit a nerve. Had she been kidding herself all along that Nick would treat her differently, that she was somehow superior to his wife and Elodie, that she would succeed where they had failed? What an ego trip that was. Lia shuddered, removing her make-up with a cotton wool pad and watching as her eyes became bruised with mascara.

She stood there for a second, staring at her reflection, before wiping them clean again.

Chapter Thirty-nine

The following morning they picked up some croissants from Hélène, Etienne's heartbroken ex-girlfriend, who stared in disapproval at Jules's blue nails, micro top and the chunky black heels that had threatened to send her tumbling to the uneven ground several times that morning.

Then they had a walk around the village, where Lia pointed out various sights and places of interest: 'It was around here that Ben and I first held hands ... this was the first restaurant we ever went to ... this is where he got his hair cut ... this is where I first met Nick.'

'You know, perhaps you should forget about doing your book and write a lovers' guide to France instead?' Jules suggested. 'You never know, it could catch on.'

As planned they had a swim and a stroll around the garden, where Lia showed her the pink cottage and they scrutinised its new occupants' laundry hanging on the line, dismissing them as has-been hippies as opposed to boho-chic hippies.

'I should take you to see Peaches, really,' Lia suggested. 'I'm sure she'd love to meet you. Only with all her classes and things, I'm not sure how much spare time she's got.'

'I think I can live without it,' Jules told her dismissively.

'Unless she's got some gorgeous son tucked away somewhere.'

'No, there's no son, just a daughter,' Lia said quietly, not wanting yet to go into her dilemma.

After breakfast they headed to a nearby town and strolled around the market stalls. Lia had never found anything she liked there before, but rather hoped that it would be here in the French countryside that Jules might find some outfit worthy of Top Shop. Jules, however, sniffed at everything she saw and it was Lia herself who ended up shopping, buying orange flower water and some almonds.

They had lunch in one of the many restaurants in the square and spent the rest of the afternoon back at Nick's house, flaked out beside the pool, a bottle of sparkling wine between them.

'So what do you think?' Lia suggested, feeling guilty at not having mentioned work yet. 'We take it easy this afternoon, hang out by the pool, and then perhaps go out this evening? I've got a few chapters I could show you and then tomorrow I thought we could drive into the hills and check out some places I've been meaning to visit.'

'Whatever,' Jules yawned, soaking up the sun in a minuscule geometrically patterned bikini. 'I'm just happy to chill out. London's got so bloody stressful, you know, it's just a relief not to be there right now.'

'So tomorrow I thought it might be good to visit this honey place in the Massif des Maures,' Lia continued. 'They make all these different types there: chestnut, strawberry tea, lavender, white heather. Of if you prefer, we could check out the lavender fields in the mountains. They should be harvesting them now. They do things like lavender puddings and sweets I thought might be interesting. I was looking on the map and I think it would take a good few hours to get there, though, so it depends on how energetic you're feeling.'

'Li, to be perfectly honest –' Jules snapped shut her book and lifted her sunglasses off her eyes – 'I hate to disappoint you but I really couldn't give a flying fuck about your heather-flavoured honey or your lavender sodding puddings. Sitting in my office, working on your book, well, yes, then maybe I'd find them all fascinating. But right here, right now, the last thing I want to do is go off on some dreary jaunt to watch someone harvesting bloody flowers. If we have to go out and about, then let's at least do something fun.'

'I thought that *was* fun,' Lia protested weakly, sipping her wine.

'God, you've been getting too much sun, lately. I don't know – where's all the glamour stuff? Doesn't Elton John have a place around here, and Joan Collins? How about some celebrity house-hunting? I'm kidding,' she added in exasperation at the look on Lia's face. 'No, I tell you what I want to do,' she said, waving her champagne flute around enthusiastically. 'Let's go to St Tropez! I want to pretend to be Brigitte Bardot and buy tiny bikinis and a sarong in the market, drink overpriced champagne and dance on tables in some trendy beach restaurant. I want to party until dawn and hitch a lift around the Med on some rich bloke's yacht or find myself in a dodgy casino at four in the morning without a clue where I am. Now *that* would be fun!'

Lia laughed – more at her own reaction than anything. Jules's idea of fun was her idea of a nightmare. 'St Tropez?' she groaned. 'It's a hell of a drive. I mean, the roads will be packed – it's a disaster once you get off the motorway. And on a Sunday? It'll take hours.'

'Oh come on, Li, what's happened to your sense of adventure? We'll have CDs on the stereo and can check out the guys in the jam. It'll be fun.'

'And parking? I don't even like to think about parking.'

'Li, what's happened to you? You're sounding like that boring ex-bastard boyfriend of yours. You've become such a little home-body. When did you last go out and do something wild? You're so obsessed with your little honeys and your lovely vegetables, you've forgotten what it is to be single.'

'Spending hours in a traffic jam is hardly my idea of having a wild single time.' Lia sighed, but her conscience was pricked. 'OK, we'll go to St Tropez, but I'll hold you personally responsible if my car conks out.'

'Your car?' Jules turned to her in surprise. 'Who said anything about your car? Didn't you tell me there's a fuck-off Merc waiting for us in that garage?' She topped up their glasses.

'Oh, there's no way—'

'And didn't you tell me that he said you could use it?'

'Yes, but then I told him I wouldn't. I just don't want that responsibility, and especially not down there, not on those roads.'

'OK, I'll drive it,' Jules said matter-of-factly, slipping her sunglasses back on and settling into her book. 'You did say that the insurance was covered, didn't you?'

'Yeah, but, there's no way ...' Lia stumbled, resenting her friend's cool confidence. 'Oh, OK, OK, I'll drive it,' she said in exasperation.

'Good, that's settled then.' Jules returned to her book, a triumphant look on her face, whilst Lia sighed grumpily, drained her glass and then slowly tumbled sideways into the pool with a splash.

'OK, Madge, Kylie, All Saints.' Striding down the stairs in her chunky black sandals, Jules flicked through her CDs. 'This lot should keep us going through the jams.'

They'd agreed on an early start to try to beat the traffic. Lia sipped her Earl Grey nervously, wondering how she would cope with Nick's car. She couldn't allow herself to look scared in front of Jules, however, knowing that she would only suggest taking over herself, which would make Lia feel truly wet. She locked up the house, unlocked the garage, and cautiously opened the driver's door. Inside, the leather interior reminded her of Nick – she was relieved he hadn't rung last night and that she hadn't been obliged to tell him what they were doing.

She started the engine, which purred obediently into life,

260

and then, her breath quickening, pulled it out of the garage and onto the drive, where Jules, in oversized purple sunglasses, floppy hat and a top the size of a handkerchief was waiting.

'Right, how d'you get the sunroof down?' she asked impatiently, climbing in.

Lia fiddled with a few knobs until slowly and smoothly the roof opened up. 'OK, here goes,' she whispered, slowly releasing the clutch and steering the car out of the drive, pausing to click the remote control which operated the gate behind her. They purred down the lane, enjoying the sensation of being up earlier than most church-goers, and she turned into the main road which led out of the village.

To her surprise, Lia found the car easy to drive, being far more responsive than her own. As she relaxed, so her speed crept up, and soon they were approaching the motor-way. The minute they turned into it, Jules leant forward and slotted the first of her CDs on the stereo, singing along to the music.

'This is the bloody life,' she called out as they swept past a Peugeot with two admiring men inside. 'You've got to marry this guy, you know Li, even if he is broke and beats you up! I want this lifestyle, I want a rich friend I can stay with on the Côte d'Azure!'

Lia just laughed, suddenly enjoying herself, and wondered why she'd ever been worried. The road down to Ste Maxime was slower, though, and by the time they had hit the coast the traffic had increased dramatically. Jules took this as an opportunity to turn the stereo up even louder and flirt with the other drivers, whilst Lia just worried about whether they would ever find a parking space.

'We'll come by helicopter next time,' Jules joked as they crawled into the town and passed the first full-up car park. With the second they had more success, and promptly headed for the shops. They spent an hour or so browsing before finding the market, where Jules insisted on buying a bikini that looked like it wouldn't fit a Barbie doll. Then

261

they strolled to the seafront and enjoyed a platter of *fruits de mer* and a bottle of rosé while watching the crowds go by.

'I'm in a bit of a quandary about Peaches at the moment,' Lia confided, when she'd had enough of staring at tanned, blonde nineteen-year-olds with bodies to die for, face-lifted septuagenarians with their tiny dogs and elegant couples who looked like they belonged in a Ralph Lauren advert. 'She told me this terrible story when I was so down about Ben,' she started, telling Jules about Peaches' daughter and the tape.

'I wouldn't get involved if I were you,' Jules shook her head, snapping the claw decisively off her crab. 'Forget you ever saw it and just stay out of it.'

'You think so?' Lia, whose every instinct was telling her otherwise, was surprised at her reaction.

'Why would you want to stir things up?' Jules waved her wine glass around demonstrably. 'She still won't know where her daughter is, so where's it going to get her?'

'She'll know she's alive, for starters,' Lia reasoned. 'And she'll hear that her daughter does care about her. I think that would be comforting.'

'I think it'll just reopen old wounds,' Jules continued attacking her crab.

'I doubt they've begun to close.' Lia picked at a prawn. 'But I feel I have this moral responsibility now, that if I don't tell her I'll be neglecting it.'

'Well, it's your call,' Jules dunked a piece of crabmeat in mayonnaise, shrugging. 'Personally I wouldn't touch it with a barge pole. Christ, look at that for an outfit!' She pointed at a hefty woman in a see-through black chiffon top and trousers walking past, and Lia knew the conversation was over. But she also knew that she didn't agree, and that she *had* to show Peaches the tape.

By late afternoon they'd found a tiny gap on the beach for their towels and had taken turns to go into the water. A couple started playing ping pong right in front of them and a man with a hairy back to their right smoked incessantly, and

Lia thought about how much she'd rather be beside Nick's lovely pool in his garden right now, reading a book and planning a leisurely supper.

In the early evening they had a drink in a bar overlooking the harbour. As Lia tried to chat, she could see Jules was more interested in making eye contact with any reasonable-looking male who appeared unattached, still hoping to be invited to a club or, better still, onto some yacht or other. Lia sipped her mineral water wondering how the return journey would be. She'd had little wine and was more than ready to leave, but feared that the traffic going out would now be at its worst. Which was the less repugnant alternative, she wondered: to hang around sipping mineral water whilst Jules flirted with dubious-looking characters all night, or to be stuck in traffic listening to CDs for the next two hours?

In the end, it was Jules who made the decision. 'OK, we're not getting anywhere here. Perhaps we'd better head for home?' She jumped off her bar stool a little unsteadily, and they took one final walk through the town towards the car.

The traffic leaving St Tropez was terrible, but nothing like as bad as that still coming in, and it was with a sense of relief that Lia finally turned onto the motorway and could put her foot down, gliding past most of the other cars. As Jules snoozed, Lia started to wonder how Nick would react about her using the car. It was as if she was pushing him, urging him to snap and reveal himself as the wife-beater he really was. But she couldn't imagine it. She couldn't imagine him turning on her, or being anything other than the wonderful man she'd now fallen for. Even her mother was in love with him, after all, and when it came to judging men, she was the most sceptical person Lia knew.

As they finally arrived at the village, Jules woke up and rubbed her eyes. 'So it's not dawn, then?' she asked.

'Half nine,' Lia told her.

'And we didn't dance on tables, or sneak onto some rich bloke's yacht?'

263

'Or wind up in a casino? No, I'm afraid not. Disappointed?' She turned into Nick's lane and searched for the remote control that unlocked the gate.

'Well, it was better than bloody lavender fields,' Jules insisted. 'And we've still got tomorrow.'

'God, I'll need a holiday after you've left,' Lia laughed, easing the car into the garage and switching the engine off. They retrieved their belongings and had showers before convening again in the kitchen.

'Hungry?' Lia asked, opening the fridge. 'I did this chicken thing the other day – it just needs heating up, and I can do some rice with it.'

'Great,' Jules said, not particularly interested. 'Could do with a drink, though.'

'There's some rosé in the fridge if you like, or I've got this bottle of red.'

Jules examined it, unimpressed, and pouted. 'Doesn't he have a wine cellar? I mean, surely everyone does around here?'

'Yes, he does, but I've never been in it,' Lia told her.

'Why not? Oh, don't tell me,' she exclaimed with delight. 'The missing girlfriend, that's where she's buried?'

'Stop!' Lia laughed. 'It's just a man's thing, I've never needed to go.'

'Where is it, through here?' Jules asked, pulling open a thick wooden door which led out of the kitchen and down some stairs.

'Jules, can you just *not* do something for once?' Lia snapped impatiently. 'I mean, can you show a little respect? I've got a perfectly good bottle of red here – now just leave his stuff alone.'

'It's a bit creepy,' came Jules's voice, ignoring her. 'I wonder if she is buried down here? Hmmm, how about a nice Margaux? Or a Hermitage?'

'Jules, stop it!' Lia called from the top of the stairs. 'Neither of us is expert enough to know what we're drinking. I mean, who knows, we might open something

264

unbelievably expensive? And let's face it, we're both tired and have had a bit already. We're not going to appreciate anything good.'

'Here we go,' Jules returned triumphantly. 'A 1991 St Emilion – that'll do.' She closed the cellar door behind her. 'Look, if he finds out, I'll replace it, OK? I'll write everything down on the label and track down another bottle, all right?'

Lia sighed, putting the chicken into the stove. How Jules could transform herself from the competent and successful editor she knew to this wild and reckless holidaymaker was beyond her. Jules busied herself with the bottle and found two large round glasses, pouring them generously half full, and then went outside to sit under the olive tree. Once Lia had put the rice on, she joined her.

'I often wonder how I'd get on doing a blind tasting,' she commented, sitting down. 'I mean, this is very nice, but I can't say it's blowing my socks off.'

She was aware of a car somewhere in the lane and thought nothing of it. But the distinctive sound of a key in the lock minutes later made her sit up straight. 'Oh, fuck,' she whispered heavily. 'It must be Nick, he's back!'

Jules giggled nervously at the bottle and the lavishly filled glasses. 'Are you sure it's him?'

'Well, funny old time for the cleaner to show up.' Lia got up and headed inside, to see Nick in the doorway, checking his post.

'Hey.' His face broke into a smile on seeing her, and she rushed into his arms. 'Where have you been? I've been calling you all day.'

'I went to St Tropez,' she told him nervously. 'What are you doing back so early?'

He turned away from his post. 'I was in London, it was raining non-stop, and I thought, "You know something, in a couple of hours you could be home with a beautiful sweet woman by your side, and tomorrow morning the sun will be streaming in through the window."' He hugged her tight. 'So, how was St Tropez?'

265

'It was fine, we just had lunch and a swim,' she told him.

'We?' he enquired as Jules walked in.

'Hi, you must be Nick,' she approached him, her hand outstretched. 'I'm Jules Neville, an old friend of Lia's, and now, of course, her editor. I hope you don't mind, but I came over to keep her company for the weekend.'

'Mind, hell no, not at all.' He smiled, shaking her hand. 'I'm glad to hear it. I hated to think of her getting lonely here.'

'And I have a terrible confession to make,' Jules continued, her confidence growing. 'I raided your cellar, and took a nice St Emilion, which I assure you I'll replace. Can I get you a glass?'

He laughed, approached the table with a look of mock worry on his face and examined the bottle. 'You know, the 90 is so much better,' he commented. 'This was kind of a mistake. Let me go fetch one.' He disappeared into the cellar and returned minutes later with another bottle. 'What's that cooking?' He sniffed the air, reaching for a corkscrew. 'And, more to the point, is there enough for me?'

'Of course there is,' Lia told him happily. This man was no wife-beater, she told herself. He was the most decent, generous, wonderful man she'd ever met, and she was totally and utterly in love with him. Seeing Jules's approval only made her feel this more strongly.

She laid the table and served dinner, and whilst they ate, was happy to sit back and let Jules grill him on everything from his business to his wine collection, watching her admiration grow with every new detail she learnt.

'So what's the agenda tomorrow?' he asked as they were finishing.

'Haven't got that far, yet,' Jules replied. 'Still a bit whacked after today, to be honest.'

'You get to Monte Carlo, yet? The casino, the Hotel de Paris?'

Jules's eyes lit up. 'Oh my God no, I'd love to go. I

266

wanted to find a casino in St Trop but Lia wouldn't let me,' she added, and Lia rolled her eyes.

'OK, let's do that tomorrow,' he decided, the matter settled.

'I'll need to put some petrol in the car,' Lia told him sheepishly, and he raised an eyebrow. 'I got persuaded.' She looked at Jules pointedly. 'Oh and I think we might have a left a Madonna CD in the stereo,' she giggled, feeling about fourteen.

'Bloody hell, Li, he's gorgeous,' Jules whispered admiringly as Nick excused himself to make a phone call. 'That Chloe girl doesn't know what she's talking about. He's totally bloody gorgeous.'

'He is, isn't he?' Lia agreed, revelling in her friend's approval.

And she was the one who'd be climbing into bed with him that night, she told herself. She was the one he'd be making love to – she, Lia Scott, was the one Nick Delaney wanted.

Chapter Forty

Nick, as usual, was up early the next morning and by the time the girls emerged for breakfast had laid the table with a selection of croissants, orange juice, hot coffee and fresh bread. Jules in particular was ravenous and tore into her *pain au chocolat*, dunking it into her coffee.

'So, what's the plan?' Nick started. 'If you've never been before, you've got to see the cathedral and take a walk around the old town. Maybe pick up lunch some-place. Then we can drive to Monte Carlo itself, and have a drink at the Hotel de Paris.'

'And gambling,' Jules interjected, her mouth full of croissant. 'Don't forget the casino – we've got to go gambling.'

Once they'd finished and Nick was starting the car, Lia, on a sudden impulse, offered Jules the front seat. It seemed the polite thing to do, as she was a guest, and it would also show how much she valued and trusted her two closest friends. She hadn't expected her to say yes, though.

Squeezed into the back seat, the CD player on and the wind racing through her hair, Lia could barely hear their conversation and felt left out, that child all over again, eavesdropping on the adults' conversation. She chastised herself for resenting Jules for having accepted her offer, when she needn't even have made it in the first place. She had foolishly been trying to prove something, and Jules had called her bluff.

It was just extraordinary how blatant her friend could be, though – letting her skirt slip higher up her thighs, her hair blowing flirtatiously around her face. Lia tried not to sulk, but was angry at herself. Every now and then Nick would call out 'You all right there in the back?' and make her feel even worse.

She kept remembering all the things Jules had done to irritate her over the weekend and wondered whether it might even be time to ease herself out of their friendship. What did she see in her, after all, if all she did was annoy her? But Jules was a life-enhancer, the one person guaranteed to make her laugh and was, for the most part, more entertaining than any of her other friends. So she had to take the whole package and get over it, she kept telling herself. And perhaps, in a strange way, she enjoyed the rivalry between them, enjoyed the challenge.

Nick parked the car and they had a quick walk around the boats before climbing upwards to Monaco itself, the older part of the principality, perched dramatically on the cliff side. They walked around the town, admired the Grimaldis' palace and dodged the little train which carried dozens of self-conscious tourists from one place of interest to another.

Inside the cathedral Lia paused at the candles as Jules raced ahead. 'You carry on,' she whispered to Nick. 'I just want to light one of these and have a chat with my dad. I usually do whenever I'm inside a church.'

Nick nodded and caught up with Jules, who was reading the tombstones of all the Grimaldis buried inside.

Lia lit her candle, shaking her head. *There I go again, Dad, pushing him closer to Jules,* she began her one-sided conversation. *Why do I do that? What is it that makes me want to torture myself? ... He's not evil, is he, Dad? Please don't be sitting up there thinking 'Oh God, what is she doing with that man?' He's a good person, please tell me he is ... Oh, and you know I got a book deal? Hardly big bucks, but it's a start. I love what I do, now, I really love it. I'm happy, Dad, I hope you are.*

She placed the candle in the centre, where the flame flickered, illuminating the air around it. *Imagine, Dad, me in Monaco! Wouldn't you be impressed?* She remembered her father affectionately. *You old rogue, Mum's so much better off without you, you know. Hope you're OK. Lots of love.*

With that, she left the candle and went to rejoin the other two.

'Look, this is where Princess Grace is buried,' Jules whispered. 'Such a beautiful woman, so sad.'

Nick paused, turning to Lia. 'Dad on good form?' he asked, and she loved him all the more.

They had pizzas in a pavement café before heading back down the hill and driving into Monte Carlo itself – the brassier, glamorous, flashier half of the principality. Its buildings were luxurious and modern and the shops all designer. Outside the casino Nick's Merc joined a row of Lamborghinis, Ferraris, fellow Mercedes and a Rolls-Royce, and the doorman graciously let them all in.

'Bit intimidating this, isn't it?' Jules whispered, taking in the marble pillars, vast chandeliers and the overdressed clientele. 'I mean, I don't actually have that much money on me.'

'Jules!' Lia cried. 'You're the one who's been banging on about casinos all this time! What do you mean you don't have any money on you?'

'You know something?' Nick interjected. 'I've got a better idea.' He led them to a different entrance where the slot machines were, hall upon hall of them, and the air buzzed with the sound of one-arm-bandits ringing and coins tumbling out. 'You get ten euros' worth each. OK?' he said, exchanging some notes for buckets of coins. 'First one to twenty buys champagne next door.'

Lia had never particularly done the slot machines before,

and found them strangely mesmerising. First she flirted around them, trying out different types in case one was ready to discharge its contents. She noticed other gamblers, though, staying with a machine until it did so and then moving on, and wondered if she shouldn't just choose her own. One woman, who must have been in her eighties but wore an obvious dark-brown wig, was hovering behind a man in the same row as Lia, as if waiting to pounce. When he finally left, she did, and was rewarded shortly afterwards with a tumble of coins to fill her already bulging bucket.

Lia tried to choose her machine intelligently, but settled instead on one which just felt right. Perhaps her dad was giving her a sign, she thought idly to herself, oblivious as to where either Jules or Nick had gone.

She lost a few, won a few and then lost a whole lot more, and her bucket was half empty when Jules appeared. 'Lost everything,' she told her. 'Let's have some of yours,' and grabbed a handful of Lia's coins.

'How's Nick doing?' Lia asked, rather defensively, having assumed that they'd be together.

'I dunno,' Jules shrugged, returning to her machine. 'I think he got a phone call.'

Lia carried on playing, looking all around for any sign of him. When her bucket was finally empty, she found Jules, who was playing her last coin.

'I was doing so well, I can't believe it,' she complained. 'Then I started losing and kept thinking *one more time, just play another*, and of course it just swallowed everything up. Damn. I'm having as much luck with gambling as I do with men.'

Nick appeared and appraised their buckets with scorn. 'I thought you girls would do better than that!' he mocked. 'Guess the champagne's on me, then.'

He changed his coins, which Lia suspected he hadn't used at all, and led them to the Hotel de Paris, where they sat in the bar and ordered a bottle.

'This is the life,' Jules sighed, stretching to pick up her glass, a cigarette in the other hand.

271

They chinked glasses but Lia thought she could see a worried look appear on Nick's face. He pushed it away, though, and turned to Jules. 'So? You enjoyed your day?'

'Loved it, thank you,' Jules gushed. 'I just can't believe I'm going back tomorrow. By lunchtime I'll be back at my desk thinking of you both under the olive tree having your lovely salads and your lovely cheeses,' she sighed.

'Well, if it makes you feel any better, tomorrow I have to negotiate with a partner who wants to sell up and a bank that's threatening to call in a loan, so I wouldn't be too envious if I were you,' Nick replied.

'Ouch,' Lia said, feeling for him but not wanting to go into it with Jules there. 'And I may well be starting my chapter on lavender-flavoured honey,' she joked instead.

Jules burst into raucous laughter. 'Oh God, please don't, she pleaded. 'Anything but that.' She turned to Nick. 'So don't you just hate fucking banks? I can't believe what mine did last year.' She began telling him all about it, her body turned towards him, starting an impenetrable conversation that Lia, now somewhat removed from them both, couldn't entirely hear.

Instead she watched people coming in and out of the foyer – immaculately made-up women in madly expensive clothing and their flashy, cigar-puffing husbands, and her mind began to wander. Had she ever contemplated, she wondered, when she was still living in Fulham and working for *Staying Alive*, that one day she'd be sipping champagne with a man like Nick Delaney in Monte Carlo? It didn't really feel like her, it *wasn't* really her – not her style, at all.

She was more at home in the village, or chatting with Peaches in her little cottage, snipping fresh herbs and sipping cheap plonk as a meal cooked. *With Ben* – the thought took her by surprise. That was where she felt most at home, with him around. And now where was he? Afghanistan, somewhere, but doing what, exactly? Heading for the opium labs again or concentrating on everyday life? It hurt her that she didn't have the first clue.

And where would he be living, and what kind of conditions would he be living in?

Suddenly the opulence of the hotel seemed strangely cruel; the extravagance of the guests' clothes ridiculous. The woman in the corner, there, she thought with indignation, her silk dress probably cost more than the average Afghan earned in one year, two, even. What was the point of sitting there drinking champagne which even Nick, apparently, actually couldn't afford? It was absurd. And what was the point in watching her best friend flirt with her boyfriend, oblivious of her own feelings? And how was Ben feeling now, and how would he be coping with it all?

'Oh, God, what a life you lead here.' Jules had suddenly turned back to her, downing a large swig of champagne. 'And it's all down to me, isn't it? I mean, the cottage, the deal, it's all thanks to me.' She was laughing but Lia caught an undertone of resentment.

'For ever in your debt, Jules,' she replied dryly, surprised to be hearing her own voice after so long. Jules was getting a bit drunk, she could see, and wasn't entirely in control. 'I'm already naming my firstborn after Nick, so I'll have to name my second after you, all right?'

'But you're happy here, aren't you?' Jules continued, ignoring her. 'I mean, it's all worked out for you since you arrived.' She lit another cigarette. 'You got rid of your boring boyfriend, you got a place with a view, got the deal you always wanted. You've been through two men since you got here—'

At this Nick raised an eyebrow.

'Jules!' Lia said urgently. 'I have not got through two men. I had one brief relationship with one and am currently seeing another, OK?'

'Well, good for you, that's more than I've had since you left. I'm so bored with being on my own.' Jules drained her glass and held it out for Nick to top up, which, obligingly, he did. 'I'm so sick and tired of it. I'm bored with going to the gym and being surrounded by other sad singles who look like they couldn't get a man if they tried. I'm so tired of getting on a train and looking around just to see if there's anyone hot in the carriage. Did you ever do that? There never is, of course – I just don't think they exist. And if they do, then I have no idea where to find them. I thought I might have the other week, but then he blew me out, didn't he?'

'You ever consider evening classes?' Nick humoured her.

'Oh God, whatever in?'

'Motor mechanics?' Lia smirked, enjoying how she and Nick seemed to be back on the same wavelength.

Jules scoffed. 'Just be full of other bloody spinsters trying to find a man.'

'Small business management?' Nick tried. 'It worked for Lia's mum.'

'Small business management?' Jules repeated huffily. 'What, and meet someone like Brian?'

'Nothing wrong with him,' Lia said defensively. 'Maybe this is your problem – you're only attracted to the difficult ones? The ones who let you down?' As she said this, she wondered if the same could be said of her.

'Yeah, I suppose,' Jules drained her glass again. 'Maybe that's exactly what I need – a stable, steady type. Keep me in check. You know, I did something really stupid last month?'

'What?' Perversely Lia was enjoying her friend's performance, enjoying how she was getting drunk and making a fool of herself.

'I answered a Lonely Hearts ad. He was supposed to be in film and loved walking his golden retriever on Clapham Common. A total jerk. Complete wanker. The dog was better company.'

'You have very high standards, you know,' Lia said impatiently. 'No one's perfect. Maybe if you'd have just given him a chance—'

'Well, you're doing all right, aren't you?' Jules swung her legs round on her chair towards her. 'Nick here's hardly Mr Boring.'

'Maybe it's time we left,' Lia suggested before Jules could say anything they both regretted. 'Let's go home, get something to eat? I've got a lamb thing in the fridge.'

Nick jumped up, clearly ready to get moving, and paid for the champagne before escorting them back to the car. This time Jules volunteered to climb into the back, and slept for most of the journey. Nick and Lia didn't say much, each absorbed in their own thoughts. Nick, Lia assumed, was thinking about the calls he had to make the next day, and about his business; while she, rather taken aback at where her mind had lead her earlier on, could barely stop thinking about Ben.

Chapter Forty-one

Lia took Jules to the airport early the next morning.

'I had a brilliant time, Li, thank you so much for everything.' Jules hugged her. 'And he's a great guy. Really, a great guy. You're so lucky.'

'I know I am.' Lia hugged her back, feeling closer to her friend again now. Somehow Jules's drunken admissions of the previous day had made her seem more human, and more likeable.

When she returned to the villa she could hear Nick on the phone in his study. He'd sort everything out, she thought confidently. Didn't all these tycoons lurch from one crisis to the next? He'd talk the bank round, she told herself, or simply find another backer, someone who'd even extend the loan to let him buy the partner out. He'd find a way to resolve things, she reassured herself. Men like Nick always did.

She worked well that morning, writing about Mediterranean herbs and their medicinal properties as well as culinary ones. Inspired, she made a quick tabouleh with mint and parsley, and put together a fresh tomato, mozzarella and basil salad, drizzled with virgin olive oil. This was what the south was all about, she thought, laying the table under the olive tree. Fresh salads eaten under dappled sunlight, made with natural ingredients bought over a chat in a local shop. You couldn't beat it.

Just after one o'clock, Nick came down, a slightly strained look on his face. 'You got lunch? You're the greatest.' He gave her a peck on the cheek. 'Your friend get off OK?'

Despite herself, she liked that Jules had become 'your friend'. 'Yes, yes, her plane was on time.' She laid the table and when she turned around, she saw Nick opening a bottle of rosé.

'You're having a drink?' she asked. 'Now?'

'I could use it,' he told her. 'You want one?'

She shook her head. 'I'm working too well for that right now.' She paused. 'So how's it all going?'

'Bit tougher than I'd hoped,' he shrugged. 'But they'll come round.'

'I hope so,' Lia said. 'Is the bank thing a serious problem?'

'I could live without it,' he drained his glass. 'One of our clients has been slow in paying us this quarter and I can't get anything out of them. That cheque alone would clear a portion of the debt – enough to pacify the bank for a while, anyway.'

'So what are they saying, the cheque's in the post?'

'I wish,' he laughed. 'But that's all boring,' he changed the subject. 'So Jules is quite a girl – makes me laugh. Jealous of you, though.'

'You think so?' Lia asked. 'I mean, all that stuff about me getting everything I ever wanted – I don't really take it seriously. She wouldn't want any of this – she'd be bored out of her brains.'

'But maybe she doesn't know what she wants yet, and that's why she's jealous,' Nick countered. 'Because you do, and you made it happen.'

'With her help,' Lia sighed, spooning out some tabouleh. 'She'll never let me forget that, now, will she?'

He laughed, helping himself to the salads. 'Not many

277

people really know what they want,' he said after a pause. 'They think they do, and they follow a dream, and then when they get it, they realise it's not what they wanted after all.'

She paused, surprised. She'd never heard him talk like this before. 'Do you feel like that sometimes?'

He shrugged. 'I guess. I wanted my own business, I got my own business. But along with it I got hassles and problems and board meetings and bankers and financiers and a whole bunch of stuff I could live without. And now I look back and think "Gee, I used to write programmes, and life was so simple."'

'But you wouldn't have all this, would you –' she gestured to the house and garden '– if you were still writing programmes. You probably wouldn't be satisfied; you'd be looking for the next challenge. We all need to move and develop to a certain extent, and I certainly can't see you standing still.'

'True.' He seemed unconvinced, eating his lunch quickly, as if it were just another distraction from the real issues of his day. 'I'd be happy in a shack on the beach,' he said quietly. 'Sometimes, that's what I think. Catch some fish, cook them on an open fire and sleep under the stars.'

'There are probably tailor-made holidays like that for stressed-out businessmen,' Lia teased. 'If someone hasn't thought of it already then maybe I should?' She paused, wondering how best to help him. 'Surely you need to build up your company, sell it off for some enormous price and spend the rest of your life doing whatever it is you want?'

'You seen the NASDAQ lately? Believe me, that was always the dream. Maybe in a few years, if we can just weather this out.'

'I'm sorry.' Lia put down her knife and fork, troubled by the way the conversation was going. 'I hate to see you like this. I wish there was something I could do.'

He smiled back at her, then his face became serious again. 'You know what?' he asked, pushing his plate away. 'There is something. I have a problem.'

278

Lia's stomach lurched and she caught her breath. Was this the major revelation? Was it on its way, now? Was this when he told her about his late wife, and Elodie, and all the therapy he'd been in, and how it had or hadn't worked? Or the business troubles, the pressure he was under and how he was nearly bankrupt? She steeled herself for his reply. 'Which is?' she asked cautiously.

He took a deep breath. 'I have this beautiful, sweet, girl-friend,' he said slowly, taking her hand, 'and she's staying with me right now. And whenever she's around, you know I can't think about anything else. And right now, the only thing I want to do is take her to my bedroom and make love to her all afternoon.'

He lifted her hand and kissed it.

'So why don't you?' she asked, smiling in relief. 'My boss is on a plane, after all.'

And later, as Nick snoozed and Lia stared at the bright blue sky from his bedroom window, she went over his words about Jules, and her jealousy. What Jules wanted more than anything right now was a stable, solid relation-ship, and although Lia could hardly boast that that was what she had, she felt a lot more secure than her friend did. And she was at least meeting men, rather than just eyeing them up on the tube.

Jules had incredibly high standards, but it seemed that Nick was one of the few men who actually managed to meet them. She'd always been quick to dismiss Lia's boyfriends in the past – Jonathan had barely stood a chance whilst Ben was rejected before they'd so much as kissed. But with Nick, Lia reflected, hadn't Jules revelled in her unease, teasing her about his reputation? So in some way, had Jules been undermining her all along, making her doubt her choices and her judgement? And was that in itself a simple deflection of her own unhappiness?

Quietly, Lia crept out from under the covers, got dressed again and returned to work, hoping that the normality of her routine would somehow dispel the confu-sion she felt all around.

279

Chapter Forty-two

She moved back to Les Eglantines the following Saturday afternoon, and Peaches greeted her at the entrance. 'It's wonderful to see you again – how well you look! Now here's your key back,' she said excitedly. 'And thank you so much again for being so understanding. I hope I didn't put you out too much?'

'No,' Lia smiled indulgently. 'I had a nice time. Nick was there quite a lot the second week, and my friend Jules came out. It was a kind of a break, actually.'

'Your friend Jules, she's the one who introduced you to us, isn't she?' Peaches asked. 'Oh, I would have loved to have met her. Well, never mind, we must have you and Nick for supper one evening. What do you say?'

'That sounds great,' Lia told her, hauling her bags though the archway. 'But there is actually something I'd like to talk to you about in the meantime. Perhaps I could pop by for tea one day or something?'

'To talk to me about, dear? You're not leaving, are you? Don't tell me.' She was getting increasingly excited, 'You're moving in with Nick! That's it, isn't it? You're moving in?'

'No, no, I'm not,' Lia rushed to assure her. 'As far as

I'm concerned I'm in the pink cottage until I get thrown out again. No, it's something quite different, but I really don't want to go into it right now.' She was kicking herself for having mentioned it already.

'Something quite different? Well, you do have me intrigued. Is it to do with your book? Or the retreat?'

'No, Peaches, please, I shouldn't have said anything yet. I'm sorry, it was stupid of me.'

'No, not at all, dear. Is it about Ben, perhaps? I haven't heard from him in a while, now, though I believe he's still coming. Or Bella. Is it about them?'

'No, Peaches, it's not. To be honest, it's about your daughter.' The words tumbled out of her mouth, if anything, just to stop Peaches' incessant questioning. Lia took a deep breath, whilst Peaches herself said nothing – too shocked, too taken aback for speech. 'I think I've seen her. On tape.' She explained about her old job, and the *Staying Alive* channel.

'Are you sure?' Peaches' voice was a whisper.

'Not a hundred per cent, no. But the ... circumstances ... are the same, and I can see similarities in your appearance.'

'Do you know where this programme is taped?'

'Chicago, I think. But it's a couple of years old, I should warn you.'

'Ah,' Peaches nodded, not really listening. 'Chicago.'

'I'm sorry. Perhaps you'd rather I hadn't brought this up, but I thought it was only fair that you should see it. It felt wrong not to share it with you.'

'You mean, you have it?' There were tears bubbling up in Peaches' eyes, and Lia nodded. 'Well,' Peaches said bravely. 'No time like the present. Shall we?'

Was there resentment in her voice, Lia wondered? Were all her emotions – the pain, the sadness, the anger at herself – all now going to be directed at Lia, for having brought the whole thing out into the open again? She heaved her bags to one side, found the tape and joined Peaches in the kitchen.

'The kettle's on,' Peaches said. 'I'll just go tell Felix.'

Lia went to the TV and video, sorted out which remote was which and inserted the tape. She cued it up to where the woman came on, her stomach churning in anxiety. There were things in life that were painful and difficult, she kept telling herself, but you had to face them anyway. Just because they were difficult didn't mean you should simply avoid them.

Felix followed Peaches into the sitting room, a look of disapproval on his face. 'You've found something interesting for us to see, I gather?' he asked.

'It was something I remembered seeing at my old job, so I got in touch and asked them to make me a recording. The last thing I want to do is upset Peaches, of course, but this might actually do her some good.'

'Of course,' Felix acknowledged, sitting down, neatly pulling up his trouser legs an inch or so as he did so.

'There.' Peaches placed a silver tray on the Egyptian pouf. 'I made Earl Grey, it's Felix's favourite. You'll have some, Lia, won't you?'

'I'd love a cup. Do let me pour.' She could see Peaches' hands were shaking, and took the milk jug from her, pouring its contents into the three mismatched cups. The tea looked weak, as if it hadn't stood for long enough, but Lia carried on pouring and offered them sugar. Then she got up and made for the television. It was worse than having to show her work to a boss, she thought, fumbling for the remote control and trying to remember all the right things to say.

'I'm not starting from the beginning of the show,' she told them. Felix looked impassive, she noticed, as if girding himself up to be supportive of Peaches later. Peaches sat there, her face lit up, trying to hide her fear, her anxiety. She nodded approvingly of everything Lia said, her lips pinched tight. She was being too keen, Lia thought, putting on too good a show, as if she just wanted the whole thing to be over.

'The first part may be distressing,' Lia warned her. 'But

282

she says one or two things later that you might find a comfort.'

Suddenly she hated herself, hated herself for what she was putting Peaches through, hated herself for her smug job in television and her access to people who could provide her with such evidence; she hated herself for her memory, for her desire to help, and for ever having thought that she could make a difference. She pressed play and sat back, sipping her insipid tea, and cringed at every word that was said.

'Oh that's her,' Peaches said immediately, a gasp of joy stifled by a sob. 'Oh, look how she's done her hair!'

Lia hoped she was paying more attention to the woman's hair than her words. 'What's her name?' she whispered, hoping to make the viewing seem normal.

'Aurelia,' Peaches whispered back. 'We used to call her Rory.'

'It's a beautiful name,' Lia said quietly, so quietly that she thought the words went unheard. All she could hear were Rory's bitter exclamations: *I will never forgive that woman! I will never forgive her!* and again she felt anger at herself for putting Peaches through this.

'Yes, I do have sympathy,' Rory had started crying now, and so, Lia could hear, was Peaches. 'I do care about her.'

The piece finished seconds later, and Lia turned off the tape, then looked around to see Peaches sobbing into Felix's neck, his arms protective around her.

'I'm sorry, Peaches,' Lia began. 'Perhaps I should never have—'

'No, no, dear, thank you!' Peaches had turned to her. 'Thank you so much! You don't know what it means to me just to know she's alive, that she's rebuilt her life, and that she *does* care. Thank you.'

Her arm was outstretched towards her, and Lia stumbled up to give Peaches a hug. A bit of her wanted to announce how she'd always known that the tape would have helped, but that would have been triumphant and self-serving. So she kept quiet, secure in the knowledge that the hug itself was saying far more than words.

'I'll leave you to it, shall I?' she said finally, pulling away. 'And get on with my unpacking.'

'The tape, dear, don't you need it back?'

'No, no, Peaches, that's for you. You keep it.'

Peaches nodded, understanding, and fell back into Felix's arms. Without another word, Lia withdrew to the garden, where she picked up her bags and carried them back towards her old home.

Chapter Forty-three

Settled again in the pink cottage, Lia tried to get herself back into some kind of routine. The nights were cooling down now and sometimes she'd choose to eat supper inside instead of in the fading light of the terrace. The year was speeding towards autumn, and Lia began to dread having to dress up again and feel herself shiver. She'd always feared winters alone, but this year, she kept telling herself, she'd have Nick, and he'd provide all the warmth and comfort she needed.

She'd once felt the same way about Ben, though, she remembered – which was proof enough, if ever she needed it, that nothing in life was guaranteed.

Nick was away for much of the month, and she told herself not to worry about his infrequent calls and the pressure he seemed to be under. Wasn't this the sort of thing these businessmen went through all the time? Someone like Nick would pull through, she kept telling herself. It bothered her, though, that when he was around they didn't see each other every night – how could he *not* want to be with her? – and she'd have to settle for a chat over the phone, knowing that he was just there, right above her, but preferred to stay alone.

Sometimes, when the midday sun and the contents of her fridge proved too tempting, she'd invite him to join her and he'd come down the quick way for some lunch of *saucisson* and black olives, fresh bread, salad and melting goat's cheese. She'd dried some of her own tomatoes and peppers, storing them in a jar with olive oil, and they'd eat them with bread and mozzarella, the oil dripping through their fingers. He told her to use the pool whenever she wanted, so she'd climb up the steep path they'd created and swim most afternoons, wondering quietly how he was getting on in that study, and when his news might one day be good.

One afternoon, as she sat on the terrace reading through a couple of chapters, she heard the gate open and Peaches appeared, followed, as usual, by the ginger tom, James. 'My dear, do you have a minute? I have two things to share with you.'

'Sit down, Peaches,' Lia leapt up and offered her a seat. 'Can I get you anything? Some tea, perhaps, or a cold drink?'

'No, no, dear, I won't stay long. We have some new arrivals coming tomorrow, and I'd better go check on the studios. How's Nick, by the way? Is he still around?'

'Yes, he is, for the time being. He's still travelling a lot, but he's using this house as a base these days.'

'Good, how exciting – haven't seen him in ages. You must come to supper, the two of you, we absolutely must organise something.' Peaches had been saying this for weeks now, so Lia was not exactly holding her breath. 'Well, I'll get the tough part over with first. I think that's the best approach. It'll give you time to digest it and then we can go over it again, if you like.' She paused, and Lia wished she'd get on with it. 'I got a call last night from Ben,' Peaches continued. 'And he's coming down here on Tuesday for a couple of weeks. I thought I should let you know.'

'Thank you,' Lia said, not knowing how she felt. There had been an inevitability to it, but the thought of seeing him again right now just confused her. 'I appreciate that. Will Bella be coming, too?'

'Not that I know of. Is this going to be terribly awkward for you?' Peaches looked pained.

'I don't see why,' Lia said bravely, wondering what Ben would make of her new relationship. But then, how could he possibly criticise her after what he'd done?

'Only he's such a regular here that I hated to turn him down.'

'Oh no, Peaches, you mustn't. No, heavens, I don't mind at all. I like Ben, I really do. It would be great to see him again – we always got on so well. Please don't worry about me.'

'That's such a mature approach,' Peaches said approvingly. 'You two made such a lovely couple. I'm not saying that you don't with Nick, of course,' she added quickly. 'But Ben has some special qualities.'

'Well let's hope Bella appreciates them,' Lia said quickly, neatly undermining that maturity she'd just shown. 'Tell me about the other thing.'

Peaches puffed herself up in readiness, a thrilled look on her face. 'Dear,' she began. 'I'm on the way to tracing my daughter!'

'Peaches, no! That's wonderful. How?'

'Well, I have a stepsister in Chicago. We're not close. In fact, we're only linked by my stepfather, who went on to become *her* stepfather when my mother died, if you see what I mean, so she's not a blood relative at all. But she's close enough for me to call her, and ask for some help. So I did, and she's going to see what she can do!'

'That's great. But what do you think she *can* do?'

'Well, I've sent photos and had one or two ideas about what Rory might be up to these days. You know she always wanted to go into retail, open a boutique, something like that. So my thought is, if she was going to reinvent herself, that's what she'd do. Millicent – that's my step sister – is going to start by checking out all the

287

independent clothes stores for me!'

'Gosh.' Lia hoped she sounded more enthusiastic than she felt. 'That'll be a huge task, won't it? I mean, I've never been to Chicago, but I imagine there are thousands of shops.'

'Yes, there probably are, and it'll probably take for ever, if indeed we find her at all, but at least I have something now; at least I *have* a location.'

'But, Peaches, just because the show's taped in Chicago, it doesn't mean she necessarily lives there. She could be in the suburbs, or out of town somewhere? I mean, I don't know the area at all, but—'

'I know, I know what you're saying. It's a hell of a long shot – I'm aware of that. You probably think I'm just this silly old woman chasing rainbows, and I'd imagine you may well be right. But it's *something*. It's something I didn't have before, it's something I can do, and that's a hell of a lot better than nothing.'

'Of course it is, Peaches. I don't mean to be negative, I'm sorry. I'm just so happy for you that you have this. It'll take a long time, I'm sure, but there *is* a chance you'll find her, isn't there?'

'That's what I keep telling myself,' Peaches began, standing up. 'And you know something? I think she wants to be found. I mean, why else go on that show? I think this was a cry for help, a cry for someone to spot her. So I'm going to do my bit.' She stifled a sob, and then steadied herself. 'Come along, James, let's not keep Lia away from her work too long.'

'You're not keeping me,' Lia started, but she was already at the gate. 'Oh, and Peaches.' Lia scrambled to her feet, and Peaches turned. 'Thank you. For warning me about Ben. Tuesday, then? Any idea what time?'

'His flight lands at two-thirty, so any time after then,' Peaches told her.

'Good.' Lia took a deep breath.

Four days' time. She cast a guilty eye up at Nick's house. Should she mention it to him? She didn't know what to do. *Ben was coming back*. Suddenly life was getting complicated, and she longed for stability, and a sense that one day, everything might work itself out.

Chapter Forty-four

The following Tuesday Lia woke up with an extraordinary sense of anticipation. It was as if an event she'd been waiting for months was suddenly about to happen, and that her life would change for ever. *It's only your ex*, she kept telling herself, sipping her morning cup of tea and watching the neighbour's cat prowl around the outskirts of her garden. *It's not going to change anything*. But despite herself she applied her make-up just a little bit more carefully and washed her hair even though it didn't strictly need it.

She wondered if she was being terribly disloyal to Nick. It wasn't as if she was expecting anything to come of seeing Ben again – she felt perfectly settled as things were. All she wanted, once she'd pulled together the tangled mass of thoughts and emotions that were going on in her head was for Ben to see that she had moved on, and for them to become friends again. Was that such a bad thing?

All day she played out various scenarios in her mind, wondering how she might first see him, and whether he'd be looking any different. Would she still fancy him if he'd had a crew cut, for example, or if he'd lost or gained loads of weight?

If his flight landed at two-thirty, she told herself, then he'd be at Les Eglantines by around four. Should she be inside, working on her laptop, or pottering about in the garden? Or would she go on-line around then, so that they wouldn't be able to talk properly? That way she'd be looking unconcerned and inaccessible, she thought to herself, and might just pay him back for a fraction of the hurt he'd caused her.

But from two-thirty onwards Lia was incapable of concentrating on anything, even the tabloid press on the Internet. Instead of burying herself in a project from which she could not be disturbed, as she'd have liked, she simply paced around the terrace, pulling up the odd weed and deadheading the plumbago, and paid frequent trips to the bathroom to check her make-up.

This was ridiculous – how many times, she chastised herself, had she put her life on hold for a man? How many times had she been incapable even of watching TV when she thought someone might call? Did men ever put themselves out like this for women? Did men suspend everyday activity for the sake of a phone call or a chance meeting? Like hell they did, she thought crossly. Like hell.

Then there was Nick – she couldn't help feeling guilty about him. She had visions of him coming to supper and Ben appearing at the front door, a bottle and some flowers in his hands. Ben wouldn't be that presumptuous, would he? Or wasn't that exactly the sort of sweet and impetuous thing he *would* do? It would be safer by far, she thought, if she and Nick were to eat out, but it would look odd if she suggested it before the evening itself. Irritatingly he'd never call before around six, so she'd never know whether to prepare a meal or to get ready to go out. By five she'd lose all concentration through wondering what to expect later on. Why was it that Nick was capable of running a business, jetting all over the world and redesigning a home all at once, yet found it impossible to plan an evening before it had actually started?

Lia tidied up the cottage, trying to remember the last time she'd ever felt this wound up, as if something huge were about to happen – something life-changing and powerful, something impossible to predict. Even her watch suddenly ran fast, as if her blood was racing through her veins and making the mechanism work double time. What if it was all a damp squib? What if Ben turned up, didn't bother to see her and just went away again with hardly a word? She ran the idea through her mind for a few minutes, but couldn't believe that he'd be so changed after just a few weeks.

But then, she'd never have believed he'd trade her in for Bella, either, so what did she know?

By half past six she found herself tumbling into depression, bemused that Ben hadn't even bothered to say hello. Had somebody got to him, told him about her and Nick, and this was his way of protesting? Lia was about to pour herself a drink when the phone rang. She raced to answer it, almost knocking over a vase on her way, and was disappointed to hear that smooth velvety American voice on the other end: 'So, how are you doing?'

'Fine ... good,' she lied breathlessly. 'Just wondering about dinner.'

'Me too. Why don't I pick you up around seven-thirty?'

'We'll go out, then? Good, perfect.'

He hung up and Lia felt cheated, as if the lack of good-byes was insulting where the lack of hellos was nicely familiar. So her scenario of Ben appearing over the dinner table was now eliminated, she thought with relief, but what if Ben were to see Nick's car?

Will you stop it! she yelled at herself, angry that she should even care what he felt. Why should it matter that she was seeing someone else? He'd made his choice all those months ago, after all, so why should she feel guilty about being with Nick? Why should she feel guilty about being happy – if, indeed, she realised the minute she'd thought it, that was how she felt? And wasn't happiness the best revenge, anyway? Hadn't she read that somewhere before?

292

But, Lia realised, it wasn't revenge she wanted, it was Ben's friendship. Friendship, and, rather strangely, his approval. Ben was different from anyone she'd met before – he made other men, with their safe desk jobs and their company cars, seem tame by comparison. Just knowing someone like him made her feel special. He was a free spirit for whom all the world was home, and hadn't she once revelled in the feeling that maybe, just for a couple of months anyway, she had meant something to him? That with her he'd found happiness, with her he'd found the contentment so lacking in his everyday life? And even though she'd lost him, she realised, now the searing pain and the jealousy had dissipated, all that really mattered was his friendship.

At seven-thirty Nick's car appeared in the lane, and self-consciously she made her way through the garden to meet him, keeping half an eye on the row of flats. She heard laughter coming from one of them and wondered who else was staying at the moment, and whether Ben was perhaps with them.

Opening the car door, Nick greeted her with that warm, open smile of his and a kiss on the lips. He smelt clean and wholesome, like a man in a razor ad – the type who'd climb mountains or go white-water rafting: someone athletic, capable and adventurous. He had a maturity Ben lacked; his whole body seemed bigger, stronger, more adult-like. He had a presence on entering the room that made even the most indifferent of waiters notice, a fuck-you attitude she'd always found sexy. He made her feel special just by letting her tag along in his world, but she never felt his equal – for the first time she could see that now.

'So how was your day?' Was there a certain tone in his voice or was Lia imagining it? She'd already told him about Ben's return, casually mentioning it after Peaches had warned her, and he'd simply shrugged as if it meant nothing.

'Quiet,' she sighed. 'Nothing interesting. Yours?'

'Discussions with venture capitalists, the usual stuff. Pretty promising, as a matter of fact, but I've got to be in New York Friday.'

'Friday?' Lia took this in over dinner, trying to conceal her disappointment. She'd hoped to spend the weekend together, to get away from Les Eglantines and its residents. But now she'd be alone again, with Ben just a short walk away. She wasn't sure how to feel about that.

He talked about his business problems and how the technology slump in general had affected his company. The partnership issue had been resolved and they'd pared down the operation to a minimum, but they still needed more funds to carry them through the next twelve months, and they were still owed money by one of their biggest clients.

After dinner, she stayed over at his house. Their lovemaking had become less intense now, but it was good just to feel his body close to hers, and to hear the sound of his breath as he slept. They would get through this rough patch, she told herself the next morning. He'd get his company's financing and the industry on the whole would pick up, and they'd look back on these months as something they saw through together.

She would consign Ben to the memory bank of exboyfriends, where he belonged. As Nick showered she wondered when she might see Ben, and where. She tried to picture his face, his hair, the clothes he might be wearing, and then chastised herself for being disloyal. What was wrong with her? As Nick returned, a large white towel wrapped around his waist, his hair floppy and wet, he playfully pulled at the duvet.

'Get up, get up, and start your day,' he trilled. 'I want to hear about a whole new chapter being written, you hear me? Now, you want breakfast, only I've got a few calls to make?'

'No, no, I'll go,' she clambered out. 'I'll shower when I get home.' She'd never seen the point in showering and then putting her old underwear back on. 'You get on – I'll see myself out. Call me later?'

She kissed him hurriedly and dressed, and then not wanting to spoil her mules on their fast slope down, walked the long way back, enjoying the early morning sun. She picked up some bread and a croissant in the village and was just walking through the citrus orchard at Les Eglantines when she heard a familiar voice calling out her name. Her heart jumped, her stomach turned over and a rosy blush spread all over her face.

Ben was standing there in a pair of beaten-up jeans, some sandals and a pale-blue shirt. He looked more tanned than when she'd last seen him and she thought that perhaps he'd lost some weight, but his eyes were still as bright as ever, and it was with obvious pleasure that he looked at her.

'You're up early,' he smiled as if he could guess why. He approached her and they kissed on both cheeks.

'Getting some bread,' Lia said awkwardly, hoping her mascara didn't look too smudged. 'So how are you?'

'Bit knackered. Glad to be back.'

'I bet.' There was a slightly awkward pause, and Lia wished they could talk naturally again. He made no particular show of wanting to walk away, though, and she wondered whether, if they parted now, each of them would come up with ten things to say minutes later. 'So, you're here for a couple of weeks, then?' she tried.

'That's right, I could do with some creature comforts.'

'I bet you could,' she said. 'How was it?'

'Good, good,' his voice brightened. 'A healing process, as Peaches might say.' He smiled. 'And I caught up with some people I'd met before, this family, and got some nice shots.'

'Good, that's great. I'm really glad.' There was another awkward pause until, deciding that she would rather be the one to break away first, Lia said, 'Well, I'd better be getting on.'

'How's it all going, anyway?' he asked as if suddenly remembering what she was doing there.

Lia told him about her book deal before turning towards the cottage. It was an awkward start, but at least they had

295

got it over with. She found herself thinking about it all morning, though, and wondering if there was anything else she could have said, and what kind of impression she might have given him, and whether he'd noticed at all that she was standing there in yesterday's clothes and make-up.

That afternoon, as she helped Etienne sow spinach and lamb's lettuce, Ben joined them, and she found it easier to talk to him in company, in the strange mix of English and French they'd come to adopt whenever Etienne was around. They could laugh again, she noticed with relief, and had lost the awkwardness of that morning.

'Come and have tea,' she suggested once they'd finished.

'What specials do you have on today?' Ben asked. 'Carrot and peach? Rhubarb and broccoli?'

She smiled, enjoying their old joke. 'I can do you a nice cup of builders', if you like. I've still got some bags left from the spring.'

As she said it, she hoped it didn't sound like a dig – the words suddenly seemed loaded with self-pity – a woman spurned, left with nothing but her memories and a handful of teabags. If Ben took it that way, however, he didn't show it. He settled on the terrace and Lia fussed around, producing tea and some orange flower biscuits she'd bought in the village.

'So is there any progress on your book?' she asked him. 'Or an exhibition?'

He shook his head. 'Not really. Though I've got more stuff to contribute to it,' he added. 'I really want to focus on it now – it's been going on too long. I've just got to make some decisions.'

Lia found herself wanting to ask whether Bella wasn't making those decisions for him, so changed the subject instead. 'I can't imagine being there,' she said. 'In Afghanistan. I tried keeping up with it on the news, but it just looks so inhospitable.'

'It was all right, actually. Far better than the last time,' he told her.

296

She nodded, feeling humbled again, and remembering that feeling from months ago. A part of her was itching to ask about Bella, but Lia couldn't; she couldn't bring herself to take the conversation up to that level. His words, his style and his phrases were all so familiar, bringing everything back to her in glorious Technicolor, rather than the tired sepia in which she'd forced them to exist in her mind – the month they'd spent in bed, their evenings together in the cottage, the trips they'd shared, everything came flooding back in that one, simple conversation.

If felt so right to be with him, she kept thinking, now that the initial awkwardness had gone. Was he aware of how right it felt too, and was he cursing himself for having spoiled everything?

And when he finally got up and excused himself, and all that was left was an empty mug and a splodge on the table where he'd knocked it, it felt equally strange to be alone again. She sat there, sipping her tea, before spotting yet another weed in the bougainvillaea and gently easing it out with her fingers.

Chapter Forty-five

Nick left for New York and once again Lia found her concentration levels in pieces, all her thoughts leading to one thing – when she would next see Ben. She made a special effort, ensuring that her lipstick was never far from reach and wearing her most flattering clothes. Instead of pulling her hair sharply back into a ponytail so it was easier to work, she allowed it to flop down onto her forehead and around her ears, where it irritated her but, she thought, looked better.

At six she poured herself a glass of red wine and sat on the terrace as the sun dipped behind the mountain. What would be her future? she thought idly, looking out across the valley in the fading light. Would she become Mrs Nick Delaney, the mother of his children, a respected food writer who accompanied him on his trips, and was Ralph Lauren chic? Would that life make her happy? Or what about – no, she couldn't bring herself to think it through, couldn't bring herself to dream like that. She and Ben were over, a thing of the past. This would be a tricky two weeks, but she'd get through them. This was still only day three after all.

She was too isolated, she told herself, pouring another

glass. She had too few friends and no one in the workplace to talk to. It was the life she'd wanted; all right, it was all that and more, but she could see now it had its downsides.

What if she were in London right now – what would she be doing? Meeting Jules for a drink, perhaps, and then going for some Thai food or Chinese? Or heading home to cook supper for Jonathan? Did she actually miss that lifestyle? she asked herself, trying to think back. Had life been better then?

She barely noticed the clink of the gate and a familiar shape appearing on the terrace. 'Drinking alone, eh? Slippery slope, you know.'

She turned and smiled broadly, accepting his offer of a bottle. 'You'd better join me, then.'

How natural Ben was, she thought, fetching another glass, how easy and self-assured. She doubted he'd spent the day wondering whether to pop round or not and fretting about his clothes.

'I love the way this view changes with the seasons,' he started, gazing out towards the sea.

She handed him a glass. How many times had she herself said that? He turned to her and she found herself too close, could almost smell his breath, sweet and warm, and she backed away, awkward and unsure.

'I'll just get some nibbles.' She jumped up, glad of the distraction, and disappeared into the kitchen, coming back minutes later with a bowl of plump green olives stuffed with anchovies. 'These have become my favourites,' she told him, trying to keep on neutral ground. 'Though you can only have so many as they're quite rich.'

He nodded, not giving a damn about the olives, and looked her up and down. 'You're looking great these days,' he told her. 'What have you been up to?'

'Same as ever,' she told him self-consciously. 'A bit of swimming.'

'In Peaches' pool? You can only do a couple of strokes before you reach one end – it's useless.'

'I go to a friend's sometimes,' she told him awkwardly,

299

hoping he wouldn't read anything into it. A woman would, she thought, straight off. Her radar system would light up, and she'd know instantly that there was another person involved. She might not ask about it immediately, of course, but the thought would be there, registered in her mind, and she'd wait for other hints to link up to it, and for a more clearly defined picture to emerge before voicing her suspicions.

But not Ben. 'Well it's paying off, you look great. The tan suits you.'

She smiled, flattered, and wondered how long they could go on without mentioning their relationship, or Bella.

'So what else? You've been busy? Made any new friends down here?'

Lia smiled. Maybe his radar system was working after all. 'Not as many as I'd like,' she admitted. 'I was just thinking about that, actually. What I'd be doing if were in London now, and whether I miss it. I don't,' she added quickly. 'But I am pretty isolated here. It's something I need to work on now the book's under control.'

He nodded. 'So no debonair Frenchman's swept you off your feet, then?'

She could hear in his voice that this was a rehearsed sentence, like the many she'd rehearsed time and again, only to come out sounding false and wrong. And she knew that this was the time to tell him about Nick, and to be honest.

'No, not a Frenchman. An American, though.' His eyes lit up with enthusiasm and he looked pleased for her, but she could tell this was a disguise, a quick reaction to conceal his shock. 'I met him through Peaches, he has a house here, though he travels a lot. It's his pool I've been using.'

'So you're seeing someone? Wow.'

'I wasn't looking for it,' she told him. 'I wasn't looking for anyone. I went through a rough few weeks after you left, and believe me, the last thing on my mind was to find someone else.'

300

'But then you did? And are you serious about him?'

'I don't know, to be honest. I don't know what being serious really means any more. Was I serious about Jonathan? Clearly not, even after living with him for almost four years. Were you serious about me? No, I don't think you were.' The words tumbled out with the wine, and she knew she'd never have said them sober.

'What do you mean, I wasn't serious? I cared about you enormously.'

Cared. Past tense. Something in Lia snapped. 'Didn't stop you running off with Bella, though, did it?'

He frowned, a kind of puzzled frown. 'What do you mean, running off with Bella?'

'How else would you put it?'

'You told me you didn't want to see me again—'

'Yes,' she interrupted him. 'But only because of her. And so you chose her over me.'

'What do you mean, I chose her?' In exasperation he reached for the bottle to find it empty. 'Look, can I open something else? The one I brought, perhaps?'

'Yes, yes, I'll get the corkscrew.' She jumped up, strangely grateful that Ben seemed to want to stay.

'I had dinner with Bella,' he started slowly, having opened the bottle and poured them each a glass. 'That was all. For one night in three months I had dinner with someone else.'

'You knew how I felt about her. And yet still you went.' Tears of rage were bubbling up in Lia's eyes.

'Look, I'm sorry. It was just a dinner. I never understood why you made such a scene about it.'

'She'd spent the entire time here ridiculing me.' Lia raised her voice now, reliving and remembering the conversations. 'She made me feel like some total loser and you somehow always defended her. And then she comes up with those ridiculous scripts telling you to dump me and sleep with her, and you went along with it! Do you have any idea how that felt? Do you have any idea how humiliated I was?'

301

He sighed, stalling for time, as if needing to get the events straight in his mind before speaking. 'Lia, I went along with her, because I wanted to hear what she had to say. I had a right to, seeing as it was all supposed to be about me. Looking back it was ridiculous, I admit, and I can see now that she was playing games, but I didn't realise that at the time. So I'm sorry, I was wrong, and I'm truly sorry. But it wasn't worth breaking up over.'

Lia could barely believe she was hearing these words. She was confused, now, needed time to think, but the wine was dulling her memory and the tears were refusing to go away. 'What do you mean, it wasn't worth breaking up over? You fucking slept with her!'

'What?' Ben's face was incredulous first, and then broke into a laugh. 'Who says?'

Lia stopped, deflated and unsure. 'Well, didn't you? I mean, you never came back to me.'

'Lia, you said you wanted nothing more to do with me, remember? If I went to dinner with her, then that was it – over.'

He never slept with her? 'And then that's exactly what you did,' Lia started, unsure of herself. 'And you never came back.'

He looked confused. 'What else was I supposed to do?'

'Ben!' Exasperated, she took a large sip of wine. 'You could have come back any time, you know that.' *He never slept with her?* 'You could have negotiated. You could have had dinner and then come back the next day, if anything just to check that I was all right. You didn't have to just walk out, you know.'

'Am I a mind reader all of a sudden?' He looked just as exasperated as she was. 'You seemed pretty clear about it at the time.'

He never slept with her? 'Ben, I needed to feel wanted. I needed to know that you cared about me. I admit I was insecure – that was partly Bella's doing. I mean, you and she had had a history, after all. So I wanted a bit of re-assurance, that's all.'

302

'Funny way of showing it, kicking me out. So what, I was supposed to come back the next day, grovelling and begging for forgiveness?'

'Yes, basically!' Lia cried out before breaking into a laugh. 'It sounds ridiculous now, doesn't it, but that's exactly what I wanted. I didn't want us to end – I was so happy, you know I was.' She put her head in her hands. 'So you didn't actually sleep with her?'

'No,' he shrugged. 'She wanted to, but I never did. I kept thinking there was more for you and me, and that I wanted to be with you.'

'So why didn't you come back?'

He sighed, and stared across at the view. 'I don't know, it was all so difficult. I didn't need the hassle, I suppose. I had a trip coming up, I had a lot on my mind, and I thought perhaps we needed a cooling-off period. I was seriously worried about Afghanistan; maybe I should have made that clearer. I just didn't want any more complications. Looking back that was stupid, I can see that now. I should have sorted everything out. I'm sorry I didn't, I can't tell you how much.' He drained his glass. 'But you, then? You and your fancy American?'

'I thought we were all over. You could have written, you know. Doesn't e-mail work from Kabul?'

'I wanted to see you in person. I thought I'd be back sooner, to be honest, but things got a bit delayed. If I'd have realised how long I was going to be I would have e-mailed, absolutely I would, but then it got too late and, I don't know, it just felt awkward. I didn't know how you'd feel, or whether you'd still be angry with me, so I thought it was best to leave it.'

'So you haven't slept with anyone since me?' She wanted to hear him say it, wanted to digest the fact, soak it all in.

'That's right. You happy now?'

'Shocked.' She looked him straight in the face, knowing that her own was pink and blotchy now, and no doubt smudged with mascara.

303

'And now you've got someone else,' he said matter-of-factly. Lia said nothing, too confused and surprised to talk. 'So, who is he?'

'A businessman.' She swallowed hard.

'Not this Nick bloke, that friend of Peaches?' He was more alert now, leaning forward. Lia nodded. 'Be careful, won't you?'

'Careful? So Chloe's got to you, too, then? You were the one who told me not to believe a word she said, remember?'

He nodded sadly. 'I so wanted it to be different,' he told her. 'I must have imagined a hundred times seeing you again. But it was never like this.' There was an awkward pause. 'I should go,' he said quietly.

She didn't look up as he walked past her down the terrace, and rushed indoors before she could hear the clink of the gate. 'You could woo me,' she called out softly, not wanting him to hear, but simply to act on her words as if they'd reached his subconscious. 'You could win me back, you know, prove that you care!'

But she knew he wouldn't. It wasn't his style. No longer hungry or in need of a drink, Lia slumped in one of the armchairs in the sitting room.

'It wasn't meant to be,' she kept persuading herself. 'It just wasn't meant to be.'

Chapter Forty-six

Lia didn't sleep much that night, but lay in bed wondering how different things could have been and how she felt she'd played straight into Bella's hands. It was as if the woman had orchestrated everything herself. She tried to remember key conversations with Ben – the first when Bella had invited him to dinner, to go over those so-called scripts, and then the second earlier that evening; but each time she ran through either of them it changed, and she had less faith in her memory. It was like seeing a movie for the second time, when scenes she was convinced she'd remembered turned out quite differently – hadn't she remembered Peaches' daughter all wrong, after all? And was she now remembering things the way she wanted to, she wondered, instead of the way they really were?

By morning, tired and almost high from that tiredness, she'd got up early, watered her plants in the gentle dawn sunlight and made some tea, planning her day. In a strange way she was beginning to see the funny side – how a simple misunderstanding could have changed their lives so dramatically. How ironic that two people whose very jobs depended on their communication skills could have failed each other so miserably. It actually *was* funny. She

305

wondered if Ben was seeing it that way. She showered and dressed and delighted in the amount of time she had before her. Not normally even waking until the scandalous hour of nine, finding herself ready to start work at eight was little short of miraculous.

Etienne had brought her two large bags of late-season figs – soft, sensuous, earthy tasting purple things – and she was determined to make jam, to fill all the jars she'd been saving in the store room and to conclude her chapter on fruits and jam-making. She didn't have a recipe as such, but had made enough in the past to know the basics, and was confident she could wing it. She warmed up sugar, lemon juice and rind and some water in a pan, added the fruit and brought the lot to the boil, before turning the heat down and letting it all cook for an hour.

She'd lined up her jars, washed and heated in the oven, and was about to begin spooning the mixture inside when there was a knock at the door and there stood Ben, a bag of croissants and some bread in one hand.

'You're up early,' he remarked in surprise.

'Couldn't sleep, so I'm making jam, only I can't interrupt the process right now, so you'd better give me a hand.'

How easy it all was, she thought in delight, how easy it was to talk to him, despite everything. As she spooned the hot jam into the jars, Ben wiped away any errant splodges and screwed the lids on tight. They worked well together, like a synchronised factory, and the job was finished quickly.

'You can have a jar for your troubles,' she told him, wiping off a chunk of fig that had found its way onto her T-shirt, 'but you're not to touch it for a couple of months.'

They sat down outside with their breakfast and there was a secondary silence between them, until each started to speak simultaneously, and they laughed.

'I've been thinking about what an idiot I was, and how I've lost something that was very special to me,' he started.

'Something?' Lia queried pointedly.

'Someone then,' he corrected himself. 'You and me – it meant a lot to me, you know.'

'It did to me, too,' she agreed. 'But the spectre of Bella was too much. I know I was jealous, and I know that that's stupid, but somehow she seems to have won, anyway. I get the impression she always wins, whatever.'

'I never saw her as such a big deal,' he told her. 'I mean, it was a brief fling a year ago and that was it, over with.'

'But the way she clung on to you, got you to take photos for her, made you do stuff with her.' Somehow it was easy to talk about her now. 'The way she kept on about your photos and helping you to organise your book or an exhibition; it was like she had some sort of control over you.'

Ben shook his head. 'I never saw it that way. I just saw her as a friend. A pushy one, admittedly. I told you, the one thing I've learnt is how important your friends are, how they carry you through things.'

'At the expense of someone more special, though,' Lia said quickly. 'You knew how much it bothered me, and yet still you went along with it.'

'I know, and looking back that was wrong. But I just don't like feeling trapped, you know? That ultimatum – see her and you'll never see me again – it was like a form of blackmail. I hate that.'

Lia cringed – had she really come across like that? She decided the best form of defence was attack. 'Yes, but Ben,' she rolled her eyes in exasperation. 'I told you this yesterday. When I said "See her and you'll never see me again." I didn't mean you'll *never* see me.' As she said it, she realised how illogical it all sounded. 'What I meant was, I'm really hurting and I'd like you to try just that little bit harder to show me how much you care. I'm feeling insecure and I need to be reassured.'

'So why didn't you just say that?'

'Because –' Lia rolled her eyes – 'because you're meant to realise that. You're meant to understand what it feels like. You're meant to have that much sensitivity.'

307

'For God's sake.' He laughed, pouring out more coffee. 'Maybe Peaches can instruct me on developing my psychic powers? How else am I supposed to get all that?'

Lia sat back, deflated, yet relieved that they could still laugh together, that this was some kind of breakthrough, and that from now on it was possible to be friends. 'Maybe we should just accept that men and women think and act differently,' she said. 'And get over it.'

'Here, here.' He laughed, breaking off a corner of a *pain au chocolat*. 'But you, though, you're happy?'

She nodded uncertainly. 'It's been a bit difficult lately, as Nick's got these business problems. But otherwise it's fine.'

'He treats you well?'

'Very,' she smiled. 'And believe me, Chloe's got him all wrong. He's just different. A grown-up, you know? It's like we're still all kids down here, bumbling along trying to sort out our lives, whilst he's got this big house and these big responsibilities and he's on a different level altogether.' She realised how difficult this was for Ben. 'Believe me,' she added softly. 'I would have liked for us not to have broken up. I would have liked for you to have come round again and for us to have made up. It could have been that easy, you know?'

'I know,' Ben said quietly. 'I suppose I've got a block about getting too close to someone, and that was holding me back. Giancarlo's death changed everything. It made me feel that as long as I'm putting myself in danger, I can't allow myself to get too close. It's just not fair.'

'You can't take a unilateral decision like that,' Lia countered. 'I mean, there are two people involved in a relationship, after all. You didn't exactly hold back when we were together, now. Was I just supposed to switch off my feelings whenever you went on an assignment?'

'I don't know.' Ben sighed. 'I just don't feel I can commit to anyone yet, you know? Get married, have a family. It's not me. I thought you wanted more than I was prepared to give. More than I felt I *could* give, even.'

'Ben, I never said I wanted to get married and have kids,' Lia cried out, embarrassed. All she'd told him was that she loved him, but then, that in itself had been too much. 'Yes, I had feelings for you, and no, I don't think I could ever turn them off – but family life? I'm not ready for that, either. If I'd wanted all that I'd have stayed in London. There are so many things I want to do with my life, the last thing I need is to settle myself into wedding bells and school runs. There's other books I want to write, places I want to visit. This is just the start, believe me.'

He smiled sadly, understanding. 'Well, I got that all wrong, then, didn't I? I just assumed you'd want all that, and it scared me. So where's your bloke?' He changed the subject. 'What's he up to at the moment?'

Lia told him about Nick's trip to New York.

'Good,' he said. 'Pizza in the village tonight? My treat?'

Lia would have liked nothing more. They arranged to meet later and, once he'd left, she took a deep breath, pleased with the way they'd got through their troubles.

And if Bella were to return, she thought, she'd be no problem this time.

They were over her.

Chapter Forty-seven

'All right, Babe?' Chloe popped her head round the front door cautiously. 'Not disturbing you, am I?'

Lia, who was just finishing her summer fruits and jams chapter, was happy to be disturbed. 'Tea?' she asked, heading for the kitchen.

'Coffee, please,' Chloe told her, following her in. 'So you and Ben had dinner last night, I hear?' she asked, a suspicious smile on her face.

'Just at the pizza place,' Lia told her quickly. 'It was nice. We sat outside in the church square bit; they've got some of those outdoor heater things.'

'So are you and he—'

'No,' Lia interrupted her. 'Most definitely not. I'm glad that we're still friends, though.'

Chloe nodded, seeming to accept this. 'Did you hear about Bella?'

Lia's stomach lurched. *Killed in a car crash? Married someone rich? Emigrated to Australia?*

'She's coming over next week. Her house is more or less finished and she's hoping to move in. Apparently she's been over a couple of times, but stayed in some smart hotel nearby.'

'Because Ben wasn't around, no doubt,' Lia said, despite herself. 'But this time she's staying here?' Chloe nodded. 'Typical. She's pretty transparent, isn't she? But it really doesn't bother me any more – she can do what she wants.'

She made some instant coffee for Chloe and some cherry tea for herself, which she sipped hesitantly.

'Got a bit of bad news a couple of days ago,' Chloe started once she'd sat down. 'My mum's sick. They think she's got cancer.'

'Oh Chloe, no, I'm so sorry. How's she doing?'

Chloe shrugged. 'I don't know, a bit shocked I think. Not really taking it in.'

'So you're going home?'

She looked up. 'Do you think I should? Etienne does, but I don't know, there's not much I can do, is there?'

'Chloe, what about moral support? I mean, even if all you're doing is driving your mum to hospital, then that's something. If all you're doing is cooking meals, that's something. This is exactly the time when all the little things count. I mean, I'm sure she'd really appreciate you being there.'

'I suppose so,' Chloe sighed reluctantly. 'I just can't bear the thought of it all, really. Driving a sick mum around, hospitals – just the smell of them makes me sick. And then being back home, sleeping in my old bedroom. I just can't bear the thought of it.'

'But it would mean so much to her, I'm sure,' Lia said, trying to coax her. 'I mean, does she have anyone else? Do you have brothers or sisters that can help? And how's your dad coping?'

'My sister's around, but she's got three kids, and my brother's at work all day. So I'm the only one really.'

'Well then I think you should go,' Lia told her quietly. 'I mean, you'd never forgive yourself if anything happened to her and you weren't there, now, would you?'

'I can't bear the thought of being around sickness and death, I just can't bear it,' Chloe shuddered.

311

'Don't suppose your mum's enjoying it that much either, but she's got no choice.'

'But what about me?' Chloe said passionately. 'I mean, here I am, leading the life I want to lead and really getting somewhere recently, and suddenly I have to go back to my old life? See all my old friends again, my family, my husband?'

Lia thought this sounded like the real issue. 'Is that what you're afraid of, running into him?'

'Well, we didn't exactly part on the best of terms.'

'Well maybe this is a test. Some kind of spiritual test,' Lia improvised. 'Maybe you have to go back and make amends, put things right. Maybe this is just a test of your strength, and how well you cope in difficult circumstances. I mean, let's face it, we're all pretty cocooned here, aren't we? World War Three could break out and we might not even hear about it. In some ways I think I'm evading reality just living here. I certainly think that's how Ben sees it. And now you're being called back, called back to face that reality.' Lia was impressing herself with her speech. 'It's a test, but one you shouldn't run away from.'

'You know, maybe you're right.' Chloe brightened. 'When you put it that way, it does seem more appealing.'

'What does Peaches think?' Lia asked, trying to keep a straight face. If Chloe felt that she herself would be getting something out of this trip, then suddenly it became viable.

'Oh God, you know she's got this thing about mothers and daughters at the moment? And now the bookings have dropped off, she's practically packing my bags and driving me to the airport.'

'I think she's right. I mean, all your spiritual development may be positive for you, but it mustn't stop you from looking out for others. From doing a truly unselfish act. All the meditation in the world can't better that, surely?'

'You're right,' Chloe set her mug down and got up. 'I'd better look into flights. Cancel all my classes. I don't know how long to stay, though.'

'You stay until it's time to leave,' Lia suggested simply.

'You'll know when that is. You stay until your mum's position is clear, until you've got your dad sorted out, you've cooked umpteen meals and put them in the freezer. I don't know, but you'll know when.'

Chloe smiled. 'For someone who's as spiritually closed as you are, you're pretty intuitive, aren't you?' Lia wasn't sure how to take that. 'Thanks, Babe.' She gave her a hug. 'I know you're right. I'll try and get a flight straight away.'

Lia saw her to the gate. 'Keep an eye on Etienne for me, won't you?' Chloe called out. 'Make sure that old bag from the baker's doesn't get to him! And you just watch yourself with all these men around!' She laughed. 'You'll never know who to trust.'

Chapter Forty-eight

She told Ben about the conversation a couple of days later. 'It's extraordinary how Chloe's spiritual development seems to exempt her from doing anything for anyone else,' she remarked, handing him a mug of tea. 'She might consider herself spiritually evolved, but she's a lousy Christian.'

Ben nodded in agreement. 'Not that I think I'd want her nursing me, particularly.' He smiled, before pausing, as if he had something awkward to say. 'I got a call from Bella earlier,' he told her, frowning into his mug.

'She's coming over soon, isn't she?' Lia asked. 'Staying here?'

'Yes, but she won't be alone, though. She's got this man in tow, been seeing him for the last couple of months. Lionel someone, a gallery owner. He's rich, mid-forties and extremely well connected, by the sounds of things. And interested in what I've been doing.'

'Not Lionel Cooper-Smith?' Lia asked incredulously.

'Yes, I think that is his name,' Ben looked surprised. 'Why, do you know him?'

'Not personally, no – he moves in far more exciting circles than I ever have. No, I've heard about him, or rather, read about him in the magazines. Bit of a playboy, has dated a few models, goes to all the parties.'

'You are in the know,' Ben looked amused.

'Only because I used to flip through *Hello!* and *OK* in the newsagents,' she told him quickly. 'Though I did see him once,' she remembered with a smile and a shudder. 'It was in an Indian restaurant in Chelsea. Very smart, in a basement. My poor ex made a spectacular entrance.' She told him about Jonathan's fall that wet spring night, and how it had indirectly heralded the start of her French adventure.

'You shallow cow,' Ben laughed. 'You dumped him because of that?'

'No,' Lia insisted, trying not to laugh. 'It just suddenly made me realise that I was going in the wrong direction. That if I stayed I'd be falling flat on my face, perhaps. I don't know, if I'd married him I'd never have got the chance to prove myself. But anyway, tell me more,' she continued, impatient to hear his story rather than carry on going over her own. 'So he wants to see your work?'

Ben nodded. 'Yes he does, next week. Thinks he might have a slot in his gallery next spring.'

'Ben, that's fantastic,' Lia enthused. 'That's brilliant – just what you were hoping for. Aren't you pleased?'

He shrugged. 'Yeah, of course I am. It's just . . . there'll be a lot to do, that's all.'

'So? That's nothing you're afraid of.'

'No.' He sipped his tea thoughtfully.

'So, what *is* bothering you, then? The thought that your babies are going out there for public scrutiny, that they'll be reviewed and discussed and with any luck sold? Is that what's bothering you?'

'Perhaps,' he sighed, staring into his mug.

'I know it is.' Lia smiled, warming to her theme. 'What you're thinking is that while you've got them to yourself, while they're packed away in their files and their envelopes, you can hang onto the dream that one day they'll be fêted, and *you'll* be fêted, and everyone will

315

acknowledge you for the great photographer you are. They're still in your control and so are your dreams. But once they're out there, even once Lionel Cooper-Smith sees them, then the game's over, and it's all for real – the discussion, the criticism, their value. And there's the danger, the slim chance, that they might not live up to your expectations. And that's frightening.'

He laughed, but said nothing, and Lia was sure she was on the right track. She suddenly felt as if she could see everyone else's lives so clearly, could so easily judge what they should be doing, and found it odd that her own should still elude her. 'So what about Bella, how involved is she going to get?'

'I don't know,' he told her. 'I doubt if she will. It'll be between him and me.'

'Coincidence, though, isn't it, that she starts dating someone who can be so influential? Don't you find that strange?'

'Lia, will you stop? If you think she's gone out of her way to pick up some bloke who might be useful to me, then you need your head examining. Bella moves in those kinds of circles – she's an artist, remember? She's wealthy and she knows people, so it's no surprise she met him. And now she's trying to do something positive for me.'

'Yeah, right.' Lia wasn't so sure. 'Totally selfless, just like Chloe. And you don't think she's going to want to play a part in the deal, to have some kind of say in what gets used, or how it gets presented, all that stuff?'

'I don't know, maybe she will,' he shook his head, frustrated. 'Maybe I shouldn't have said anything.' He started getting up. 'I just wanted you to know, OK? I just wanted you to know that she'll be down next week with lover-boy. There's nothing more to it than that.' He headed towards the gate.

'Ben, what's the matter?' Lia stood up and tried to stop him. 'I'm sorry, I didn't mean to sound jealous, or however I sounded. I just don't trust the woman – you know that. She fucked things up for us and I'll never

316

forgive her for that. I can't help but be a bit suspicious.'

'*She* fucked things up? You'll never take responsibility for that, will you? It'll always be *her* fault.' He looked genuinely angry. 'Well, now that you've got someone else, what do you care? Why do you act so protective towards me when you're settled and happy? Why do you keep having to go on about her?'

'Well, why do you keep defending her? Why do you refuse to accept that she went all out to get you? Why can't you see how I felt?'

'Felt? Thanks.' He opened the gate. 'I really – want – us – to be friends.' The words came out choked. 'I really want that. But it's just not that easy, is it?'

'Ben, wait,' Lia called, but he'd disappeared into the orchard and down towards the studios before she'd had a chance to stop him. Confused, she sat back on her chair and sipped her tea, before pouring it angrily into a flower bed. Somehow Bella's influence was always present, she thought bitterly. It smothered them, trapped them, tore them apart. Bella was still winning, after all those months. Lia shook her head in frustration, as if trying to shake off the woman's influence.

Bella was still the one in charge.

317

Chapter Forty-nine

It was a relief to hear Nick's voice a couple of days later. She'd kept her head down and managed to avoid running into Ben in the orchard or around the village, and was beginning to tire of her self-imposed isolation.

'Where are you calling from?' she asked him breathlessly.

'Take a look,' came his casual reply, and she bounded out into the kitchen garden, looked up and there he was, towering up above her at the furthest point of his land. She waved excitedly.

'Now, are you coming up to me or am I coming down to you?' he asked.

'I'll be right there,' she told him, not bothering to say goodbye before changing her shoes and bounding up their secret path towards him. He met her halfway, under the olive tree, and she threw her arms around his neck, holding him tight, thrilled to be seeing him again. 'I missed you,' she told him. 'I missed you so much.'

'I missed you too, Honey,' he whispered. 'Come on, I've got something for you.'

Holding her hand he led her up towards his house, warning her of any thistles or loose stones he'd come across. She would move in, she told herself excitedly. She'd had enough of the madness at Les Eglantines. She'd move in with him, and be there to support him through the bad times as well as the good. She couldn't carry on worrying over every last word she said to anyone, and how it might be interpreted; couldn't face seeing Ben stuck for ever under Bella's spell; couldn't bear to waste another evening listening to Chloe's self-centredness and Peaches' lunar escapades.

Nick was her salvation, she told herself, Nick was her future, her love, her rock. Why had she ever questioned that, she wondered, when all he'd ever shown her was kindness and warmth?

'So how was New York?' she asked once they'd got to the smooth lawn of his garden.

'It was OK,' he told her noncommittally. 'One step forward.'

'Without the two back, I hope?'

He just smiled. 'It's good to see you,' he told her. 'Drink?'

'Why not?' She laughed happily. 'I'm not going to get any work done now, am I?'

He went inside and she wandered to the pool, crouching down to dip her hands in the water. It was getting noticeably cooler now, and she knew her swimming days would soon be over. Nick returned minutes later with a bottle of champagne and two glasses, a carrier bag swinging from his wrist.

'For you,' he told her. 'With love from the Big Apple.'

She peered inside it to see a neat package wrapped in tissue paper, which she pulled out and opened carefully. Inside was a simple but elegant silk wrap in moss green and beige. 'Nick, I love it!' she exclaimed. 'It's perfect for this time of year. Thank you so much.'

He just shrugged, easing the cork out of the champagne bottle with a practised thud, and then poured some into each glass. 'I thought it would match your skin tone,' he told her, and she smiled. How many men would consider

319

a woman's skin tone when buying a gift, she asked herself? Not Ben, that was for certain – it would never occur to him. And how many men would just buy a gift anyway? How special and sensitive Nick was, she thought dreamily. He was in a different league altogether.

They chinked glasses and had a sip. 'How's your friend?' He paused, trying to remember her name. 'Jules?'

'Haven't heard from her for a few days,' Lia admitted, secretly pleased that he'd almost forgotten it. 'Which means she's fine, probably bonking someone new.'

'Is that so?' He looked amused.

'Yes, yes, I know what she's like. When she's bored and got no one she's on the phone or e-mail all day, but when she's seeing someone you barely hear a word. It's only natural, I suppose. And then over here, some smart gallery owner's coming to see Ben's work, Chloe's grudgingly gone off to be with her sick mother, and Peaches is busily looking for a needle in a haystack. All the usual madness, really,' Lia sighed.

'Getting tired with all the excitement around here, huh?'

She laughed. 'It's a bit intense, like being in a dormitory or something. I mean, individually they're all nice people, but put them all together and it just gets a bit much.'

'So, what are you going to do?'

'I don't know.' Lia leant in towards him, nuzzling him, feeling the strength of his chest. 'Maybe I need rescuing. Maybe you should just take me away from all this!'

'You know something?' He sipped his champagne thoughtfully. 'Maybe I should.'

'Sell your business, sell the house, sell the car, and let's run away somewhere. A little island in Greece, perhaps? Or somewhere in Italy?'

'I thought you'd already run away once,' Nick told her. 'You know, you can run all you like, but you'll never run away from yourself.'

She pulled away, sensing his seriousness. 'I know, I'm joking – of course you can't.' She straightened up, feeling slightly foolish. 'You're still lumbered with all the old baggage you brought with you in the first place. You think you can leave it all behind, you think you can escape from it all, but you can't.' She paused, realising how unhappy he looked. 'Are things still bad?'

'They're going to be bad for a couple of years, I guess,' he said evenly. 'Just got to get used to it. I don't see anyone pulling out of this unscathed.'

'I'm sorry. And what about that big client? Have they paid up yet?'

He shook his head. 'Something's going down there, I just don't know what.' He rubbed his eyes.

Lia shuddered. 'How can I cheer you up?' She turned to him. 'What can I do to make you feel better?'

He stroked her hair tenderly. 'Just being with you is helping.'

'Anything else?' she asked with a knowing smile.

'You know, there might just be something,' he replied smiling before gently leading her indoors and up the stairs.

Chapter Fifty

'Dear? Are you there dear? Why, I haven't seen you in ages!' Peaches' head appeared round the door. 'My, it smells divine in here – have you been baking bread?'

Lia had decided that this mid-season period, when it felt too mild to start on hearty soups and stews, but not summery enough to carry on making salads and fruit dishes, was the ideal time to try out different breads, and so had trawled through all her recipes and started adapting some. She'd made batches of garlic bread rolls with olives and rosemary, a round loaf flavoured with coriander seeds and oregano and a herb focaccia sprinkled with polenta and coarse sea salt, and then given them to Nick and Etienne, who had been particularly appreciative.

Today she was working on a *pain d'épices* with honey, cinnamon and nutmeg, which she'd heard was a surprisingly successful complement to foie gras, and a real autumn treat.

'Have a slice,' she suggested, cutting them each a piece, and they sat on the terrace in the sun.

'Oh, this is delicious,' Peaches said approvingly, scattering crumbs over the table. 'You are such a clever cook.' She paused for a second. 'How are you getting along?'

'Just fine,' Lia smiled, knowing it wasn't her book Peaches was referring to. 'I wish Ben and I could be friends, but it just doesn't seem to be working out that way. Every time we get on to the subject of Bella we end up having a row. I don't know how to avoid it.'

'I don't think she's really the problem,' Peaches said quietly, brushing some crumbs off her shirt. 'Ben's sore that you're with someone else now – that's the problem.'

Lia thought about this for a second, realising that she'd never once imagined how jealous and hurt Ben might be feeling. How dare she – in his eyes, anyway – continue criticising Bella when she herself was with someone else?

'Just as well I've been keeping my head down lately,' she smiled sadly. 'And Nick's been here all week, so I've been spending time with him. But how is everything? Bella OK? And what's Lionel like?'

'Oh, he's quite a charming fellow,' Peaches enthused. 'And so handsome! Bella's really a very lucky woman.'

Lia smiled. 'I hope she appreciates it.'

'I think she does, you know, this time. I actually think she does. They decided against staying in one of the studios, you know – they thought it too cramped. They're staying in a hotel nearby, somewhere terribly smart. Money seems to be no option with him!'

'Good, I'm glad.' Glad that Bella might now leave Ben alone, perhaps – the thought raced through her mind. 'And do you know if he's interested in Ben's work?'

'I believe he is,' Peaches told her. 'I believe he wants to do something with it in the spring. He has a very smart gallery in London, you know. Mayfair, somewhere. Really quite prestigious.'

'Yes, I know,' Lia said. 'I've read about him. That's great news,' she added simply, meaning it. 'Ben deserves some recognition. I hope it goes well for him.'

'I wish it could be easier between you two,' Peaches said. 'I get the feeling he's a little lost at the moment, although this project is going to keep him busy enough. But there's something else.' Peaches' eyes lit up and there was obvious excitement in her voice. 'I can't keep it back another minute. I have something really rather wonderful to tell you! I got my wish from the comet,' she began excitedly. 'Millicent's found her!'

Lia was stunned. 'Peaches, that's incredible! How on earth did she manage that?'

'Well, it was so obvious, really. You remember I told you she'd wanted to go into retail? Well, Millicent was doing all this research, going through the phone directories and what have you, when one day she was on her way to meet a friend for lunch in a neighbourhood she didn't know at all well. They were trying out a new restaurant – some Italian place her friend had heard about that had gotten rave reviews. Anyway, she took a wrong turning and found herself down some back street, all lined with stores – nothing too fancy, just good, basic family stores.' Lia began to wonder if the story would ever end. 'She stopped to get her bearings, and just saw it – a children's wear store. Called Lily Starlight!'

'Lily Starlight?'

'Oh, that was her full name – didn't I tell you? We are from California, you know!' she added with a giggle.

'And so you're sure this shop belongs to Rory?'

'Positive. The next day Millicent went back and this time she actually went inside. I'd sent her photos, of course, and she recognised her immediately. And you know what? She's expecting again!'

'Oh my God, Peaches, that's wonderful. So did Millicent speak to her?'

'She didn't, no. They don't know each other, you see – they've never actually met. So she wanted to discuss it with me first. To be honest, I'm not entirely sure what to do next. That's why I've come to you. You have such a clear, logical way of thinking.'

'You make it sound like a fault,' Lia chuckled. 'But I don't honestly know what to suggest. Are you thinking of going out to her?'

'Well, you know how I feel about planes,' Peaches

324

giggled nervously. 'And Felix couldn't possibly travel.'

'But surely you have to see her?'

'I know. I do, don't I? There really is no other way.' Peaches suddenly looked frightened.

'It's not the sort of thing you can do over the phone,' Lia continued. 'It might be tough, but I think you've got to go. If you *want* to, that is. I mean, maybe this is enough, just knowing she's alive and well?' Lia could see that Peaches longed for more. She took her hand. 'I think you have to go. Peaches, I don't think there's another way.'

'I mentioned it to Binkie, and she's offered to keep an eye on Felix for me, cook him some meals, that sort of thing. But it's such a long trip—'

'And you don't know what to expect at the end of it. I do understand. But you'll never know unless you go to her. I think it's just one of those things you've got to face. And I think you'll have to expect her to be difficult at first. I don't see it being easy.'

'Oh, my,' Peaches' face crumpled into a sob, and she covered her eyes with one hand. Lia sat with her, trying to comfort her.

'I think it'll work out,' she said softly. 'I think she'll come round. If she's having another baby, well, she'll be taking huge comfort from that. It feels like this is the time, Peaches. Didn't you say after all that her going on that show was a cry for help? And isn't it weird that Millicent just found the shop unexpectedly like that? It almost feels like a sign.'

'That's what Felix said.' Peaches sniffed. 'But you're right.' She pulled away, straightening herself out. 'You're quite right. I must summon up my courage, catch that plane and go find my daughter. It's what I must do. Even if she kicks me out of that store of hers, I will have made the effort.' Suddenly she brightened. 'Felix has promised to make a tape for me for the journey, a soothing meditation to calm my nerves.'

'Wonderful,' Lia tried to sound encouraging. 'I'm sure

that will help. Just don't expect her to be all smiles and welcomes at first. She might be far from it. But it'll be a start, and from that point you can write to her, call her, mount some kind of campaign to win her back. Whatever, it'll be a hell of a lot more than you've got now.'

Peaches got up, a determined look on her face. 'Well, that's settled then. I'll talk to a travel agent this afternoon. You'll be all right here alone, won't you?'

Lia smiled, and then hugged her friend. 'I think I'll manage,' she told her, relieved that Bella wasn't actually staying at Les Eglantines. 'I think somehow I'll cope.'

Chapter Fifty-one

As the clocks went back, so the comet disappeared from the sky, and Lia couldn't help but feel a certain sadness in its departure, as she did in the relentlessness of the oncoming winter, and the steady darkening of the nights. She tried to imagine how life might be in the months to come, snuggled up on the sofas in Nick's villa or seeing her own breath in the pink cottage – but no firm picture came to her, as if her future were so undecided it might not exist at all.

On one particularly mild evening she suggested that they ate in the pizza place in the village, which was still serving at tables set up in the church square. Nick, who was embarrassed at the number of meals she'd been cooking him lately, agreed at once. They had just ordered – a sweet potato soup for her followed by some chicken liver pasta, and pâté and a grilled steak for Nick – when Bella, Lionel Cooper-Smith and Ben appeared, taking a table in the far corner from their own. Nick had never met any of them before, but from the look on his face as he watched Lia's reaction, he knew exactly who they were.

'Does it bother you that they're here?' he asked.

'No, no, of course not,' she replied truthfully, turning

away. 'They've got business to discuss. I told you about it
– the older chap has a gallery and wants to put on a show
of Ben's work. I'm glad for him.'

'And so the woman's Bella? She's attractive.'

'Don't I know it.' Lia shuddered. 'As well as manipulative and venomous and a complete bitch. But if you'd like
me to introduce you—'

He laughed, interrupting her. 'There's no other woman
I need to meet.' He held her hand briefly before the waiter
laid their first courses in front of them.

Lia smiled, relieved, urging herself to believe that Nick
was the one, her future, her love. So why, then, did her
eyes keep straying over to where Ben sat, just to keep track
of the way he looked at Bella, to see if there was a hint of
anything in his eyes. Bella, she could see, was all over
Lionel, touching him affectionately on the shoulder as they
laughed, clearly happy in each other's company. And Ben?
He just looked out of place, somehow, and a little alone.

'Enjoying your soup?' Nick asked, clearly frustrated by
Lia's lack of attention.

'Yes, it's delicious,' she snapped back, angry at herself.
'They haven't stinted on anything, and the flavour's really
good.' What was Ben ordering, she wondered, noticing the
waiter hovering around them. And had he spotted yet that
she was there?

Suddenly she shrank back as Bella's eyes had turned to
meet her own, and she tried to focus on her soup, and on
Nick. Her cheeks burned, as she knew Bella was probably
telling the others that she'd seen her.

'You know, we could always leave,' Nick suggested
sarcastically.

'No, I'm sorry, I really am. It's that woman. She
somehow always manages to make me feel awkward.
There's just something about her, you know, something
superior, as if we're all just minions around her. It would-
n't matter if we had all sorts of things in common, if she
shared my love of cooking, or I shared hers of painting, or
if we'd been brought up in the same neighbourhood or

328

gone to the same school – there's still no way we could ever be friends. To be honest, I doubt she actually has that many female friends, you know – she's much more a man's woman.'

'And that's all that's bothering you?' Neatly, Nick was spreading some pâté on a piece of toast.

She laughed, embarrassed. 'Yes. Well, of course it's strange being in the same restaurant as your ex, I can't deny that. And it's strange to feel so distant from someone you were once so close to. I mean, how would you feel if Elodie turned up? Wouldn't that make you feel uncomfortable?'

He looked shocked. 'Elodie, wow, that's a tough one. Yeah, I guess it'd be awkward. But that was a long time ago. I haven't thought of her in ages. Your shawl looks very pretty, by the way.'

'Oh, this?' Lia laughed. 'It's a great colour, don't you think? It matches my skin tone.' How clever he was, she couldn't help but notice, to avoid discussing his previous relationships like that.

Their main courses arrived, and as Lia picked at her chicken livers, her eyes met Ben's, and they nodded to each other in friendly acknowledgement.

'Everything OK?' Nick asked tersely.

'Delicious,' she told him quickly, surprised at the tears which had suddenly started welling in her eyes. Her future was with Nick, she kept telling herself, pretending to have a problem with her contact lenses. This was the man for her. This man would be her husband, the father of her children. She'd be a fool to lose him now.

They decided against puddings, and Nick asked for and paid the bill. As he stood up, he turned to Lia.

'We've got to go say hello, you know that, don't you? You've got to introduce me.'

'OK.' Lia nodded weakly, knowing he was right. He always did the right thing, she thought grimly, wishing they could just sneak the long way out round the church square. She geared herself up to being the extrovert type she'd always envied, and approached the table, bursting into their conversation. 'Hi – enjoying your food?'

'Lia, how are you?' Bella reached up and air-kissed her on both cheeks. 'I thought that was you over there. Now, do introduce me.' She eyed Nick approvingly.

Everyone was introduced in an awkward display of outstretched arms and false niceties, and Lia couldn't help but wish that they hadn't stopped, knowing how irritated she'd feel at having to watch her food grow cold while making polite conversation. Bella swiftly began engaging Nick in a discussion about his house, his architect, and the contractor who designed his pool, leaving her standing dangerously close to Ben.

'So how are things?' he asked her quietly.

'Good, good,' she told him awkwardly. 'You?'

'Fine. I'm off to Kashmir soon. On the early flight to London tomorrow, and then heading off from there.'

'Kashmir? That's a bit dangerous, isn't it? I thought you'd had enough of all that.'

He shrugged. 'They asked, and I couldn't see a reason not to go. It'll be interesting though, and very photogenic.'

'God, be careful,' she implored. 'I thought you were busy sorting out your exhibition?'

'I was, but once I'd got a deadline, I got through it. I've worked on it solidly all the time I've been down here. So I'm taking all the material to my sister's and then when I get back I'll get everything printed and mounted properly.'

'Well, I'm really pleased about the exhibition. I'm thrilled for you. But I wish you weren't going away again. At least not there.'

'I'll be all right,' he laughed. 'And you? What's happening with you? You've been rivalling the baker's, I hear from Etienne. So what about all those rolls I wasn't offered?'

Lia laughed, but wanted to cry. Why did she always think it would be hard to talk to him, only to find it so easy? 'I felt sorry for him,' she said. 'He was showing me how to treat peach leaf curl the other day and saying how

330

much he missed Chloe. I had to do something.'

Ben glanced in Nick's direction and Lia realised his conversation with Bella had come to an end, and that he was now waiting for her. As Ben stood up to say goodbye, she couldn't help but lean forward and hug him.

'You take care of yourself, you hear me?' he whispered.

'You, too.' She held him tightly, oblivious of the others, just willing him to be careful and not to fall into any traps, or into the line of fire, or to be taken hostage, or any of the other things that might happen there. Finally she pulled away, suddenly appalled at what she'd just done. 'He's off to Kashmir,' she told Nick, trying to make light of their hug. 'Can you believe that?'

'Good luck.' Nick shook Ben's hand. 'You're a braver man than I am.'

They finished their goodbyes and walked to Nick's car, which was parked just below the square.

'He wasn't going to do any more dangerous stuff,' Lia started saying as she climbed in, trying to defuse what had just happened. 'He's got this exhibition coming up, and he wasn't going to do that kind of thing any more. But Kashmir's still dangerous, isn't it? I mean, anything could happen there.'

Nick said nothing, just continued driving towards his house.

'What did you think of Bella?' Lia asked. 'She was asking about your pool, wasn't she? She probably wants to install one herself. Her house is beautiful, you know, stunning.' She knew she was waffling, and could almost detect a level of panic in her voice. 'Did you talk much to Lionel? He seemed pretty smooth – perfect for her, I suppose.'

Nick pulled the car into his driveway and switched off the engine. She hopped out, hoping that things would be back to normal again once they were inside. She followed him to the door, waiting as he put the key in the lock and opened up, and then went in ahead as he stood politely aside for her.

Although she tried to, many times afterwards, Lia couldn't remember exactly what happened next. She felt herself being banged hard up against the wall, and her shock at how suddenly it had happened. She could remember gasping as a punch struck her on the side of her face, and then another, lower down, in her ribcage. She remembered reeling down from the shock and the pain, tumbling forward onto her knees and then a kick to her side, and then another, and then another. She couldn't remember if she cried out, or if she'd begged him to stop, couldn't remember if she tried stopping him, or indeed, if she'd have been able to. All she could remember was the shock, and the pain, and the feeling of complete and utter defencelessness.

And the next thing she knew he was holding her, crying over her, begging her to forgive him.

'Honey, I'm sorry.' She could hear the words being spoken, but couldn't register what they meant. 'Forgive me. I got so mad and so jealous seeing you two together, and I couldn't stop myself. I was so wrong. Please, forgive me. Let me help you. I'm sorry, I'm so sorry. I can't believe I did this to you. Please, Honey, forgive me – say you'll forgive me.'

She wanted to lie still, to hug herself, to hide away, to be alone and to gather herself, in her own time. But his voice kept pounding at her, irritating her like a plane flying overhead, or a fly buzzing at the kitchen window.

Finally she brought herself to look at him, to look deep into his watery, contrite eyes, to look hard at the face that she'd kissed, held and loved for months, and as firmly and as evenly as she could, she just said to him, 'Take me home. Now.'

Chapter Fifty-two

She woke up the next morning to the sound of the phone ringing. Not that she'd slept much, but had just lain there, in stunned disbelief at what had happened. He'd driven her home, tearfully apologising all the way, and she'd gone inside and run herself a hot, deep bath and sat in it until it was almost cold, and then carefully towel-dried herself before climbing into bed.

And now the phone was ringing, a particularly determined-sounding ring, and she lay there, unable to raise herself to answer it. Physically she didn't know if she could walk, and she had no desire either to catch a glimpse of herself in the mirror or to pore over the bruising on her body. She lay there quietly, long after it had rung off, until the need for her morning pee became unbearable, and then carefully, flinching as she did so, she pulled away the covers and swung her legs down to the floor.

To stand upright hurt, she discovered, so she walked, stiltedly, to the bathroom, holding the walls for support. Avoiding the mirror, she made straight for the loo, but once she'd finished, was faced with her own image as she washed her hands. But was it her? She looked like a victim of a mugging that she'd sometimes see in the paper, an aubergine-coloured bruise spreading halfway across her face, and her right eye swollen beyond recognition. Taking in the rest of her body she could see similar bruises all over her ribcage and buttocks. No longer afraid of what she might find, she stared at the marks, stopping only to go back to the bedroom to peer at them in the full-length mirror inside the wardrobe.

It was, she decided grimly, a work of art. She felt she could become an exhibit in Lionel Cooper-Smith's gallery – a living work of art, the living proof of Nick Delaney's fury. She dressed carefully, in loose clothing, and went downstairs to make a cup of tea. The phone started ringing again, and reluctantly she picked up.

'Hey, how are you?' Nick's voice began. 'I'm sorry, Honey, I'm so sorry. Can you ever forgive me?' She hung up, and returned to the kitchen, to boil the kettle.

Her tea made, she sat aimlessly at the dining table, wondering what to do. She could hardly go out and face the world with a face like that. If only Peaches were there, she kept thinking, she would be such a comfort. Along with Jules, Peaches was the only person she could talk to. She looked at her watch – it would be too early for Jules now, she'd be on her way to the office. She hated calling her friend anyway, as she was always either busy or en route somewhere or another call would come in or she'd be in the middle of something. Funny how all the communications tools in the world just seemed to make communication so much harder.

Why couldn't Peaches come back, she wished miserably. Why couldn't she appear in the doorway with strange warnings about Mercury being retrograde and sit with her and hold her hand and just *be* there? As it was, she could hardly go and ask Felix when she was due back. Even Chloe, she thought, even Chloe might be good company now. Or then again, perhaps not.

The phone started ringing again, and she ignored it, until suddenly it occurred to her that it might be Jules, or news of the others, and so she went to pick it up.

'I know you're mad at me,' Nick was crying now. 'But we have to talk. Please, give me a chance. Please. I love you. You're the last person I want to hurt. Please, Lia, let me see you, let me talk to you, please.'

She hung up, struck by the thought that this was the first time Nick had ever told her he loved her, and how it had never bothered her before that he hadn't. She finished her tea and made another cup, each movement awkward and laboured, accompanied by a flinch of pain. When the phone started ringing again she yelled at it to leave her alone, before sinking back into her chair.

She could call her mother, she thought as the phone continued to ring. Could she talk to her? But what to say? 'I got beaten up last night, Mum, by the man I've been sleeping with. Oh, and by the way, I was warned before I even met him that he'd do it'? She couldn't admit to something like this, couldn't admit to her stupidity and hubris.

The phone had stopped and then started again, and irritably she went to pick it up. This time she'd speak, she told herself – that was, as long as she still *had* a voice; she didn't know that for sure. This time she'd tell him to fuck off and leave her alone and never to call her again.

Buoyed up by the thought, she lifted the receiver.

'You'll never guess in a million years who I ran into last night?' So Jules had decided to do away with the usual hello's and niceties as well, then. 'Jonathan. In this bar in Soho. He was with some associates and looking really bored, so I went up and said hello.' Lia could tell that Jules was on the street, and probably heading towards the office. 'We had quite a nice chat, actually. I think he's lightened up a bit. He even took my number, saying perhaps we should meet up for a drink sometime.'

'Jules, he hit me,' she spat the words out, bursting into tears of relief as she did so. 'He fucking well hit me.'

'Oh, my God, Li, I don't believe it. What on earth happened?'

Lia's cries were too much for her to speak, and she

335

tried to control them. 'We were having dinner,' she began carefully. 'Last night. And then Ben and Bella and her new man turned up at the restaurant.' She took several deep breaths. 'I was distracted, I admit. It was my fault—'

'Li, it was not your fucking fault, don't even begin to think like that,' Jules said sharply. Then her voice softened. 'So what happened next?'

'As we were leaving we went up to talk to them – he actually said we should. I got talking to Ben and he told me he was off to Kashmir soon, and I was scared for him. We had a big hug goodbye, and I knew the minute we'd done it that I was in trouble.' She started crying again, her chest wracked with pain from the tears, and her ribcage hurting more with every sob. 'He drove me to his house. I should never have gone, I should have just gone home, but I wanted to save things; I kept trying to save them.'

'So what happened next?'

'I don't know, the minute I was inside he started hitting me, kicking me, I don't know, I don't know what happened, I was so shocked.'

'Oh, God, Li, you poor thing. Are you all right? I mean, nothing broken?'

'No, I mean, I'm fine. Just sore. Bruised as hell and so ashamed.'

'Ashamed? Come on, Li, you've got nothing to be ashamed of. Don't talk like that.'

'But I knew, didn't I? I fucking well knew!'

'Look, I knew too, but I was taken in. It was all so hard to believe, or maybe we just didn't want to believe it? Oh fuck, I've got another call coming. Hold on a minute and I'll get rid of them.'

At this, even Lia had to laugh. A few seconds later Jules was back. 'Sorry about that. Look, I'm almost at the office now. Why don't I call you from there? I'll even come over if you like, you know – I bet they'd let me. I could jump on a plane and be there in the afternoon?'

'No, no,' Lia said quickly. 'Please don't tell them, don't tell anyone. I really don't want anyone to know. It looks so stupid. I am not a battered wife; this is not me. Please don't say a thing, OK? Promise?'

'If you insist,' Jules agreed. 'Look, I'll call you a bit later, OK?'

Lia hung up the phone and went back to the bathroom to reassess the damage to her face, wondering hopefully whether she could cover the bruising with make-up. It was impossible, though – nothing would disguise that colour. She would just have to work, she told herself, get on with her work and let her bruising heal.

But once she'd turned on her laptop and opened the files she'd last been working on, she couldn't do it. How to write about bread when she felt she'd been viciously kneaded herself, or describe aubergines when she pretty much looked like one?

She went back to the kitchen for more tea, only to notice how low she was on milk, and how few provisions she had left. She'd been meaning to go to the supermarket that morning, but there was no way she could go now. Cursing, she checked all her cupboards to see how much food she could live off, not that she felt like eating anything. She thought she heard the chink of the gate, and her heart leapt – was Peaches back? Not daring to go outside, though, she waited for the sound of her footsteps, or the familiar warmth in her voice, or for an angry admonition of the neighbour's cat, but none came. It was too soon, she told herself – Peaches would be another week at least.

She was preparing to go on-line when the phone rang again, and she rushed to answer it. Instead of Jules, though, as she'd hoped, it was Nick.

'I left you something outside,' he started. 'And I'm praying you'll forgive me. At least let's talk? At least let me explain. Please, Honey, give me that much.'

She hung up, before he could say anything else, and gingerly opened the front door. On the step were two bulging supermarket bags with a bunch of mixed flowers lying on top, and quickly she took them all inside. One bag contained milk, some cheeses, a steak, butter and bread;

337

the other some fruit and vegetables, biscuits and pasta. She found herself laughing gently at his thoughtfulness, and then her laughter turned into tears again – great, painful, sobbing tears.

Pulling herself together, she unpacked the bags and put the flowers into a vase, wondering whether she was wrong to accept them. A stronger person might just take them right back to his house and leave them on his doorstep, but she wasn't feeling that strong yet, and was simply grateful not to have to go anywhere herself.

When the phone started ringing again, she was sure it was him, and picked it up. 'Thank you,' she said quietly.

'For what?' Jules's voice came on the line.

'Oh God, he was just round here. He brought two bags of goodies and some flowers. It was sweet of him – the last thing I wanted was to go to the supermarket.'

'It was sweet of him?' Jules repeated. 'He beats the shit out of you last night but now you're saying "Never mind, it was sweet of him to do this"?'

'I know, I know, don't be hard on me,' Lia agreed. 'A poor choice of words. But it does get me out of going outside today.'

'Well, how much does that save you and how much him?' Jules challenged her. 'It hardly reflects well on him if his girlfriend is seen looking battered and bruised, now, does it? So if anything, you're doing him a favour by not going anyway. He's not doing this for you, you know, he's doing it for himself.'

'Oh God, I suppose you're right. It's just, he keeps calling, keeps asking me to forgive him; he sounds like he's crying and, I don't know, he just sounds so bad.'

'Don't even think about it,' Jules was firm. 'Don't even think about talking to him, let alone forgiving him. You hear me? This is what they do, these men, and the women feel obliged to take them back. And then, sometime later, the beating starts up again. Don't fall into that trap, what- ever you do.'

'Oh God, what am I doing here? Why did I ever think

this was a good idea? Why did I ever leave?'

'Li, come on. I just spent twenty minutes stuck on the Northern Line. I practically choked on the pollution on my way to the office. I came in to twenty-four e-mails, seven new synopses to go through and a major production delay on one of my biggest titles. I'd give my eye teeth to be where you are now, though maybe not exactly in the same state. You're doing fine, believe me.' Her voice was softer now, caring. 'Everyone loves your work. I don't think I've told you that before, but they really do. They're hiring a great photographer to illustrate it and everyone's getting really excited. Don't even think about giving up.'

In spite of herself, Lia started crying again. Perhaps it was hearing Jules's words of encouragement that did it. She thanked her friend and slumped down in front of her laptop. She would go on-line, she told herself, plugging in the modem. She'd read the papers, scour the gossip sections and have some fun. Anything to take her mind off what had happened.

And once she'd done all that, she decided she'd do something rash, and for her, quite brave.

She decided to e-mail Ben.

Chapter Fifty-three

He stopped calling after a while. Lia stayed quietly in and around the pink cottage, talking to Jules and trying to think about something that wasn't her bruises and didn't involve getting beaten up. She went to bed early, making sure all her windows and doors were firmly shut, feeling for the first time in her life that she was in danger.

In the morning, she woke at her usual time, studied her bruises in the mirror to find them little changed and made herself a cup of tea. Jules had suggested photographing them, as evidence, and talked about contacting the police, but Lia had no desire to go that far. She couldn't, she *wouldn't* become a victim. And she'd known what she'd been letting herself in for all along.

By the time she was dressed the phone started ringing.

'What say I take you to dinner?' He sounded brighter now, less remorseful and desperate, and inwardly she groaned. 'Your favourite place, you know? The one with the table under the olive tree. They do a mean grilled steak and I've got a bottle of that St Emilion you love especially on order. And you know the best thing? It's just a short, uphill walk from your place to get there, so no one need see you. We need to talk, Lia.' His voice softened now. 'I really need to see you. So, let's say I'll meet you there tonight, around seven-thirty, OK? I'll be waiting.'

She hung up, but the call unsettled her. Just knowing that he was a few metres above unsettled her, and she couldn't face pottering in the kitchen garden in case she saw him. She'd stopped crying now and was feeling more resolved. She decided to go on-line to see if there was a reply from Ben. She didn't expect anything, though; it was too soon. Would he be spending much time at his sister's before heading off, and where exactly did you fly to in Kashmir, anyway? Restlessly she waited as her server loaded, and her breath quickened at the sound of the three words she most wanted to hear: *You have e-mail.*

She opened her mail box, cursing how long it was taking, only to see the Mailer Daemon message returning her e-mail to Ben. Damn! She must have got his address wrong. He'd told it to her once, and it had seemed so obvious at the time that she hadn't bothered to write it down. She tried another variation, using his initials, and another putting a dash between his names, and sent them both off with an introductory sentence explaining what had happened.

She wanted to make tea but had drunk enough Earl Grey for one morning. She went in search of some herbal, pulling out box after box from the cupboard, looking for one she thought might be comforting: strawberry and vanilla, caramel, apple and almond, peach and black-currant, verbena and orange-flower, raspberry and grapefruit, lime-blossom and honey – each one seemingly more enticing yet actually more revolting than the last. No box had more than two or three bags used, and Lia was appalled at her own waste. Why had she collected them so avidly, she asked herself. What had she been expecting from any of them? They'd become a kind of addiction, and yet far from providing the comfort she'd longer for, all they'd done was clog up valuable cupboard space with their pretty boxes and their insipid smells.

341

She would throw them all out, she decided; clear out the clutter in her life and start again. It would be therapeutic. She began emptying the bags themselves into the bin, regretting all the waste, while flattening the boxes ready for a future trip to the recycling depot. Then she'd go through the rest of her cupboards, she told herself, and clean them all out thoroughly, scrub all the kitchen surfaces, even behind all her storage jars, before turning her attention to the bathroom. In cleaning the house she'd be doing something tangible, something positive, feeling suddenly energetic and driven.

She was tipping all the boxes into her recycling bags when there was an ominous tap on the front door, and the voice she least wanted to hear rang out.

'Lia? Lia? Are you there?' She heard the door open and cursed herself for not having kept it locked. 'Are you there? Only I wanted to invite you and that divine man of yours to—' Bella stopped, startled at the apparition which appeared through the kitchen doorway. 'Oh my God, what on earth happened to you?'

A selection of answers flashed through Lia's mind. She'd had a car accident, fallen down the stairs, walked into the wardrobe. 'That divine man of mine,' she said instead, with a wry smile.

'Oh my God, you poor thing!' Bella dropped her handbag and rushed towards her. 'Are you all right?'

'I'm fine,' Lia said tersely, furious for not having locked herself in.

'He seriously did this? He did this to you?' Bella was scrutinising the bruising on her face.

'Right after we saw you. He didn't appreciate me saying goodbye to Ben like that.'

'I don't believe it. What did you do? Have you contacted the police?'

'No, no, I don't want to do anything like that.'

'Are you sure? I mean, he shouldn't be allowed to get away with it. And what about him, anyway – has he been in touch?'

342

'Yes, yes,' Lia sighed, wishing Bella would just go, yet at the same time kind of appreciating her concern. 'He never stopped ringing yesterday, and today I've had an invite to dinner.'

'Well, you're not going, are you?'

'No, of course not.'

'Look, is there anything I can do? Do you need a doctor? I know a marvellous man—'

'No, no, I'm fine, really I am. Just a bit sore, that's all.'

'I can't believe it,' Bella sat down at the dining table with a thud. 'He seemed such a wonderful person, and Peaches never stopped raving about him.'

'I was warned,' Lia sat down too. 'Chloe knew. She used to massage Elodie, his ex.'

'Well, who'd believe that silly girl? I certainly would-n't. Where is she, anyway?'

Lia explained about Chloe's mother. 'Would you like something to drink?' She suggested, heading towards the kitchen. 'Coffee, tea? I was just clearing out some herbal stuff when you arrived.'

Bella peered at all the boxes disapprovingly. 'I don't blame you. I'll have some coffee, please, with milk.'

Lia made a cafetière, strangely glad that Bella was there. She seemed so mature, so responsible, that Lia almost felt safe. They sat at the dining table with their mugs.

'Does anybody else know?' Bella asked.

Lia shook her head. 'I wish Peaches was here. She's the one person I'd like to talk to. But I haven't seen anyone else. I've been keeping my head down, for obvious reasons.'

'It's nothing to be ashamed of, you know.'

'That's what my friend Jules, in London, says. But you still feel, so stupid, really. I mean, I was warned. But I got taken in by it all – the charm, the generosity, the warmth. It was so hard to believe he could turn.'

'I know, I'd probably have felt the same. It's funny, I'd always rather wanted to meet him myself, before, but I was never here at the right time.'

343

Lia smiled. She could almost see them together. 'Lionel seems very nice,' she offered.

'He is, isn't he? Such a relief to meet someone genuinely fun and interesting and creative. I've quite fallen for him.'

There was a brief pause as both sipped their coffee. Then Bella said, 'You know, I don't expect you to like me. I know I've done and said some terrible things, and I apologise for them. I didn't take you seriously, or rather, I didn't take Ben's feelings for you seriously. I knew all about what happened to him in Afghanistan, and why he was so reluctant to commit to anyone, and so I rather dismissed you as a fling. And I was just stuck in this horrible, dark place after my divorce came through, so negative and insecure and jealous. But now, since I met Lionel, the cloud's lifted, and I can see again. So I want you to know how sorry I am. I wasn't myself.'

Lia nodded, not knowing what to say, and then finally said a subdued 'thank you' before starting to cry again.

'Look, come and stay with us,' Bella suggested. 'Don't be here, all by yourself, not with him right there above you. Come and stay. The house is vaguely habitable these days – that's why I was hoping to have you round. Let's go and pack some things.'

Li shook her head. 'Really, that's very kind, but I'm fine here. I can't let him drive me out of my own house.'

'Are you sure? I feel so bad, there must be something I can do. Some shopping, perhaps? Is there anything you need?'

'He thought of that already.' She told her about the groceries Nick had left.

'You're not thinking about going tonight, are you? Promise me you're not thinking about it?'

Bella was beginning to sound like an over-protective mother, and Lia hated feeling like that little girl all over again. 'I'm not thinking about it, believe me.'

'Oh God, is that the time?' Bella had suddenly caught sight of her watch. 'I have a meeting with some pool people at twelve. Look, take my mobile number, and if anything happens, or you need anything, just call me, OK?' She wrote it down on a piece of paper. 'I know I'm the last person you'd probably want to contact but it looks like I'm the only one around, so you're just going to have to face up to it, OK?'

This last comment was delivered with a mild laugh. Lia joined her.

'Thank you,' she said firmly. 'I really do appreciate it.' Then she thought of something. 'Is Ben still in London? Have you been in touch with him at all?'

'Ben?' Bella looked surprised. 'He's only just left. All I know is that he's leaving England shortly, and will contact Lionel once he gets back about the exhibition. We're really not that close, you know.'

Ask her for his e-mail address, ask her for his e-mail address, the thought raced through Lia's mind, but she stood, paralysed, not wanting to admit that she'd tried to contact him and failed even to do that much. How much more humiliation could she heap onto herself?

'Did you help him sort out which photos to use in the end?' she asked instead, a strangely neutral question that was still important to her.

'God, no,' Bella laughed. 'He knew exactly what he was doing – he certainly didn't need my help. He just needed a kick up the backside, that was all.' She began heading towards the gate, and then turned. 'Seriously, Lia, if there's anything you need, or if you change your mind about staying, please contact me.' She gave her a quick hug and was gone.

Lia sat back on her chair on the terrace, in stunned disbelief.

Chapter Fifty-four

By the evening Lia was feeling bored. This was her restless time of day, when she would be making dinner preparations and looking forward to some company, and the thought of yet more hours on her own was filling her with dread.

She wondered whether to call Bella, but wasn't ready for that just yet, and the last thing she wanted was for someone like Lionel Cooper-Smith to see her the way she was. Perhaps she should have got Jules to come over, but then, she hardly wanted the publishers to know what had happened, either. So she was stuck with her solitude, unless, of course, she went to join Nick.

All day she'd been pushing that thought from out of her mind, but now, as darkness fell on the terrace, she let the idea play out in her mind. She'd climb up the hill, no mean feat in her state, or perhaps just drive round. She played with the hill theory, and imagined herself arriving at the top, amidst his cypress trees on the neatly tailored lawn. He'd be standing there in some elegant chinos and a fleece, lighting the barbecue and wiping its utensils clean. Perhaps he'd be having a beer. He'd turn as she arrived, and she'd be looking suitably frail and drawn.

He'd come towards her and scoop her up in his hands, kissing her hair and begging for forgiveness. At this point Lia's stomach lurched – the thought of being in his arms again, of smelling that nice clean smell of his, of feeling his skin against her own – she couldn't do it, couldn't allow herself to go through with it, couldn't trust herself not to fall for him again.

She stopped the fantasy there. It was ridiculous anyway, as it was far too dark to walk and she wouldn't be able to see a thing, so she'd have to drive. She pictured herself entering his gates and pulling up outside a door which used to feel like home, and then promptly imagined herself having to run away, jumping back inside the car, only to stall it as he ran after her.

She couldn't go. She'd shut the shutters, lock all the doors and pour herself a glass of wine.

But as she did all that, her thoughts kept turning to him. He would be up there now, getting everything ready. He'd be preparing to tell her what happened – to tell her about his wife, perhaps, and about Elodie, and about how he was going to change. It was funny how only a few days ago she had decided he was the one for her, and now he'd become the last person she could allow herself to see.

It was over, but she'd miss the good Nick, the nice Nick, who treated and spoiled her and who took her and Jules to Monte Carlo, and who was funny and kind and generous. She'd miss him. And she'd miss the house, she thought guiltily, and the pool and the car. All the trappings, she thought grimly, and there she was, herself trapped in the pink cottage, a victim of her own foolishness and vanity.

But what if he could change? she asked herself. They'd been together for months now with no sign of any violence, what if this were the last time? What if he'd got whatever it was out of his system, and was now ready to be a good husband, or lover, or whatever it was he could actually be for her?

She could at least hear him out, she began telling

347

herself. She could at least go up there, not allow any physical contact, but just listen to what he had to say. She played that scene out in her mind – the barbecue, the beer, the chinos – but there would be no hug, she'd shrink away from that. Instead, she'd just sit down and listen. But then what? Would she walk away if she didn't like what she heard? Would she turn away and never see him again?

She felt herself crying again – crying because she missed the good person that was inside him, the good person that was genuinely there. She wanted that person back. She looked at her watch – it was almost seven o'clock. She could shower and change, drive round to his place and hear him out. She would not let herself succumb to his charm, or to his excuses – she would simply hear him out, and leave.

Decided, she raced upstairs, pulled off her clothes and stood under a warm shower for five minutes. Then she dressed, pulling on some thick, loose-fitting trousers, a jumper and her fleece. There was nothing she could do about the bruising on her face, she thought regrettably, before telling herself off. The last thing she wanted was to make herself attractive for him. She applied some lipstick, which was all she could manage, and out of habit sprayed herself with perfume, before chiding herself for having done so. This was not a date, she kept repeating to herself. This was closure.

She was just on her way downstairs when she heard the chink of the gate – had he come to collect her? Would he be so bold? She held her breath and then released it again at the sight of Bella marching towards her, a bottle of champagne in one hand.

'Lia!' she cried out. 'What are you doing? You were going to him, weren't you? I don't believe you, I really don't. Well thank God I decided to come.'

'I only thought—' Lia began.

'What? That he deserved a chance? That you would hear him out? Oh come on, we both know what would happen. He'd mount the charm offensive to end all charm

348

offensives and you'd just fall for it. I'm not going to let you go, now, you hear me? I can't believe you were seriously thinking of going. Now, where are your glasses?'

Meekly Lia went to the kitchen to find them, whilst Bella set about opening the bottle.

'And I ordered a Chinese takeaway – it'll be here at around eight,' Bella continued efficiently, pouring out two glasses. 'Lionel got a call from one of his clients – turns out he was staying nearby, and they're having dinner. I could have gone but something told me I'd be needed here.' She passed Lia a glass. 'Just as well, really.'

Lia sipped her champagne guiltily, feeling like a schoolgirl who'd been caught smoking. She began to understand how Ben must have felt, caught up in the force of Bella's personality. 'You're right,' she said finally. 'I was going. I was going to let him explain himself, and to find out about what happened to his wife and his ex. I just thought I needed that one conversation, that was all.'

'Well, like I said,' Bella sipped from her glass. 'We both know it wouldn't have ended there. So just as well I came. Cheers.'

Lia was aware of the time, all the time. She was aware when it was seven-thirty and had still got that mental picture of him fussing around his barbecue. By eight she thought she could almost smell the charcoal burning. As Bella jumped up to greet the Chinese delivery boy, and she disappeared into the kitchen for plates and bowls, she could imagine him sitting there, warming himself by the barbecue, the opened bottle of St Emilion on the table.

'Oh Nick,' she said softly, rummaging in the drawer for chopsticks. 'Why did you have to ruin everything? Why?' She could almost feel his remorse and for that second wanted to hug him, to tell him she forgave him and to go back to the way they were.

'Right,' Bella's voice boomed out behind her. It was as if she was deliberately playing the role of schoolmistress, bullying her into forgetting about him. 'We've got chicken

349

and cashew nuts, egg fried rice, sizzling beef, which has probably lost its sizzle by now, and some spring rolls. Help yourself.'

Lia began to laugh. The thought of sitting in her dining room, eating a Chinese takeaway with Bella DeVere was so ludicrous it was comical. 'This is very kind,' she began. 'I was getting very down on my own.'

'That's why you should stay with us,' Bella chided. 'I know how it feels, and the last thing you want is to be alone.'

'You know?' Lia stopped, a spoonful of chicken and cashew nuts perched precariously mid-air above her plate. 'Did your husband—'

'No, no, nothing like that,' she replied quickly. 'He just liked to fuck secretaries.' She laughed, but then her tone changed. 'I can't have children, and that became a big deal for him. He started screwing around, fell in love with his PA and has just become the proud father of twins. No, I know what the loneliness feels like, and the sense of being unattractive and undesirable. It hurts like hell.'

'That's when you came here? To the retreat, I mean?' Lia asked.

'That's right. My –' she searched for the right word '– dalliance with Ben was the first after he'd left me, so I suppose it took on a great significance. Deep down I knew that there was nothing to it, but like you are now, I kidded myself that maybe it could work out. I behaved badly – I've told you I'm sorry. It's funny how when you're inside it, that terrible depression, you can't imagine that it'll ever lift, and then it does, and you can't quite remember it ever having been so bad. You look back and think "My God, did I really do that?"'

'Those scripts—' Lia started.

Bella shrugged, embarrassed. 'Yes, sorry about that. He must lie with the goat. My little joke, I'm afraid. My spiteful little joke.'

'I can laugh about it now,' Lia told her. 'At the time, though, I couldn't believe how everyone was so taken in.

350

They all made me feel inferior because I was being so "closed off" spiritually.'

'I'm not proud of all that,' Bella admitted. 'But I hope we can get over it. When Ben gets back, I hope you two can be close again. I really do.'

'Me, too.' Lia paused, suddenly trusting Bella, understanding what had motivated her. 'I sent him an e-mail yesterday. Told him about what happened, and asked him to stay out of trouble and to get back safely. And then the bloody thing came back. I've tried variations on the address but they both came back too. You don't know it, by any chance, do you?'

Bella shook her head. 'Not wired up I'm afraid,' she told her. 'Can't particularly see the point, although Lionel's started nagging me. He might have it, though. I could ask him.'

'If you would,' Lia tried not to sound desperate.

The phone started ringing and they looked at each other for a second before Lia jumped up to answer it.

'Just calling to confirm your reservation,' Nick's voice came on the line. 'Your table's all ready.'

'I'm not coming,' she told him firmly. 'You can cancel it.' She hung up.

'You can't stay here with him towering above you like this,' Bella insisted. 'Come back with me tonight,' she suggested. 'And we'll take it from there. Let's get you out and about a bit more. It'll do you good.'

Lia smiled, gratefully. Bella was right, of course. 'Yes, I will,' she told her. 'And thank you.'

Chapter Fifty-five

Lia spent the next few days at Bella's house. It was uncomfortable and many of the rooms were covered in dust, but she felt safe there, and rather enjoyed being somewhere completely new. The garden was a delight, and she'd spend any free time she had wandering through the cypress and olive trees, exploring. Bella and Lionel were staying at a hotel a few miles away, but would join her each morning for breakfast before planning their day. They usually had galleries or exhibitions to visit, or Bella would have a meeting with yet another contractor, and so Lia created a makeshift office in her bedroom where she tried to work.

Lia found that, far from being difficult, as she'd rather imagined, Lionel was funny, considerate and kind, and he and Bella made her feel protected, like a stray kitten who'd pitched up from nowhere only to be given the best place to sleep by the fire. Wasn't that exactly what Ben had been to Bella, she reflected one afternoon – a stray she could nurture? So, had Bella always needed to be needed, perhaps, making her husband's rejection all the more painful?

Lia found herself fascinated by her new friend, watching

her knock up meals in her reduced kitchen, pouring generous glasses of wine and shivering, laughing, by the paraffin heater as the evenings wore on. She had a marvellously practical side to her that Lia had never expected, and an earthy sense of humour that caught her by surprise. Suddenly there was a new dimension to the woman – a capable, light-hearted side Lia had never imagined possible. It was as if a 3D Bella had emerged from the cartoon cut-out she was before, and Lia felt as if she was seeing her for the first time.

Instead of feeling in the way and self-conscious about her bruises, Lia felt at home and wanted. Each morning Lionel would make a point of scrutinising her marks, making her laugh with descriptions ranging from squashed fig to over-ripe banana as they lessened with every day. He wasn't around much, though, but would disappear off to meet with clients or artists, or to take Bella somewhere glamorous for lunch, and although she rehearsed telling him about that fateful night in the Indian restaurant off the Fulham Road a hundred times, she somehow never quite managed it.

Likewise she got nowhere with Ben's e-mail address – Lionel had just looked vague when she asked him, saying that he thought he had it somewhere, but never actually producing it. She asked him twice and then gave up, persuading herself that she'd come up with it eventually. Mentally she composed several e-mails, though, telling Ben what was going on, and knowing how funny he'd find it all; but as Bella's phone line had yet to be connected, she had no means of getting in touch.

She returned to the pink cottage only when they left for England, determined to buy plants for some of Bella's urns as a thank-you present. The pink cottage felt stuffy and lifeless, and she found herself peering up nervously towards Nick's toffee-coloured house for any sign that he was there. Her bruising was coming down now, much to her relief, and she could almost disguise it with make-up. Bella had given her the contents of her own fridge – some pâté, cold meats, milk, jam and eggs, so there was no immediate need to present herself to the world.

Once she'd sorted herself out, put a load of washing on and gone through her post, Lia went on-line. Still nothing from Ben, she found to her disappointment, wishing that she'd been tougher on Lionel. She tried another couple of variations on his address, read the papers and logged off again, deciding to call Jules.

'Isn't it weird how it's all turned out,' her friend said. 'I mean that Bella of all people would be so supportive?'

'Tell me about it. It's like everyone's changed since I first met them. And talking of about-turns,' Lia remembered. 'So what about you and Jonathan? Weren't you going to meet up with him?'

'Yeah.' Jules didn't sound too enthusiastic. 'I'm supposed to be seeing him later this week, actually. A quick drink, that's all, but I'm going to make sure I've got something to go to afterwards.'

'You won't tell him about me, will you?' Lia asked. 'I'd hate for him to know.'

'No, of course I won't,' Jules agreed. 'Though God knows what we *will* talk about. Oh shit, someone's on the other line, I'd better go.'

Lia felt deflated, as she always did when Jules had to cut her off, but got back to work on her autumnal mushrooms chapter. She planned a few recipes, knowing she'd have to go out sometime, if only to buy ingredients. She was just gearing up for a trip to the supermarket, when Chloe appeared in the doorway.

'Hello stranger, there you are!' she said. 'I was beginning to get worried about you.'

'You're back.' Lia was surprised at how pleased she was to see her. Now perhaps Les Eglantines would get back to normal, she thought, fondly remembering her first night at Peaches' house. How long ago it all seemed.

'What on earth happened to you?' Chloe was already scrutinising her face.

'Guess.' Lia shook her head.

'Oh my God, I did warn you.'

354

'I know you did,' Lia assured her. 'I accept full responsibility. And I don't really want to talk about it, if you don't mind.'

Chloe looked a little disappointed. 'That bastard,' she hissed. 'That complete bastard.'

Lia found herself wanting to defend Nick, but stopped. 'Coffee?' She offered instead, making them both a cafetière. 'How's your mum doing?'

'She's OK. You were right, she was really pleased I went back. It meant a lot to them both. That's why I've come up to see you. I'm leaving here, I'm going back home.'

'Chloe, are you really?' Lia found herself feeling strangely upset.

'Yeah, it's for the best. It was never going to work out, you know, Etienne and me. We're too different. Talk about not even speaking the same language. He's a lovely guy, and I've really enjoyed our time together, but he's not the one for me.'

'But I thought you two were really close?'

Chloe shrugged. 'I did a lot of thinking, you know, back home. And I realised how much I've grown, how much I've learnt about myself, spiritually, I mean. And I realised that this whole place here, my reason for being here, was to develop and grow, and to find myself. And now I've done all that, I feel I'm ready for the next stage in my life.'

'And what's that, then, do you suppose?' Lia tried to remember every word Chloe used, thinking how much Ben would enjoy this.

'I'm getting back together with my Ian, my ex. Moving back in with him, in fact.'

'Wow.' Lia tried to hide her surprise. 'I mean, I bet he's thrilled.'

'Yeah.' Chloe sounded less certain. 'And I am, too. He is my husband, after all. I'm ready to commit to a proper relationship, you know, to starting a family and building a new life together.'

'But what about all his financial problems?'

355

'Well, he's got himself sorted,' Chloe brightened. 'His uncle helped him out, invested quite a bit in the business and then took over some of the management. It's all worked out, and he's even buying a new house.'

Suddenly it was all making sense. 'Somewhere nice?' Lia asked.

'Lovely.' Chloe's eyes lit up. 'In an area I've always liked. Really beautiful houses, with nice gardens. So I'll be moving in with him there, it'll be great.'

'And what about Etienne? How's he taken all this.'

'He'll be all right. He was upset, of course, but he understands. He was an important part of my spiritual progress, and I think he realises that. Tell you the truth, I wouldn't be surprised if he doesn't get straight back together with Hélène, from the bakery, I know she's been waiting for him.'

'Gosh, big changes, then. And have you heard anything from Peaches?'

'Not really,' Chloe told her. 'Felix said something about a family reunion, but I wasn't really listening.'

Lia tried not to react – Chloe's self-centredness knew no bounds. 'And so you're leaving, like, straight away?'

'This afternoon. That's why I was glad I caught you. I kept trying yesterday. I've just come back to pick up my things.'

'But what about Peaches? You can't go without seeing her, surely?'

'She'll be all right,' Chloe started getting up. 'But tell her goodbye from me, won't you?'

'You won't even see her before you go?' Lia asked in disbelief. 'I mean, after all this time?'

'She'll understand.' Chloe said confidently. 'My place is with my sick mum and my husband. I'll get earning again and have a nice house to live in. I'm just following my path. It's what's right for me.'

'And Ian, your husband,' Lia raced to get all the facts, knowing she'd only kick herself later if she didn't. 'He was thrilled to see you again, I bet?'

Chloe didn't seem so sure. 'He'd started seeing someone else, to be honest,' she said indignantly. 'A girl from the local pub. I soon broke that up,' she added with a laugh. 'I wasn't going to let her have his nice new house. After what I went through with him – you know all his worries, the business going down – I'm the one who deserves all that, not her.'

Lia tried not to laugh, but hugged Chloe affectionately at the gate.

'I'm going to try for a baby, the minute I get back,' Chloe confided. 'That way he can't change his mind.'

'I'm sure a baby would be a very . . . spiritual . . . thing for you both, and I wish you well.' Lia tried to keep a straight face. 'You don't happen to have Ben's e-mail address, by any chance, do you?' she asked. 'Only I thought I did but I've obviously got it down wrong.'

'E-mail?' Chloe frowned. 'No, he's never given it me.' Her tone changed. 'Now you're not going to see that Nick again, are you?' she asked.

Lia shook her head. 'Not if I can help it,' she told her. 'I'll miss you,' she added, realising with surprise that she actually meant it.

'You've changed, you know, since you got here,' Chloe called out from the orchard. 'You're much less uptight than you used to be.'

Lia laughed back. 'Maybe it's a spiritual thing,' she suggested. 'Maybe you've all got to me at last.'

Chapter Fifty-six

The washing gave her away. She knew it would – realised it the minute she started hanging it out in the kitchen garden, and decided she almost wanted it to; she wanted their inevitable conversation to take place.

He arrived that evening, a bunch of red roses in one hand and a bottle of Côtes du Rhône in the other. She wasn't frightened by his appearance, uninvited, at the door, but was mentally prepared to see him, and felt strong enough to deal with it.

'You've been away,' he said, handing her the gifts. He looked tired and drawn, but had shaved and smelt of shower gel. He was wearing jeans and a white T-shirt under a moss green jumper, and she had to look away not to feel attracted to him again.

'At Bella's,' she told him, depositing the bottle on the table and unwrapping the flowers.

'You OK?' he asked. 'You look good.'

'The bruising's gone down,' she answered, trying to sound casual, cutting the bottom off each stem and then bashing it lightly with the handle of her scissors. 'And you?' she asked. 'How have you been?

'Terrible,' he told her, approaching the kitchen. 'Can I

open this?' He indicated the bottle, and she nodded towards the drawer where she kept the corkscrew. 'I've been wanting to talk to you for days.'

'I'm sure you have.' Lia arranged the flowers in a vase before taking them to the sitting room.

He opened the bottle and reached for two glasses, and they sat at the dining-room table. She couldn't look at him, but stared at her wine or at the grain of the wood instead; anything to avoid being seduced by those eyes, and that smile, again.

'I've been wanting to tell you how sorry I am. You're the last person I want to hurt. If there was anything I could do – if I could turn back the clock and for it not to have happened, then I'd do it. I feel guilty and ashamed. I want you to know that.'

'But it did happen, Nick.' Lia sipped her wine. 'And it's not going to again.'

'No, you're right, it won't. I have a problem,' he started, and she was reminded of the afternoon, just after Jules's visit, when he had said the same thing. That conversation had led them straight to bed, she remembered, determined not to succumb today.

'I've started therapy again,' he continued. 'I have anger management problems, and I get jealous easily.' He paused, and she noticed that tears were welling in his eyes, and turned away again quickly. 'And things have been rough lately, with the business, you know that. It sounds like an excuse, but I've been under a ton of pressure. But I'm back in therapy, and I'm making progress.'

'Nick, it doesn't matter. I mean, good, I'm glad for you, you obviously need it, but that's it. We're over. I'm not going to live like this. I can't live with the doubt and the worry that any time I so much as smile at someone—'

'But I'm getting there,' he insisted. 'Please, Lia, hear me out. I'm working hard, and I'm getting there. But I can't do this alone.' His voice started breaking. 'I need you. Please, give me another chance. I can't do this alone.'

She shook her head. 'It's not a risk I want to take. I'm

359

sorry, but like I said, I can't live like that.'

She could see him fighting for the right words, battling her. 'Do it for me, I beg you. I'm in a real dark place now. You're the one hope I have. Please. Come see the therapist with me. He wants to meet you, wants us to go together. He'll tell you how far I've come.'

'And how far's that? That I haven't committed suicide yet – is that the measure?' She felt her own voice crack, and the tears springing up. 'Or that I haven't been forced to flee, to run away while you were on business? So that's the big improvement?'

He shook his head. 'You knew? About my wife?'

'And Elodie.' Lia nodded. 'But I didn't believe it. Couldn't believe it of you.' She paused. 'So how did your wife do it?'

'Sleeping pills. She took an overdose.'

'You must have put her through hell.'

He looked down and she could see his hands were shaking. 'Believe me, I've worked hard since.'

'And Elodie? How long did she put up with it?'

'A couple of years.' His voice cracked and she could see he was forcing back the tears. She had to stop herself from reaching out to him, comforting him; from holding him and telling him she'd stay.

'Nick, I'm sorry,' she said. 'But I'm not going to be another martyr. I appreciate everything you've done for me, really I do, but that's it. I can't trust you. And without that, I've really got nothing.'

He sat there in silence, as if not really taking in what she was saying. She felt strangely cruel, as if she herself were inflicting some terrible pain.

'I think you should leave now,' she told him quietly. 'I don't want to see you again. I don't want to live in fear. If you have any genuine feeling for me, you'll respect that.'

Saying nothing, he hauled himself up and made for the front door. Watching him, Lia fought back the tears. It could have been so different, she kept thinking; everything could have been so different. A part of her wanted to run

360

after him, agree to see his therapist and to commit herself to working with him. But the larger part just felt relief that it was over.

She called Jules. In the background, she could hear the sound of a London bar, and for a second tried to picture the scene, wondering whether she herself would like to be a part of it.

'I think you'd better move house,' Jules advised her. 'You can't live like this, not with him just up the road.'

'You know, I think it'll be all right. I don't think he'll come back, I really don't. I'm not going to see him again. Don't ask me why, but for some reason I'm quite sure about that.'

'Well, I hope you're right. But make sure you lock all your doors and windows tonight, won't you?'

Lia had to smile. 'I will. I'll let you get on with whatever you're doing. Have fun.'

She poured the rest of Nick's wine down the sink and then methodically closed all the shutters and locked the doors before moving into the sitting room.

Maybe Chloe had a point, she wondered. Maybe she, too, had exhausted her life down here, and it was a job and the company of friends she needed, rather than this constant battle against loneliness. She tried to picture herself in London again, sitting in a bar with Jules, knowing she'd have to struggle in the rain for a taxi home. She tried to picture herself at a TV station, producing yet more trivial shows, and climbing uncomfortably up the corporate ladder.

She even tried picturing herself with Jonathan again, wondering if he wasn't becoming more attractive now that Jules was in touch with him. And she pictured Ben walking up to the front door, wrapping her up in his arms and holding her. And that was the picture she clung on to, as the patter of rain started beating down on the roof, and a storm broke out all around her.

When would he be back? she kept asking herself. When would he be back, and would he even give her the time of day?

Chapter Fifty-seven

She was heading towards the driveway the following morning when Lia heard a faint call, and turned to see Felix, a stick supporting his weight, standing in the doorway.

'There you are, dear. I haven't seen you for ages,' he said quietly, clearly pleased to have caught her. He was looking rather frail, she thought, suddenly feeling guilty at not having spent any time with him since Peaches' departure.

'I spent a few days away, to be honest,' she told him. 'Have you been all right?'

'Yes, yes, Binkie's been looking after me a treat. I've just put the kettle on – would you like some coffee?'

'Oh, Felix, I'd love to, but I've got to get to the supermarket before it closes,' Lia checked her watch. 'Is there anything I can get you?'

'No, no, dear, that's all right. Binkie's been doing the shopping.'

'Good.' She started to leave. 'Any news of Peaches? Will she be back soon?'

'Yes, quite soon, I think. It's been a good trip. But don't let me stop you. I tell you what, Binkie was going to buy some paella for this evening, ready made from a *traiteur* somewhere nearby. Why don't I ask her to get two portions, and we can have a nice chat later? That is, unless you've got plans, of course.'

'No, I've no plans,' Lia smiled. 'I'd love to, I really would. What time shall I pop round?'

They made arrangements and Lia was careful to find a decent bottle of wine in the supermarket. She felt oddly excited at the thought of having supper with Felix, as if the evening would prove to be significant in some way, and she might learn something powerful and important.

She arrived to find him sitting in his armchair with Keith, the black cat with two white paws, fast asleep on his lap and the BBC World Service radio on in the background. It was a little loud for her liking, but she didn't like to ask him to lower it.

'Shall I do the honours?' she asked, indicating her bottle, and then trawled through the kitchen to find a corkscrew and two glasses. 'I bet the cats have been missing Peaches,' she joked.

'Yes, damned things. Don't know what she sees in them. They've got her into more than enough trouble in the past, as it is. So, have you been with your chap these last few days?' Felix asked as she handed him a glass.

'No, no,' she told him. 'That's all over, I'm afraid.' She sat down opposite him, wondering if he could see her bruises in the soft light. If he could, he certainly didn't show it.

'Oh, what a shame. Peaches will be disappointed. She had great plans for you two, you know.'

'I'm sure she did,' Lia laughed. 'So, tell me how she is?'

'Well, I'll let her tell you on her return, which should be early next week, but the trip was a great success, and she's very happy. I can't tell you how grateful we both are to you, you know, for having found that tape.'

He made it sound like something she'd stumbled across as she was clearing out the attic.

'So she's seen Rory?' Lia asked.

'Yes, yes, and met her husband, and their child.'

'They've got a child already? So Peaches was a grandmother without even knowing it?'

'That's right, with another one on its way. I think it was all rather strained at first, but then they found a middle ground. The husband, I think, helped there.'

'Well, that's wonderful news. I'm thrilled. And delighted of course that she'll be back soon. I've missed her, and I bet you have, too?'

'Oh yes, the place seems slightly darker without her. One exists, but one does not live.'

Lia sipped her wine awkwardly, wishing she'd been more attentive. It wouldn't have hurt to have popped in from time to time, to have had a coffee with him now and then, invited him to lunch. She'd been too wrapped up in her own affairs, she realised, to have thought about anyone else – the very thing she'd always mocked Chloe for.

'So Chloe's left?' she asked, remembering. 'That was a bit of shock.'

Felix smiled. 'Yes, Chloe, a law unto herself. Peaches will be upset, of course, but I think we'll cope. We'll need to get some winter tenants in, though, so if you know of anyone, do tell us.' Then he turned to her. '*You* weren't planning on leaving us, were you?'

Lia shook her head. 'I've had my moments when I've wondered what I'm doing here. Last night I found myself thinking back to London, and wondering whether I could ever go back. I suppose we all feel unsettled from time to time.'

Felix nodded knowingly and started climbing out of his chair. 'Let's start heating this paella, shall we?' he suggested, heading towards the kitchen.

Lia helped him find a large enough pan and to warm the mixture thoroughly. Binkie had done well – it was full of healthy-sized chunks of chicken, pieces of squid, some plump mussels, sausage and giant pink prawns. She laid the table in the dining room and refilled their glasses.

364

'So you weren't thinking of leaving, then?' Felix repeated once they were sitting down in front of the vast dish, forgetting what she'd just told him.

'Not seriously, no,' she shook her head. 'But I have my wobbly moments.'

'Wobbly?' He smiled. 'Don't we all. You fit in here,' he continued. 'You were brought here for a reason, and I think you should stay a while longer.'

'A reason?' Lia repeated, helping herself to a spoonful of paella.

'Well, you certainly didn't come by accident. You've been a messenger, after all, leading Peaches to her daughter. Never underestimate the importance of that. When things happen, when they fall into place, you know you're doing something right,' he continued. 'We can never know what our destiny is, or where this life is meant to be leading us, but coincidences are always a good guide. What you've done for us, for Peaches, has been invaluable.'

'Well, I'm thrilled,' Lia said self-consciously. 'Thrilled that it's all worked out.'

'You see, everything happens for a reason,' Felix continued, carefully cutting a piece of chicken. 'It all slots into place like a jigsaw puzzle. You came here to do Peaches the most enormous favour, but I'm sure that you, too, will reap some kind of reward in time.'

'It's been a bit of a roller-coaster ride, to be honest,' Lia laughed gently. 'If I came here for some peace and quiet then I got it completely wrong.'

'I'm sorry things didn't work out with Nick Delaney – that's a great shame.'

'He has a few problems,' she told him carefully. 'And a tendency towards violence.' Felix nodded as if she'd just told him Nick enjoyed rugby and cricket, and she wondered if he had trouble with his hearing. The radio was still on loud, distracting her, but he didn't seem to notice. 'But you know Bella's been pretty good to me lately,' she offered. 'I never thought we'd be friends, but somehow I think that we are now.'

365

'She's a good person underneath it all,' he told her. 'She just does her best to disguise it. This paella's rather good, isn't it? I must say Binkie's done us proud. Has there been any news of Ben, by the way?' Felix looked up. 'Where is he again these days, Tashkent?'

'Kashmir,' Lia corrected him. 'And no, I haven't heard anything. I've been listening out for any stories on the news, but it all seems to have gone quiet.'

'He's a special person,' Felix frowned. 'It would be a great shame if he stopped coming here. You and he were rather close once, weren't you?'

'Yes, once,' Lia smiled fondly. 'I rather messed things up. Around the time of Bella's scripts. I got the wrong end of the stick and overreacted somewhat. I wish things were different.'

'Don't,' Felix told her with surprising force. 'Don't wish anything was different. As I said before, everything happens for a reason. The coincidences, like you and that tape, are there to bring us forward, and the problems, or misunderstandings, or blocks, are there to slow things down when they're moving in the wrong direction. Whatever happened, or however you think you messed up, just wait and see. If something's right, if it's meant to be, then it will have benefited from that delay. Don't try to force anything through, whatever you do; just let it work at its own speed. The world can be a magical place if you let it.'

'Maybe that's my trouble,' Lia admitted. 'I'm too impatient. If something doesn't go my way then I want change, like now, straight away.'

Felix smiled. 'Then perhaps that's the reason you're here? To learn to slow down, to work at a different rhythm. It may be frustrating, and it may be hard, but it's the best way. I can't tell you how much I used to emphasise this to my groups. Life isn't the destination, it's the journey itself, the getting there. There are no destinations, of course, because life itself doesn't stop. Just when you think you're settled and at ease, then, bang, something

366

happens to change it all. These are the tests, the challenges we all face. And we *all* do, you know. Everyone has to go through them to some degree or other.'

Lia nodded uncomfortably, wishing there was something intelligent she could add, or a meaningful question she could ask. But her mind, that wondrously logical and unintuitive thing, stayed stubbornly blank.

'The trouble today is that everyone wants control in their lives,' Felix continued, as if sensing her awkwardness. 'They charge around changing this and demanding that, and all too often ignoring the magical things that are happening around them. And there is always magic, you know. Forces, up there, that are pointing the way.'

'I don't know which way they're pointing me,' Lia laughed.

'Then wait,' he told her simply. 'Just wait. Get on with your work, tend to your garden, and let the magic work for itself. Don't try to control anything, and just see what happens.'

'Isn't that all being a bit passive?' Lia tried. 'I mean, surely there are some things you simply have to control? We can't all just sit around expecting things to happen to us, surely we've got to create the opportunities, or at least, some of them?'

'Quite right,' Felix nodded. 'Of course there are things we have to create. You did just that, for example, by moving out here, and deciding to write your book. But once you've made a major decision like that and followed it through, then you must let it go. And that letting go is the most exhilarating part of life, I assure you. Letting go can be just as exciting and rewarding as making a major decision. It's hard to understand, I know, but if you try it you will.'

There was a brief pause as both ate their supper. In the background the BBC had turned to business news, and a major scandal unravelling about a multinational company which had been hiding losses from its shareholders, and was now on the verge of bankruptcy. Lia didn't quite catch

367

its name at first, but slowly realised that it was the very client that Nick had been chasing for months.

'Ah, these corporate rogues,' Felix chuckled. 'They're all getting their comeuppance. Did you know I used to be a stockbroker, once, in another life, many years ago?'

'Felix, no I can't imagine it,' she said, her stomach twisting into knots.

As he started telling her, the radio continued, and Lia was torn between two stories, but heard enough to know that Nick's was bad: *one of the biggest corporate scandals in history ... missing pension funds ... enormous shareholder losses ... numerous creditors being defaulted.*

'I saw the error of my ways,' she heard Felix saying. 'I was burnt out by forty-five – divorced, alcoholic and a total wreck. Ended up in India, checked myself into an ashram, and from there I never looked back.'

Lia nodded, wishing she'd heard all his story, but couldn't stop thinking about Nick, and what the scandal would mean to him. Should she call him, see that he was OK? Or maybe he'd been paid before it had all happened, and had nothing to worry about?

When the meal was over, it was obvious that Felix was tiring, and Lia washed up, thanked him and headed back to the pink cottage. She wasn't to think about Nick any more, she kept telling herself; he wasn't her responsibility. She could well have got the company's name wrong, anyway. She tried to remember what Felix had said instead, wondering if she was indeed part of some great mystery which was leading her forward.

Everything in her life, every decision she'd made, every step she'd taken, had been a practical one, she could see now, up until her move to France. Then she'd stepped off the ledge of security and jumped into the unknown, and hadn't that been the best feeling of her life?

And now she was free again. In the bathroom, she paused to study her bruises in the mirror. Felix hadn't even noticed them, she remembered with a smile. He hadn't even noticed them, or if he had, was far too polite to comment.

The bruises would fade, Peaches would come back and life would return to normal. She couldn't wait, she thought, brushing her teeth, before remembering that that was the very thing she was meant to be doing.

Have patience and wait, she told herself, climbing into bed a few minutes later. The world was a magical place, according to Felix, anyway.

And somehow everything would work itself out.

Chapter Fifty-eight

Peaches came back the following week, and suddenly Lia's world was full of lunar gardening, chatter about the cats and forthcoming plans for Rory and her new family to visit. It was as if a void had suddenly been filled again. Even the garden seemed happier, with bushes that had hung forlornly throughout her absence suddenly perking up, as if her daily chats really did make a difference.

The reunion had gone well, Peaches told Lia, after some initial difficulties. These had involved Rory trying to throw her mother out of her shop and even threatening to call the police, but had gradually moved on to something warmer and altogether less hostile.

'Eventually she softened,' Peaches confided over a cup of jasmine tea that Lia had discovered she rather liked. 'And started telling me all about her husband and their child, a little boy.'

'And this is a new husband?'

'That's right dear, she wasn't married before; she hadn't been in touch with Lily's father in years. But now she's married to a lawyer, a charming man, very respectable; the store's doing well and she has a whole new life!'

'So you met him, and the son?'

'I certainly did, he's perfect for her, and the little boy – Robert, they've called him – is just adorable. Oh, it was difficult at first, of course it was, but you know I think we've gotten somewhere, I really do. I explained about the tape you'd found and she admitted that for some time after going to that show she'd felt bad about me. The other guests, you see, they'd all encouraged her to contact me, as did her husband. In a way I think she was pleased I just showed up and took the responsibility away from her.'

'That's fantastic, Peaches, it really is. And so you'll stay in touch with her now?'

'Absolutely – they're even considering coming to France next year. Won't that be wonderful? You'll be able to meet her – I mean, you'll still be here, won't you? You've got no plans to leave?'

'Not that I know of,' Lia told her, wondering just what exactly she *would* be doing. Her life was no longer predictable – she could say that much at least.

'It's been a strange year,' Peaches went on. 'Not doing the retreat properly and only having a few rentals. I've let the place go, somewhat, I'm aware of that. Starting from now I must decide what to do with all the flats.'

'Will you set up the retreat again next year?' Lia asked.

'I don't think so, dear, it's such hard work, and Felix isn't really up to it these days. I think we'll just rent them out, that's all. Put a few ads in the papers, that sort of thing. I was rather hoping Chloe might look after all that for me again, but it seems she has other fish to fry. Oh well, dear, thanks for the tea.' She started to get up. 'I'd better go see how the invalid's doing. He very much enjoyed your company the other night, by the way.'

She set off along the path, and Lia was relieved that she hadn't asked anything about Nick or what she'd been doing over the last few weeks.

She filed more chapters and started thinking about future projects and the other Mediterranean countries she could write about. Rather than heading straight to Italy or Spain,

371

as she'd initially imagined, Lia found herself drawn to the flavours of North Africa and the Middle East. What could be more appetising, she thought excitedly, than the earthy taste of hummus and the aubergine dip, baba ganoush, or spicy grilled chicken, or a lamb and apricot tajine piled high onto some freshly steamed couscous? How healthy and tasty the classic green tabouleh, how nutritious the proportion of pulses and vegetables to meats, and how comforting the puddings made of dried fruits, cardamom, rose- and orange-blossom water.

As she e-mailed her initial ideas off to Jules, Lia realised that just thinking about these countries and their foods made her feel closer to Ben. How did he feel about her? she kept asking herself. Could they ever go back to the way they were, or was it too late for that? She wished she could trust in Felix's magic, and simply believe that they would be happy again, but somehow everything seemed to get in their way.

She read the on-line papers and re-read all her previous attempts to reach Ben, wondering what the magic formula could be. She was sure she was just a letter or a hyphen out – it was as frustrating as starting a crossword puzzle where she had most of the letters but still couldn't come up with the answer.

She'd just logged off when the phone started ringing, and Jules was on the line, wanting to talk through her new ideas. She was very positive, saying that as they'd just published a major book on Italian cuisine they needed to focus on a different area, and she thought the Middle East would be ideal.

'So you've still not heard anything from Ben, then?' she asked once they'd finished discussing work.

'Nothing,' Lia told her. 'And everything I've sent him comes straight back. So what about you and Jonathan?' she remembered to ask. 'Weren't you supposed to be having a drink with him some time?'

'Oh, I blew him out, couldn't be bothered in the end,' Jules told her casually. 'Sometimes you just know that there's no point, and that it's all going to be an embarrassing waste of time.'

'Felix would disagree with you there, you know,' Lia told her. 'You should stop trying to take control of everything, you know, and let the magic work. It's the only way to move forward.'

'What? Oh Christ, Li, don't you think it's time you moved? That place is getting to you. You'll be chanting some mantra down the line to me next. Oh shit, is that the time? I'd better go, I've got a meeting in a minute.'

Lia hung up feeling rather sorry for Jonathan, as if he'd reached out to someone different, only to be unceremoniously dumped before he could make an impression. She'd rather liked the idea of Jules seeing him and discovering a good side; it would make her feel vindicated, somehow, as if she hadn't had hopeless taste in men after all. But now he sounded like the type you'd avoid sitting next to on a bus, and that thought rather tugged at her.

As the days grew shorter and the magazines became full of grey being the new black and boots being the new shoes, Lia found fabulous mushrooms in her local shops – ceps, chanterelles and boletuses – and began to experiment with them, trying everything from mushroom stroganoff to risottos, pasta dishes and warming coq au vins. This was the chapter she'd been looking forward to all along – with the type of food that made it all right to be cold and stuck indoors for hours at a time; the kind of food that made winter feel like a privilege and not a burden.

On the days that Etienne worked at Les Eglantines she'd try and help him, and together they made compost, cleaned out beds and borders and planted the last of the winter garlic, all under the guidance of Peaches' lunar calendar. If he felt the time was right to do something but Peaches insisted he waited a couple of days, he'd laugh, shrug his shoulders and duly do so, only to make it perfectly clear afterwards how much better the conditions had been on his day, after all.

As Chloe had suspected, Etienne moved back in with

Hélène. When Lia asked how he felt about Chloe, and her decision to leave, he just laughed the entire episode off, as if it hadn't meant anything to him, anyway. He'd always loved Hélène, he insisted, and had never stopped loving her, despite Chloe. She was faithful and loyal, he said, and best of all, she adored him, and that, he maintained, was what a relationship was all about.

Lia didn't like to ask what exactly *he* brought to the relationship, but was glad that things seemed to have worked out.

She'd got used to not hearing from Nick, now, and respected that he was leaving her alone. Every now and then she'd look up at his lovely toffee-coloured house and wonder if he was there or travelling, and how badly he'd been affected by his client's meltdown. Every now and then she'd allow herself to remember her old fantasies of being Mrs Nick Delaney, international traveller and food writer, before pushing them out of her mind and checking herself back into reality.

And then, late one morning, Peaches appeared, dabbing her eyes with a handkerchief, and clearly using all her strength not to break down completely.

'What on earth's the matter?' Lia asked, as Peaches took her hands in her own. They felt cold and dry, and Lia found herself imagining the worst. 'Has something happened to Rory, or her baby?'

'No, dear, they're fine, thankfully,' she managed to say before breaking into a sob.

'Not Ben, then? Peaches, please tell me, you haven't heard anything about Ben, have you?'

'No, no, thank God, I'm sure he's fine. Oh dear, I don't know how to tell you.' She sat down with a thump, and Lia sat opposite her. 'It's Nick Delaney. He's dead. He shot himself.' She started to cry again, as if she could only have held back the tears until she'd got the words out. 'He'd been suffering terribly from depression and was seeing someone about it in Cannes, I believe. Apparently he'd had dreadful financial difficulties for some time, and had put

374

his house up as collateral a while ago. Then one of his big clients crashed. There was a lot about it on the news when I was in Chicago, you know – they'd been cooking the books for years, but he lost everything. In the end, he was ruined.'

Lia just sat there, too shocked either to cry or speak.

'Binkie Hardcastle told me this morning,' Peaches continued. 'You know they shared a cleaning lady? She found him, the poor woman, in his study. Can you imagine?'

'I just can't believe it,' Lia said eventually. 'And when? When did this happen?'

'Yesterday. Binkie called just now. It's too dreadful. I really am so sorry. You hadn't seen him in a while, though, had you?'

'No, no, I hadn't.' Lia shook her head, trying to understand that her Nick was now dead. Had she heard anything strange yesterday, she tried to remember – the sound of a gunshot, perhaps – that she'd assumed was a hunter? Or police sirens – had she been unaware of those, too?

Peaches blew her nose, composing herself. 'You know, I did his chart once, just for the fun of it – not that I ever gave it to him, of course,' she started, trying to brighten. 'I doubt he'd have been interested. But I do remember now that he had Mars in Cancer, which can be difficult sometimes, leading to great moodiness, especially in the home. Which is hard to imagine, I know – I couldn't relate that part to him at all. But the charts don't lie, do they, so maybe there was something in it, after all?'

Lia thought for a second, and then, taking Peaches by the hand, told her everything.

Chapter Fifty-nine

A few days later, Lia was drying her hair when she realised the phone was ringing. The tone had an urgency to it, an insistence that compelled her to charge down the stairs, her hair a split personality of dry and sleek on one side, damp and tangled on the other.

'Lia, is that you? I wasn't sure I had the number down properly. It's Bella. I'm just calling to say how terribly sorry I am. I just heard the news about Nick, and although what he did was completely unforgivable, it must still be a dreadful shock. How are you doing?'

'I'm OK, thanks,' Lia told her, surprised to be hearing her voice. 'Numb, I suppose – that's the best way of putting it. I just can't imagine that he's gone. I keep remembering all the good, decent things about him, and can't help feeling that somehow, in some way, I contributed to his death.'

'Well, for God's sake don't think that,' Bella retorted. 'Don't blame yourself, whatever you do. He wasn't a risk you could take, you know that, and anyway, by all accounts it was because of his finances, and not because he was jilted by some girl down the road.'

Quietly Lia laughed at being so forcefully put into her

place. 'How did you hear about it, anyway?' she asked.

'It was in the papers; Lionel saw it. Didn't get much of a mention as it was tied in with that big corporate scandal. So how is everything there?'

'A bit strange really. Peaches was gearing herself up to be questioned by the police and for herds of journalists to come sniffing around, but it's all been very quiet. His brother came, apparently, to retrieve his effects and fly the body back to the States. I don't know what'll happen to the house – it'll be sold by his creditors, I suppose.'

'What a total bloody nightmare,' Bella breathed down the line. 'But you're OK?'

'Yes, thank you, I'm fine.'

'Did you get hold of Ben, by the way?' Bella's tone changed. 'Weren't you looking for his e-mail address before?'

Lia shook her head, exasperated. 'Yes, Bella, and I still am. You thought Lionel might have it.'

'Yes, he did. Hang on a sec, I've got it here somewhere. Been carrying it around in my bag for some time now. I've just been so busy I'd forgotten all about it.'

Lia could have screamed. She wondered what Bella's idea of being busy was – not having time to buy shoes in between facials, manicures and lunch, perhaps?

Bella dictated the address, and Lia realised that Ben had a new service provider, and that that had been the problem. He must have changed it over the summer and neglected to tell her, which was hardly surprising under the circumstances.

Once she'd hung up, Lia logged onto the Internet, deciding to write him a whole new letter. She told him all about what happened the night she'd last seen him, and about the changes at Les Eglantines. She told him about Nick's suicide, and the feeling of shock that had reverberated around the village. She told him about how much she cared about him, and how she hoped he was staying safe. She told him about her strange new friendship with Bella, and

377

about how she finally understood his loyalty. She told him about her ideas for a second book, and about the travels it would entail. And she told him about how she'd never stopped thinking about him, and how much she wished they could start again, from scratch.

And as she hit the *send* button, her stomach churning over with excitement, it occurred to Lia that Bella had been a kind of messenger, just as she herself had been for Peaches, and that although she could have been a more efficient one, perhaps the delay was for a good reason after all. Wasn't this a better e-mail, less hysterical and desperate than the last?

She was just reading the papers and a horoscope, for the fun of it, when the familiar voice told her she had a new e-mail, and Lia raced to her inbox to see Ben's name there. This time, though, it stood alone, unaccompanied by the dreaded Mail Daemon message, and she took a few seconds to savour the look of it before opening the cyber envelope to read:

What great timing – have just arrived back in London after gruelling few weeks in Rajouri, north of Jammu. No phone lines, no connection, not much decent food but some great shots. Sorry you've had such an awful time, and wish I'd been there for you. Was just about to call Peaches – think I'll come over next week. My sister's having another baby and needs my room, so will have to look into something more permanent. Can't tell you how much your e-mail meant to me. I feel the same way, and look forward to seeing you soon.

She read and re-read it again, not quite believing it was really from him. She could have murdered Bella, but in a way, was beginning to see how the delay had worked for her. If her initial message *had* got through, after all, and she'd received no reply, Lia would have felt terrible, rejected, and might even have ended up going back to Nick. As it was the timing had worked totally in her

378

favour. Suddenly she began to understand what Felix had been talking about.

On her way to the village the next day she popped in to see Peaches, who was chatting to a pink oleander bush as she cut its overgrown stalks right back.

'Well, that's better,' Lia overheard her say. 'You needed a good haircut so quit complaining! Oh, hello, dear.' She swung round to greet Lia. 'I am so behind with tidying up this place. How are you?'

'I'm fine, thanks. I was just wondering if you'd heard anything from Ben, only I got an e-mail from him yesterday saying he was coming over some time?'

'Oh, yes, that's right, dear, he called last night. I was meaning to tell you. He'll be arriving Monday. Now, is that good news or bad?'

'Good,' Lia smiled confidently. 'Definitely, good.'

Chapter Sixty

She wondered whether to meet him at the airport. She wondered whether that would be a thoughtful and sweet gesture, or just too pushy by half. In the end she dropped him a quick e-mail, to which he replied that as he was on such an early flight, he'd just take a taxi and be done with it.

The nights were getting colder now, and as she pulled the shutters to as early as five-thirty, she couldn't help thinking of the months they'd spent together, and the evenings they'd shared just watching TV and chatting and making love. How blissful and uncomplicated life had been then, she reflected, and how much confusion and hurt she'd gone through since. And now, suddenly, her enemies were either dead or had become strange new friends. And so there was nothing else, theoretically, anyway, standing in their way.

She'd done some shopping and taken it to his little flat, where she helped Peaches to make up his bed and give everywhere a thorough clean. She left a note telling him to come up any time, saying that she had no plans other than to work at her desk all day. She spent the morning hearing phantom chinks of the gate and fiddling with her hair, which refused to be pulled back into a neat ponytail, and flopped stubbornly over one eye.

And then, just as she heard a real chink and his voice, finishing off a conversation with Peaches, and caught sight of his hair, and his frame, through the dining-room window, and just as her stomach started doing a double somersault and her chest contracting in excitement, the phone rang. Cursing, she rushed to answer it and get rid of the caller as quickly as possible.

'So I went out with Jonathan on Friday,' Jules's voice came on the line, without bothering to say hello first.

'Good,' Lia said hesitantly, signalling to Ben to stay and that she wouldn't take long. 'Look, it's not a great time right now. Can I call you back this afternoon?'

Ben was now standing on the terrace, admiring the view, and all she wanted was to be with him.

'You can, but I'll be tied up in meetings,' Jules answered irritably. 'But just to let you know, we spent the entire weekend bonking our brains out.'

'What?' Lia pulled herself back to the phone, despite having nearly dropped it. 'You what?' she found herself laughing excitedly, dying to hear more and yet desperate to welcome Ben.

'I thought that would get your attention,' Jules said matter-of-factly. 'I can hardly believe it myself, but we just got on really well.' She sounded surprised. 'He's a different person without you, you know.' Lia wasn't sure how to take this. 'And he's fit, and really quite good looking. I wonder why I'd never noticed before.'

'I can't believe I'm hearing this, Jules, but, much as I want to hear all the gory details – *not* – I really have to go. Ben's just arrived, I'm sorry.'

'Oh bloody hell, has he? OK, I'll let you go. Oh, but one other thing – they're pretty keen on the Middle East idea, so I need you to come up with a treatment and chapters again, same as before.'

'Oh my God,' Lia gushed, not really taking any of it in. All she could see was Ben – a tanned, sexy and highly amused-looking Ben, clearly enjoying the one-sided conversation as much as her panic. 'I've got to go, but, gosh –' she stumbled for the right words – 'well done.'

She hung up and then laughed out loud. 'Well done? My best friend's bonking my ex-boyfriend and I tell her "well done"?'

Ben just laughed, staring at her affectionately. 'So things have been quiet and dull around here, then, just as usual?'

Lia went to kiss him on either cheek, but he pulled her towards him, kissed her briefly on the lips and then held her tight, stroking her hair with one hand as the other crept down towards her bottom.

'You have no idea how much I've dreamt of this moment,' he whispered. 'How much I've missed you and wanted you.'

'Oh God, I've been the same,' she cried, feeling tears welling up in her eyes. 'I've just so wanted things to be the way they were, you know? Back in the spring.'

'They will,' he assured her, pulling back and stroking her hair, taking in her face, her eyes, her body. 'They will. This time I'm staying around for a while. I've got the exhibition, I've talked to my agent about a book, and this time I'm going to do it seriously, I promise. I'm not going anywhere, believe me, and I'm not going to let you down again.'

They kissed and held each other as if neither ever wanted to let go. Finally, remembering her other good news, Lia pulled away.

'And I've got another book to write,' she told him proudly. 'They really like the idea.'

He held her hands in his, concerned. 'Are you serious? I mean, Lebanon? Syria? As a blonde alone you'd get no end of hassle. But, come to think of it,' he frowned thoughtfully. 'There's a lot more I could do out there, I mean photographically, so maybe—'

'We could combine a trip?' Lia said excitedly, before backtracking, scared of frightening him off. 'I mean, I don't want you to feel hemmed in, of course, but it might make sense, mightn't it, when the time comes? If we still

382

like the idea, that is. I mean, nothing definite.'

He laughed, understanding her concern, and pulled her in close. 'Right now I just want to stop here for a while, wake up every morning beside this beautiful girl I know and finally get my act together,' he told her. 'But who knows, next year, perhaps? Knowing me, I'll be restless again by March.'

'Look.' She pulled away, trying to restrain the urge to haul him up to her bedroom and tear off all his clothes. 'Can I offer you something? Some tea, perhaps?'

'Oh God.' He pulled a face, teasing her. 'What's the special today, then, baked bean and banana? Lentil and lychee?'

'No, I'm over all that.' She laughed, heading for the kitchen and putting on the kettle. 'I discovered good old simple jasmine tea. It's very light, very refreshing and has no overpowering flavour.'

She spooned some leaves into a pot, explaining. 'It was this boring tin that put me off,' she started. 'I was always looking for something more exotic, more colourful, more daring, you know? A bit like in life, really. Always looking for more and then getting disappointed. And then I found everything I wanted in this tea,' she joked, feigning a happy housewife expression and holding the tin up as if in a commercial. 'Right here, for a fraction of the price of all the others.'

'Or we could just have sex,' he suggested dryly, and giggling, she had to restrain herself yet again.

She poured a mug and then handed it to him. He was smiling at her as if there was no one else he'd rather be with in the world, and as if this tea was the most precious gift he'd ever been offered.

'Trust me, it's good,' she urged as, hesitantly, he took a sip.

'It's not bad.' He smiled, putting it straight down again. Then he pulled her in closer, kissing her forehead, her eyelids, her cheeks and nose. 'But now I've tried that,' he smiled, 'what about my suggestion?'

The Ex-Factor
Andrea Semple

When Martha Seymore finds out about her boyfriend's one-night-stand she doesn't know what to do. And Martha's business *is* relationships. She's the girl who gets paid to sympathise with the cheated and jilted, the under sexed and over attached at *Gloss* magazine. Realising she's just as clueless as her hapless readers, Martha finds it increasingly difficult to continue giving relationship advice whilst dealing with her own heartache. Also, there's the distinctly unattractive prospect of admitting a failed relationship not only to her colleagues, but also to her oldest friend, Desdemona, whose irritatingly perfect lifestyle would make even a saint harbour murderous tendencies.

Worse, Desdemona's new fiancé is Alex, Martha's first ex-boyfriend, who, contrary to all expectations, has matured into an infuriatingly sexy and talented chef. Life just isn't fair. Tired of always doing the right thing, Martha starts to wonder whether her new flatmate has the right approach to relationships after all: is the best way to get one man off your mind, at least temporarily, to get another one into your bed?

A novel about sex, relationships, and other natural disasters

Praise for *The Ex-Factor:*
'Andrea Semple's book about an agony aunt's agony will make you laugh, cry and make you want to call up your friends and tell them how much you love them. Refreshingly original – it's like an advice column but much, much better.' Faith Bleasdale
'A bright and sunny read, whatever the weather' Matt Whyman
'Very witty – it made me laugh out loud' Deborah Wright

The Cupid Effect
Dorothy Koomson

What's love got to do with it?

Ceri D'Altroy's hero-worship of Oprah Winfrey is beginning to have serious repercussions. Bored with London life and writing yet another 'black is the new black' fashion feature, she's decided to take Oprah's advice and follow her heart's desire. Going back to college might not be everyone's dream but all Ceri has ever wanted to do is teach . . .

But though her professional life seems to be sorted, Ceri's personal life is still a no-go area. After six long, long, months without so much as a snog, she's given up hope of ever finding anyone who'll put up with her various idiosyncrasies. In fact just lately, her pent-up energies and frustrations seem to have been diverted into solving other people's romantic problems. Since arriving in Leeds she's reunited a happily uncoupled couple, encouraged her new flatmate to do something about his unrequited love and outed the closet relationship of two of her new colleagues. All this, in spite of her new life resolution to mind her own business. But is Ceri destined to always play Cupid? Or can she use some of her powers where they're needed most – to help herself?

Praise for THE CUPID EFFECT:
'One of the funniest, most unusual books you'll ever read. Be careful, this book may change your life (and viewing habits).' Mark Barrowcliffe, author of *Girlfriend 44*
'A laugh-out-loud, feel-good page-turner.' *She*
'Dorothy Koomson makes an impressive debut with a quirky, original, wise novel. This is a totally enjoyable story full of believable characters and situations.' *New Woman*
'If you're looking for a great read, then check out *The Cupid Effect*, a fantastic new debut novel written by Dorothy Koomson. A funny look at love, life and matchmaking you won't be able to put it down!' *All About Soap*
'A hilarious read.' *OK's Hot Stars*
'A funny, quirky read.' *Company*

Brief Encounters
Neil Rose

Charlie Fortune is a hard-working lawyer for one of the city's most ruthless firms. Charlie's determined to make partner or die in the attempt. Sadly, Charlie's troubled by the one defect no self-respecting laywer should have – a conscience. He feels guilty about hiking up his billable hours. He's also a sucker for the sob stories he hears helping out at his local legal advice centre *pro bono!* All in all the partners at his firm are beginning to suspect that Charlie lacks the killer instinct it takes.

They have no such doubts about new recruit Elly Gray. She's ruthless, talented and determined. She's also Charlie's ex-girl-friend. And a woman he'd sooner not see again, let alone share an office with . . .

Praise for Neil Rose:

'Move over Nick Hornby, Neil Rose is in town!' Maurice Gran, co-creator of *Birds of a Feather* and *The New Statesman*
'wickedly funny' The Telegraph
'Woody Allen-meets-Portnoy's-Complaint-meets-Adrian-Mole kind of novel . . .' *Guardian*
'Well-written, entertaining read' The Times
'Warm . . . often amusing, incisive' *Jewish Chronicle*

Olivia's Sister
Claire LaZebnik

At 21, Olivia Martin has mastered the art of cynicism. Maybe
that's inevitable because of her dysfunctional family – a
desperately needy, alcoholic ex-model mother; a rich, ill-
tempered father with an imperious new wife; and a spoiled
half-sister. Olivia's modus operandi has been to ignore them all
and just drift through life, tough and alone.

However, just as she is in danger of falling in love – or at least
in lust – for the first time, Olivia's familial responsibilities
come crashing down about her. Her father and his second wife
are killed in a car crash, and she is left to inherit both their
considerable fortune and guardianship of her four-year old
half-sister. Despite Olivia's view that 'If I'd wanted to be
saddled with a kid at this point in my life, I'd have grown up in
Oklahoma,' she has no choice but to do the right thing and try
and raise a child she's only met a handful of times.

The Shape of My Heart
Tiffanie DeBartolo

When I was twelve, a fortune teller told me that my one true love would die young and leave me all alone. Everyone said she was a fraud, that she was just making it up. I'd really like to know why the hell a person would make up a thing like that.

Wry yet vulnerable, Beatrice Jordan isn't the sort of woman who usually answers personal ads but she is unable to resist the following: 'If your intentions are pure, I am seeking a friend for the end of the world.'

In doing so, she meets Jacob Grace, a charming, effervescent thirty-something writer, a free spirit who is a passionate seeker of life. He possesses his own turn of phrase and ways of thinking and feeling that dissonantly harmonise with Beatrice's off-centre visiion as they roller coaster through the joys and furies of their heart-wrenching romance. Along the way they try to come to terms with the hurt brought about by their distant fathers who, in different ways, forsook them.

Praise for *The Shape of My Heart:*

'Funny, fresh and sharply contemporary: a romance that defines off-beat but is as deeply felt as any' **Eileen Goudge**

'a star-crossed romance in the hipper outreaches of Los Angeles. De Bartolo's combination of one-liners and three-hankie tearjerking is skillful ... This generation's *Love Story' Kirkus Reviews*

The Dive From Clausen's Pier
Ann Packer

Carrie Bell was born and raised in Wisconsin. She's had the same best friend, the same good relationship with her mother, the same boyfriend for as long as anyone can remember. She is already quietly bored with Mike when he is horrifically injured in a diving accident at Clausen's Reservoir. Now the future that Carrie was only beginning to rebel against looks set in stone. Everyone thinks they know what Carrie will – and ought to – do. But Carrie is caught in a maze of moral dilemmas and is forced to question everything she thought she knew about herself. It is a moment of terrifying confusion, but also of mesmerising possibility.

Praise for *The Dive From Clausen's Pier*:

'The Dive From Clausen's Pier is one of those small miracles that reinforce our faith in fiction. It is witty, tragic and touching, and beguiling from the first page' SCOTT TUROW

'beguiling first novel. Packer's ample talents reveal a sure sense of pace and pitch, a brilliant ear for character' *New York Times Book Review*

'A densely enveloping book, presented with uncommon assurance for a debut novel ... deeply satisfying' *New York Times*

The Mango Season
Amulya Malladi

The Mango Season **is a lush and beautifully written novel from a highly acclaimed writer. With vivid descriptions and compelling characters, it takes the reader on a trip into the heart and soul of contemporary India.**

Priya Rao left India when she was twenty to study in America. Now, seven years later, she has returned for a visit to discover her parents are intent on arranging her marriage to a suitable Indian boy. She has arrived home in time for the harvesting of mangoes – the hottest time of the year and a time full of ritual and ceremony. As a child she had loved this season best but, after years away, Priya finds the heat of an Indian summer overwhelming and everything about India seems different – dirtier and more chaotic than she remembers.

Her extended family are also consumed by talk of marriage – particularly the marriage of her uncle Anand, and his decision to marry not only for love but to marry a woman of a much lower caste. Priya can only guess a what reaction her own engagement would provoke if she were to reveal that she has left behind a fiancé in America, a fiancé of an entirely different race and religion . . .

Praise for Amulya Malladi's *A Breath of Fresh Air*:

'[Malladi] draws us into the novel with her characters, who are refreshingly free of stereotype. . . . Their voices are clear and strong, each one carefully modulated to be different' **Chitra Benerjee Divakaruni, author of** *The Mistress of Spices*

'a complex exploration of love, recrimination and forgiveness . . .' *Time*

'Malladi's writing style is unadorned and simple . . . Along the way she sketches some remarkable women . . . and treats her male characters with compassion' *San Francisco Chronicle*

'Gemlike . . .' *San Francisco Weekly*

391

A SELECTION OF NOVELS AVAILABLE FROM
JUDY PIATKUS (PUBLISHERS) LIMITED

THE PRICES BELOW WERE CORRECT AT THE TIME OF GOING TO PRESS. HOWEVER JUDY PIATKUS (PUBLISHERS) LIMITED RESERVE THE RIGHT TO SHOW NEW RETAIL PRICES ON COVERS WHICH MAY DIFFER FROM THOSE PREVIOUSLY ADVERTISED IN THE TEXT OR ELSEWHERE.

0 7499 3354 2	The Ex-Factor	Andrea Semple	£6.99
0 7499 3343 7	The Cupid Effect	Dorothy Koomson	£6.99
0 7499 3386 0	Brief Encounters	Neil Rose	£6.99
0 7499 3403 4	Olivia's Sister	Claire LaZebnik	£6.99
0 7499 3378 X	The Shape Of My Heart	Tiffanie DeBartolo	£6.99
0 7499 3363 1	The Dive From Clausen's Pier	Ann Packer	£6.99
0 7499 3433 6	The Mango Season	Anulya Malladi	£6.99

All Piatkus titles are available from:

www.piatkus.co.uk

or by contacting our sales department on

0800 454816

Free postage and packing in the UK
(on orders of two books or more)